# Nine-Tenths

## J.M. FREY

Cover Art: Bianca Armbruster
Cover Design: J.M. Frey
Map: Christopher Winkelaar
Graphic Elements: Canva Pro
Editing: Donna Frey & Ruthanne Reid
Interior Design: J.M. Frey
Fonts: Over the Rainbow & Libre Caslon
Author Photo: Marion Voysey
Interior Layout Created on Atticus



ebook ISBN: 978-1-7381485-6-1
Paperback ISBN: 978-1-7381485-5-4
ASIN: B0F7WV53SR

www.jmfrey.net

*This book is for you.*
*I am so happy you're here.*
*The world is a better place with you in it.*
*Stay.*

GREAT LAKES REGION
ORILLIA
TORONTO (CASTLE FRANK)
ST. CATHARINES
NIAGARA
BRITISH NORTH AMERICA
ONGUIAAHRA NATION
DUTCH NORTH AMERICA
NEW AMSTERDAM
GREAT BRITAIN
CARDROSS
GLASGOW
SCOTLAND
HADRIAN'S WALL
ST. FFAGANS
ENGLAND
LONDON
UPPER CANADA
LOWER CANADA
ONGUIAAHRA
D.N.A.
BRITISH NORTH AMERICA
WASHINGTON
UNITED STATES of AMERICA

# content warnings

Profanity
Sexual Content
Discussion of past Death of a Parent / Grief
Anxiety and Panic Attacks
Kitchen Fire
Mild Fantasy Gore and Violence
One scene of mildly Dubious Consent
One scene of pseudo-Monsterfucking
A few homophobic slurs
A few anti-Indigenous slurs
Abuse of Perfectly Innocent Coffee Beans

# The Rules

1. No assuming interest unless it's spelled out.

2. No more charming narcissists.

3. Don't mistake lust for Love.

4. Relationships are work. So you gotta work at them.

5. Not every partner has to be The One, so don't stress if they're not.

6. Don't give up on the idea of soulmates, but don't hinge everything on the belief of it.

7. You are worthy of love.

# chapter One

There's this thing in stories called the "inciting incident".

And mine? It's a goddamn doozy.

It's the part of the book, right at the start, where you pinch the pages between your fingers, and whisper to yourself: *here we go.* It's the bit where the lovers have their meet-cute, the farm boy leaves his family behind for the wider world, the Chosen One is attacked by her first evil monster, blah, blah, blah. You know what I mean. It's my favorite part of the book. It's the place where everything opens up and you have no idea what you're in for—only that it'll be exciting.

I know all about Inciting Incidents because I was going to be a writer.

No, I *thought* I was going to be a writer. Historical romance, that's my jam. Dukes, rakes, wind-blown-gowns, dropped handkerchiefs, cliffside confessions—I am a slut for that stuff. Forget real history (totally flunked 'We're-Feeding-You-Colonialist-Narratives-Disguised-As-Education101'). Give me made-up kingdoms and far-flung pirates. Give me the fantasy of a happily ever after that lasts beyond 'the end'. Give coffee and *stories*, and I am a very happy boy.

But right before he got sick, in the summer between my first and second year of university, my Dad and I had a serious talk about writing. How much work it is. How long it takes to start paying off, how little mid-list writers make. Backup plans.

And then... *after,* I thought, well, he wasn't wrong. If life was going to be pointlessly, stupidly, cruelly short, then I should spend my time trying to do something good, right? I switched majors. Science makes sense. Science is logical. Science creates vaccines and saves lives. Science can bring species back from the brink of extinction.

Science doesn't break your heart.

All of this is to say that I can—with complete and utter certainty—point to the exact moment when my life became a trash fire. It was my twenty-fourth birthday, and my big sister Gemma gave me the dumbest, but most totally plot-initiating gift: a sunrise alarm clock.

My Inciting Incident starts like this: in Mum's pokey poppies-and-roosters kitchen, with Gemma turning over the box that the wrapping paper reveals, trying to figure out where the English description is hidden.

"It's an alarm clock," Gemma says, when I don't comment immediately. She's leaning on the back of my chair, the braid hanging over her shoulder long enough to tickle my neck. I flick it away.

"I have a perfectly good alarm clock." I hold up my phone, then let it slap back down onto the plastic tablecloth. "Goes ding when there's stuff."

My sister heaves the kind of sigh only eldest-born siblings make, indulgent and frustrated at the same time. I love making her make that noise. It's hilarious.

"It wakes you up gently," Gem says. "So you're not cranky."

"M'not cranky."

Everyone laughs. I may have snapped at Stuart just this morning when he shook my foot through my childhood bed sheets like an aggressive chihuahua.

Okay.

So I'm cranky in the mornings.

"I don't see how it's supposed to work." Stu grabs the clock. "How can you see the light if your eyes are closed?"

As the younger brother of twin siblings, I am used to having the toys I'm playing with getting pulled out of my hands. Instead of trying to snatch it back, I fiddle with the iridescent green bow that was on the box.

"The same way you can see sunlight through your eyelids. It just works, okay? I've been using this exact same one for months. I promise you'll wake up in a better mood."

"You know, it's rude to give someone a present that benefits yourself," I say, playing with the tape on the bottom of the ribbon. I stick it to my ear. Mum smirks at my accessory, but otherwise her prim little 'all my babies are home to roost' face stays in place.

Makes me feel a bit shitty, because I'm the only one of us who went away to school, and *stayed* away. Gem came back to live with Mum straight after she finished her undergrad, so Mum wouldn't be alone in the house after Dad. Stuart never left the city, though he's got his own place now. But that's *why* I stayed away after I graduated last year. Mum and Gem don't need me, and if I came back, Stu would try to get me to join his construction crew.

To be fair, I *do* go weak in the knees for the kind of person jacked enough to pick me up and consensually throw me around. Standing on a roof next to a whole crew of pretty roughs trying to help them replace shingles? That's gonna lead to me swooning, falling off, and dying of a broken neck. Stu doesn't want that on his conscience.

Because she's a bossy know-it-all, Gem takes my present from Stu and opens it to show me how it works.

Suddenly empty-handed, Stu helps himself to another piece of my birthday cake, licking the icing off his fingers *and* the serving knife.

Mum slaps the hand holding the knife, and Stu flushes up and sets it down in the sink. He descends on his third piece like a wolf, but at least now he's watching his manners.

"There's instructions," I point out as Gem tosses the booklet on the table. "I don't need you to do it for me."

"The day you read the instructions," Mum says, "is the day I'll know for sure the fairies swapped you back."

It's an old joke, me being the Changeling child. I'm the only one of them with dark hair. The rest of my family are blond as heck.

Mum's grinning at her own cleverness, lips curving into that little curl in the side of her mouth that holds secrets. Dad always called it Mum's 'Peter Pan Kiss'. It's the spot where her sense of humor lives. He'd wrap his arms around her waist and kiss that corner, and Mum would swat at him for ruining her lipstick.

Thinking about Dad reminds me that he's dead.

I hate the swoop-and-stab sensation in my chest that comes with remembering. Especially when there's a moment you want to share, and you think *I should say that to Dad*, and you straighten up a bit and take a deep breath, and turn your head to his chair and start composing the sentence in your head: "Hey, Dad, Mum's doing that—" and then you stop.

You stop composing. Stop turning. Stop thinking about sharing. Stop breathing.

Because that chair is empty.

Dad's dead.

And you'll never get the chance to point out the Peter Pan kiss again. Or watch Mum swat him. Or listen to him tease us for falling for Mum's Old World fairy stories. Or hear his stupid *har-har-har* donkey laugh, thick with his Lower Canada accent.

It's my birthday.

He's not here.

I'll have another birthday, next year, and he won't be there for that one either.

I try to control my breathing, but Mum hears it hitching. I'm already staring at Dad's terrible empty chair, so it's not like I can hide what I'm thinking about. Mum curls her fingers over my knuckles.

"I wish he was here too, *mo leanbh*," she says softly.

Stu and Gem go quiet.

"Sucks," I cough out, deciding to give no one the pleasure of watching me actually cry. I'll save it for later, when I'm back in my own apartment. Not because of any kind of 'real men don't' toxic masculinity bullshit, but because I hate the fuss. They take the shit my therapist tells them about being my support network too much to heart.

"More tea, Mummers?" I ask instead, standing, breaking her hold on my hand to pick up the teapot on the counter beside the decimated cake.

"Time for something stronger, don't you think?"

"I've got it," Gem says, leaping at the chance to be helpful. She pops my gift back into the box and pushes the whole thing into my arms, forcing me back down into the chair. "Four glasses?"

"Extra ice in mine," Stu calls at Gem's back as she breezes into the living room and over to the booze hutch. We all pretend Gem's not wiping at her eyes. "I gotta drive."

"You're not staying for dinner?" Mum asks him.

"One of my guys got in the weeds with something at the museum, and the city wants it done before the kids start showing up for summer camps."

"But Colin's come all the way from St. Catharines," Mum protests. "I thought you'd at least spend the night."

"I have a perfectly good bed a ten minute drive away, Mum."

Mum's lips pucker. I hate seeing her unhappy, but what am I gonna do? Tie Stu to the chair?

Ha.

"Could use your advice," Stu says to me. "Figure out the best place to—"

"I know what you're doing, and the answer is no," I say, but I force a smile through it. "Try all you like Stu-pid, I'm not coming to work with you."

"It'd be nice to see both my boys working in their Dad's company," Mum says, trying to keep the peace.

"I need a landscaper for the summer—"

"My degree is in environmental and sustainable tourism," I remind everyone. "I wrote my thesis on biodynamic viniculture. Y'know, the science of eco-forward vineyard management? Not grass-cutting."

"It's all outdoors and nature, isn't it?"

"Give it a rest."

"It's just a job," Stu presses. "I know you're still figuring out the career thing, but you gotta make money in the meantime—"

"I have a 'just a job'. Hadhirah pays as good as you, and I don't have to get eaten alive by bugs in the backwoods—"

"Orillia is hardly the 'backwoods'," Mum tuts.

"I'm happy in St. Catharines," I say, trying to stay firm but non-confrontational, like Dr. Chen taught me. "I like my friends, and I like Beanevolence. I don't want to work for Stu when he has no idea what it is that I actually do."

"It's not like I'm going to kidnap you and force you to wear a tool belt. Don't get your feathers in a ruffle, *mo leanbh*," Stu says, in his best imitation of Mum's Scots brogue.

Mum was seven when she and my Nan emigrated to Canada to get away from Nan's horrid husband, and Mum still has that pretty Scottish burr. Doubly so when she gets off the phone with her half-sister Patricia. I wish you could inherit an accent.

"Thank you for the offer," I say, baring my teeth. "But I decline."

"Suit yourself," Stu says. He rubs his hand through my hair, which, *rude! Some of us actually style our hair and use product, like civilized people, Stuart!*

"Plan to." I take a sip of my cold tea before I can say anything that will turn this into an actual argument.

"Need help, Gemmy?" Mum asks. As a way to change the subject, it's not a subtle one.

"I'm coming," Gem says, over the clink of glass tumblers on Dad's mid-century bar tray. Dad had a thing for cocktails and James Bond. Mom has a thing for a good peaty scotch, so it was a match made in a shaker.

Gem sets down four Old Fashions, extra ice in Stu's, and extra cherries in mine. Our "*Slàinte mhath*!" is maybe too forced, but whatever.

Casting around for something to start a new conversation, Gem says: "I like your shirt. It's not black."

"Oh, yeah," I say, stroking the olive button-down. It's a tight fit, one of those tailored shirts that makes me look gawky and skinny, but Mum always appreciates the effort. Gem is wearing one of those cute dorky matching summer-dress-and-cardigan sets that makes her look like the librarian she is, and Stu is in a bright blue tee-shirt and dark jeans that are actually free of construction debris or paint. Which *is* dressing up, for him. "Beks picked it."

Mum perks up. "And where is Rebekah? I expected her to drive you."

"Mum," I groan, and it's a waste of Dad's good Scotch and Gem's artful work, but I down the cocktail in one go.

"What?" she asks.

"They broke up last year," Gemma reminds Mum gently.

"Doesn't mean she's not still your friend. She could have driven you up."

"It's five hours, Mummers," I protest. "I don't want to be in a car with her that long."

"Maybe all you need is the chance to have a good conversation, sort out—"

"There's nothing left to sort out," I cut in sullenly. "Yeah, we're still friends, but that doesn't mean I can just let you ambush her—"

"Ambush!" Mum echoes, looking guilty enough that it's obvious she totally had plans. "I would never."

"You *have*," Gem reminds her. None of us have forgotten Gem's high school crush, and the inflatable kiddie pool.

"Well," Mum says, flustered and caught-out. "It still would have been nice to see her."

"You could have brought Caden," Gemma says with a sly eye-side.

"Choke and die." I offer up a sharkish smile.

"Colin!" Mum scolds.

"Who's Caden?" Stu asks. My himbo brother likes gossip just as much as his twin.

"Breach of confidence!" I snarl at Gem.

"There was no NDA," Gem says through her own knife-slice grin.

"Who's Caden?" Stu asks again, amused.

"He's no one," I insist.

Gem scoffs. "That's not what you—"

"He's no one *now*," I amend, fiddling with my glass, watching my ice cube melt and wishing I hadn't drunk it all in one go. I always feel like a jerk if I get up and refill before everyone else has finished. I'm not, like, an alcoholic, but I don't want my family *thinking* I am one. They already watch me like a time-bomb when it comes to mental-health shit.

"Oh," Stu says, catching what I mean.

"You'll just have to try harder next time," Mum says. It's meant to be pleasant and understanding, but I literally grind my teeth together so hard Gem shoots me a startled look. "I don't know what I've done wrong, that you can't *keep* a partner, *mo leanbh*."

"Gem and Stu are single right now too, Mum, it's not like—"

"Just remember what Dr. Chen said about needing stability, Colin. It's not good to jump from relationship to relationship like this."

*That's skirting dangerously close to calling me a 'greedy bisexual,'* I think, but don't say, because that's not a conversation I feel like having right now.

"Cut Colin some slack," Gem says gently.

"I just don't know why Rebekah couldn't come up with you," Mum says, wringing her hands. "She was such a nice girl, and you were going to get—"

"You said you weren't going to bring that up," Stu stops her.

My stomach bottoms out, and I shove away from the table.

"Just forget I said anything, okay?" Mum says. She pats my shoulder lovingly, and leaves to go turn on the TV. I hate when she does that. Can't argue at her back, 'cause she can't read your lips that way. Mum keeps her hearing aids turned down so she can't hear anyone or anything that isn't directly in front of her. It always bugged her when we screamed across the house.

The TV flicks on, the channel flips, and Stu stands up to peer into the living room when it stops on a program with someone singing in that high, signature '70s tone we are all very familiar with.

"Mum's watching Lawrence Welk reruns again," Stuart says accusingly as Gem starts to tidy up.

"Rebekah broke up with *me*," I remind them.

"We know," Gem says. "Stu, when were you planning to leave?"

"Might as well be right now," Stu grunts. Then he comes around the table and wraps me up in a bear hug that has me dangling a few inches from the floor. "Have a good trip back tomorrow."

"Thanks," I wheeze, nose smooshed.

He sets me down and slaps my shoulder in a manly, hetero way. "Happy birthday."

"Just one year away from my quarter-life crisis. I'm thrilled."

"Will you have figured out what to do with your fancy degree by then?"

"Har har."

"Oh!" Gem says, and turns away to rifle the junk drawer. She sifts through archeological layers of take-out menus, dried up pens, and loose Canadian Tire money. She emerges with a rumpled, used-to-be-white envelope. "This came for you. Like, last year."

"Why didn't you forward it?"

"I'm not your secretary."

I take the envelope. "I was here at Thanksgiving. And Christmas. *And* Easter."

"I'd forgotten. Mum found it when she was looking for the birthday candles."

I slip the letter out of the envelope. The paper is textured and expensive. The letterhead is crowned with maple leaves, and a little flame. Underneath it says, **From the Office of Lt. Gov. Francis A. G. Simcoe.**

**Dear Colin Fergus Levesque;** the letter reads, in a computer-generated handwriting font. **On behalf of the office of the Lieutenant Governor of the province of Upper Canada, and in the name of her Royal Majesty, Elizabeth Regina, we are pleased to congratulate you on the occasion of your graduation from your post-secondary studies...**

...blah blah blah.

"What is it?" Stu asks, looking over my shoulder. "Oh, one of those."

"Yeah." I chuck it into the recycling bin under the sink. "Just the same thing the dragons always send. Nothing special."

# chapter two

As soon as I shoulder open my apartment door, someone shouts "surprise!" from behind my sofa.

"Shit!" I drop my bag on my foot in shock, grabbing at my shirt over my heart.

The shout is followed by coughing, which *doesn't* surprise me. It hasn't been vacuumed back there since my roommate Katiya left on her grand Backpacking-and-Smelly-Hostels Tour of The Continent with her fiancé. Happily, this means I get the place to myself for the rest of the summer. Even more happily, it also means she's not bugging me to spin the chore wheel every weekend.

Less happy for Dikembe, my fourth year lab partner, who is crawling out from behind the sofa, streaked with gray dust.

The "surprise!" is echoed from a few other hiding places around the apartment—not that there are many, it's just a two-bedroom, first floor of a crummy, crumbling row house in the student-ghetto part of downtown—and two more people tumble laughingly into the front hall.

"This is a gross misuse of the emergency key I gave you," I say as Hadi steps out of my front closet.

"Happy birthday!" she jeers, detangling the back of her purple hijab from the Velcro on one of my coats.

"Keep your shoes on," Dikembe says. "About face."

He pushes at me until my nose is nearly against the front door.

"No, no, no," I complain. "I've been on a train all day. I want to go to bed."

"You want to go with us to the bar and get waaaaaasted!" Mauli says, coming in from the kitchen. They're in their Party Skirt, the sparkly blue one, which means they are planning to really properly drink tonight. Shit, is that the last of Katiya's vodka swinging from their fist?

Dammit, I'm gonna have to buy a new bottle before she gets home. Make it an apology present to sweeten her up to the idea that I might not be moving out after all. The hope was that I would find a job and be outta her hair before January. But I'm starting to think that won't happen.

"It's a school night," I protest.

"You graduated a year ago!" Mauli reminds us.

"So it's a worknight." I aim an elbow at Dike so he'll back up.

Hadhirah makes a noise like an old-fashioned telephone and lifts her palm to the side of her face. "Hello? Yes? Hmmm, you don't say. I'll let him know." She drops her hand. "Your boss says it's fine."

"Har har." I let them manhandle me outside and down the grungy cement porch to the broken sidewalk. "Just don't be on my ass tomorrow if I'm hungover."

"Hey, they're not *my* tips at risk."

We end up at The Brass Monkey, just down from Beanevolence. My apartment is a few blocks north of the main street, where both the bar and the café are located. It's one of the few advantages to living in a place where the smells and stains of a hundred students who rented it before me are ground into the carpets.

Hadi spends a few minutes chatting with the bartender, while Mauli opines on the wonders of microbreweries. Dikembe makes eyes at the girls at the table next to us, and tries to look as cool as he can with a Chez Levesque dust bunny stuck in his twists.

One of the other nice things about living and working within the same few blocks is that you get to know everyone else who does the same. And sometimes, because of it, they give you free shit.

"Turn that frown upside down, grumpy gus," Hadi says in a syrupy voice when she comes back with a basket of Roasted Cauliflower Bites. There's a candle in the curry mayo. "Look, on the house."

I didn't realize I was frowning. The train trip must have worn me out more than I thought. I blow out the candle, and Mau and Dike pound me on the back like I've scored a winning touchdown. Our tasting flights come with an extra shot of Jaeger for the birthday boy, courtesy of the table of girls, and I tell Dike to go thank them for me. I even brush the dust bunny away first.

"You're not going with him?" Hadi asks as I down the shot.

"Nah, too bagged. Long day."

I'm not...

I'm not going to do it.

I'm not.

Somehow my phone is in my hand already, though, and from a distance I hear myself saying: "Rebekah usually has Mondays off. I could—"

"No!" Hadi shouts, so quick it's actually kinda insulting.

Mau pulls the phone outta my hands. They're tipsy enough that they fumble it. If they drop it into one of their glasses, I'm going to eat their soul. But they shove it down the front of their skirt instead, right into the boxers below it.

"Don't think I won't go in there after it," I say, pointing at their nose. "You know the saying about a bi person sticking their hands in someone's pants and being happy with whatever they find."

"Buy me dinner first," Mau says, sticking out their tongue. I make a swipe for it and miss.

"What do you call this?" I Vanna White the cauliflower.

"Didn't buy it. No Gs, No Os."

"I can get my own Os!"

Hadi snorts, and I realize what I just said.

"I can do *that*, too," I say, leering cartoonishly. "Masturbation is a normal and healthy part of—" She shoves me. "Abuse! Abuse! This is homophobia!"

Hadi finally breaks out a real smile, instead of that tight, sardonic thing she likes to call one. Score.

"If you can get your own, go get one from them." Mau leans across the table and flicks their eyes at someone at the bar. Their back is to us, but they're still moving enough to make it clear that they were turning away quickly. Like they didn't want to be caught. "They've been staring at you since we got in."

I turn to glance over my shoulder and—

*It's him.*

My heart jumps into the back of my throat, and I'm halfway off my stool before my brain catches up with what I'm actually seeing. In the light of the overhead lamps, the guy at the bar's hair only *looks* ginger, their dirty blond hair reflecting the reddish light of the barback.

*Not him.*

"Snacky," I stage-whisper all the same, committed now that I'm on my feet. Mau drops my befouled phone into my hand.

"Colin," Hadi says, grabbing my sleeve before I can head over. "Hey, be smart, okay?"

"The Rules?" I tap my temple.

"The Rules," she agrees, and lets me go.

As I work my way through the crowd, I try to shove away the weird flutter that even thinking I had spotted *him* caused. It's a stupid thought. There's no way someone like him—upright, posh, *snobby*—would sit and shoot the shit with the bartender for funsies.

So why had I been *excited* when I thought it was him?

People like him don't date people like me.

Do they?

It's just curiosity. It has to be. Because of the *access*, right? It would have been the perfect excuse to finally bridge that customer-service gap. Sidle up to him, actually meet in a place where I didn't work to distract me, where I could casually drop the fact that it was my birthday and I wouldn't say no to a celebratory drink.

Actually get a conversation out of him.

Yeah, right.

He never *talks* to me. I stopped trying to start a conversation with him over a year ago, because he'd always looked like

I'd smacked him between the eyes with a wet fish whenever I tried. It seemed kinder to just let him hide behind his newspaper—an honest-to-god *paper* paper—and stare at me.

And he *does* stare. Sometimes I think the staring is the kind you do when you appreciate the look of another person. Sometimes, I think it's some weird split-tongue thing. It's gotta be, 'cause if he was into me, he would've said something by now, right?

The part of me that's still a writer sometimes makes up stories about my fussy regular. Why he's here. What he's thinking about. Whether he really sleeps on a pile of gold (if that's not a speciesist stereotype.) What the no-doubt beautiful maiden he goes home to every night thinks of his morning routine. Or if maybe he's into something a little more me-shaped.

Oh my god, I am such a romance novel cliché right now.

Also, *dammit Colin.* Maybe focus on the person you are *actually* trying to get between the sheets?

"Hi." I slide onto the bar stool beside the guy.

"Hi. I hear it's your birthday." his voice is softer than I expected and I look again. Not a guy, but a butch gal. Still snacky.

"Yup." I flash her a smile.

It's about half the wattage I can usually manage.

I'm tired. The long train ride, the unexpected surprise... and I remember doing this with Caden. And from Caden, my brain jumps to Rebekah, and how last year for my birthday we'd done one of those boat cruise dinners at Niagara Falls, and I'd had a ring burning a hole in my blazer pocket, and...

... I just don't wanna anymore.

"Sorry," I say, before she can suggest anything. "I thought you were someone else. I shouldn't have... my bad."

I don't wait for her response and slink back to the table.

"Not into you?" Mauli asks.

"I'm not up for it."

"*Up* for it," Mauli snickers, and I pinch them hard on the shoulder.

I leave at closing time, after a few beers too many, frustrated and manhandling Mauli into one of the cheap cabs that prowl downtown for desperate fares. Dike had headed off with one of the ladies hours ago, and Hadi had bailed before I'd even returned from my failed attempt to hit on the guy at the bar.

*Happy birthday to me,* I think morosely as I trudge home. Alone.

# chapter Three

You remember what I told you about the Inciting Incident? Well, this is where it matters.

Because that alarm clock?

It *sucks.*

Stu was right, and I can't tell when the light gets bright. I am stupid-lucky my brain wakes up on its own, shouting *something is wrong*! It takes me thirty solid seconds of staring at the display to figure out what 'something wrong' is.

I am very late.

I am also hungover as *hell.*

I run the four blocks to Beanevolence, throbbing head down, gulping on air to keep from puking, and hoping I don't bowl someone over. I'm envisioning a line of pissed off suits waiting by the door, tapping expensive shoes on the filthy pavement. Or Hadi writing out a pink slip to fire me. She'd do it, too, even if she had to go buy the pink paper specifically for the dramatic gesture.

Rounding the corner, I'm both relieved and horrified to see there's only one person waiting. Shit. I've totally screwed the morning rush. That's hundreds of bucks Hadi is out.

Hard fail.

Then my stomach swoops, because it's *him.* The guy I'd thought, for a hopeful split-second, had been at the bar last night.

*Now is not the time to be kicking yourself.*

Now is the time to open the goddamn door, and make some coffee, and steal some of the weapons-grade painkillers Hadi keeps in her desk. Hangover headaches are the worst. The fact that I did it to myself makes it even worse-er. Worser? Whatever, I hurt too much right now to care whether that's a real word or not.

Worser-er than even that is that I look like something that crawled out from under my bed, and he looks unfairly delicious.

He's in his usual uniform: a button-down, and a matched tailored-within-an-inch-of-its-life waistcoat and dress pants. This time it's the hunter green with the yellow oversized check and matching shirt. Flattering, but not my fave of his looks.

The newspaper under his arm is in French today. He looks slightly desperate for his caffe tobio. That's a short pull of espresso doppio'd into drip-coffee in equal amounts. Hard core. If I didn't know what he was, I'd say it was a macho drink ordered to intimidate, like dudes who eat hot sauce that's too spicy to look cool. But who knows what caffeine does to people like him? Maybe coffee alone isn't enough to give him his morning perk. Maybe he just likes the taste.

"Sorry," I say, as I swoop in.

The split-tongue steps back, gesturing to the door. This close to him, I can tell he's got that weird aftershave on. It's smoky-amber, with musky deep undertones of fermenting grapes that one field trip too many to peninsula wineries has tattooed on my brain.

"You're late—" he starts, and I shouldn't call him a split-tongue, even in my own head. It's not polite; it's verging on a slur, really. Being hungover is no excuse for meanness. Especially since he doesn't actually lisp.

What he does do is talk in a skin-tinglingly precise accent that's British in the vowels and hard Canadian on the conso-nants. It's arresting, and lyrical. He even rolls his 'r's a little and, okay, I *have* wondered how you get a forked tongue to do that. The point is, it's the kind of accent no one else has had in decades. Maybe centuries, I don't know.

I mean, I have no idea what the dude's name is, let alone his age. Kind of a rude thing to ask.

"I'm aware," I grunt.

"Allow me—" It takes me a second to realize he's trying to get at the door to, what, open it for me? Like some sort of romantic hero?

Oh, no.

No.

That's cute.

That will not do.

This close, I can feel his body heat , and my brain is seriously not online enough to separate last night's fantasies from reality, and arrggggh, it's too early for this.

"I got it," I say, a bit stronger than is polite.

His eyes snap wide. This close, the sunflower yellow of them is flecked with sparks of warm amber. He blinks a few times, the gold-leaf freckles that dance across his cheeks and the bridge of his nose getting lost in a mortified flush.

Shit, I'm being an asshole.

"Sorry," I say again. "Can you just... let me actually unlock it?"

He stands there, all handsome and forlorn. "I thought you might be ill—"

I drag my under-caffeinated gaze from his mouth—this close I can see that the upper peak of his lips are so perfectly shaped they look like they've been tattooed there. I don't think I've ever seen his elegant face composed into anything except a politely thoughtful expression of near-nothingness, sort of like if resting bitch face had a refined older brother. But now he looks hang-dog.

I want coffee.

I want him to back off.

(I want to kiss him.)

I'm *so* hungover.

He is so pretty in the morning light.

I'm being so uncooly feral.

*What is wrong with me today?* I bet if I'd actually gotten laid last night I wouldn't be staring at him like he's the last donut.

"Alright, come in."

He heads for his usual front corner table. He *must* know he looks good sitting there. Possibly he likes this table because he likes his back to the wall, and an eye on all the exits. Hadi painted the support columns of the old black building the same blazing bronze as her logo, and they do frame the view of the street nicely. And the view of him, from the sidewalk. Or maybe he just likes the warmth from the windows—it could be a cold-blooded lizard thing. But honestly, I really think he's doing it just to torment me.

'Cause when the sun hits the front of the building just right, it sparks off his spun-copper hair, lines his high cheekbones and beaky nose in gold, gilds his shining freckles, and lends a flush of warmth to his otherwise cream-pale skin.

(What? I'm still a writer at heart. I've already decided exactly how I'd describe him on paper. Don't judge me.)

God, I'm *thirsty.*

I lie to myself and pretend I mean I need something to drink.

The fact that I can almost hear the syrupy anime love theme every time I look at him is the unfairest kind of bullshit imaginable. I am a trashperson, lusting after him when the most we've ever spoken before today was the time he miraculously asked for a second caffe tobio (he'd had bruises under his eyes like thumbprints. I'd wanted to ask him if he was okay, but he was back to his table so quick and—)

Maybe Gem is right and I do need to lay off the romance novels.

(Never.)

Thirsty. Focus on the coffee.

Right.

Maybe I need a glass of ice-water instead.

Maybe just a whole-ass cold shower.

I get all of the gear flicked on, checking water levels and pulling the wands out of the sanitizer, then grind the first pot for the perc. As the espresso machine chugs its way to wakefulness, I peer into garbage cans and inspect tables. The till is counted out neatly, with a post-it note reminding me to buy a roll of quarters stuck to the crisp purple stack of tens.

Obviously Min-soo closed last night, 'cause she always kills it.

In the dark kitchen, I crank the industrial oven up as high as it will go to pre-warm, scoop dough from the huge bowl Min-soo left in the fridge last night onto trays, and climb the step-ladder to dump a burlap sack of fresh beans into the massive stainless steel bean roaster in pride of place in the corner of the kitchen.

In my back pocket, my phone starts playing a punk version of *You're the Cream in My Coffee*. Shit. That's my alarm to start the second batch of scones. Dammit. I don't have time to let the oven preheat properly. I shove the tray in.

Then it's back out to the front, where *he* is sitting primly in his corner, eyes on his newspaper.

Yeah, I'm a basic bitch and prefer coffee that's more sugar and froth than bean juice, but there's something so good about a fresh-brewed black coffee first thing in the morning. That's art in its own right, my loves. I interrupt the drip machine to pour myself a mug, and take one selfish minute to revel in a perfect sip.

But what is usually a soft symphony of my mornings is instead a self-inflicted cacophony. The plink of coffee into the carafe, the hiss of the espresso machine, the hum and clunk of the bean-roster in action, all punctuated by the crisp rustle of his newspaper? Agony.

A year ago, I would use this quiet time after the morning rush to work on my thesis. Before that, it would have been an essay, or a lab, or something else I'd procrastinated. Now, I have nothing to work on. Nothing to do but this. Nowhere to go but here. No career, no demand, no drive, just...

Me.

And him.

And the stretching, hissing, clunking, dripping, painful silence.

"Ugh, get your ass in gear, you embarrassment," I mutter to myself.

"Beg pardon?" he asks, voice raised politely.

*Shit.*

"I said, uh, the espresso machine is warmed up. Caffe tobio?"

"Please." He crosses his legs. There's a flash of turquoise at his ankle. I only catch it for a second, but it looks like he's wearing socks with cartoon dragons on them. Huh, okay... that's more playful than I expected him to be.

"Coming right up."

"I appreciate it. And you *are* well?" he asks, which is the longest string of words I've ever heard out of him.

"Yeah." I turn to the machine, tapping out a careful twenty-seven seconds with the toe of my chucks, timing as the espresso fills the demitasse. So I'm completely in my head, and totally not expecting it when his voice comes from somewhere much too close, just over my left shoulder.

"Oversleeping could be the sympto—"

"Gah!" I shout, and *Christ no*, the wand in my hand goes flying up, up, sprinkling boiling-hot grounds like freaking pixie dust.

He ducks and snaps the newspaper over his head as they rain down. The sharp clatter of the wand hitting the tile makes us both wince. In the aftermath we stare across the counter at one another, eyes wide, with what I assume are matching shocked expressions.

"Are you—" he starts again and I hold out a hand to stop him.

"I'm fine."

"I've never known you to—"

"Shit, you're chatty today," I say, and it's accidentally catty. He flinches, stung. A glob of espresso grounds plops off his shoulder and splats on the tile floor. "Sorry, sorry! That came out wrong. I'm not... I'm not having a good morning."

"My apologies," he murmurs mournfully, and aw, no.

"I'll make you another one," I say quickly. "On the house. Just... sit, and I'll—"

"Perhaps I should go." He lowers his paper and flicks grounds off the toe of his shoe. Oh, shit, are they expensive? Am I going to have to pay for, I dunno, shoe dry cleaning?

"No, please. " That lurch in my stomach again, and it's only because a morning that has started terribly (and has only gotten worse) would really become awful if he wasn't sitting in the sunlight, glimmering quietly. "Please stay."

It would be just *wrong*.

"If you are ill, you ought to be taking care of yourself first," he insists, instead of acknowledging my plea. "Don't you have a colleague who could cover—"

"I got a new alarm clock, I didn't wake up, it's fine, it doesn't matter."

"It does to me." He crunches the ruined paper in his hands, flexing and twisting. "In fact, I, er, perhaps it is time I confessed that... I smell something burning."

"You smell burning?" I swig another mouthful of coffee from the mug I'd left by the till, and take a deep breath to calm myself. Wait. "I smell it, too."

His gaze flicks to the door behind me, slit pupils dilating. "The kitchen."

"The scones!" I squawk and spin on the spot. I slip in spilled espresso, toppling sideways. Before I can hit the ground, he lunges across the countertop, catching my arm in a grip that's stronger than I think he realizes. It also prickles.

Trying to get my stupid feet under me, I catch the barest flash of red scale and black, long-tipped nails. Then his hand is back to a perfectly pale peach, fussily manicured, and human.

I shrug him off and push through the door. I shouldn't have gasped, that was a stupid thing to do when the air is heavy with smoke. But I do, and jerk to a stop, folding double, coughing. He runs into me. I nearly topple. That prickling grip pulls me upright again.

"What can I do to—" he starts, but the fire alarm cuts him off.

"I forgot to turn down the goddamn oven!"

"I'll get it." He reaches out with his free hand. It's covered in deep red scales, his fingertips ending in delicately curved claws.

Holy crap.

He's dexterous, able to work the knob, then swing down the oven door. Black smoke, oily with burning fats, cascades into our faces. I cover my mouth and nose with the edge of my Henley, eyes burning.

"Oven mitts!" I warn.

"Not necessary!" He's got the tray balanced in his claws. "Where should I—?"

And that's when the fire suppression system kicks in.

It lets out a sharp, high whistle that startles him so badly the claws of the hand holding my arm spasm. They go right through my shirt and into flesh.

I holler.

Five things happen at once.

First, he drops the tray of scones. It clatters off the tile, sending burnt pucks of dough into the air. One smacks into my leg, and two pelt him as we dance away.

Second, he yanks his claws out of my arm, blood on the tips, and freaking hell, it stings.

Third, white foam pours from the pipes that ring the kitchen ceiling, coating every surface in a bitter-tasting cloud. Including us.

Fourth, the guy makes a sort of gurgling belch noise, then a sharp bony click accompanied by a spark on his lips that looks exactly like the kind you get from a lighter.

Fifth, he spits fire.

Right into the corner. Where the giant custom bean roaster is. The drum is perforated, and the beans inside it immediately go up in flames. They're so hot they burn blue. The steel drum starts to goddamn melt.

"*Coc y gath*," he gasps in horror, dithering on the spot.

"Holy shit," I say, clamping my hand down over the punctures in my arm.

"I'm terribly sorry!" he shouts over the sound of the alarm and the hiss of the foam deflating around us. "I didn't mean to—I was startled!"

The urgency of the situation suddenly hits home, fire crawling up the wall toward the ceiling, and I scream: "Put it out!"

"What do you want me to do? Suck it back up?" he shouts back, all his cool calm evaporating in the heat of the inferno. "I'm a dragon, not a fire extinguisher!"

Well.

Fuck this meet-cute straight to hell, then.

# chapter four

**"Y**ou destroyed my roaster, set the kitchen on fire, and clawed up my employee," Hadi snarls ,counting off the dragon's sins on her fingers. She shouldn't look as frightening as she does, standing there in pajama pants, a rumpled hijab, and a bright purple hoodie she somehow hasn't realized is on backwards.

But he is *cowed.*

"I'll pay to replace them," he replies, so miserable that I genuinely feel sorry for him. His forearms are black with ash from where he clawed the burning beans out of the roaster and scattered them on the floor so I could attack them with the extinguisher. His shirt is now raggedly short-sleeved.

Hadi snorts. "Damn straight you will. And in the meantime? How am I supposed to make *coffee?*"

"We'll rush-order it." He fumbles for his wallet. Soot smears all over everything, but he manages to hand Hadi an hon-est-to-god paper business card. She pinches a clean corner between two fingers. "Have your insurance company contact my people with the information of the upscale model. Hire professional cleaners and contractors. I'll cover it all."

Hadi looks over at me. "You heard that? I have a witness?"

From my perch on the rear fender of the ambulance, I give her a thumbs up and a goofy grin behind my oxygen mask. This is hilarious. I'm not feeling even remotely hungover anymore.

That might be the shock talking.

The garage-door style windows at the front of the café are open, letting out the last of the ugly smell. Inside Beanevolence, the fire fighters are checking over their gear and preparing to go. There's a small crowd around the outside of the police tape cordoning off the sidewalk, mostly folks from the buildings on either side of the café, which were evacuated for safety. Luckily, nobody but me has to be treated for smoke inhalation.

A sharp pain on my right bicep startles me hard enough to make a very not-manly noise. The paramedic dousing the place where the dragon's talons pierced my skin in disinfectant *tsks* at me and reminds me to stay still.

Right.

Smoke inhalation *and* puncture wounds.

Everything between the bottom of my right ear and my right elbow fucking *burns*.

"I'll call when I'm done with that idiot," Hadi says, jabbing a finger at me. "Right now I have to go with him to the hospital."

"I can go by myself," I crackle, distorted by the tight dryness of my throat.

"I'll go," the dragon says, and everybody ignores me when I protest a second time. "Please, it's the least I can do. This way you can stay with the shop."

I pull off the oxygen mask long enough to shout "I said I can go by myself!", and then start heaving another round of hacking coughs.

The paramedic, now packing wads of sterile gauze into the five neat dime-sized wounds, *tsks* again. She pushes the mask back over my face, and says, "Actually, *I'm* taking you." She points at the dragon. "Loverboy. Get in if you're getting in."

"He's isn't—"

"I'm not—"

"Don't care," the paramedic interrupts. She removes my mask briskly, and steps up into the box to stow her gear.

I don't need babysitting, so I stand and try to clamber one-handed up the fender. Okay, I haven't had breakfast, I'm dehydrated, I've lost blood, and I'm having trouble breathing, so it's a dumb move, right? I'll cop to that. My foot doesn't land on the fender, and I scrape my shin as I slide down, scrabbling for the rails.

I'm gonna add a broken jaw to my list of injuries and it'll be *mortifying—*

The dragon's arm is around my waist before I hit the pavement.

"Whoop!" I shout as my feet come off the ground. "I'm sorry, are you... actually holding me up like a sack of potatoes?" I twist my neck to stare up at the guy. He's not even straining. "Uh, as fun as this is, can you put me—"

"Of course," he blurts, and carefully sets me back on my feet. "Oh, your shirt."

His attention isn't on the new black streaks decorating the waist. He's looking at where the paramedic cut off the sleeve, the tape on my skin, the spots of blood blooming against the gauze.

*It's really not this guy's day. Really not mine either*, I decide, and flap my good hand at him when he tries to hand me up into the ambulance like some Jane Austen heroine. Yes, I've read Jane Austen. One, the books are good, and two, I appreciate a well-crafted narrative. Also, it has nothing to do with being a pining hopeless romantic, no matter what Gemma tells you, so there.

"Sit," the paramedic barks. She points at the bench along the side of the box.

Like two naughty school children, we obey in unison.

The paramedic closes the doors, glares once to make sure we stay put, then turns her attention to paperwork. The driver pulls away slowly, gently easing around the firetruck.

The dragon's a soothing warmth beside me in a way a *homo sapiens* can never be, and the adrenaline spike from the near-disaster has me woozy enough to want to lay my head on his shoulder. I don't though, obviously.

"Awww," I say after a moment. "No sirens."

The dragon stifles a laugh.

"What?"

"I was hoping for the sirens, too," he admits in a whisper.

And then he smiles at me.

It punches all the air right out of my lungs.

The skin beside his eyes crinkle up into shallow crow's feet. It hits me for the first time that he's more than just objectively handsome. I'd noticed, in a distantly-aesthetic way, before now. But shit, he really is *attractive* in a way only someone whose face you've seen transform with honest, intimate emotion can be. With the color still high on his face from the fire, it makes him all English-rosy and glowy and, yeah, *no*, let's back this train up.

Now is a bad time for this kind of thing.

I yank my gaze to where my left hand is cradling my right elbow tight against my tummy to keep my arm from moving. His gaze must follow it.

"Does it hurt?" the dragon asks softly.

The scoff is out of my mouth before I can catch it behind my teeth. "What do you think?"

I'd meant it to be funny, but he flinches, and shifts so there's a careful inch between us. It's not until he's gone that I realize how soothing it was to have him pressed all up the side of me, curled toward me to protect me from the cold glare of the evil paramedic.

"Sorry, that was a shitty thing to say."

"I do apologize again," he mutters. "I have a wretched temper and I must control it better."

"It was an accident."

He does a sort of half-shrug, head shake move that's awkward as hell, and *oh fuck*, cute. Dammit. *Dammit.*

*The Rules*, I remind myself firmly. *Don't forget The Rules.*

"Been wondering," my mouth says without any input from my brain, and okay, so that shot of whatever it was the paramedic gave me before she started packing my wounds is kicking in strong because I can't feel my face any more. "Why do you come in and stare at me every morning?"

"*Stare* at you?" he echoes like an offended maiden aunt.

It's hilarious, so I laugh. And then I wince, and grab my elbow harder. Goddamnit, that *hurts*. The paramedic heaves a sigh, grabs a roll of fabric out of a box by her feet, and leans over to wrap my arm in a sling.

"Ouch," I complain as she ties the knot behind my neck.

"Your fault. I told you not to move it."

"I'll make sure he stays still," the dragon says to her with a sort of condescending solemnity.

Is he taking the piss?

I think he's taking the piss.

"You're not my keeper," I snipe back, smirking to show that I'm teasing, that I'm trying to get that light mood back. That I want him to lean back in and press all of that delicious body heat against me again.

"I've injured you. It's on me to ensure—"

"Fun as that would be, this isn't actually a draconic romance novel," I interrupt. I want to put my hand on his knee. Good thing it's trapped in the sling. "I get it. You're being nice, but like, you don't *owe* me a debt of honor or any of that possessive Harlequin stuff."

A smile breaks out across his face, and *thank fuck*. This one is a sarcastic little thing, curling up just one side of his mouth. "Read many draconic Harlequins, do you?"

"Man, shut up," I grump, but I can't seem to control my matching grin. "You can't shame me for my taste. There's nothing wrong with liking happily ever afters."

"Nothing at all," he murmurs, but it's so soft I decide he didn't mean for me to hear it. Fine, I can pretend. I'm in too much pain to pick a fight, anyway. Or, to continue picking it, or... whatever this is that we're doing.

We're not *actually* fighting, are we?

My stupid brain-weasels grab that idea between their sharp teeth and run away with it, and suddenly I wonder if I've misread this whole thing. Just because he's attractive doesn't mean he's attracted to *me*. Fuck, maybe he's just doing this because he feels guilty for torching my place of employment and clawing me up.

What if he doesn't even want to be here?

I hate taking pity-favors from people. If that's what this is, I'd rather do this alone. No one needs to see me being whiny. It's not cool, and it's not sexy. And I want very much to be cool and sexy for him.

Choking on my humiliation, I say softly: "You didn't need to come."

"I really did," he replies, infuriatingly calm.

"We'll probably have to wait for hours."

"I would have been sitting in the café, anyway."

"I will be *annoying*," I threaten.

"I'm certain you will be."

"I hum terrible classical music earworms when I'm bored."

"I especially like your rendition of *Peter and the Wolf* when you're mopping," he says, but it's small, careful.

Despite him being taller than me, and fit as hell, *everything* about him is carefully controlled. *Gentle*, that's the word. *Precise*. From the shine on his shoes to the crease ironed into his slacks, to the usual careful lay of his hair, this man has never once looked or sounded anything but mindfully curated.

He makes me feel loud, messy, and childish. I thought dragons were supposed to be brash, confident, and charismatic, but he's never been demanding, and I've never heard him speak above a gentle murmur (unless he's yelling about fire extinguishers).

He catches my look of confusion and says, "My apologies."

"No, it's—" I start, and then literally bite my tongue because I have no idea how to end that sentence.

*Is* it fine? Beanevolence is a public space, and I don't have to hum at work if I don't want to. So is it creepy he's noticed? Or is it charming? I have *no* idea.

"You didn't answer. About why you come into the café every day?" I prompt. He clears his throat and a flush climbs up from his collar. It's not red enough to be scales. Is he embarrassed? "What, you're such a wealthy man of leisure you have nothing better to do?" I joke.

"Quite," is all he says.

*Holy shit, what?* I have the time to think, but not say, because the ambulance stops.

"Alright, everyone out," the paramedic says, stepping over us to fling open the back door with urgency. I don't blame her. The burnt-coffee reek is pretty acrid.

The dragon descends first and holds a hand up for me to take and, yeah, okay, I've got a sling now and it friggin hurts to move so, sure, I can let him Mr. Darcy me onto the sidewalk. There's that smallness again. He's not even a bit impatient for me to accept his help. I don't want to think about it. I also make a point of not letting myself think about his skin, or its warmth, or, or what shape his fingers are when I finally slide my hand into his.

Nope. This is *not* a tropey repressed hand-touch moment. I refuse.

The paramedic walks us through getting signed in at the admission desk. Then we're directed toward the uncomfortable waiting room, without an answer about how long we're probably going to have to wait.

"Plastic chairs," I whine as I sink into one, just because I can.

I'd promised the dragon I'd be a bastard. I might as well live up to it. It'll be fun and kill time, if nothing else.

The dragon looks around and then down at his blackened hands. "Would you mind if I—?"

"Go. Scrub." I wave him off.

"Will you—?"

"I'm fine." I pull my cell phone out of my back pocket. There's already half a dozen texts from Hadi, and one each from Gemma and Stuart, who must have heard the news already, and a missed call from Mum.

He hesitates, and I pointedly bow my head to make it clear that I've already dismissed him, turning my attention to the family group chat:

**im ok oven caught fire not my fault**

The dragon doesn't currently have a tail, but when I glance up, he's walking up the hall with enough shame that if he did, it would be tucked between his legs.

# chapter five

"**S**o what do I call you?" I ask when he gets back. I'm trying to offer an olive branch, or whatever it is when you've been an ass to the regular who has accompanied you to the hospital, even though he didn't have to.

Part of my question is because I don't know his name. But part of it is me realizing he's a dragon—I mean, I knew he was a dragon this whole time, the eyes give it away—so he's probably got a fancy title. Duke McSootyClaws or something.

They're always dukes in books.

"Oh." He freezes. "Dav, I suppose."

"You suppose?" I slouch, trying to find a position where my arm doesn't throb. I'm not having any luck.

"Alva-draig Tudor." This is the first time I've heard him actually sound miffed.

He looks out of sorts for the first time, too. His pants are creased and smeared with ash, and his waistcoat is hanging open like a regency rake. His hair, normally straight out of an Errol Flynn flick, with a severe 1940s part and careful swoops on top, is a sort of frizzy orange flop across his forehead. He pushes it back irritably. He's rolled up the ragged ends of his sleeves so his shirt looks less like he stuck his hands in fire—which he absolutely did—and more like it's a sartorial choice. And wow, *forearms*. Trim, and muscley, and flecked with more of those intriguing gold-dust freckles and spun-copper hair and, *yes please and thank you*.

It makes something in my middle flippy. Or maybe that's the pain meds? One or the other. I'm too hot, and too cold, and sticky with pain-sweat, and kind of nauseous, and I want to close my eyes and lean against his shoulder and *sleeeep*. Ugh.

"Dav it is," I concede. "Middle name for a middle name, then. Colin Fergus Levesque."

I squirm around until I can get my free hand aimed in his general direction and he shakes it awkwardly. I'm blinking dumbly, I know I am, my eyelid s heavy in a way that sucks because there's no way I a) could actually fall asleep here, and b) *should* fall asleep here, and c) will probably not be able to sleep later when the shock of being lightly-stabbed in the middle of my first (and hopefully last) industrial fire has worn off.

"A pleasure," Dav says as he sits. His whole face twists up when he realizes what he's said. "Well, not the part where I hurt you—and set fire to the—it's not *actually* been a pleasure—"

"No, I get what you mean," I say, cutting off his increasingly-desperate word-deluge.

I shimmy, looking for some moment of *relief* because this is awful. I just want to *cry* and I'm not going to, I'm *not*. The fingers of my right hand have started to tingle. Maybe something's wrong with my arm. I could be paralyzed, or disfigured for life.

*Shit*.

"Though, *draig* is not my middle name," he adds softly. His voice sounds like it's coming through a tunnel. "It simply means *dragon*. We often append that to our given names. Rather like saying, ah, Joe and Not-Human Joe."

"Huh?"

"Dear lord." His voice is now deep in the cave, his face suddenly blocking my eye-line to the scuffed linoleum floor. One slender hand cradles first the back of my neck, then my cheek, then is laid against my forehead, then is gone. Gosh, he's warm. A miserable full-body shiver crawls over me. I wish he'd put his hand back on my nape. "You've gone dead pale. Colin?"

I wiggle my fingers, to prove to myself that I can, and the pain it stirs up is excruciating.

Am I about to vomit?

I might be about to vomit.

That wouldn't be even remotely cool and sexy.

"Stay here," he says, and then he's gone.

*Ha, like I have anywhere to go. Or the ability to get there.*

The flip in my stomach is starting to feel more like a flop.

"He's coming out of shock," a new voice says over my head. A blanket whumps onto my lap. "Keep him warm. The painkillers have started to wear off."

"Then give him more," Dav says, and this is the first time I've heard him sound confident and leader-ly. "He should be lying down."

*I bet he's a duke. Maybe a baron. Do I address him as 'Lord' or...? Boy, he sounds authoritative. Why is he never bossy around me? It's sexy.*

"There's no beds," the nurse (the voice must be a nurse) says. "We'll push him up the queue."

"I'll get you some water," Dav says, and the nurse tells him not to. No food, either. He tucks the blanket around me, aggravated, and I swat him away.

"Hurts," I tell him when he yanks. "Knock it off." He steps back, lets out a frustrated sort of hissing noise that I had no idea dragons made, and is absolutely not adorable. "Go for a walk or something."

"I don't—"

"There's a Timmie's in the lobby."

"Their coffee is wretched."

"It's hot."

"It's not *yours*."

At some point my eyes closed, because I need to pry them open to squint at Dav.

"Say what?"

"It's not..." he starts, but my head is swimming and I don't catch the rest. "...-lin? Colin?"

"Don't drink it then. It's just an excuse to get you to stop fussing."

"Do you want me to go away?"

His stupid wounded expression hooks into me, tugs at the squishy bit behind my breastbone where my heart is working overtime. A part of me wants to, so badly, say *No, please stay, hold me. I'm actually scared. I want my Mum.* Instead I say: "I'm fine on my own."

"I don't think you are," Dav says quietly. He crouches down in front of me again, slacks pulling tight across his thighs. Woof. "The nurse said no food or water. Is there anything else I can do for you?"

I open my mouth to say *shush and let me sleep*, but what comes out is: "My sister used to read to me when I was sick."

Fuck.

I did not mean to say that.

Now he knows I have a sister, and maybe he thinks I'm some sort of lame pansy for reading romances, and I'm not *ashamed*, but what if *he* thinks it's something shameful, and how could I ever like someone who thinks having a nice relationship with his sister is shameful and—

*I'm panicking*, I realize belatedly. *This is a panic attack. I am in the emerg, and my arm is bleeding, and I can't breathe, can't breathe, can't breathe*—and I can't say it, because I can't suck in the goddamned *air*, and Dav's hand is back on my forehead, the soft touch of cloth beside my eyes (I'm not crying! I'm not!), and it's a friggin' *handkerchief*, and he murmurs, "I'll be right back," and then he's gone, he's *gone*, and I reach up, try to grab his wrist, but I am already alone, I don't want to be alone, I don't, I was wrong, I'm not fine, I'm shaking and I can *feel* the blood oozing from the holes, feel it sliding down my inner elbow, am so focused on it I can practically *hear* it, and I want his warm hands again, and I am scared and I am a liar and I want, I want, I *want*—

"Lord above, Colin, *breathe*," Dav says. He drops something on the floor, but that's okay because his hands are back on my face, cupping my chin. "That's it. Big breath in."

Oxygen shudders into my lungs.

"And out."

The exhale sounds thick and gross. Dav doesn't care. A smile blooms on his face, and even though it's tight, there are furrows on either side of his mouth, not quite deep enough to be dimples, but kind-looking and honest.

"In again, Colin, there's a lad."

Right, Dav's rarely-before-witnessed-smile, that's one thing I can see. A small paperback on the floor, white text against a field of familiar lurid purple. Two. A candy bar beside it, black wrapper. Three. Dav's dress shoes framing both, smeared with ash and dried espresso. Four. The stretch of wool over his knees, a faint stripe of orange in the check I hadn't noticed before. Five.

On to touch: Dav's palms against my cheeks, scratchy on my scruff. Two, the blanket over my lap, weighing me to the earth so I can't go flying off. Three, I tap my chucks against the linoleum floor, plasticky and hollow. Ground. Four, I wriggle in my seat, the thin padding pressing against my skinny-ass hip bones. Grounded.

Sound, now. I can hear Dav's voice, *In, out, that's it, Colin, well done.* Muzak in the waiting room, a clarinet rendition of something by Lizzo. Behind the desk, the administrator on the phone, trying to soothe someone, telling them to "bring her in, honey. We'll take care of your baby." That's three.

Two for scent—I can smell charred fabric and the acrid stink of over-roasted beans.

And I can taste salt from my own tears pooling at the corners of my mouth.

"That's better," Dav says softly, and he's not speaking from the end of a tunnel anymore.

"So," I say, and my voice sounds trembly. I reach up with my left hand, wrap my shaking fingers around his wrist, pull his hand back far enough to get a good look at the sodden square of lemon-yellow fabric that matches his pre-burning button-down. "An honest-to-god handkerchief, eh?"

Dav blinks at me for a second, a sweep of copper eyelashes over high cheekbones. Then that smile gets deeper, settles into his face. I sort of expected his teeth to be pointy, or for him to have fangs, but the only draconic thing about him in this shape is his tongue and his eyes. I wonder if he can change them to look more *sapiens*-esque too, if the sunflower color of his irises and the slightly-slit pupils are a personal choice.

If they are, I hope he never changes them.

Dav passes me the handkerchief in question. I appreciate him not saying anything about why I need it. Then he scoops up the book and the candy. I've never seen him order a dessert, so yeah, I'm a nosy jerk and point to the chocolate bar.

"For after," Dav says, and he's being *cheeky*. "If you're good for the doctor, you can have a sweet."

"Awww, thanks daddy," I say, making sure the sarcasm is audible. "But that'll keep me in here."

Dav frowns. "The chocolate bar?"

"Yup," I say, popping the 'p'. "But I appreciate the gesture."

"Is it the nuts? I've seen you drink almond milk."

"The cocoa," I correct. "A rare but annoying food allergy. Do you know how many restaurant desserts have chocolate in them? *All* of them, is the answer." It feels good to be bantering with him again, feels normal, and natural, and not at all like I just had a freak-out in public in front of like, two dozen people. Some of whom are *still staring*.

"*Chocolate*," he murmurs, chagrined.

"Don't tell me you're one of those people who is going to weep for me because I can't have it. Cause I'll tell you, to me it just tastes like puking after birthday parties."

"Vivid." He wrinkles his nose.

"You eat it for me," I tell him.

Dav pockets it instead. "I'm not fond of sweets."

"It'll melt in there."

He makes an annoyed growl-purr sound, and hands the chocolate to a wrecked-looking mom holding a sobbing infant a few seats down. She seems grateful.

"And what's that?" I ask, pointing at the novel.

He hands it to me and retreats into himself, as if waiting for me to find something wrong with this offering, too. "I had nothing to read to you, so I went to the gift shop."

A scantily clad woman in a white Gothic dress smolders up at me from the cover. The dress is mysteriously cling-ing and wet while her flowing blonde tresses are dry. She's leaning back against a dude with a faint bluish tinge to his dark skin, slit-pupiled eyes the piercing color of a Polynesian sea, rippling biceps patterned with tattoos, and his forearms peppered with cobalt scales. Both models are showing the same amount of cleavage—which is to say, *lots*.

Yum.

"*The Azure Ariki's Royal Bride.*" I read aloud. The flop in my stomach turns back into a flip. "Are you making fun?"

"No?" Dav says. "You said you liked draconic romances."

I did, didn't I?

"That's... thoughtful," I allow. "Thanks."

Oh god, he's actually *nice*.

It's weird.

It's cute.

Oh, fuck.

"Shall I read?" He holds out his hand, waits for me to relinquish the book. The gesture is small, polite, like he's not comfortable with touching me now that my panic attack has passed. He hasn't taken me accepting it once as blanket permission to keep at it, and that's, yeah, that's thoughtful, too. That's *attractive*.

I'm exhausted, and still sweating, and aching, and I wish like hell I could get comfortable in this chair. I want to be read to. I give him the book.

Dav leans on the armrest between us, so he's close enough that he won't be interrupting anyone else. I wish he would wrap one of those careful arms around my shoulder.

"Chapter One," he begins gently. I let my eyes slip closed and lean as far into his space as I think I can get away with. "Yalente's father had been a missionary during the Wars. He had uprooted them from Zeeland in 1844, and it was 1846 before Yalente again found herself between four walls in a place she could call home."

Dav is a lovely reader, and when I realize his shoulder is just the right height to rest my aching head on, well, I can blame it on the exhaustion, right? Panic attacks take it right out of me.

"It was a... ah, a small reed house," he reads, voice hitching as I get comfortable. "And newer than the little stone cottage over which her dying mother had left her mistress at the tender age of fourteen. Now twenty, Yalente was losing her second home, for the Māori Rangatira had triumphed. The Pākehā had lost, and were now being evicted from the land they had stolen. Including Yalente, who began to understand what it meant to have unknowingly and unwittingly been a thief..."

# chapter six

The doctor had put neat little stitches into each of the five puncture wounds, and assured me I was going to heal up perfectly fine, with no danger of nerve damage. I'd also had a tetanus shot, just to be sure. Which was a bit insulting to Dav, to be honest.

"I'll walk," I say as I sway to a stop on the evening-cool sidewalk.

The sun is setting. *How* had we been in the hospital that long?

"You will not," Dav counters, already thumbing at his phone. "What's your address?" He makes a face when I tell him.

"It's cheap. And my roommate's backpacking through Europe. I have the place to myself until January."

Although, how I'm supposed to save up to move out now, since I have no workplace and, shit, likely no job, I have no idea. Ugh.

Also, I am *not* leaning on Dav to stay upright.

It may look like I am, but I'm actually not.

It's just... it's been along day, okay? So what if he's the perfect height for my head to rest on his shoulder, it's not a big deal, and I still haven't had *any coffee*. Tragedy. I can be excused.

Dav slips an arm around my shoulder, careful to place his hand on my ribs, rather than my bicep. Gosh, he's so warm. June though it is, this is Canada. It's chilly when the shadows get long. And I hadn't worn a jacket to work because I'd expected to be home by now.

When the car arrives, the posh bastard opens the door for me. Either it's the second round of painkillers talking, or I'm starting to like him. Once we're settled and I've won the silent battle of wills to strap my own damn self in with the seatbelt, Dav fills the awkward silence by staring a hole through his phone. Right, fine by me. I can just lean back and close my eyes and...

My stomach grumbles.

Mortifying.

Dav jerks his head up, startled. Then his expression melts into something closer to amused.

"No," I say immediately. "You don't have to order me dinner."

"I haven't even—"

"*No*," I repeat. "All I want to do is go to bed." I don't add: *And I don't want your apology-money or pity-time*, because that's what I fear this *actually* is. I don't want it to be that, even though I can't define *that* right now, because I'm...

I like spending time with Dav.

I like his gentle manners. I like his precise way of moving, as if every gesture is calculated for maximum elegance and efficiency. I like his fussy clothes and his stupid hanky. I like that he's the right height to lean on, and that his very presence makes the chill evening air tolerable. I like his voice when he is reading me romance novels. For a dude who hates to be fussed over, I'll admit... I even kind of like Dav's fussing. 'Cause when he does it, he *enjoys* it. He's not just doing it because he thinks he should.

Dav is nice, but like, *thoughtful* nice. I used to worry he was a split-tongued creep, but he's never actually done anything creepy. Just sat in the corner and read.

I might even be *enjoying* today, in a masochistic way.

It—*stupidly*—feels like a date. A date that started with impatience and flying espresso and fire, and is ending with blood and localized freezing and stitches. But honestly? It's still not the worst I've ever been on, and nope, this is dangerous territory to be letting my drugged-up brain wander into. I have been burned by thinking there was something there before. Many, *many* times before. This is why I have The Rules.

So no, I am not going to let him buy me dinner because he feels bad about lightly stabbing me by accident. Dinner would be way too *actual* date-y. It doesn't matter that he's now 'Dav', the handsome and well-dressed dragon who beleaguers nurses on my behalf, and buys me candy when I am hurting. He is still *just* a customer.

That's *all.*

He actually harrumphs. "Very well."

Victory.

He turns his attention back to his phone. After a long few moments, he makes that annoyed, put-upon kitten-purr-growl noise again. Does he even realize he's making it? It's... adorable.

"What?" I ask, because I'm a glutton for punishment.

*Get it together, Colin.*

"Hadhirah Bakush, your boss," he starts, then stops and makes the sour-lemon face again. "As you're already aware she is..."

I cover my mouth as I chuckle, afraid he'll think I'm laughing at him. "Yeah?"

"She has spoken to her supplier and the bean roaster can't be shipped for at least a month. She's checked all the other national suppliers at my behest, and it seems that anything large enough to be worth her while are all similarly unavailable."

"Like there's some sort of global shortage crisis?" I ask.

"Evidently," he sneers at his phone. "How inconvenient."

"Bad news," I agree, slumping back in my seat and imagining how blue the air around Hadi must be. "We have an ancient manual, but it's *tiny*. There's no way to make the quantities we need on a daily basis."

"Surely you can buy pre-roasted beans?"

I make a show of clutching my non-existent pearls.

"I'll take that as a no, then, shall I?" Dav says, arching his fussily shaped eyebrow with sardonic nonchalance.

My heart goes pitter-patter.

Fuck.

What, I like the dry-humored straight-men types, okay? I am a smol bi disaster bebe and sass is my domain; my partner has to be someone I can springboard off.

*Not a date!*

God, I need sleep. And food. And sleep. And water. And sleep. And to text Hadi to tell her the doc said I had to be off for at least a week. And sleep.

"Is the only issue with the manual roaster the quantity?" Dav asks as the car pulls onto my street.

"We'd need two people on shift to use it. Except this time of year, without the students at the university, Hadi can only afford one opener."

Dav pets his floppy hair back again irritably. Then he says, slowly, "What if I were to, ah, volunteer my services?"

"You?" I squint, trying to gauge his expression in the passing pools of lamplight.

"I am usually in the café all morning, anyway. How difficult would it be for you to show me how to make the beverages, and work the till so you could be in the kitchen?"

"Oh, the till?" I say, as the car slows to a stop. "That's not what I thought you were going to say."

Dav's shoulders jump up to his ears, defensive. "What did you think I was going to say?" he asks softly.

A sound that's closer to a giggle than I would like to admit flitters out of my mouth as I unbuckle. "Maybe it's the meds talking, but I just had this sudden, stupid vision of you, I don't know, doing your fire spitting thing and roasting the beans yourself."

Dav smiles at my glee, the deep-cheeked sweet one that turns his furrows into full-blown dimples. "If you had a stock-pot sturdy enough, I could likely do so."

I pause halfway out of the car. "What, really?"

"Really," he says, holding out the dog-eared romance novel.

"Keep that. You can read me the rest during the next time it's slow at work," I say, before my brain can catch up to my mouth.

*Oh brilliant, Colin.*

*Idiot.*

"Oh. Well." He retracts the book awkwardly. "Yes."

"Uh. I'll, um, check in with Hadi, and let you know."

"You'll need my contact information." He hands me his phone. "Put yourself in, and I'll text you."

*Not a date, not a date, not a date*, I scream at myself as I poke at the screen one-handed. "So, um, should I EFT you for my part of the ride or...?"

Dav snorts like I've made the funniest joke he's ever heard. "Good night, Colin," he says gently.

"Good night, Dav," I reply, hand him back his phone, and shut the door.

My phone buzzes while I'm toeing off my chucks and kicking them into the front closet. The text reads: **Take care. I'm sorry.**

I save him as Snacc-Dragon.

What?

Don't judge me.

In the cold light of day, my head unclouded by pain-meds, it's a stupid idea. Hadi disagrees.

"I'll take his free labor," she says over speakerphone. I haven't told her about the part where Dav thinks he could roast with his breath, just the java-slinging. "How long will you be armless?"

"I haven't lost a limb." I'm laying in the bathtub, puncture wounds and gauze wrapped in cellophane. My phone is on the closed toilet seat, and I've tied my sling to the towel rack so my arm is supported. "I just can't do any heavy lifting or stretching, anything that'll rip the stitches."

Hadi makes a grump noise that reminds me, sharply, of Dav's annoyed growl-purr. That gets me thinking of Dav's smile, Dav's mouth, the light dusting of ginger beard that had appeared on his cheeks at the end of the day...

*Not a date!*

"How long will that be?" The way Hadi says it makes it clear she's repeating herself.

I blink back down to Earth. "Uh, two weeks? Probably?"

She grumbles again and I stare at the cracked seafoam-blue tiles to keep my mind on the conversation. There's a prescription for pills balled up in my jeans pocket. I should fill it. Ugh, but that means putting on clothes and shuffling to the pharmacy, and that's all the way on the other side of downtown, and *ugh*.

"I guess that's not so bad. We can't open until it's been cleaned, and we've been inspected by the city. The rest of the kitchen is fine, but that whole wall needs to be taken back to the studs. Thank god for oldey-timey architecture, because they're iron and not wood."

I wince. I haven't admitted it's my fault the scones got scorched in the first place. Maybe in this situation it's best not to fess up. The real damage came from what happened after, anyway.

"How long will that take?" No Beanevolence means no pay cheque.

"Not as long as it could have," Hadi says, and I detect a note of grudging respect. "Your boy must be as rich as they say dragons are, 'cause I've never had contractors hop to it so fast."

"He's not *mine*."

"Ten bucks says he'd like to be."

*Not you too. First I'm being bullied by my own hopeless romantic tendencies, and now my boss.*

"How long?" I growl.

"About a week for everything but the bean roaster. That could be a few months."

"*Months* with the old manual?" I blow out a breath. "Gross."

"A few months of being cooped up in the kitchen with your dragon," Hadi says, warming up to the fantasy of some sort of clandestine affair between us.

"Stoppit," I grump. "I have learned my lesson."

"Oh? And what lessons are those?"

"Numbers One, Two, and Three of Hadi's Seven-Step Rules for Colin's Happily Ever After," I recite. Christ, I can't believe she made me memorize these. "Right now those are the only ones that apply."

"Good boy," Hadi says, smug. "Doesn't change the fact that he likes you. If you are gonna work beside him for a while, I want you to keep them in mind. Especially Rule One."

*Right,* I think. *Don't get carried away.*

"Fine. Thanks, mom-friend."

"Mom-friend? Clearly not. I am the wine-aunt friend if nothing."

"You don't drink."

"I can still be a wine-aunt."

The truth is, Hadi is more like some weird amalgamation of an older sister, mentor, and best friend than a boss. She's only two years older than me, and we'd been in the Environ-mental Tourism program at Brock University. She'd gone on to open Beanevolence immediately after graduation, with some serious grants from the city. They'd been impressed by her as-local-as-possible plans. Pretty much everything except the growing of the raw beans themselves happens within a few kilometers of the place: milling, roasting, fruit growing, dairy and milk-alternative production, all of it.

I'd been there from day one, her first eager little barista.

And it's been great. Okay, I didn't *dream* about being a barista when I was a kid. Who did? But it pays better than minimum wage, Hadi lets me pick my hours, I'm practically managing the place myself, and all the nooblings have to obey me. It's worth holding on to. At least until I've found a real grown-up job.

Like the kind that Hadi made. Like the kind it seems that literally every other person I graduated with *already has*. The kind that would mean I haven't wasted the last five years and the chunk of the money I'd inherited from Dad on tuition.

Ugh.

Adulting *sucks*.

It sucks even more when it seems like you had all this *possibility* and *potential* and then, like... *nothing*.

Of course, it wouldn't have been actually for nothing if Rebekah and I had... Well, Hadi had been there for me then, too. For *every* horrific dating disaster I'd been through for the last five years, really. Thus, The Rules.

"Hey. Colin?" Hadi asks, uncertain in a way she rarely is.

"Yeah?"

"Are you okay? I mean really, are you *okay*?"

My breath catches in my throat, eyes suddenly burning. "Yeah," I choke out. My voice is still scratchy from the smoke inhalation. At least, that's what I'm blaming it on. "I'm fine. Really."

"I was scared," Hadi confesses. "I was so worried you'd been burned... and then when I saw all the *blood*... I'm coming over."

"I have no pants on."

"That has literally never stopped me before."

I groan and roll my head back against the bath pillow. "Okay, fine. But give me an hour, okay? No, actually two. I gotta figure out how to wash my hair." I turn to look at the bottles jumbled along the edge of the tub. It pulls on the wounds. "Shit."

"Have you taken your meds?"

"Forgot to get 'em," I admit. No point in lying to Hadi. She'd know.

"Your dragon didn't insist you stop at the pharmacy in the hospital before you left?"

"He's not *mine*."

"Sure. I'll swing by, grab your prescription, and pick 'em up for you. I've got medical EI leave forms for you to fill out anyway, and I'm buying you enough take-out to pack the freezer so you don't have to cook for a week."

Another hot surge of emotion crawls up my throat and I swallow it down roughly. I hate being treated like an idiot little brother who can't do things for himself. I hate being babied. But you know, sometimes someone just steps up because they care.

It's not that I subscribe to toxic masculinity bullshit about how dudes can't express their feelings. Nah. It's just that I hate to ask for help and she knows it. So she maneuvers me so I don't have to.

Thoughtful bitch.

I love her.

"Don't you have shit to manage at the café?" I ask, instead of blubbering.

"It's all over the phone at this point. I can do that from your horrifying sofa."

I chuckle. It is pretty awful. My first roommate and I had saved it from the curb, and it looks like the '70s had vomited all over it. "Pfft, see? I was right."

"About what?"

I swish the water around, stirring up the glitter from my bath bomb.

"You're totally the mom-friend."

"Lies and slander," Hadi says, and hangs up.

# chapter seven

I spend the next week sleeping, and reassuring the fam there *is no need* to cross the province just because I had a few stitches, I am *a big boy*. My brother and sister both text back with the exact same emoji of a face with a long Pinocchio-is-lying nose (either they did it on purpose to annoy me, or they really do have that twin-mind-reading thing.) I eat leftovers, am diligent about my meds, send a thank you card to Auntie Pattie for the bottle of birthday Scotch, read romance, work my way through the massive To Be Read pile of novels I'd neglected during Uni, and convince myself that I'm being a dumbass about Dav.

Dragons are hella secretive. Websites are scanty. Wiki entries are lists of facts and dates, with little speculation. Medical texts are vetted before they're published. Nearly none of them have social media. So there's zero evidence that Dav a) likes dudes, and b) likes *me*.

Why would he? He's hot. He's charming. He's got style, if a bit old-fashioned. He's presumably rich, being a dragon. (If that's not a speciesist stereotype.) He's probably in politics, they always are. And he's got a big care-taking streak; he'd spent as much time mother-henning the other people in the waiting room as he had me, popping up to grab tissues for the mother with the baby, translating for someone who'd only spoken French, helping an elderly man to the washroom.

And he clearly has excellent taste in coffee.

No way he's single.

And if he is, there's no reason he'd be into me. I'm all elbows and ears, skinny but not fit, and a plush bum that no kind of coin could bounce off. I dress like I shop in bargain stores, because I do. I have permanent late-night-studying bags under my eyes, scruff that I can never seem to shave all the way down, and no idea what to do with my mess of hair, so I do nothing at all. I am a *barista* for christssake. I don't own anything but my student debt and an unused degree.

I'm not lazy, and I'm not a fuck up. But my bed and my TBR pile call to me a lot more strongly than career ambition. Stu says it's normal to flail around after university, because the schedule and stress are gone. The dumpster fire has to burn down to ash before you can move the thing, right?

But it's been a year.

Gem had jumped right into her Master's of Library Science after undergrad. She was back with Mom and working with the local branch on diversity programming within weeks of graduating.

And Stuart had followed Dad's footsteps and joined the family construction company as soon as he'd gotten his Bachelors in History. It was only meant to be a summer job, but Stu had liked the work. Considering our hometown is full of Heritage Buildings that need constant attention, he'd married his love of old shit and making things, taken some online courses, and turned himself into Muskoka County's foremost expert on heritage restoration.

That's not 'flailing.'

And me? *Nothing*. No spark, no calling. No interview has been successful. No job posted in our alumni group has sung its siren song.

I like solving people's first-world problems with a smile, a coffee, and a chat. My own personal Coffee Shop AU. But

I don't want Beanevolence to be my forever home. This is Hadi's dream, not mine.

My dream had been the one I'd been co-planning with Rebekah.

And that was over.

So now what?

I hate to be told what to do, which Dr. Chen says comes from being the youngest sibling. And, unfortunately at most jobs, is the standard. Then there's my issues with *change*, with being forced to make *decisions* that fucks me up so bad I can't make a choice at all. Dr. Chen would say *that's* from my dad dying suddenly, and everything being yanked out from under me. But those sound like reasonable and logical reasons, so of course my brain weasels do their best to convince me it can't possibly be true.

Clearly, *I'm* the issue, not my trauma.

Right?

Right.

I hate to be such a goddamned stereotype of a bisexual, shooting finger guns at my problems instead of solving them but, I'm on the fence about next steps. Going with the flow is easier.

Maybe it's also why I'm such a gullible shit when it comes to romance—because I keep keeping on with the keeping on when people hurt me, or take advantage of me, or cheat on me, or are just a plain bad match. Better than breaking up, right?

Although in this case, maybe it's a good habit to have.

*Just keep on keeping on with Dav*, I spend a week telling myself. *He's just a customer. He's just a co-worker for the next few months, or for however long it takes for him to get bored of playing barista. Don't think about him in any other context, and it will be fine.*

I mean, Dav hadn't even texted me again. He never asked how I was feeling, never added anything besides a thumbs up emoji when I'd told him he should show up at 8am on Monday.

There's no reason for someone like *him* to be into someone like *me*.

I'm on time, because I traded away that sunset alarm clock on a neighborhood app, and got a a real, metal jangly one in exchange. Maybe a dick move, as Gem gave me the clock as a gift, but better a dick than fired.

Hadi and I meet early so we can look over the work Dav paid for before the guy himself shows up. The kitchen walls are in and painted, with a taped-in gap where the new oven is going to go. Until then, Hadi's arranged to get pastries from a woman doing all-local, all-organic catering from her own kitchen. The roaster is still on backorder, though.

"Don't worry, he won't last that long," Hadi says, having been the recipient of a panicked phone call last night about how I had somehow developed some stupid-ass crush on the man who had stabbed me with his hand. "And Min-soo said she'd come in if you need help. Not that you will in dead-time."

That's the thing about St. Catharines—when Brock University and Niagara College let out for the summer, the place is like a lockdown-era ghost town. The only people who actually live here are retired artists, folks who work in customer service, or exhausted teenagers manning tourist attractions by Niagara Falls. Without the drunk students to block the view, you realize that downtown is sad and pathetic, filled with wretched pensioners who have nothing better to do than ride the bus and smoke outside of malls, and rundown dive bars that are barely passable in the daylight, splintered and scuzzy. The Business Association has been working hard to revitalize St. Paul Street, posh upscale bistros and fancy boardgame cafés clustering around the new performing arts and arena venues, but the rest of the street is slowly rotting in stale beer and decomposing glitter.

Hadi is at the forefront of the business owners trying to make the downtown appealing and useful year-round, but the tourists are slow to pick up on the idea that there's more to St. Catharines than a wine festival and a few sagging art galleries.

"Yeah, okay." I shove my right hand into my jean's pocket to keep my arm still and supported. I don't need the sling any more, but I try not to jostle it. I walk out to the front, past the counter, marveling at how everything sparkles. "Jeeze, this is impressive."

"Tudor's team does good work," Hadi agrees.

"Tudor?" I ask.

"Your dragon."

"He's not *my* dragon! Do you think they're related? I've never heard of other Tudors but the queen."

"Her Majesty is a cousin, on—" Dav says from the door, his rich accent rolling across the empty café.

I jump, wounds twinging. *Oh shit,* I think, and check my watch. 8am exactly. Of course the posh bastard is punctual. *Did he hear Hadi call him 'my' dragon?*

"On my mother's side," he finishes slowly, coming to a cautious stop, as if afraid he's scared us. Okay, to be fair, we *are* both standing behind the counter with wide bunny-in-the-headlights looks on our faces, but it's only because we had *just been* discussing him. Hadi hasn't reconnected the little electric bell over the front door yet and I'd never realized before, but Dav walks softly.

*Like a predator*, the scared-bunny part of my brain whispers, and yikes, that's an unpleasant thought. I'd never considered it before, but yeah, dragons do have very sharp teeth to go with the claws that can slip through flesh so easily.

*My flesh*, the bunny-part adds.

*Shut up, weirdo,* I tell the bunny.

"Why are you staring? Am I late?" Dav asks, glancing down at his wristwatch—heavy gold, like the buttons on today's waistcoat.

"Um, uh, no?" I splutter.

*Shit. He's not as handsome as you remember, cut it out.*

Ah, who am I fooling?

Because he is.

My stomach flops at the sight of his hair back in its usual Errol Flynn swoop, and his slacks seem especially well-tailored today. The sleeves of his navy-blue floral button-down were already rolled up to his elbows, ready to work, and *get it together you absolute trashfire.*

Hadi invites Dav behind the counter, offering him a nickel-tour. She hands him the binder of nifty laminated infographics that show how to layer the drinks.

"There's no caffe tobio," Dav says, flipping the book back to the front to search again.

"Colin learned that one special for you," Hadi says, the nosy wench. *I thought she was supposed to be on my side. Whatever happened to bloody Rule One?*

Dav makes that uncomfortable clicky noise. "I didn't mean to put you out."

"Not a problem," Hadi assures him, and slaps his shoulder chummily. He flinches so slightly that I don't think Hadi notices. He stares at her hand, befuddled, then down at his arm where she'd touched him. "I'mma leave you to it. Don't let Colin bully you."

Dav draws himself up like an affronted pigeon. "He would never—"

"He would," Hadi assures him, sliding out from behind the counter. She eels out the door with a "Lock up after me!", the conniving bitch.

I lock up after her. Dav's still at the espresso machine, his lower lip rolled in and pinched between his teeth.

"This is, ah, a role reversal, wouldn't you say?" he asks softly, gesturing between us with one finger.

He is trying *so hard*.

And it is so *cute*.

Dammit.

Not ready to pack into the pokey kitchen just yet, instead I sit at his usual table. I perch one ankle on my knee, and mime opening a newspaper and peering over the top.

"Yes, I can see how that'd seem disconcerting," he berates himself.

"Why do it, then?" I ask, dropping my hands. "Don't you have somewhere better to be?"

*Ha*, I applaud myself, *I remembered my mental note. Good job, self.*

Instead of answering, Dav turns to put away the binder. The line of his back is tense, his shoulders practically up to his ears.

"Dav?"

He winces again, like my voice is a gunshot. From this angle, the freckles on his neck shine like golden ink on vellum.

"Hey." I slide behind the counter to touch his sleeve. He jerks as if I'd pinched him. I step back, palms out, nonthreatening. "Sorry."

"No, I—"

"I should have asked."

"It's me, I—" He makes that throaty click-spark noise and screws his eyes shut. A curl of smoke trickles out of the side of his mouth.

"Am I stressing you out?" I step further back. "Because I can back up—"

"No, please!" His hand shoots out, claw-free, to snatch my wrist. It's the arm with the still-healing punctures. I try not to make a face as it's pulled straight, but fail. He drops my wrist in horror. "Oh, Colin, I'm so *sorry—*"

"Okay, stop, shhh, stop!" I say, forcefully, but not unkindly.

Dav scrubs his hands over his face. Before he can push them through his hair I say, gently, "Don't."

He freezes and looks up at me.

"I like your hair. Don't muss it up."

He looks at me with an expression that twists so quickly, I can only parse the surprise and self-recrimination. There's just something so *lost* about him.

"Let's go roast some beans, eh?" I ask, and Dav nods miserably. "And from now on, I won't touch you if you can't see me coming, how about that?"

"And I'll mind your arm," he says softly.

"Thanks."

"How's it healing?"

"Just fine. Barely hurts any more." I shove my hand back into my pocket to support it all the same.

His mouth twists to one side. "You needn't lie to me, Colin."

"I'm not."

He looks at me like he can read the truth on my skin, but leads the way all the same.

# chapter Eight

D av inspects the kitchen's refurbishment with proprietary
interest. Which makes sense, as he did pay for it all.

Everything gleams, but the layout has stayed the same: prep
station on the wall to the left of the door, washing station on
the far left wall, oven and roaster on the right, and cabinets
and industrial fridges framing the second exit on the wall
opposite. St. Paul Street backs onto a ravine, so the rear exit
opens onto a dingy deck on stilts, populated by a rusting bistro
set.

A stainless steel table takes up most of the remaining floor
space in the kitchen. If there's more than two people working,
you have to scootch, and you *will* get flour, or soap bubbles,
or coffee dust on your ass.

I show all of this to Dav before we come to the *piece de
resistance*—the old manual roaster. I trained on this beast,
back when Beanevolence first opened. It's fourth-hand, all
Hadi could afford when she started this venture. And it pretty

much takes up the whole table. It's shaped sort of like a steam train engine. Except instead of smoke coming out of the big funnel, that's where we pour in the green beans. The conductor's cabin is a cylindrical drum turned by hand crank, heated from below with a row of flames fed by a camping propane cylinder. The cow-catcher out front of the train is a basin, where roasted beans are raked out of the cylinder to cool.

Have I mentioned the kitchen is small? Dav is standing so close I can feel the soothing heat coming off him. So I wasn't hallucinating his warmth in the hospital, even if I was seeing something more there. I wonder if his human friends fall asleep around him all the time. It'd be nice to cuddle on a sofa and—*whoa, no, time out.*

"Ready to get cracking?" I force a laugh at the in-joke before I realize he doesn't get it.

"I thought we were meant to see if I could roast the beans myself instead of using the machine?" Dav asks.

"We can try that after lunch," I say, opening the pantry. It's already been stocked with fresh, big sacks of beans. My stupid heart is fluttering in my throat, and I focus on the job instead of the fact that I just implied we'd be having lunch together. *Not a date!* "That way, we'll at least have one batch ready for tomorrow if the you-roasting doesn't work out. Grab that."

Dav hefts up one of the big bags with no visible effort. I swallow hard, absolutely *not* watching the way his shoulders flex through the silk backing of his waistcoat.

"And now?"

"Uh, a third of the bag, into the funnel. We need, um, scissors, hold on," I turn in a circle, looking for them. Behind me there's a quick, delicate ripping noise, then the ping of hard beans dancing inside the copper funnel. I whip back to catch Dav pulling his finger out of a neat, vertical slice in the bag, already human-shaped again.

"They're sharp."

"I remember," I reply, touching my wounded arm, and before he can apologize again, I jump back into the instructions. "I'll light the pilot."

I'm crouched to peer up under the machine, struggling with the matches, when Dav's face appears through the gap on the other side.

"Where are you meant to be lighting?"

I show him the spot, and move to hand him the box, when he purses his lips. The bone-click is softer this time, but no less startling coming from a human-looking throat. He blows a thin flame at the touchpoint. The propane ignites with a soft *fwump*, and the rest of the burners pop on gently.

I stop breathing.

Flames in my face, the whoosh of oxygen igniting, the particular brimstone-scent of dragon's fire... bright orange in the center of my vision, my arm throbbing... *shit*! I fall hip-first against the prep counter behind me, sharp and painful. I turn and clutch the edge of the counter, squeezing hard to ground myself in the bite of it.

Five things I can see—the wall in front of me, covered in stainless steel shelving, filled with bowls and pans. My hands, shaking. Fresh bins of flour under the worktop. A balled up napkin in the corner, where Hadi had missed the garbage. The inside of the door with its hand-written sign: *Knock on the door, don't knock out your coworkers.* Four things I can touch—my feet on the ground, my palms to one another, the napkin as I nudge it into the bin, the smooth steel of the worktop. I hear the susurrus of the flames, the pop of the drum heating up, the clink of the beans settling. I smell the first rich aroma of coffee, the spice of my deodorant being put through its paces. I taste clean air, no trace of oily smoke.

"Colin?" Dav says when I finally release a deep breath and straighten.

"I'm fine. I was just... it surprised me. Um," I swallow hard, pushing through, and turn to face him. I try to look non-chalant, not like I just fended off a panic attack in front of him. Again. "I... had a sense memory moment. Fire in my face. But it's passed!" I add when his fussy eyebrows do that complicated wiggle of guilt.

Dav growls at himself, hands jammed into his pockets. "I can never seem to get it right—"

"Just a bit of warning next time." I dare myself to mean it. My heart twists to see how hard on himself he is. "You didn't mess up anything."

"I *will*, though," He chuckles, but it's a dry, cruel sound. "I do. Every time."

Whoa, now. Who told this kind, smart, hot man that he was a fuck up?

"You haven't, though," I assure him. "Except for the part where we're burning the beans."

"And now we're burning the beans!" Dav throws his hands up into the air and rolls his eyes, distraught.

"Turn the crank, drama queen," I deadpan. "No, slower. They need to settle against the side a bit. Yeah. See? Crisis averted."

Dav gives one of those growling, self-deprecating scoffs.

I'm not used to being the one who reassures people. That's usually Hadi. And she's usually reassuring *me*. Still. I reach out, making sure he can see it coming this time. I pause with my palm just above his shoulder, giving him the space to pull back if he doesn't want me to touch him. He stays where he is, so I let it land.

"You haven't screwed anything up, Dav," I tell him again, earnestly. Those sunflower eyes search my face. I don't know what he's looking for, but I keep my expression as reassuring as possible.

He straightens, confidence restored. "Now what?" he asks.

I let him go. "Now you keep at that until your arm gets sore. We want the beans at about two hundred degrees. We'll do the light roast first."

"Light roast at two hundred degrees" Dav repeats determinedly, like he's memorizing for an exam. The muscles of his bicep press and release against the fabric bouquets, and that shit should *not* be allowed in public. It's obscene. "Is roasting time the only difference between light and dark?"

"Light roasts sort of taste like spring, and dark roasts like autumn."

Dav crinkles a grin at me. "A poet as well as a barista."

My mouth goes dry. "Uh, hardly. I just... like words. Like stories."

"I recall," he says meaningfully.

"Yeah, uh... It'll take about twenty minutes for the first crack." I wrench my brain back on topic. "Decant the beans right away so they don't keep cooking."

"First crack?"

"They crack open when they're done, let out the CO2."

"Which is important because...?"

"No one wants carbonated coffee."

"Ah! No, I suppose not," he says with an almost-dimple.

"Then the beans cool for a day, over here." I show him the big metal bowls stacked on a wire rack in the corner. "And then they go out to the front whole. They go stale if you grind 'em more than ten minutes before using them."

"What an art," Dav says, appreciatively. "As delicate as wine-making."

"Pretty similar!" I laugh, insides fizzy with his flattery. "You even get better coffee if you aerate it." I mime pouring from high.

"Oh! I thought you were just being showy."

"I do like all the cute boys looking at me." I punctuate it with a flirty wink and then immediately regret it. "So, uh, call me when you hear the first crack, okay?"

"Yes," he murmurs, his own head lowered and his face made unreadable by the angle. I've made him uncomfortable. *Fuck.* "And what will you be doing?"

"Restocking."

"Perhaps I ought to—your arm. That will be quite a lot of lifting."

I arch an eyebrow at him. "Oh, so you know where everything goes, eh?"

"Ah," he catches himself. "Not as such, no."

"Just cause you're here every day doesn't mean you know how this place works." I say it lightly, but his shoulders still hunch up like I've landed a physical blow. Even coming at the topic from the side has him squirrelly. "I can stop asking."

Dav takes a moment to consider this, forked tongue flickering out to wet his lower lip. A surge of lust drops directly into my pants like an overheated cannon ball.

*Stand down.*

"I do owe you an answer," Dav says at length. "But not just now?"

It's a request, and one I'm happy to honor. "Sure thing. Now, keep cranking, bean-wench."

We have a quick lunch of to-go sandwiches. I was curious what Dav would pick —something stereotypically meat-on-bone? Instead he gets the turkey sandwich, same as me. *That's not very dragon-y,* I decide. We eat out back, sunlight burning away the earlier awkwardness.

While Dav stays pretty mum about his professional life—and I don't poke, like I said I wouldn't, which is *hard,* I am *curious*—he's happy to tell me other stories. When he compared the art of coffee to winemaking, it turns out he knows what he's talking about. He owns a small vineyard, and soon has me snorting all the way through a story about his horse, and the mess it caused when it decided that the Crushing Room seemed like a good place for a stroll when it had slipped its paddock. The horse, formerly white, was purple up to its gaskin, somehow inside the tub, and chomping merrily away at the grapes. They had to throw away the whole batch out of fear the horse had 'contaminated' it. By which Dav meant, pissed in the vat. He doesn't provide a firm date for when this happened, and Dav has to explain to me what part of the animal the *gaskin* is, but I get the sense that it was more than a few decades ago.

When was the last time people rode horses as their main form of transportation?

If I'd known I would one day befriend a dragon, I would have paid attention in those hated history classes.

*Are* Dav and I friends?

We can be friends.

I'm cool with that.

His grin while I return the favor fills me with warmth. I offer a story of the time my university buddies had gone to the Goth nightclub with a bunch of Drama kids. One had convinced me to wear her blood-red corset, but it was a real one, with steel boning. Trying to be macho, I'd told them to lace it as tight as they liked, and I'd fainted after one Jaeger bomb. Dav makes noises about knowing how tight corsets can get, and I decide he means because he's old enough to remember women wearing them every day, and not because he's worn them himself.

Ooof.

I have a sudden vision of Dav, with his freckly, creamy skin and strong shoulders on display, waist nipped in by a shiny black leather corset and tiny lacy panties barely covering his dragon-hood.

*Jesus.*

This is getting ridiculous.

"Coffee, "I croak, balling up my sandwich wrapper.

"Please," Dav says, following me back inside.

Hadi keeps an emergency stash of whole roasted beans in the back of the freezer. Thank god it survived the fire, because I refuse to go down the street for a franchise latte on principle. I show Dav how to work the electric grinder, and we fill two mason jars with first the coarser drip-coffee grind, and then I demonstrate the trick of using short bursts to make the powdery espresso grind. Dav stands right over my shoulder.

*If I turned around fast enough, I bet I could kiss him*, I think, and shake my head to knock that thought loose. *No, no, no, kissing coworkers is gauche.*

I hip check him to get him to take a step back, and he snorts and hip checks me back. We scuffle like schoolchildren and I'm not gonna lie, I kind of love watching Dav get all flustered and giggly.

His laugh is a breathy *eh-eh-eh* noise that hisses out between his teeth.

Even his joy is careful and small.

Out front, I show him how to load the porta-filter wand and tamp down the grounds, and in a few minutes we're java'd up.

"Time to set fire to some beans?" I ask, loving the way his eyelids flutter in pleasure as he sips his tobio. His spun-copper lashes are *pretty*.

"Indeed!" He's *excited* and his butt looks *so good* in those pants as he heads back into the kitchen, and it occurs to me with the speed and impact of getting unexpectedly smashed in the head with a frying pan, I am fucked.

So fucked.

He moves the roaster to the pastry table (he's so strong, *damn, don't think about him heaving you up against the wall, about wrapping your legs around his waist, shit*). I unearth a large cauldron with a thick base, leftover from Hadi's failed attempt to serve soup and panini.

We spend the next hour testing the usefulness of Dav's firebreath. Dav has the ability to change the stream-width, but not the heat, according to the thermometer he keeps spitting on. We eventually decide a thin stream, hissed out between pursed lips like a whistle, is best. He can dance that over the beans, while shifting them around with his own fire-proof hand, making sure they get touched evenly. The experimenting is fun as hell. It reminds me of everything I liked best about my environmental bio labs.

And watching him actually *do* it is fucking *gorgeous.*

I want to press my cheek between his shoulder blades, put my arms around his chest, feel him inhale, hear the click of the firelighter bones deep in his throat, feel the steady surge of his exhale. I don't touch him because first, I already know that he startles easily, and frankly, we're not burning down this kitchen again. And second, *No, Colin.*

Eventually the beans crack, and we crowd around the bowl like proud parents, cooing at the perfect color and the intense, smoky aroma. It's a shame we have to wait until tomorrow to taste it.

# chapter Nine

The coffee is *divine*. It's smooth, and bitter in a floral, almondy way that sits beautifully on the tongue, thick on the finish, and fills my stomach with sunlight. Coffee is already the nectar of the gods, but this is a fucking *delight*.

"It tastes normal to me," Dav says the next morning, over his own cup.

"You have no palette then," I accuse. "This is *magic*." I slurp down another hot mouthful. I don't care that it burns my tongue. Feels good. Feels *right*.

"My palette is perfectly refined." He flicks his forked tongue out at me.

"Then maybe it's because you spent yesterday breathing fire and it's screwed up your tastebuds, but believe me, this is incredible."

I toss the rest of the coffee in my mug down my throat, and top myself up. It doesn't even need milk, or sugar, or anything fancy.

It's...
You know what it is?
This is finally a coffee that *tastes* the way coffee *smells*.
"So you like it, then?" he teases.
I shoot him my biggest, dopiest grin. "Keep making it like this, and I might just have to marry you," I say before my brain can throttle the conduit to my mouth.
Dav twitches once all over, like he's been shocked by a live wire, and then sends me a super-fake smile. "No, you wouldn't."
He retreats to the kitchen.
Well.
Huh.
That... happened.
Not sure what else to do, I stay on this side of the door to get the front in order, and drink the whole carafe of our test batch by myself.
Beanevolence goes through about two kilograms of coffee each day. These are individually roasted to different strengths. Each pot of drip coffee is ground as needed, but as the espresso takes more time, we do it by the jar. There's three long glass tubes attached to the wall of the bar-back with copper striping for the unground beans. Clear glass isn't preferable for storing beans, but as we usually use it all up within a day, the sun doesn't have the time to do any damage. And they look damn cool, like a mad scientist's lab. There's even a copper hand crank at the bottom of each tube to dole out the beans in pre-measured batches.
So, Dav has a lot of beans to work through to get us up to snuff. That's the excuse I give myself, anyway, for being too cowardly to go into the kitchen and apologize for... whatever it is that offended him just now.
Around noon, he comes out front anyway, red-faced and winded.
"Yikes," I say. "Need a drink?"
"I've had quite enough coffee."
"Water, I meant." I set down the box of sweetener packets. I had been refilling the jars on the table where customers can personalize their drinks. Hadi provides four different kinds of sugar, including a rotational seasonal special. Personally, I do not get the appeal of dehydrated strawberry sugar in coffee, but it's a hit in July. "The water from the bar sink is drinkable."

I turn away quick when he helps himself to a glass. His waistcoat is missing. His top *three* buttons are undone. His face is lightly sheened with sweat and there are a few dark-red curls of chest hair peeking out of the vee of his shirt. His Adam's apple is *lickable*. I want to find out what dragon sweat tastes like.

He's endearingly, temptingly rumpled, his hair product melted away, leaving it floppy and damp. There's a peek of dusky rose nipple as he raises his arm and I just, I just want to *bite it*. Those bare forearms, the flex of strong fingers around the glass—I remember the feel of them through my shirt—I want those arms to hold me down—I want—

Shit.

*Shit.*

A loud noise startles us both, and Dav whips his head around to track it, slit pupils narrowing, predatory and *hnnnnnnf that's sexy*. Of course, he's looking right at *me*, because the noise was me dropping the box.

Welp.

*Yeetus yeetus, time to self-deleteus.*

"I'll help—" Dav starts.

"No, I'm fine." I start scooping the packets back into the cardboard box. "Just, stay over there." I add, and okay, that might have come out a bit desperate, but the front of my jeans is not currently fit for public viewing and the last thing I want is to make Dav uncomfortable again.

I pop back up, box held in front of my fly.

"I, ah, bathroom." I leave the box on the station and dart for the gent's. I splash cold water on my face and the back of my neck until everything calms the fuck down.

When I get back, he's buttoned his shirt and waistcoat, cool and collected again. Thank fuck. My nerves would not have been able to take it.

"Now what?" he asks.

"Huh?"

"I finished. Should I do more?"

"Uh. Wow, yeah, that was fast. Okay. I guess I can show you how to make batter?"

"So long as you promise not to burn them." He twinkles out a smile.

Sassy-Dav has started to resurface, and I like the bitch.

Am I forgiven, then?

"Shut up," I snipe playfully. The kitchen is heavy with dragon-generated heat, and I prop open the back door to clear out the last of it. "I'll make you bake them, instead."

"They may actually be edible, then."

Making sure he can see me reaching, I pinch his arm.

"Owww," he complains theatrically. "How cruel."

I'm sure the recipes for the baked things must be written down somewhere, but I talk him through from memory. Once the scone batter is in the fridge, the basic oat muffin batter gets portioned into four bowls.

"Blueberries in this one, the whole basket," I tell Dav, "Raisins here, bananas and peanut butter there, then chocolate chips here."

Dav frowns. "Should you be handling those?"

"I'm not anaphylactic."

"Still, it's a shame," Dav says, popping one of the chips in his mouth. It's organic and made small-batch from an ethical-labor, sustainable farming operation. "Chocolate is one of my favorite things about the New World."

" 'The New World'?" I huff. "D'you still call historic Toronto 'York', too?"

The corner of Dav's mouth twitches down. "Only when speaking of His Excellency's territory."

"His... Excellency. Right," I say, blind-sided by the reminder that the man standing beside me is hundreds of years old. And in every culture in the world, dragons are chieftains, or tribal leaders, or autocratic royalty like the Russian Czars and our own British Empire monarchs.

I have no business getting a crush on a man who, for all I know, may be an actual prince. That's one step too close to taking draconic romance novels seriously, thanks.

"What did you do to it?" Hadi asks, glaring at us over the rim of her mug. Her lips and hijab are both a vibrant crimson this morning, and it just makes her look more annoyed.

"Who says we did anything?" I offer what I hope is an endearing smile.

So basically, totally confessing.

"Do *not* bullshit me about my own coffee."

I sigh and give up on the smile. It felt tight and weird, anyway.

"Dav has some... expertise, and suggested a tweak. Don't you like it?"

"I fucking love it, that's the problem," Hadi says, turning to Dav.

He's buttoned all the way up today, in black trousers and a waistcoat, with a shirt in a burnt orange that matches the Beanevolence logo. He's wearing an honest-to-god pocket watch, with the fiddly little chain and everything. I feel like a slob next to him.

Dav had proudly presented the first cup of coffee he'd made all by himself to Hadi when she'd come in to oversee the installation of the oven this morning. The two gals in the back doing the installation were both given coffees too, and I can hear the one saying "Holy shit, this is good," through the door.

"Why is it a problem?"

"Because you *changed* something. Colin, the key to building a customer base is *consistency*. Can you honestly tell me you can do this every time?"

I look to Dav, who gives a little contained eyebrow wiggle that I interpret as an 'of course'. Then I look back to Hadi. "Yes."

"Even when the new roaster arrives?"

Dav and I exchange another look. Busted. We didn't think of that.

"Look, show me what you did different, and I'll see if I can adjust the machine."

"Ah," Dav says, and spending two days with him has made it much easier to read his body language. His face stays serene, but his posture seizes up like a soldier called to attention.

"He can't," I say, jumping in before Dav feels the need to lie. "That's, um, kind of a dragon secret?" I make up on the spot.

"Is it?" Hadi asks Dav.

"Yes," he says, calmly and firmly. "My apologies. As I am already here daily, I'd be happy to volunteer my services to roast your beans, even after the roaster arrives."

"I can't afford another employee right now."

"I believe I said 'volunteer'," Dav points out.

Hadi heaves out a sigh, hands on her hips. "If today goes okay, if people like it, *then* we can talk." She flicks one of my ears. I duck away because ow, and also, I don't like it when people point out my stupid jar-handles. "Don't change anything else, okay?"

"Okay," I promise, flattening my hair over the sides of my head.

She goes into the kitchen. Before the door closes, the installers clamor for a refill of the cups I'd sent them in with.

"C'mere." I lead Dav over to a table far away from Hadi's ears, where I'd been writing a sign when she'd arrived. It reads *COFFEE IS ON. BEVS ONLY UNTIL 2PM*, which is when we expect the oven installation to be complete and safe to turn on. As I tape it to the window beneath our 'Closed' sign, I ask: "*Is* it a dragon secret?"

"In a way," Dav says. His hands are folded behind his back as if awaiting a commander's inspection. "It's only that it's..."

"What?" I prompt, lowering my voice and stepping close. His eyes pop wide before settling on my face, and I realize I forgot to ask before getting into his personal bubble. He's prickly about that.

"I... it's simply that..." he licks his lips, nervous, and I fight to keep my gaze up on his eyes instead of his mouth. "It's *unseemly.*"

"Oh." I guess I'm surprised? He'd agreed to try it out readily enough when I'd made the joke, but then again, Dav doesn't seem real big on standing up for himself. Shit. "Have I put you in a bad position? Sorry, I didn't mean—"

"You haven't," Dav says, in a rush. "I wanted to try it. However, my family is quite against using our, ah, *genetic advantages* in menial ways. Trivializes us, you see? Makes dragons look like a tool or a beast of burden, not a person."

I take a second to process that. "Does every dragon think that?"

"Most of what Elizabeth-dragoun Virginium Bonum Magna Tudor sets down as best practices for her court, others adopt. Or were forced to adopt, under British rule."

"I don't get it," I say, leaning on the table with my left arm. My right still itches, but the stitches have dissolved. "I'm not trying to be combative here, but using the advantages you were born with, surely that's not 'unseemly'?"

Dav's eyes drop to his hands, which he carefully folds before him in what appears to be an attempt to keep himself from fidgeting. "Do you know who Thomas Seymour was?"

"No," I admit.

"He married Katherine Parr, Henry Rex's final wife, after Henry's death. Seymour had a little dragonblood himself, but it was much weakened by intermarriage with humans. He was also maternal uncle to little King Edward, and so Seymour felt he ought to be closer to the crown than he found himself. He, ah... was unsavory toward Elizabeth Regina when she was still a princess. After Edward Rex died so suddenly, under such mysterious circumstances, and Lady Parr passed, Seymour attempted to marry Her Majesty. To *rule* her, and through her, the country."

I scoff. "You can't rule a dragon. Everyone knows that."

Dav looks up at me, sunflower eyes meeting mine with surprising intensity.

"You *can* rule a dragon. There are ways," he says earnestly, but doesn't elaborate. His whole body sways toward mine, then back again, like he's become momentarily dizzy.

"Seymour groomed Elizabeth Regina to obey him," he goes on. "At first he asked small things—fetch that candlestick, wear that blue gown. But then he asked for bigger, more uncomfortable things. He encouraged her to light household fires with her breath, dig fields with her claws, provide transport on her back as she flew. When she wore her dragonshape, he spoke to her as if she was a dumb beast. As if she were less than human."

"Fuuuuuck," I breathe. "That's uncool."

"Indeed," Dav hisses out. "If she were nothing more than a beast, he could take her crown. There was even rumor that he meant to challenge the tradition that dragons shepherd their human hoards. He thought humans should rule humans."

"That's stupid," I chuckle. "It never works. Hello, look at America. They had a whole failed revolution about it."

"Indeed. What Seymour did, it was..." he shudders, chest rising and falling rapidly. "What's *worse* than 'mortifying'?" His jaw clenches so hard his teeth squeak.

"Hey, breathe." I touch his elbow gently, making sure he can see me coming.

Dav blinks hard, and shakes himself out. "Only when she took the throne did Elizabeth Regina understand what Seymour had been trying to accomplish. He was executed for his audacity, and his suspected involvement in the death of his nephew."

"Hold on, I thought Edward Rex got sick? That's why he died."

Dav gives me an 'oh come now' look. "There are very, very few diseases that can touch a dragon."

He's admitting more than he should, I realize. "Okay. So then, if Seymour is dead, then why can't you make coffee?"

"It became unspoken and unwritten law that we were never to use our draconic abilities in service of humans. But this is dragon knowledge, so you mustn't spread this around, Colin. I should not have told you."

"I promise to keep it secret." I offer up my pinky finger. Dav cracks a small smile and wraps his own around it, accepting my childish vow. We shake briefly before his fingers skitter away. "So I get it. I'd be pissed too. But it's been, like, five hundred years. I'm not saying it's right to treat you as if you're lesser than boring *homo sapiens*. But I guess I just wonder... if dragons can do things humans can't, I don't see why they shouldn't, if it makes everyone's lives easier?"

Dav snorts. "You sound like Onatah."

"Who?"

"She holds the territory next to my own." He gestures gently to the east, toward Niagara Falls.

"Oh, you *do* have friends!" I tease. "Did you meet her when you were sent out from Elizabeth Regina's court? Did you wear a *ruff?*"

I can't help my curiosity, okay?

"Oh no," Dav huffs, like I've said the funniest thing he's heard in weeks. "That is to say, yes, I was sent from court and we met shortly upon my arrival here. But not that long ago, not in a *ruff*. Heavens, Colin, how old do you think I *am?*"

"I don't know!" I laugh. "That's why I'm asking."

"Perhaps I'll make you guess." And just like that, we're back to happy, sassy Dav.

The Dav I like best.

"That's not fair," I whine, gathering up the sign-making stuff. "Your name is Tudor, isn't that an old family?"

"My mother is a thrice-removed niece of the royal Tudor line. My grandfather was Welsh, descended directly from Y Ddraig Goch himself."

"You say that like I'm supposed to know what it means," I throw over my shoulder, stashing everything away.

"The Great Welsh Dragon," Dav says, following after me. "They say he was King Arthur's wisest counselor."

"Now you're just talking shit. King Arthur wasn't real. It's a fairy-tale to explain why human-only Round Tables are a shitshow, and we need draconic monarchs."

"Wasn't he?" Dav raises a mocking eyebrow. "Don't you think a *draig* would know?"

"Stoppit," I laugh, then gesture to the carafe beside me. "We open in ten minutes and that's empty."

"Sir, yes sir," Dav tosses out with a lazy salute, and gets grinding.

# chapter Ten

T he physiotherapist gave me a set of exercises to do, but Beanevolence is hopping, and I get all the exercise the doc could want by pulling espresso, lifting cauldrons of beans, and hefting around crates of milk, platters of scones, and jars of sugar.

And Hadi had worried that the new version of our coffee wouldn't be popular.

Ha.

Our first open Monday, the usual morning customers boomerang back in that afternoon, which isn't normal. On Tuesday, they've brought their friends along. By Wednesday, there's an honest-to-god line up at the counter.

Dikembe and Mauli swing by to get a look at our new employee and send me text messages like **Isn't that the dude you want to climb like a tree?** And a string of frankly obscene emojis. I try to run them off with free lattes, pointedly in *to go* cups. Instead, they slide into the leather club chairs and refuse to move for the rest of my shift, which means I'm forced to introduce them. Dike offers a congenial handshake which Dav takes with all the calm seriousness of a soldier greeting the spouse of a commanding officer, and Mauli invites him for drinks at the Brass Monkey.

I'm desperate for Dav to say yes, but I'm not surprised when his posture goes ever so slightly stiffer, his lips roll inward, and he flicks his eyes at me like he's afraid of disappointing me.

"S'cool if you have other plans," I offer, giving him the out.

Dav retreats gracefully, and Dike and Mau spend Wednesday evening waggling their eyebrows at me and coming up with increasingly lewd scenarios for me to 'accidentally' fall into Dav's embrace. We drink about twelve pints of craft beer between us, as Dike keeps a running list on his phone of every romance novel trope Mau can look up on theirs.

I don't tell them that I'd never actually do any of these things to Dav.

One, some of them are kind of sneaky. Two, the rest would startle him so bad the whole block would catch fire. Three, he doesn't like me like that.

The next morning, Hadi 'likes' every single photo posted of us in increasingly ludicrous and drunken arrangements, recreating front-cover poses. Or, at least, *trying* to recreate them. At one point the waitress had brought over a table cloth, and a birthday girl at a nearby table had donated her tiara. In the cold hung-over light of morning, I decide that I'd look very pretty in a wedding dress.

By Thursday, I'm worried we're going to run out of green beans before the weekend. Hadi's already put in a second and a third order. Friday morning, there's a lineup snaking past the entrance of the darkened comedy bar next door when I arrive to open. Dav waits for me on the cement planter box by the entrance, dressed this time in a sharp blue waistcoat and trouser set that should look costumey, and instead just looks delectable. His shirt is the color of his eyes.

"Shit, man, you're making me look bad." I shake his hand in our new daily greeting. Dav likes formality. I like touching him. "I'm gonna have to up my style game."

Dav perks up. "My tailor could—"

"Whoa up. Five-packs of shirts is all I can afford. Let's open before the mob riots."

With Dav's help, it takes just fifteen minutes to get the first two pots of coffee going and the initial batch of scones and muffins in the oven. When we let them in, Dav mans the cash, charming the panties off everyone, regardless of their gender and sexual orientation. I handle the drinks, barely able to keep up. Our summer morning rush used to last about half an hour, and if it was a good day, it consisted of maybe twenty orders. During the school year, it's usually about an hour, and maybe a hundred cups.

Today it lasts two and a half hours and I don't know how many people we serve, but I make over twenty pots of coffee and god knows how many lattes. It feels like we just caffeinated the entire non-student population of St. Catharines. By the time I've got the chance to sneak to the back for a glass of water and one of the muffins that had come out wonky, it's practically noon. I'm sweaty and, ugh, so not attractive right now.

"That's all of them," Dav says, coming to join me. Wonder of wonders, he's got a caramel latte for me. "I noticed that you didn't get any for yourself."

I have just enough manners not to stick my nose right into his attempt at foam art. The coffee is everything it's been all week, tasty in a way I can't pin down. The flavor is different, yeah, but there's something *satisfying* about it. I made up the Beanevolence dark roast that I keep in my house yesterday just to compare, and the difference was like trying to put skim milk on toast instead of the best salted butter you've ever had.

My mouth gets ahead of my brain again, my traitorous taste-buds acting as a distraction.

"I love you," I blurt, as soon as I come up for air. Dav makes a noise like a pinched kitten. "Sorry, dumb joke."

"Joke," he echoes, but it's strangled. Dav shutters up, like I've pulled the cord on his emotional blinds. He sets down his own mug on the metal worktop with a clatter.

*Oooooooh, fuck, what have I done?*

"Dav, uh—"

I'm not sure what I was actually going to say just there, but it's fine, because I don't get the chance to get it out, anyway. He's already retreated to the front, slow and calm like he hasn't a care in the world.

*I've offended him,* I think. *He's having a freak out. Shit.*
*I didn't mean it!*
I did mean it.
*Shit.*

Before I can screw up my courage to face Dav—to say what, apologize? Be honest? Oh, fuck—the electronic door-chime goes off.

I can hear Dav speaking to the customer. I curl my fingers around the edge of the worktop, arms rigid, claw wounds twinging. I let myself take ten whole seconds to bite my tongue hard enough that it begins to hurt, to punish myself for my stupid mouth.

Then I straighten up, stick on my Customer Service smile, and go out to make coffee.

I don't work Saturdays. So when my phone rings at 11am, Hadi's name jangling obnoxiously across my screen, I'm already halfway into my jeans before I answer.

"Y'ello," I say, struggling to hold my phone against my head and pull on a shirt.

"We're slammed and your dragon won't let us into the kitchen."

"He's not mine," I repeat, jamming my feet into my chucks.

"*Colin*!"

"I'm already out the door," I reassure her, and jingle my keys next to the mic. She hangs up on me without saying bye, like she's some character on TV or something. It bugs me, and Hadi knows it.

Someone tries to give me guff when I slip through the door ahead of the line, but I toss "Man, I work here," over my shoulder at him. I offer a wave to Min-soo at the cash, snag up the bin of dirty cups, and shoulder into the kitchen.

Okay, so the other reason I wanted to come in was that I didn't like how I left things with Dav yesterday. He'd spent the rest of the day avoiding me. Not keeping his distance from me like we were opposite ends of a magnet, but emotionally. Like a life-sized model decoy of Dav.

It sucked, and it was my fault. I had hurt or offended him, though I wasn't sure how, and it had something to do with jokingly professing my love. He'd clammed up when I'd teased about getting married too, and yeah, okay, I'm an asshole because I'm just realizing that there's a pattern there.

*Clearly not into me.*

Maybe he's even the kind of rigidly straight that can't even handle queer teasing.

So I had to make sure he was okay, and find a way to be his friend again.

He looks up as I slam in the door, red-faced and disheveled, waistcoat and pocket watch missing and wearing only a slight-ly sweaty tank top—*holy fuck, shoulders*!—and scowling.

"I believe I asked you to knock before—Colin," he says, surprise making his eyebrows bounce once before that painful non-expression slaps into place.

"Hi," I say, which is both inadequate and stupid.

I set the bin down, swap out the clean mugs in the industrial dishwasher and return them to the front, then knock before I come back to start grinding beans. Seeing him standing there, hair floppy, exhausted, tight lines around his eyes, another wave of guilt slams into me.

"You know you don't have to do this if you don't want to."

"I want to," Dav says, chin lifted, jaw set.

"You don't actually owe us." I turn away to start filling the big grinder.

"I *want* to be here. Colin, I—"

It's a dick move, but I turn on the machine before he can make another excuse or tell me another lie. He clearly *doesn't*. Or at least, he doesn't want to be around *me* anymore. That much is obvious by the upright way he holds himself (the stiff way he used to be, before he let me doze on his shoulder in the hospital waiting room as he read me a love story), the way his nostrils keep flaring as if I'm something disgusting, the way he keeps the table between us.

My homophobic student rez roommate in first year did the same.

Okay, fine; so Dav isn't the only one who's upset, alright?

"You need me," Dav says, as soon as the noise from the grinder isn't jamming up my hearing. I scoop grounds into a glass jar. My hands are shaking. I spill a little hill of coffee on the worktop.

"We don't, actually," I say, and it's *mean*, but I can't stop myself. My brain is outside my body watching my mouth move and willing it to stop, but it's not. "It's *unseemly*, anyway."

"Colin—"

I turn to face him so fast I scatter the hill of grounds in an arc across the floor.

"What was it?" I snap. "What's pissed you off so much you won't even talk to me?"

"I *am* talking to you," Dav says darkly.

"What I said, it was a *joke*."

"Was it?" Dav asks, but it's not a question. It's more like a challenge. "And do you often proposition your colleagues? Profess your love over sloppily made lattes?"

"Yes!" I say. "*As a joke*."

"So it was meaningless, your confession?"

"Yes!" I throw my hands up, and wince when my right bicep burns.

Dav steps around the table, hands flexing, fingers opening and closing.

Steeling himself.

"What if I don't want it to be?"

I think I'm getting whiplash.

"What?" I ask.

He stops so close I could count the flecks of deep orange in his irises.

"What if I don't want it to be a joke?" Dav asks, leaning in, voice rich with that draconic rumble.

*Holy shit, is he about to kiss me?*

I can't help it, I lick my lips, drop my eyes down to his, wonder if they're as fussily cared for as his hair, his manicures, his waxed eyebrows. Does he sugar-scrub his lips? Will he taste sweet?

"Colin!" he growls when I haven't answered. "Tell me. What if I don't want it to be a joke?"

"Uh... um..." I say, oh, so cleverly, and lick my lips again. My mouth is suddenly so dry my throat clicks.

Is this happening?

I think it's happening.

Oh, *shit*, this is happening. "Dav, I..." Fuck it. You know what? *Fuck it.* Screw Hadi's rules. I don't even care if I regret it. I will regret it more if I *don't* take a shot at it. So I stretch up my neck, aim for his—

Dav takes my hand.

I freeze.

It's gentle, but it feels like he's pushed a bolt of lightning through my skin. His long fingers caress my palm, skim lightly across the sensitive underside of my wrist, over my pulse point. I gasp like one of the protagonists in my books, light and surprised, because I *am* surprised.

I watch him lift my hand, gaze locked on mine, making sure I'm watching him do it. Then, gently, he presses his lips to my knuckles.

And it's... it's *intimate*.

The feel of his breath on my skin, the slight dampness, the heat. His lips are warmer than the rest of him, and I want to know if it's because he's been breathing fire, or if this is another dragon thing. Is his mouth always this hot?

I want to put my tongue against his to gauge it.

Dav's watching me, carefully, thumb brushing across the spot he'd kissed. It sends goosebumps racing up my arm, to shiver along my scalp. Every part of me feels honed in on that single, sweet point of connection between us. It's erotic in a way I would never have written, and yet, to have him standing so close, practically sharing the same air, my hand in his...

"Dav..." I whisper. I have no idea what to say. What to ask for. I should be apologizing, but would that ruin the gravity of this... what is this? A confession? "I don't—

"Hey assholes!" Hadi snarls from the other side of the kitchen door.

Dav springs back so fast he slams into the table. He is back to prim posture and folded hands, though this time his attention is on the floor, on the footprints marked out against the white tile in spilled coffee. I feel bad that I've wasted his hard work like that.

When I look over, Hadi is peering around the doorframe. "If you're going to have a domestic, don't do it in my kitchen. Everyone can hear you two shouting. Fuck." She pinches the bridge of her nose. "You know what, Dav hasn't taken lunch. Colin, get him out of here for an hour. Work out your shit."

She yanks the door closed behind her, slamming it with a ringing *thunk*, and turns up the café muzak.

My face *burns*, and the blush must match Dav's, because he's as red as a tomato, freckles lost in the flag of color, eyes obscured by the flop of his hair. It's not a good look for him. And yet I just want to *grab* him, throw him up against the fridge door, and cover his mouth with mine, and *shit*, yeah, Hadi was right.

Time for a break.

# Chapter Eleven

D av kissed my hand.

It's all I can think about.

I don't want to sit out the back of Beanevolence for our break. I need to be in public or I won't be able to trust myself.

"Let's go out," I suggest, as Dav dons his shirt and waistcoat, attention laser-focused on his buttons. He's suddenly bashful. For being caught in just his under-shirt? (How cute, he still wears an under-shirt.) Or being overheard by every customer? Or being shouted at by Hadi? Or kissing my hand? "How about the board game café at the top of the street?"

"As you like," he agrees softly.

*I'd like you to mean this. Please, don't let me misunderstand. Please don't let me fuck this up.*

Dav said he didn't want my love confession to be a joke. Then he'd kissed my hand.

Butterflies and fizz bubble up in my stomach as I lead him through the crowd of people out front. The lunch rush has dwindled, so there's only half a dozen people in line now, though all the seats are full. We get the stink eye from a few, but someone applauds when I grab Dav's wrist to speed him along. The backs of his fingers brush my palm when I tug him through the front door.

*Dav kissed my hand.*

I float the whole block to the resto. The owner, a woman with bright red corkscrew curls and an infectious smile, offers up some free craft beer when she finds out we're part of the café crew, and begs us to let her know when we'll be selling packets of our new roast so she can start slinging it here.

When she's dropped off our lunches, Dav twirls his spoon through his chili and, like he's ripping off a band aid, blurts out: "I have nothing else to do."

I look up from my burger, caramelized onion dripping out the corner of my mouth. *Oh, yeah, real attractive. But Dav kissed my hand, so he doesn't care.*

"Sorry?" I dive for a napkin, because I'm still replaying that kiss like a looped GIF in my mind, and this isn't where I thought this conversation would start.

He sinks back into the banquette, the closest thing to a slouch I've seen from him. "You've asked me, repeatedly, why I came to the café every day."

"Okay." I give him the space to elaborate, instead of making a joke about how it's obviously because he thinks I'm cute. You don't kiss the hand of people you think are not-cute.

Dav stabs his chili. His spoon stands straight up. "I have nothing else to *do*." For the first time since the kitchen, he meets my eyes. His face is unshuttered again, that's something, but he looks deeply unhappy. I want to kiss the worry away, but I don't know if we're there, yet. I don't know if that's actually what he wants.

I decide to focus on the conversation he clearly wants to have, instead of the one Hadi interrupted and I'm dying to get back to. Who knew I'd be all *communicate-y*. I've never been the one who likes to talk it out in a relationship before. Dr. Chen would be proud.

*Relationship*, I think, biting down the goofy grin that's threatening. *Dav kissed my hand.*

"That can't be true," I press. "Everyone knows dragons work in government, or head charities, or, or wealth management portfolios, whatever those are, or all the important shit for maintaining an estate."

One corner of Dav's mouth curls into a self-deprecating smirk.

"Odious letters of business," he says, paraphrasing *Pride & Prejudice*, in the bit where Caroline is pestering the dragon Darcy as he tries to attend to his correspondence. Dav remembers that I like Jane Austen. It makes me giddy. Maybe we can read them together.

*He kissed my hand.*

"Yeah, like that."

Dav shakes his head. "Not me."

I open my mouth to ask *But really?*, and stop when I realize he is genuinely miserable about this. "I don't understand," I say gently, instead. "You can explain if you want, or I'll shut up."

"Don't shut up," Dav says immediately. His hand makes a move toward mine, but never quite lands on the table. "But, please, you must understand, it's terribly... *mortifying*. For a dragon to have no *purpose*..."

I snort. "Your purpose is to stare at me like a thirsty creep. But don't worry, I don't mind it, now."

He makes a distressed whining noise that's entirely inhuman. "Please forgive me. I didn't intend... I simply enjoy watching you *serve*."

"Okay, explain *that*." I wave a fry in his direction before popping it in my mouth.

"There is a deep-rooted instinct in the *homo draconis*," he begins softly. He splays his hand against his chest as if to keep his heart from thudding right through his ribs. "A desire to ah, to use the crude pop culture vernacular, to *hoard*."

"Yeah," I say, nodding along, because this isn't news to anyone. "Land, wealth, titles. I know."

Dav looks stricken. "You understand, then, that in the colonies, European dragons claimed for themselves overlarge swaths of territories, as if they were utterly unoccupied. And when they were seen to be occupied, but not by us, not managed in the way *we* manage them. it was called 'underutilized' and therefore free for the rescuing from those Indigenous dragons doing it *wrong*." He makes that hiss-spit noise, and I'm reminded that there must be some interesting architecture in the back of his throat.

*Maybe I'll find it with my tongue when I finally get to kiss him properly.*

"So, colonizers," I say carefully, wondering if my opinion on this is going to put us at odds. "I'm following so far."

"Thieves," he sneers in agreement, and yeah, whew, okay. We're still on the same page. "Save for what the Empirical dragons so *graciously* allowed the Indigenous Peoples to retain. Pah." He catches himself, eyes darting around, and he hunches down again.

Interesting. Probably not a topic he's supposed to be having opinions about in public. Not as the beneficiary of those 'thieves'.

"So, what," I say slowly. "You don't, uh, have any place?"

He's going to give himself whiplash, the way he keeps snapping his head up at me. "I most certainly do maintain territory!" he hisses with indignation that, in a human, might have suggested I had said something nasty about his ability to get it up.

"Sorry," I say, hands up, *don't shoot*. "I'm just trying to understand."

Dav does something I've never seen him do—he looks actively upset, like he's going to *cry*. His nose scrunches up and his eyes go red-rimmed and squidgy. He blinks a few times and his lashes spike.

*He's beautiful*, I think, watching him struggle. *He kissed my hand*. I want to return the favor, kiss each digit one by one.

I also don't want to move too fast. He's clearly got some notions of how things are supposed to go. I don't know what they all *are*, but I can damn well respect the lines he's already drawn.

"I know, and I appreciate that," he says. He heaves another sigh. "You needn't worry. I have both territory and nesting grounds—a small estate—out in Canborough."

Not sure why he thinks I'd be worried he doesn't have territory. Or nesting grounds.

But good for him, I guess?

I wrack my brains and realize his 'estate' is a twenty minute drive from Beanevolence, in the middle of vineyard country. I assumed he lived within walking distance. Why else would he even know Beanevolence exists? But I've never seen a car.

*Maybe he flies in.* I imagine Dav with big leathery wings protruding from his back, soaring in the mist above Niagara Falls, dancing in and out of the mist plumes. He's being serious with me right now, though, so I cover my grin by taking another big bite of my burger. Half the topping squirts out the bottom.

"Of course, because I manage an estate, it is only right that I have a housekeeper for the house, a manager for the farm, a head vintner for the grapes, and a winemaker for my cellars," Dav goes on softly. "It's all very proper. And so even at home, I have nothing to *do*."

"And you're not involved in, like, I dunno, local government or BIAs? I thought there's always a dragon on committees and stuff."

"No." He's actually *squirming*.

"So what does this have to do with you liking how I serve?"

Dav puffs out a breath. He stares out at the street, watching the passersby. He's not avoiding my question, he's trying to figure out how to answer it, so I let him be as I try to shove the pickles back in my bun with mustardy fingers.

Why did Dav ever kiss my hand?

At length he says, "Along with the desire to hoard comes one to serve that which one hoards. One creates a community and then one... *protects* it. Cares for it. But I am—" he stops, voice crackling, the rims of his eyes red, his face splotchy. "I am unnecessary."

"Dav, you're not—"

"Please, Colin." He holds up a polite hand. I splutter to a stop. "You do not know our society, and I know you mean well, but believe me when I say I am *utterly* unnecessary. I am an unneeded soldier, saddled with vital but meaningless territory, with no place within the politics of the country or the legacy of my family."

The way he phrases it, it sounds like he's repeating something he's been told. And if that's true, then that's fucking awful. An invisible fist of pity and grief for Dav squeezes the top of my lungs. Some family, if they call him 'unnecessary' to his face.

"That's... harsh." I want to comfort him, but I don't know what I'm supposed to be—or allowed to be—saying here. "But I know you. You're compassionate. You're clever. You can do more than just be a soldier."

"No, Colin, I can't. There was a, hrm, a disgrace, and I am prevented from... participation. Perhaps one day I'll be asked to, ah, contribute to the propagation of the bloodline... but I doubt it."

I have no fucking clue what to do with *that*. Ask what the disgrace was? No, if he wanted me to know, he'd tell me. Make a crack about propagating the branches of his family tree?

No, I don't actually want to think about him having sex with anyone who isn't me.

He looks wretched, and fuck if it doesn't make my heart do a somersault. I want to say something cheeky, something sharp and funny, but when I open my mouth what comes out is: "If I can ask..." I say slowly, waiting for his nod. "What do you mean, unneeded soldier?"

"My only purpose is to fight." He spreads his hands. "And there is no war on this soil at present."

Great. Now I have no appetite.

"You just sit around and wait for the bombs to fall?"

"Essentially."

"Fuck, that's bleak. So you come in and torture yourself by watching me do what you're not allowed to?"

Dav makes a noise that sounds more like a sob than he'd probably like to admit. "At least the scenery is fetching."

My heart gives up on somersaults and starts cartwheeling. *Fetching*.

Fuuuuuck.

"You are very good at what you do," Dav says. His shoulders have dropped, as if he's set down a heavy burden for the first time. "There is a nobility in serving. The essential workers of The Great Pause taught us that, if nothing else."

My stupid jar-handle ears go red. "I'm just a barista."

"You're much more than that," Dav admonishes, that furrow beside his mouth deep and honest. *I want to kiss it*, I think suddenly, and bury my stupid face in my own lunch before I pull some sort of complete numbskull move and try. "People come into Beanevolence grumpy, or upset, or stressed from their work day, and you take the time to offer them a smile, to hand them a cup. You love everyone you serve, and in that moment when you connect, when your eyes meet, they love you back."

"The heart-eyes are for the caffeine."

"Don't sell yourself short," Dav says, and then turns his attention back to the window.

His freckles are a constellation of golden stars in the syrupy slant of the summer sun. He pushes his hair back off his face, seems to be steaming out the wrinkles his confession had creased into him from the inside. Once he's smooth and refined again, he turns and digs into his lunch mechanically, like a soldier bolting back his rations.

*'When you hand them coffee, they love you back'*, his voice echoes in my head, and all I can think is, *I hand him a coffee every morning.*

"I'm sorry for pushing," I say, when our plates are cleared.

"I would have told you, one way or another."

"There's no reason I needed to know."

"But there is." When he meets my eye, there's *meaning* there.

*Wait, something important just happened, and I don't think I caught it.* "Come again?"

Pink flickers along the tops of his ears, backlit by the window. "Surely I've embarrassed myself enough today."

"Wait, I—" I stop, lick my lips, not sure I'm understanding what I'm supposed to understand. "Sorry, no, I—"

"*No?*" he echoes, sinking further into himself. "I'm a fool, I—"

"No, wait, no, not *no*. That's not what I meant. Auuaugh, I don't know what I mean." My heart is thuddering so hard my neck is throbbing. "Can we, hold on, can I have a second to process what it is that I even *think* you're trying to say here?"

"Have I not been clear?" he asks, aghast.

"Yes?" I hedge, "But I'm an idiot sometimes, and Hadi made me The Rules to *keep* from being an idiot, so I want to be sure."

"The Rules," he repeats, confused.

"Dating Rules. I will recite them for you one day, but not right now." I take a deep breath. "For clarity, is this you telling me you're, um..."

Dav nods. "Attracted to you, yes. I thought I made that clear."

*He kissed my hand.*

"Fuck." I flop my arms onto the table, pressing my forehead into my elbow.

He brushes a so-gentle-its-almost-not-there touch on the back of one of my knuckles. I rest my chin on my forearm and look up at him. God, he's so unfairly handsome. I wish he'd smile, though. I hate seeing him so pinched.

"Is that unwelcome?" he asks.

"No," I confess. "It's ... shit. It's just that I spent the last three weeks trying to convince myself I was seeing something that wasn't there."

"It's there," Dav says at once.

I'm flooded with relief so palpable that it splashes fresh-water-sweet against my senses. He turns his hand over to run the tip of his pinkie finger, feather-soft, along my life-line. Goosebumps trickle up my wrist.

"Yeah, I'm getting that." I hook my own pinkie finger around his wandering one, and it's childish, but it also feels absurdly intimate. Another vow. "So what now?"

"Now," he says, and there it is, the kind, satisfied smile is finally back where it belongs. "Now we roast beans. And afterward, perhaps you will allow me to take you to dinner?" His finger tightens around mine. It should be awkward and stupid, but it isn't.

"You're sure that's okay? You're already spending all day with me."

"My dear." The endearment makes my stomach wriggle. "I'd like nothing better than to fill all my free time being close to you."

"Okay." I feel simultaneously wound so tight I can hear myself creaking, and so loose with joy that I could noodle right off the chair. "Okay. Just don't expect me to put on my 'serving' show when we're out."

When Dav laughs, when he *really* laughs, it's absolutely beautiful.

# chapter Twelve

As we walk back to Beanevolence, I decide that it's a lovely day to set myself on fire.

Not because Dav and I have still got pinkies curled around one another—it's disgustingly twee, and I freaking *love it*, okay—but because when we get back, Hadi is standing at the window with her stupid phone out. The garage door-windows are open, so she has a clear and unobstructed sight-line when she snaps what I assume is going to be an embarrassing photo.

"Do you have to?" I ask her as Dav drops my hand to open the door. Like the gentleman he is. Not like a sneaky sneak friend stealing pics.

She wouldn't hold the door for me.

She wouldn't kiss my hand either.

I'm okay with that.

"What'd she do?" Dav asks, a puzzled look on his face putting a vertical line between his eyebrows. I just want to, like, kiss it away. But there are a dozen people in the café, and Hadi is grinning at us, and Dav, I'm figuring out, likes his privacy. So no PDAs.

"She's being a punk." I hold up two fingers at her when we get inside. "Rules One and Two, okay?"

"Okay," she says. "You look cute."

"Fuck off."

Hadi laughs and drops her phone into her hoodie pocket. "We're completely out of all the baked stuff, my nerds."

"I'll put in some trays," Dav agrees, rolling up his shirt-sleeves.

I hand over the sandwiches Dav had suggested we bring back from the restaurant for Hadi and Min-soo—he'd paid for all of it, even though I told him he didn't have to—and relieve Min-soo at the till. It's not so busy now that I can't take orders and make coffee at the same time. We tend to taper off in the evenings, with no student study groups to fill the sofas and tables.

"That's thoughtful." Hadi peers into the take-away box at the roasted veggie sammie I knew she'd like. "Thanks Colin."

"Thank Dav."

He gives her a little wave as he disappears through the kitchen door.

As soon as he's gone, Min-soo crowds me up against the front counter.

"So?" Min-soo asks, lit up with intense delight. "Is he a good kisser? I bet he's a great kisser. Did he dip you? He looks so Hollywood!"

"I don't know?"

"Is that a question?"

"I don't know," I repeat. "He hasn't kissed me yet. I mean, my hand, but not my—"

"He kissed your *hand?*" Min-soo squeals, and it's loud enough that I clamp my palm over her mouth.

"He can probably hear us!"

"No, I can't," Dav calls from behind the kitchen door, and my lungs constrict with mortification.

"Sorry!" I push Min-soo back so I can wash my hands.

"By all means—please keep flattering me. My ears are burning." His voice is tinged with embarrassment, and it knocks me for a loop that I can tell.

"I'll set the rest of you on fire, too, if you don't cut it out!"

Dav laughs in that beautiful baritone. I am so gone on this guy. This is *ridiculous.*

Min-soo honest-to-god clutches her hands together over her heart. "It's like *Desires Aflame in a Time of War.*"

I know that's her favorite K-Drama because the little witch got me hooked on it too, and now it's *my* favorite K-Drama.

"It absolutely is not. Now either go on your break or help me with the recycling."

Min-soo hates taking the recycling bags down to 'The Murder Basement'. Just because the stairs are old and open, the walls are lumpy with years of inept tenants trying to plaster, the floor is uneven from an untold number of renovations, and the lightbulb doesn't always turn on? There's nothing scary about that. (The monster mask Hadi propped up in the corner? *That's* scary.)

Min-soo grabs her own sandwich box, and knocks on the kitchen door.

"Yes, alright, come in," Dav calls after a minute, and his voice is low and husky from the flame. He must have just started roasting, but it sounds like something else, though, like his voice is husky for another reason and I stick my hand in my front pocket to try to adjust the lay of my skinny jeans as subtly as I can.

Min-soo darts through with a quick, "Congrats, Dav," and then I hear the back door open.

"Congratulations?" Dav mutters in echo. I can't tell if he's surprised or annoyed.

Hadi is still standing at the far end of the counter, *looking* at me.

"What?" I snap.

"I'm trying to figure out why you're not squirrely."

"I don't get squirrely."

"You do. The first week of you in love is like trying to corral a tree-rat on speed."

"It's not!"

*It is.*

She offers up a flat glare.

"I dunno what's different," I admit softly, hoping Dav can't hear me over the sound of breathing fire. "I just... he's so calm."

"He's a nervous wreck," Hadi corrects. "Although, only around you."

"Gee, that makes me feel special."

"Maybe it should." Hadi gives me a bro-pat before taking her lunch downstairs to her office in the Murder Basement.

Fuck. Does it?

Dav was quiet beside me on the way to lunch, withdrawn and contemplative. He'd walked with his hands jammed in his pockets, radiating *don't talk to me* vibes so loudly my ears rang. But at the table, he'd opened up. He had been *honest*. He'd finished his sentences. Which I'll admit was probably because I'm making a conscious effort to stop cutting him off. I'm getting that he doesn't blurt shit out like me, and needs time to work through his thoughts.

But maybe Hadi was right. Maybe he was nervous before.

It's gotta be the other dragons that have him looking over his shoulder, minding his words. It can't be *me. Not allowed to serve*, he'd said. *Because of a disgrace.*

The more time I spend with him, the more I see that he downplays things. I flop my poor bleeding heart out all over the place, pinned to my sleeve and oozing down my arm; Dav's heart is under seven layers of plate armor at the bottom of a dry well.

And I basically forced him to share an uncomfortable truth. I'm an asshole.

But maybe it's this calm willingness to be vulnerable that has me so mellow. This, whatever this is, whatever it is we become, this feels... different from every other time I've had a crush. The crush-part feels the same. But this bit, the getting-to-know-you bit, the let's-go-on-a-date bit, this part feels sturdier, somehow. Nicer. Easier. Grounded.

*God, don't screw this up, come on,* I chide myself. *Don't get in your own head too much. Let it stay easy.*

"So are you gonna send me the pic?" I ask Hadi, a few hours later.

"Pull it off our social media feed."

"You *what?*" I yank my phone out of my back pocket.

I had it on silent. Gemma has texted **Who is that?** with a heart-eyes emoji. There's a missed call from Mum, and an email from Auntie Pattie that reads, **I didn't realize it runs in the family.** I'm too annoyed someone forwarded the picture to her to ask what she means. And there is one text from Rebekah. All it says is **I approve.**

*Christ.*

"Hadi!" I whine. "Did you have to?"

"Customers were asking who he was. Sorry, not sorry."

And the photo itself is... shit, it's *nice*.

Dav's hair is pushed to the side by a breeze, loose and casual, glowing in the sunlight. He's walking a few steps ahead of me, body angled so his torso is pointed toward the camera. God, his shoulders look amazing, his trim waist nipped in. Today's outfit—a copper dress shirt with the sleeves rolled up to his elbows and his top button undone, under a sharp waistcoat-and-trouser set in a deep chocolate—makes him look like some sort of bronze statue come to life.

I look like a scarecrow, caught mid-stride. I've got my chin tilted up at Dav, a wide smile on my face and a splotch of mustard on my shirt collar. (I check now, and yup, it's still there. Dammit.)

Our near arms are angled toward one another, his hip blocking most of our hands. If you weren't looking for it, you wouldn't even notice Dav and I have our pinkie fingers locked together.

Hadi's put a deep-shadowed syrupy-amber filter on the photo, so it looks like something out of Vanity Fair.

Underneath it says: *Welcome to Beanevolence's newest (volunteer) employee, "Dav". He's been helping us out since the fire, bringing his secret bean-roasting technique to the back room while we wait for our new machine to come in. No, he won't tell us what he's doing differently either, but trust us, you gotta taste the results.*

The comments are mostly congratulating Beanevolence for reopening, and a few hellos from regulars. There's an **EW** in the photo's comments from Mauli. Someone replied to their comment **You better be joking,** and Mauli backtracks in the replies with **just teasing my friends**.

And, holy shit, there are like ten different thirst comments. I wonder if Dav even knows what an eggplant emoji is for. And then I wonder if Dav knows what *sexting* is, and you know what, I am at work right now and this is not freaking appropriate.

My phone pings with a DM from Dike. It's a copy of the photo, but with our hands pixelated out as if we're doing something x-rated.

This is too much, all at once.

I text my Mum a quick **Will talk after work**, and a middle finger emoji to my sister. Stuart hasn't weighed in yet, so I'm gonna assume it's only because he hasn't had the chance to check his phone in the middle of whatever job he's at.

By the time we're done with the afternoon rush, the pic has racked up more comments than any other post Hadi's ever made, Dav has finished roasting two batches, baked two dozen scones, and ground enough espresso that each mason jar is packed, and Min-soo has decided she's making herself a latte. The day's emotional rollercoastering has me worn down, and I ask if she'd mind making me one, too.

The latte she hands me is rich in a way I'm not used to, with the new flavor of the coffee, but it's tasty and frankly, I'm bushed, so I'm not ashamed to say I chug it. Min-soo and I are discussing what kind of provisions she'll need to prep for Hadi's opening shift tomorrow when the boss herself comes upstairs.

"Alright, if we've got it all under control now, kids, I'm gonna let Colin and Dav go. I'll stick around until seven, Min-soo, and you can close at nine like usual."

"Actually, I'd like to do one more round of each roast," Dav says, sticking his head out of the kitchen door. "So perhaps tomorrow won't be so much of a mad scramble. If that's alright with you, Colin?"

"Sure," I say. "I, uh, I think I'll go home and take a shower before we go out. Change into a shirt that's less, you know, *mustardy.*"

Dav makes a noise I have decided to classify as a clicky-dragon-giggle. "Right. Also, I meant to tell you earlier, but there's mustard on your shirt."

"Gee, thanks, honeybun," I sneer with mock anger.

Dav's face does something startled, and affectionate, and complicated at the silly pet-name.

"Aww," Min-soo coos.

"Eugh," Hadi teases. "If you guys are gonna get gross, keep it out of the café." I punch her arm playfully and she swats at me in retaliation, but I'm too light on my feet, too fucking delighted with the world, to get tapped back.

"Right, see you losers later. Lemmie take my mug to the back, and I'll be on my way."

"That's Min-soo's mug," Hadi says, when I grab it.

"Nah, it's mine."

"But that mug was a chocolate latte."

"Yeah," Min-soo says. "Colin asked me to make the same thing I was drinking."

"Colin can't have chocolate," Hadi says, suddenly intense.

"Shit." I stare down at the bottom of the cup. Brown sludge still clings to the side of the cup. How could I have not noticed? No wonder it tasted weird. "*Shit.*"

"What?" Min-soo asks, and then her eyes pop wide. "I forgot."

"And you *drank it*, you dipshit?" Hadi snarls at me, grabbing my shoulders.

"I didn't... the new coffee, I couldn't tell, I—"

"*Colin,*" Dav says, pale with horror.

I clutch at my stomach, waiting for the first terrible cramp. Hadi ushers me into the kitchen, shoving me up next to the sink for either water or vomiting, whichever need comes first. Dav's wringing his hands, and Min-soo keeps apologizing.

It's like I'm a trained monkey. They're all waiting for me to perform my big trick. Only... "I think I'm okay?"

Usually I go from zero to Aubrey Posen in about five minutes flat.

"What do you mean?" Dav asks.

Hadi studies me with narrowed eyes. Then she pins Min-soo in her sights. "Are you sure you made him a chocolate latte?"

"I made both at the same time."

"I feel *fine,*" I insist. "Though I'm not loving the aftertaste now that I know what it is. But I don't think I'm going to vom. Uh. It's a Christmas Miracle, I guess?"

"It's June," Dav says, deadpan, and I'd kiss him right there if he didn't look so stricken.

# chapter Thirteen

I insist that we're not changing our plans simply because I *didn't* have an allergy attack, and go home to shower. I stink of my fear-sweat, stale-coffee, and whatever lunch I spilled. And I need to wash the creepy-crawly sensation of *not* being sick off my skin, and get the taste of chocolate out of my mouth.

I couldn't kiss Dav if it tasted like yuckiness. And I absolutely plan on kissing Dav tonight. Not on the hand. On the mouth.

I wanna see what that forked tongue can do.

Would it be too forward? Dav's old-fashioned, yeah, but he isn't a swooning miss in need of a fainting couch. It just seems like his manners—and his hairstyle—are stuck in the past. Working at Beanevolence may be the first time in decades he's been surrounded with common people.

"That's depressing," I tell my towel.

I don't have much in the way of fancy going-out clothes, but Dav isn't going to take me to some black-tie extravaganza on just a few hour's notice. I hope.

Shit.

I dive for my closet.

I've got a decent pair of dress pants, which I'd bought specifically for a fundraiser I'd gone to with Rebekah. They're tighter than I remember. Too many caramel lattes.

*Or chocolate ones?*

By rights, I'm supposed to be curled up on the floor beside my toilet, clutching my ribs and fighting off a pounding migraine. As I flip through my closet, looking for the black dress shirt that goes with these pants, I set my phone to speaker and call Mum.

"Hullo, *mo leanbh*," she answers. Her voice makes all the tension tucked up behind my lungs melt away. It makes me feel like I'm right back to being a kid next to her on the sofa for story time. I used to play around with having an accent like hers as a kid, to confuse my teachers, and I still put it on for funsies at the bar.

I wonder if Dav would laugh at me, or *with* me, if I tried it with him.

"Hullo, Mummers," I say, sliding on the shirt.

"That's a pretty man in that photo," Mum says, not even bothering with the pretense of small talk.

"That he is."

*Deodorant*, I remember as I'm doing up the last button so I have to unbutton the whole shirt again.

"Is he *your* pretty man?"

"Maybe. Depending on how tonight goes."

"Och, Colin, I don't want to hear about that."

"Dinner, Mum," I laugh.

"That's alright, then. Wear that nice cologne your brother got you for Christmas."

"Good idea." I spin around on the spot, trying to remember where I put it. Ah-ha, sock drawer.

"And brush your hair, for goodness sake."

Right. This is why I don't tell Mum about these things. My family is bossy.

She's not wrong though, so I comb it back off my face, and put in the nice frizz-killing hair oil.

"Hold on, I'll send you a photo to prove I have. There, sent."

Mum tsks. "You didn't shave? What about beard burn?"

"I thought you didn't want to hear the details," I chuckle. "Besides, he's a dragon. He's probably got a tough hide."

Mum goes so quiet so quickly, it's like an explosion.

"Mum?"

"He's what?"

"A dragon," I repeat. "Minor one, not involved in politics. Just a nice guy." I feel bad for underselling Dav, but his dirty laundry isn't mine to air.

Especially if there's no guarantee that this is a forever thing. I don't know if I want it to be a forever thing.

(I think maybe I do know.)

*The Rules*, I remind myself. *Don't get ahead of it.*

"Colin," Mum starts, and then stops. "I don't know..."

"You didn't freak when I came out." I sit down on the bed, socks hanging from my fingers. "But you're freaking now?"

This hurts in a way I didn't expect.

"I know you like your Harlequins, but those are just books."

"And this is my life. I like Dav, and he likes me. I don't care that he's not *homo sapiens*."

Mum is quiet for another chasm of eternity.

"It's just a date," I say softly.

"His life is just so different from yours," Mum says, tentative.

"It's really not."

I put my socks on and a sourness curls through my guts. Fuck. I shouldn't have called her. I don't want to feel small, and stupid when I see Dav again. Like I'm making a mistake.

"Okay then," Mum says finally. "Just be careful."

"I have two condoms in my wallet, and I've already checked the expiry dates," I joke, desperate for a return to levity, even as I'm speaking through a clenched jaw.

"Colin!" Mum laughs, scandalized.

"What? You work in healthcare. Don't act like you don't know what men my age get up to."

"I don't want to think about it!"

"Fine, fine. Oh, actually, there was something I wanted to ask. Mum, you're a nurse."

"I'm aware," she says, and there's the nice light banter back. Whew.

"Can food allergies ... vanish?"

Mum makes a thoughtful noise. "People can grow out of food allergies. But yours have only gotten worse. Why?"

"I had a chocolate latte today by mistake."

"And you're going on a date? I'm sure he'll understand if you cancel—"

"No, that's what I mean. I feel fine."

"Maybe it wasn't real chocolate?"

"You know Hadi would never stock crap."

"I don't... I don't know what to say, then. Maybe you were lucky this time."

"Maybe? I dunno."

"Has anything else changed? Are you on any new meds?"

"Dr. Chen hasn't changed anything," I confirm.

"Keep a list of what's different for the next week," Mum says. "I'm glad you're fine."

"Me too."

"And, Colin?"

"Yeah?"

She hesitates, and then says, carefully: "Have a good time tonight."

Thank god.

Affection, warm and bright, bursts through me. "I will. Bye." I hang up and go digging through the dirty laundry at the bottom of my closet for a decent pair of shoes.

When I resurface, I take in the state of my room.

Yeah, no.

There's nothing cool or sexy about this. Quick as I can, I jam all of my dirty clothes into my hamper, shove what other crap I can under the bed, and change the sheets.

Hopeful?

Yes.

Likely to happen?

No.

Will I be filled with regret if it *does* happen, and I end up fucking Dav on stale bedding?

Yup.

I have literally just enough time to dash into the kitchen and shove all the dirty stuff from the sink into the oven before the doorbell rings. I take a quick look at myself in the bathroom mirror on the way to the door— red-faced from rushing, but otherwise, as good as it's gonna get. I snag some Chapstick from the dish of keys-and-coins detritus as I'm unlocking the door and shove it in my pocket, all the same. Just in case.

Dav is standing on the front step, hands in his own pockets, relaxed and happy. It's a damn good look on him.

He's also wearing a different suit. Did he go home, too? This one is a slate gray, with a bold blue check. The buttons are silver instead of the usual gold, and a quick glance at his wrist confirms his watch and cufflinks are as well. This time he's wearing the matching jacket, and oh my god, his shoulders look squeezable. The blue of the check is matched perfectly by his shirt, and he's wearing a pocket square printed with bunnies inside wine glasses.

I can't help my smitten grin, and he follows my eyeline and huffs out a chuckle. "Gift from Onatah. She thinks I take myself too seriously."

"You do. Is she also the gifter of the socks?"

"Absolutely."

"Do I need to put on something fancier?" I ask, gesturing him inside as I head back to my bedroom. Thank god I tidied up. "I, uh, I have a jacket?"

I pull a plain terracotta sports coat out of the dry cleaner bag, and yank it on. Rebekah had picked this out, too. I don't have a whimsical pocket square, but there's a pile of enamel pins in a rice bowl on my dresser, and I fish out the squirrel driving a blue car.

Blue, to match Dav.

I'm such a sap.

Dav's lingering in the doorway, taking in my space (*really glad I tidied*). I spread my arms, give him some sparkle fingers, say "tah-dah!"

His pupils get fatter and slightly more oblong.

Boy likes what he sees.

Nice.

"Will I do?"

"Yes," he croaks. This isn't a dragon-noise. It's just plain old choking on his words. "You look very well."

"You get more British sounding when you're nervous."

He harrumphs, and steps into the room. Dav leans forward, slowly, giving me the chance to pull away. I don't. He lays his cheek against mine for a soft, gentle greeting kiss.

He smells like burnt sugar.

"Hi," I say softly, kissing his cheek back. His skin is soft, not like scales at all. Maybe I *should* have shaved.

"Hello." His hands settle on my elbows.

I want to unbutton his blazer and grab his ass with both hands.

I don't, because I'm not feral.

"Dinner?" I remind him, because if he keeps sweeping his thumbs along the inside of my arms, I'm gonna back him up until he tips over onto my freshly-made bed and get him messy.

"Right." Before he can retreat, I hook our pinkie fingers together. Dav glances at our hands, startled, then back up to my face. Confidence slides into his posture. "It's a short walk."

He doesn't let go of my pinkie, not even when I need to pause to lock up, not until we're seated side by side at the table, the tips of our shoes brushing in the shadows where no one else can see.

Our waiter at Twenty Wine Bar turns out to be one of Beanevolence's regulars. So when she recommends the gnocchi and some perfectly crisp Pinot Grigio, I trust her. I wrote my thesis on sustainable winemaking, and Dav has a vineyard, so when he asks if I'd like to hear about his own Pinot crop, I say yes. I spend dinner watching Dav come alive with pride about his vines, and his people. It's pretty fucking charming.

"Of course, the wine from my land is only for my table," he says. "Or my staff. I give them cases for the holidays."

"'For your table.'" I put finger quotes around it. "Hoity-toity winemaker and his private reserve."

Dav's ears go delicately pink. "I'm only a winemaker because there's little else to do, and the crop is ideal for what arable land I have to call my own."

I don't like hearing Dav talk about what he's not allowed to do. Since I can't fix it, I ask him to order dessert. The raspberry cheesecake arrives with two spoons and an unexpected chocolate sauce swizzle on the plate.

"I'll send it back," Dav says.

I've had enough wine to feel like throwing caution to the wind, and frankly, I'm still keyed up over the fact that I *should* have had an allergic episode and haven't.

"Colin!" Dav hisses when I swipe my finger through the sauce and pop it in my mouth. I'm not going for sensual, though I realize as soon as I lick my finger that maybe I should have.

Do you have to seduce someone when they're already a sure thing? I guess it's only polite to put in some effort. Too late now.

I don't *like* the taste of chocolate. It reminds me of too many hours spent heaving until there's nothing left to come up but thin, frothy bile. But this goes down smoothly. There's nothing.

*Nothing.*

"Shit," I say softly. "This is weird."

"Are you okay?"

"Yeah? I just don't know *why*."

I have the sudden fear of a delayed reaction, of puking on Dav's shoes as he moves in for a goodnight kiss, and regret testing myself. We finish the cheesecake together, and I pick around the chocolate, deciding that I've tempted fate enough for today.

The conversation about food allergies and my Mum's advice takes us through to the bottom of a second bottle of wine, and I am more than tipsy enough to lean heavily on Dav as he walks me home.

"Do dragons get drunk?" I ask, watching my footing on the uneven sidewalk.

"Of course," Dav says, bending in closer to my ear to whisper. "But not on so little."

I snort at the thought of Dav sitting at the table in the fancy Italian Bistro drinking wine out of the bottle with a crazy straw.

Dav favors me with an indulgent smile that I want to taste. He paid, too, and wouldn't let me leave anything but our tip, and only when I argued that it's not fair to the power balance of our relationship if he's going to be the one handling all the expenses. He's pouting now, actually *pouting*.

I want to bite his lip.

"C'mon, man." I butt his shoulder with my forehead and give him my best Bambi-eyes. "Stop moping."

"I understand your concerns," Dav protests. He's taller than me, but only by enough for my eyes to be exactly level with his mouth. He licks his lips and a hot thread of desire unspools from the base of my neck, curling into my pelvis. "But Colin, please. I am wealthy, with little to do but to figuratively sit upon it. I am happy to stimulate the local economy. And, of course, it's satisfying."

"Feeding me all day is satisfying?"

Does he mean sexually?

It'd be weird if he meant sexually, right?

That should be a turn off, a red flag, potentially a sign of a controlling partner.

Unless it's kinky?

"Colin, you remember what I said about serving."

It *is* kinky.

Also, turns out, *not* a turn off.

"I remember. It's just... I don't want you to serve me."

He flinches, neck scrunching unattractively and I wonder what that little fat roll tastes like. Salt and brimstone? I could push him under one of the trees lining the sidewalk, get my tongue under his ear and if the shadows are thick enough, flick open his fly and—

*Down boy.*

"Not like that," I add, when the hurt look flashes in his eyes again. "Not like... ugh. I don't want you to think you *have* to serve to be around me."

"I like it, though," Dav says. "Draconic instincts dictate—"

"No, I get it." I pull us to a stop now, at the bottom of the crooked cement porch that leads up to my rental. I take one step up. It makes him have to tilt his chin up, and I like this angle. It's intimate, as if I was sitting on his lap.

I want to invite him in. I don't know if I should, though. I like him too much to want to have sex with him on the first date.

Does that make sense?

I'm going to decide that it makes sense.

"I don't think you do."

"I want you to like spending time with me. Not because your draconic instincts tell you that you're supposed to provide for me. But because *you* want to be here."

Dav's free hand brushes my arm where the punctures were, lingering. Then he cups the side of my face, the tip of his thumb tracing the outline of my bottom lip. His eyes are on my mouth, but he's not *doing* anything.

He's *listening*.

He's giving me space to finish my thoughts.

Fuck, that's sexy.

"I don't want you *because* you're a dragon," I whisper in the quiet evening darkness. I set my palms on his hips, under his jacket. "I don't want the pile of gold, or the perks of being on your arm." I wish I was feeling bold enough to slip my fingers up under his waistcoat, feel the warmth of him through the thin material of his shirt. "I just want Dav."

"Good Lord," Dav whuffs out, as if I've punched him in the gut.

I don't have time to ask him what he means, because then his mouth is on mine.

*Finally.*

His lips are soft, and he slides both of his hands across my cheeks to cup the back of my head, to direct the kiss, and I let him because it's so *good*. I don't know how long I've wanted this but it must have been longer than I thought. Since before the hospital waiting room and his posh voice reading me a love story, since before the ambulance and giggling while a paramedic glared at us, since before burned metal and fire and blood, since before rude words at a door.

Maybe even since before I ever met him.

Because this feels *right*, and his tongue is wet and soft when he licks my bottom lip carefully, once. I open up to him, invite him inside, but then the absolute *bastard* lets go and takes a step back. I try to cling to his belt but he's too quick, and my fingers are kiss-stupid.

"Whuh?" I manage to say, ever so intelligently, cranking my eyes open.

Dav is rumpled. His mouth is wet and red. I lean in to keep going, to give at least as good as I got, but he ducks his head and chuckles.

"Good night, Colin. See you tomorrow."

"You could see me more right now," I whine. I have completely changed my mind about not wanting to have sex with him tonight—now I like him too much to let him go.

"No," he says gently. He takes my hand and *kisses the back of it*, and then he's off down the street, strolling towards where I assume he parked his car.

"You're an asshole and I hate you!" I call after him.

"No, you don't!" he calls back, raising one hand in a fond salute.

# chapter fourteen

"Wipe the cardamom honey around inside of the glass, okay, now the espresso, good, and now the foam," I say, talking Dav through assembling a latte for some influencer-type waiting impatiently at the end of the service counter. Hadi is needed in the kitchen to make more scones, so Dav's joined me in manning the machines.

"There you are," he says to the influencer, and all her irritation vanishes when he turns on his charm. She winks. *My* irritation spikes. As soon as the latte is out of his hands, I tug on his belt loop to get his attention, and peck a quick kiss off his lips.

Dav's Customer Service Charm melts into something besotted. I send a catty glance at the influencer, because I'm a possessive bitch, okay?

But she just says "cute", and takes the last empty club chair by the front window to give her latte a glamour shoot. It's gonna be cold before she takes a sip, but that's not my problem.

Every new social media post is free advertising for us.

Predictably, my back pocket vibrates about five minutes later, when I catch her actually drinking her latte out of the corner of my eye. I've got the Beanevolence accounts on my device today, because Hadi couldn't keep up. Prepping to add the influencer's post to our stories with one hand while I pull espresso with the other, I nearly drop my phone into the compost bin when I actually *look* at the thing. The first photo of the series isn't of the coffee, or even the café itself.

It's me and Dav.

Kissing.

I send her another glare and she winks again.

Fuck if it isn't a good pic, though.

It's a dramatic angle, the lower edge of the photo framed with the beaten-copper counter. Dav's hair has been color-corrected to match it, both of them gleaming. The kiss itself is light, like that optical illusion of the silhouettes nose-to-nose so it looks like a chalice in the negative space between them. Except there's no chalice, just the steam rising from the espresso machine like fairy tale fog. Dav's profile is classic: the carved-out lips, the beaky British nose, the groomed eyebrows, the classic swoop of hair. I look like an exhausted trash goblin: weak chin covered in scruff, unravelling yarn ball-esque hair, the knobby nose I inherited from my nan, the perpetual bags under my eyes that moved in at the start of my first-year exams and never packed off.

But I look happy.

I *am* happy.

Dav looks happy, too.

I hope he is.

I waffle for a second—my kisses don't need to be all over Beanevolence's social media feeds—and then I think, *What's wrong with putting a little happiness out in the world?*, and hit 'repost'. It's not like there isn't a rainbow flag sticker right above the door handle. If showing two men kissing on our feed loses us some customers? Well, we don't want homophobes in our café in the first place, anyway, thanks very much.

Then I get back to the rush of making complicated coffees and 'accidentally' bumping into Dav whenever I get the opportunity.

Okay, so it turns out she was not *just* an influencer. She was a reporter from a lifestyle website famous for listicles. A day later, suddenly **Eight Things We Are Dying Over At This Cute St. Kitts Café** is out there, and hundreds of thousands of people have been emailed a copy of the picture of me kissing Dav in their newsletter.

Shit.

It's Gemma who alerts me to it with some pop-eyed emojis and a link.

I'm standing in the kitchen, having popped back for a glass of water and a quick check of my phone. Dav's abandoned the cauldron, resting his chin on my shoulder, arms around my hips, when I make a choked squeaking noise.

"What is it?" he rumbles into my ear and yes please, that's nice.

"The kiss heard round the world. Fuck. Sorry, babe."

Dav turns his attention away from where he was snuffling behind my ear (tickles!).The website lists the attractions of Beanevolence in the following order, with high-contrast, luscious photographs designed to make your mouth water.

**1. The Coffee**

This is a close up of our canisters behind the counter, the sunlight glinting off the glass.

**2. The Bean Roaster**

Somehow the influencer got a candid shot of Dav that I am totally saving to my spank bank. He's standing in the doorway, leaning one shoulder against the jamb, head cocked as he laughs. Dav's started wearing an apron over his nice clothes (he accidentally scorched his pants the other day) and it pulls *just so* across his chest and hips.

**3. The Coffee**

Our drip pots, elegantly framed by the clean sleek black of the machines.

**4. The Sustainable, Local, Organic Model and Female Ownership**

Hadi, though she clearly posed for this one because she's giving the viewer a cheeky grin. Her hijab is a bright blue that contrasts gorgeously with the black and burnt orange decor of the café itself. Hadi looks cool and confident—a queen in charge of her empire.

### 5. The Coffee

This shot is of my hands, making the honey cardamom latte. I'm in the middle of pouring the milk foam in the little honeycomb pattern that took me months of practice to get right. Shit, I need to do something about my bitten-up nails.

### 6. The Cute Barista

Oh lord, it's me. I suppose my ears don't look *too* big in this picture. And she caught my face at an angle where it actually gives me a jaw. Moving on.

### 7. The Coffee

I don't remember making her companion's drink, but this shot is obviously of somebody's drip-coffee from above, on one of our café tables.

### 8. The Romance!

And there's the kiss. Oh god, Mum's gonna print this out and put it on her fridge.

It's a flattering, well-shot feature, for all that my consent wasn't asked for the pictures. Irksome.

"That looks good." Hadi appears over my other shoulder, and tucks in close to sandwich me between her and Dav.

On one hand—aww, my two favorite people. On the other—invasion of personal space much? Just to cement the violation, she touches my screen to zoom in on the kiss.

"Could you not?" I say.

"It's cute."

"It's *everywhere*. Bee-are-bee, gonna go throw myself off the back deck."

"Do a flip," Hadi says, deadpan.

"Please don't, actually," Dav says, strained. He sounds like he's talking through a wired jaw, but it's not my potential nosedive that has him spooked. "How many people have seen this?"

"I dunno," I confess. "There's over four hundred comments on it already."

"Shit." Hadi whips her head around to stare at the wall that separates us from the front, as if she can hear the thunderous footfalls of the approaching mob of thirsty coffee nerds. "More beans!"

"Yes, ma'am," Dav says without any trace of irony, offers her a perfectly crisp salute, and gets cracking.

By nightfall, three other major social media feeds have featured the article, and Hadi has fielded half a dozen calls from industry publications. *The St. Catharines Standard* and the Brock University Alumni Association have sent around reporters and photographers. Mauli and Dikembe stopped by to congratulate us and wheedle freebies, and Mum and Auntie Pattie have both sent me embarrassing GenX memes masquerading as congratulations.

We stay open late to manage the evening interest. Hadi heads home at nine, shooing Min-soo out in front of her and locking the door when she goes. I've agreed to stay a few more hours to prep for the morning, and suddenly Dav and I are alone in the kitchen. He's working on the last of the beans, and I'm trudging through dishes and dough prep. I'm desperate to open the back door for some cooler air, but Dav is paranoid, as if other dragons are hanging around the bottom of the slope behind the street with long lenses, just waiting for him to fuck up.

Who knows, maybe they are.

"I'm not keen on this article," he says while we lock up, just before midnight.

*Christ*, I am not looking forward to being in for six, but Min-Soo's got morning summer classes, and Hadi's reluctant to hire someone to share my shift with in case this burst in popularity is a blip.

Dav looks wiped, and I feel the same. We had plans for take out and hangs tonight. Instead we're both slumping back to my place, feet aching, backs sore, limp from the heat of the kitchen. I'd been hoping I could convince him to sleep over, but I think the only kind of sleeping that might actually happen is *sleeping*.

"Asking permission would have been nice," I agree, leaning into Dav as we wait for the traffic lights to change. "Consent is sexy."

"Indeed." He slips an arm over my shoulders. His fingers ghost over the puncture wounds—now dime-sized red dots, slowly shading to white. "Though I did like the pictures themselves. But that's not what I mean."

"Then what?"

"I worry what might be said."

I look up at him. The streetlight lines all his sweet edges in amber. "You think you'll get in trouble?"

"I think I am a dragon who has been forbidden from service, photographed in a café serving humans."

"But not *really*," I push.

"I am seen to be employed, Colin." He rolls his bottom lip in and bites it once, nervous, then seems to catch himself at it and lets it go. "That may be enough."

Rage frazzles up in me so fast, I actually gasp. I'd forgotten I was still so goddamn angry that Dav's own family says he's supposed to be small and disposable. Dav's one of the kindest, most emotionally aware, and thoughtful people on the planet. It's *cruel*.

"They're *that* serious about you just being a soldier and sitting around waiting for orders to go out and, I don't know, fucking *die* in some pointless bloody trench?"

"Peace, darling," Dav says softly, and leans down to gift me with a gentling kiss. It's chaste, and peters off into little pecks at the corner of my lips. We end up missing the light entirely, standing in the soft, breathless summer night.

"Don't think calling me pet names is gonna make me any less pissed," I tell him when we finally separate, a whole cycle of red lights later, and cross. I reach out and hook my pinkie finger around his. It's fucking twee, but it's kind of our thing now. In his other hand he carries a tote, which he's been keeping secret from me all day.

As we walk, Dav's face scrunches. His shoulders ride up, and his grip gets uncomfortably tight. A flush of red climbs up his neck from the collar of his dress shirt—unbuttoned three holes, the unrepentant hussy—and the next time we pass under a streetlamp, I can see it's not a blush, but the first prick of red scales.

"Whoa, okay," I say, and tug us to a stop. "What's going on?"

"I... I just..." he lets go of me and presses his hand against his chest. "I can't stop thinking... they're going to be so *angry*, especially after—" he cuts himself off with a hard gasp, and I don't have time to ask *after what* as I press my own hand over his, lacing our fingers together. His teeth are suddenly sharper. "I should never have, I should *never*—"

"Okay, stop, stop," I shush him. "Come on now, big breath in, follow me. Good, in, two three... out two three. Hey. I'm here.

Look at me, hey." I thread my hands through his hair, press my palms against his ears—lengthening into points—blocking out the rest of the world. He drags his eyes up, slowly, stopping to stare at pieces of me, to latch onto the buttons of my Henley, the notch of my collarbone, my bottom lip, before he meets my gaze. "Another breath, in, in, in, out, out, out, out. Hey, you're good."

The red fades. Under my fingers, the shells of his ears shrink and smooth. The fangs recede. His pupils round out a little. Slowly, carefully, I rock up on the tips of my toes and kiss him. This is a comfort kiss, slow drags and little soothing noises. *Hello, I'm here with you. I'm here.*

"It's already done," I say gently. "Whatever they think, whatever happens now, it's already done."

"I know."

"And you enjoy it, making humans happy?"

"Yes," he says fiercely. "Very much."

"Then we'll deal with what comes next when it comes."

"We?"

"It was my idea, wasn't it?" I ask, rubbing my other hand through my hair. Ugh, sweaty. Maybe I can convince Dav to have a shower with me. No, knowing my luck, I'd slip and crack my head open. "If you end up in the shit, I'll stand in it right there next to you."

Dav huffs a scrunch-nosed laugh. "Charming image."

# chapter Fifteen

I'd cleaned, okay? I just want that to be clear. I knew he was coming over, and I'd cleaned. While Dav helps himself to the kitchen cabinets, I order a pizza. It's not what we planned, but good enough is good enough.

He meets me in the living room with the only two soap-spotted but perfectly usable wine glasses I own, and the Grape & Wine Festival promotional "yay guy" opener. (Because the arms go up as the little neck twists down and he goes *Yay! Wine Time!*) From his tote, Dav produces a dark wine bottle with a hand-printed label that reads *2017 Pinot Noir* in one color of sharpie, and *Miracle Year* in another, a later addition. The lettering is elegant and old-fashioned, as even and beautiful as my old nan's, and I realize with a surge of warmth that I'm seeing Dav's handwriting for the first time.

Dav sits primly on the wonky sofa and makes the wine guy go yay. His socks today are boogying grapes. Onatah is already my new best friend and I've never even met her. I slide over until there's no space between our thighs, and Dav un-prims and slumps against me.

"Hi," I say. "You brought me wine from your cellar?"

"Yes. I hope that's okay?"

"It's fucking hot is what it is." I slide my nearest hand up the inside of his thigh, stopping just south enough that I can feel the edge of his underwear. He's a briefs man. Nice. "Look at my dragon, providing for me and shit."

Dav shudders once all over, eyelids fluttering. Well, now. That's a reaction that I last saw in a boyfriend when he was trying not to come too fast during a blowjob.

*Very* nice.

"Really?" I ask, delighted.

"Hush. You'll make me spill."

He does this fancy bartender *thing* with his wrist as he pours, and the wine *leaps* into the glass with a mid-air twist to aerate it and *holy shit*.

"Not to be horny on main," I say, holding very still so I won't jostle him. "But do that the fuck again."

Dav laughs and pours the second glass with the same sexy flourish. I want to appreciate it, I really do, but there's something else I want to appreciate more first.

"Oh my god, put that bottle down right now, come here."

I flop back, yanking him on top of me. Dav laughs joyously. It makes his stomach bounce against mine. He's heavy, and *real*, and it's wonderful. I want to leave bruises on his hips, grab greedy handfuls of his gorgeous ass, lick all the way up his spine. All I can reach right now is his mouth, though, so I bite it. Dav groans and props himself up on his elbows, fingers carding through my hair, and I fist my hands in his shirt so he can't get away.

"Colin?" he moans, and I fucking *love* the way he says my name.

"Just kissing for now," I reassure him. I like knowing the endgame when it comes to being naked and vulnerable. That way, I can enjoy what's happening instead of worrying myself over what may or may not be coming next. I flatten my palms against his chest, sliding my thumbs up to trace the slutty, slutty vee of skin revealed by his collar with my thumbs.

"Hm, yes," Dav agrees, and gets to it with a fervor.

Holy shit, he has *not* kissed me like this before. Like he wants to thoroughly map all the vectors of what *just kissing* can entail. I'd dragged him into the cradle of my thighs, but he props his hips back, polite. I'm already half-mast, but I can't tell if he's getting hard, and the fact that he's not making that my problem by grinding it against me makes me want to grope his polite ass even *more*. Goddamn.

"Unk," I manage to moan when he slides that beautiful forked tongue of his out of my mouth and up around my ear, then uses it to great effect on my neck. There's going to be a hickey high enough up for *everyone* to see tomorrow and I don't even *care*.

"Budge back," Dav says an eternity of *warm, wet, soft* later.

I'm too high on the taste, and feel, and smell of him to do anything but obey. Propped up against the sofa arm, Dav lifts one of the glasses to my lips.

"Drink." His voice is like smoke and fire, dark and rich, and deep. I give one of those full-body shudders of my own.

The wine is like his voice—deep and smoky. Also kind of like blackberry jam? I know a lot about *growing* wine, but not a lot about tasting it. But I know what I like, and this is *good*.

"That's amazing."

"I'm glad you think so." He kisses a spilled drop from the corner of my mouth. My brain flashes to every romance novel I've ever read where the love interest does the same. It's much nicer in person than on the page.

"You brought me wine from your own cellar," I repeat. He offers another sip, and this is so fucking *romantic* my whole body is buzzing.

"I thought we could try it with this." He sets the wine down and retrieves something else from the crumpled tote bag. It's a small box with a purple ribbon that reads *Laura Secord Chocolates*.

"What if it was a fluke?" I sit up all the way now. "You don't want to spend all night holding my hair back."

"I would, if you wanted," Dav says, sitting back. "I thought perhaps you've never had the opportunity to experience quality chocolates before."

"I'm curious as hell, I'm not gonna lie."

He hands over the box. Inside, two small truffles nestled in purple paper grass shine like glossy stones. Then the smell hits me. It's the scent of childhood misery and hours in the bathroom.

"I can't do it," I say, handing it back. "I'm sorry, I hate to waste your money—"

"It is no waste." He ties the box back up. "I'll give them to Hadi."

"I just don't want to risk it. This—" I gesture between us, and he licks his lower lip, which is still kiss-bitten and that is *illegal*, sir, you cannot just *do that* in front of me. "This is too nice to fuck up with puking."

And once he's seen how gross and pathetic I am, curled up on the tile and praying for death, he won't ever want to kiss me again. That's something I absolutely can't allow.

"Understandable," he concedes.

"I've been thinking about my food intake, and nothing's different. I'm eating the same stuff, using the same condiments. Except for the lunch at the boardgame pub, and Steph's burgers are good, but I don't think they're 'cure a food allergy' good."

"I don't know of anything that can," Dav agrees, sitting back and letting only some of his weight rest on my calves. We tap our wine glasses together and sip in tandem. "It's funny, I don't recall food allergies being so severe in my youth."

"What, a thousand years ago?"

"Hush." He taps my thigh with a teasing grin. "You're wretched."

"Ouch!" I pantomime pain. "So cruel. So old, and decrepit, and *cruel*, and *ancient*—"

"I'll show you ancient, you brat." He pulls the glass out of my hands, places it on the coffee table, and pushes me back down into the flat throw pillows. "Just kissing?" he checks in as he slides his legs over mine, trapping my knees between his on the cushions.

"Roger, roger."

"Dav," he says, with that silly, eye-crinkling grin as he lowers his face. "In case you've forgotten."

"Yeah, no, that's not very likely."

We fall asleep like that. The slow, wet slide, the soft push-pull lures us into dreamland. I wake up with a crick in my neck and a dragon asleep on my chest when the pizza guy rings the doorbell. I poke Dav upright, and before he can muzzily apologize, I chivvy him toward my bed. He's face-down in the pillow by the time I get back inside with dinner, so I stow it in the fridge and move the wine glasses to the sink.

I'm tempted to strip him down for his own comfort, but that's one intimacy-step too far for tonight. I wake him a little, make myself *not* have a heart attack over how cute he is when his face is all scrunched up in half-sleep, and leave him alone to wrestle into a spare pair of pajama pants. When I come back from pulling on my own pajama pants in the bathroom, he's dead asleep on his back, one arm thrown up over his head. He's also shirtless, and the pants are so tight around his hips that he didn't do up the string.

I am exhausted, but that doesn't stop my mouth from absolutely *watering* at the sight of his *everything* so casually on display. He's got a soldier's body, lithe and conditioned power with a sweet, concave tummy, and no belly button. I guess that's normal, dragons coming from eggs. He still has a treasure trail though, spare and brilliantly orange, arrowing down from the sparse spread across his chest to a thin line that disappears into his waistband.

That's *nice* nice.

*Stop being a perv*, I tell myself and crawl in beside him.

Sure, I could sleep on the sofa. Or even in my roommate's bed.

But there's a snuggly dragon sleeping in mine, and to paraphrase the girl with the golden locks, he looks just right.

The alarm startles Dav so bad he shreds the pillow. Good thing I was jetpacking, curled up against his back and lovely pert bum with my arms around his middle, or it might have meant another trip to emerg. We have enough time before we have to be at the café to mutter apologies and tumble around one another in the bathroom. Dav washes quickly, then I jump in the shower as he rifles my barren fridge for breakfast.

We end up munching on cold pizza. I was planning to seduce him, why don't I have something that isn't mustard and half-finished margarine to feed my conquest in the morning? Ugh, *fail.* At least I have a stash of spare toothbrushes from dentist visits.

We don't talk about last night, and though it might actually make a blood vessel burst, I refrain from any jokes about having Dav in my bed. He's already sheepish about showing up to Beanevolence in yesterday's clothing. I'm not about to scare him off by being obnoxious.

As we're pulling on our shoes, I say, as casual as possible: "I'd like to see your place sometime." I don't want to push, but Dav's walked me home or been in my apartment nearly every night for the last three weeks, and I've never even seen his *car*. Dav's face makes me add: "Sorry, is ... is that something I shouldn't have asked for?"

"It's fine." His expression is doing a complicated dance between confused, and scared, and delighted. "You cannot realize how serious a request that is. It's not common for us to allow humans who are not, ah..." he scratches the back of his neck. "Not *collected* to be allowed into a dragon's keep."

I snort as I usher him out and lock up. "I'm not asking to marry you, bro. I just wanna see your place. You've seen mine."

Dav smirks, and there's something gorgeously lecherous about the way he raises just one of his sculpted eyebrows at me. "Indeed I have."

"Hey, if it's not cool, it's not cool," I back-pedal. "I don't mind us going to mine all the time. Though I'm gonna have to get bread and eggs or something."

"Maybe one day," Dav allows, wrapping his pinkie around mine. "But it's a very big step for the present."

"I won't push. Rules Two and Three."

"Yes, what *are* these Rules?" Dav asks. He reaches up and flicks what turns out to be dried toothpaste out of my scruff by the corner of my mouth, and I think, suddenly, without any warning: *I love you*.

Oh.

*Shit*.

Yeah, so that's...

That's a thing that just happened.

"Colin?"

"Hm?" God, his eyes are so *golden* in the early-morning light.

"The Rules?" He tugs on my finger and I realize I've stopped walking.

"Ah! Yeah!" Fuck, am I blushing? I'm blushing. Shit. "It's, um... I make bad romantic choices. Not you! But, uh, I have sort of a history of having bad taste."

"I'm making an effort not to be offended," he says, but his tone is light.

"So, after like, every romantic disaster a bi dude could suffer, and trust me, dating multiple genders means there are multiple ways shit can get bad, Hadi wrote rules for me. She broke into my locker at the school and taped them to the inside of my door. They help me do gooder."

"May I know what they are?"

"Er, yeah, I—shit, it's embarrassing. I've never shared them before," I say quickly, before he can offer an out. But being un-conscious together in the same bed is physically intimate, you know? Something like that deserves some kind of emotional intimacy to go with it. And admitting that one is a dumbass when it comes to romance to the guy I am romancing seems only fair.

"Colin, I don't want to push you."

"No, no, I—" *I love you*, I think again, suddenly. *I thought that just now. I looked at you and thought 'I love you'. Fuck.* "So, ah, One: No assuming interest unless it's spelled out. I tend to, you know, read into shit."

"I believe I've made my interest explicit," Dav says softly, dropping into that rumble-purr from last night. It gives me a sudden sense-memory of the burst of perfectly aged pinot noir on my parched tongue.

Damn.

"Um, Two: no more charming narcissists. I have a habit of falling for charismatic people who are, you know, *only* charismatic and not much else."

"I wouldn't call myself a narcissist, I hope," Dav says with a frown. "And I'm certainly not charming."

"Eeeeehhhn." I make an obnoxious buzzer sound. "The judges disagree. You're charming as fuck." I pat his ass, and he flicks my cheek in retaliation. The cheek on my face, I mean. I'm laughing when I say, "Three: don't mistake lust for love."

The 'L' word makes both of us clam up. I speed through the rest. "Four: relationships are work. So you gotta work at them. Five: not every partner has to be The One and don't stress out if they're not. Six: Don't give up on the idea of soulmates, but also don't hinge everything on the belief in it. And seven: I'm worthy of love."

Dav goes quiet and thoughtful. This is awkward as hell. I wish I was wearing a scarf so I could hide my face in it, but it's July.

At length, Dav says: "Ah, I see why you enjoy the literature you do so much. Who doesn't dream of a soulmate who believes they are worthy of the love they share?" He is looking up at the sky, though, as he says it, throat working like he's choking back something. The gooey-caramel hopeless romantic center of me burbles. He lifts my hand to kiss the place where our fingers are hooked together. "I like your Rules very much."

"Technically, they're Hadi's," I crackle out.

He swoops down, right in front of Beanevolence, for a belated good-morning kiss.

It's the kind of kiss that blocks up your hearing, pins your focus on the person whose face is mashed against yours. Or at least I assume it is, because I don't hear my boss until she's close enough to speak right into my ear: "Stop making out in front of my café and open it."

Dav springs back like he's been caught with his hand in the cookie jar.

I waggle my eyebrows at Hadi. "And good morning to you, too, Oscar."

"Ew," Hadi says, reaching between us to unlock the door.

As much as I don't love getting up early for work, Hadi is the *worst* at mornings. I have no doubt whatsoever the minute she's sure she can afford another summer employee, she'll be getting someone else to replace her. Oooh, hey, maybe that means *I* can get off opens, too.

I head straight to the machines, and Hadi waits until Dav has retreated to the kitchen before pressing her finger directly over the hickey on my neck.

"Nice," she says. "Rule three?"

"Rule three."

And we leave it at that.

# chapter sixteen

"**Y**ou *called* me," Gemma says instead of 'hello'. "Is the world ending?"

"See, this is why I *don't*," I grumble, fumbling to get the phone on the counter before I drop it in the dishwater. I poke at it with a sudsy finger to turn on the speaker.

"Hold on," Gemma says, and then she's on speakerphone, too. I can hear Stuart in the background shouting at Mum to come to the living room.

"Oh, Christ, I'm hanging up."

"No you're not!" Stuart says. "Mum! *Mo leanbh*'s on the phone."

"Only Mum gets to call me that." I point a soapy knife at my brother's voice. "I didn't call for a family roast. Gem, can we talk for a minute without the peanut gallery?"

"I've got to get the chicken out of the oven, anyway. Be right back, *mo leanbh*," Mum says, and *great*, by all means, give Stuart more ammunition. I groan.

Gemma clicks off speaker. "What's the what?"

"Auuugh." I'm not sure what to say now that I have her alone. I check the door behind me—still good. "I just... so, I'm seeing someone."

"No, really?" Gemma deadpans.

"Fuck off. I think... I really like him. Like, maybe love him?"

"And you're scared shitless?" she asks kindly.

"That's just it," I admit, rinsing a wine glass. "I'm not. But not being scared is scaring the crap out of me."

"What do you want me to do about it?" she laughs. "Besides telling you to stop worrying yourself into knots."

"I'm not."

"You are. When did you last speak to Dr. Chen?"

My confidence curdles. I haven't talked with my therapist since Beanevolence got torched. I've been riding too high on the amazing coffee and wonderful dragon kisses to make a new set of appointments. I try not to be flaky. I don't see her every week, like I used to right after Dad died, in that first terrible lockdown summer when the whole world went to shit, but we still do tune-ups via video chat.

*"Ah,"* I say, caught out.

"So item number one: appointment," Gemma orders.

"Yes," I grumble. I *hate* giving any of my family any reason to boss me around. They think just because I'm a big fat mental health wreck that I'm still a child. I want to be *better* than that, to get all my own adulting right, no chiding or babying.

"Are you writing it down?"

"I'm writing it down!" I scribble it on the white-board stuck to the fridge.

"Good. So," she prompts when I don't add anything else. "You love him?"

I cut my eyes back to the front door in a panic, but no, Dav hasn't snuck in. Thank god. My life is already my own personal Coffee Shop AU, I don't need any other tropes to tiptoe in.

"Yeah, but what if he's secretly regretting everything and he's gonna ghost me? What if he sees what a trash goblin I am—"

"Whoa," Gemma cuts me off. "Where is this coming from?"

"Gem, he's *perfect*." I whine, wiping off my hands and throwing the towel over my shoulder as I turn to lean back against the counter. I glance at the door. Still safe. "He's nice, and polite, and he's *such* a great kisser, so obviously he's regretting every second he ever spent pining for me and he's secretly planning to fuck off and never come back, and I don't even know where he *lives*. I like him *so much* and this is *such* a stupid mistake. What am I doing? Should I end it?"

"What *are* you doing?" Gemma asks. "Are you actually asking me to help you think up reasons to break up with him because you've convinced yourself he's gonna leave you without even saying goodbye?"

"*Yes*."

"That's just the brain weasels talking."

"There's no reason why a dragon like him—"

"*What?*" Gemma screeches. The silence that follows it echoes like shattered glass.

"Did Mum not tell you?" I ask softly.

"No."

"Surprise?" Even though she can't see them, I add jazz hands, which just end up flinging droplets of gray dishwater all over.

"Okay." She sounds like this is something she's decided to freak out about later. "*Dragon*. Wow. Okay."

"How do I keep him from vanishing?"

"The cute dragon," Gemma clarifies.

"Yes. The cute dragon."

"The cute dragon who came into the café every morning for like a year and a half."

"Yes, that cute dragon." I don't add that Dav only came in because he was lonely and aimless.

"The cute dragon who looks at you like a besotted idiot in every single photo I've seen?"

"*Yes*, that cute dragon," I snap. "Have you inherited Mum's bad ears?"

"I'm just being sure," Gemma laughs.

"Don't tease! I'm serious."

The thought of Dav just changing his mind and leaving is *stupid*. Today has been great. He wanted to cook dinner, so he went out to the farmer's market around the corner and I said I'd stay behind and do the dishes. As soon as he left, I'd been smashed with this sudden, black-dog, steel-wool, terrible thought: *What if he never comes back? What if I end up standing here in this stupid, yellow, horrible kitchen watching the door and it never, ever opens again?*

It's awful and dumb.

It's my goddamn brain weasels and I *know* that.

Doesn't make it any *less* awful and dumb.

"Listen," Gemma says gently. "Not everybody you love will leave without the chance to say goodbye. He's not Dad."

"That's not why I—"

"*Colin.*"

The way she says my name stings. A hot wave of sorrow crowds my larynx, climbing up my throat into my sinuses, stinging and terrible. "Fine. Maybe it is."

"Did you take your meds today?"

"Yes?"

"Is that a question?"

"No?"

"Okay," Gemma says. "You're *sure* you took them."

"*Yes.*" It's the one thing I never forget. I hate where my mind goes when I'm not balanced. *If you can't make your own serotonin, store-bought is fine.*

"So cute dragon," Gemma says again. "Just enjoy being in love and take it one day at a time, okay? And call Dr. Chen."

"Okay."

"Can I put the rest of the fam on now?"

"Yeah."

She turns on the speakerphone and Mum is right there saying hello. I wonder how much of Gemma's side she heard.

I grimace, but force my tone to stay light. "What's up with you losers?"

Mum *tsks* at the affectionate insult, and launches into a run down of the dinner she's making, the changes in the garden, what the neighbors' kids are up to, how Gemma's broken up with that nice young man—"He turned out to be a red pill weirdo, Mum!"—and how Stuart's new client wants him to divert part of a nearby wetland through their property to become a pretty babbling brook.

"Don't do that, Stu!" I interrupt.

"No?"

"Obviously!"

"Obviously," he repeats, mocking.

"Not obvious to me," Mum says.

"Have you even *checked* where the watershed runs? Where local fish stocks spawn? What the average water table depth is every year? Never mind destroying a whole micro ecosystem, if you move water closer to a historic property with no modern foundation, it'll flood every snowmelt. No way, man, tell them to walk their asses to the riverside if they want to enjoy nature. Don't fuck around with the current saturation levels."

"Language!"

"Sorry, Mum."

"If I don't," Stu goes on. "They'll just get someone else—"

"Take it to the city, then. Or actually, you know what, get one of the guys out from Nipissing University to assess the property, talk to the owners. There's gotta be a professor up there specializing in environmental protections. Uuuuh, and the Heritage Board... I forget what it's called... I think Ruthanne from high school's on it? Point is, come up with something that makes everyone happy."

"Listen to you, using your degree and stuff," Gemma says, pride radiating from her voice. It still makes me preen, even though her mother-henning bugs the shit outta me.

"Dad would have been proud," Stuart says softly, and that's enough to make me drop the pan I'm scrubbing back into the greasy water and take a few huge gulps of air.

Dad never got to see me graduate, so it hits hard when Stuart says shit like that. We were in lockdown and construction had been deemed an essential service, and we had all been *so careful.* Fuck the Covidiots, anyway. If that asshole electrician had worn a mask, then Dad would never have—it doesn't matter.

Dad did.

So did the asshole electrician.

And that's all there is to that.

"Don't let them do it without making them *think* about it, okay?" I ask, working to keep my shit together. Stuart's a jerk.

"Yeah, *mo leanbh,*" he warbles in imitation of Mum.

Seriously, Stuart's a *jerk*.

A noise from the doorway catches my attention, and yeah, of course Dav is there, setting down his tote bag and watching me get slammed with one of those deep moments of long-held grief. He makes a gesture between us, holds out his arms, *you want a hug?* I really, really do want a hug. Because the first thing that sings through my blood is: *He came back!* Followed by: *Of course he came back, you idiot. He's 'besotted.'*

*Christ, and you love him.*

But more than anything, I want him to hold utterly still and be totally quiet, *oh my god.* If the fam catches on that he's in the room, they'll force me to introduce him. I am *not* ready.

"Right, I'm hanging up if you're gonna be mean," I say. "Blame Stuart for cutting off the call, Mum!"

"Oh sure," Stuart says, laughing. "It's all on me, like always."

"You're the big brother," I agree. "It's your job for it all to be your fault, Stu-pid. I'm just the innocent little kid who follows you around, even into the middle of a dock that unmoors—"

"That wasn't me!" Stuart yelps. "How many times do I have to tell you, I didn't untie it!"

"Sure, sure," Gemma says. "Bye Colin."

"Bye Gem. Bye Mum."

*"It wasn't me—"*

I press the hang-up button, give myself a moment to scrub my face with my water-wrinkled hands, and then nod and open my arms to my cute dragon. "Okay, hugs now, please."

Dav crosses the dingy linoleum in his lemon-yellow, monkey-printed socks, and wraps me in his arms. "That was fun."

"That was the worst ordeal of my liiiiiife," I moan into his shirt. "I can't believe my Mum didn't like, sense you there with her magical Scottish Mind Reading Magic."

"Would it be so bad?" Dav asks, stiffening.

I wriggle to prop my chin on his collarbone and look up at him.

"Hey, it would not be a bad thing to introduce you to my family. Just... not yet."

"Okay," Dav says, and then peels away to fetch the tote and root through the dishes drip-drying in the rack. He starts doing something fancy with butter melting in a pan, then a knife and the biggest leek I've ever seen in my life. "I liked hearing you talk with your brother—Stuart?"

"Yeah." We sort of dance around one another as I set the table, an echo of the way we move in tandem in the café's much smaller kitchen. Noticing how well we move together evaporates the last of the grief. "Stuart and Gemma are twins."

"Stuart and Gemma," Dav says, committing it to memory. It occurs to me that if he has siblings—clutch-mates? Egg-lings?—he's never mentioned them. "I liked hearing you use your expertise. You're clever, Colin."

I clear my throat, trying to sound cool while my heart jumps up to double time: "My thirty thousand dollar piece of paper should be worth *something*."

Dav's knife slams down hard into the cutting board, scattering leek everywhere. *"How much?"*

"Thirty thousand bucks."

"That's absurd."

"Welcome to late-stage capitalism. Still have all your fingers?"

"What? Oh, yes," he waves his intact hand at me, wiggling said fingers cheekily.

"You sure? Maybe I should check." Feeling silly and bold, I take his hand and make a point of kissing my way down the backs of each of his fingers, ignoring the fragrance of onion. By the time I'm done, Dav's let the knife clatter to the counter and is pitched toward me like a magnet to iron. His free hand brushes lightly up the side of my hip, fingers dancing across the denim. "Yeah, all good."

His kiss, when it comes, is hot, and heavy, and open-mouthed. He crowds me up against the corner, and I am happy to let him push me up to sit on the countertop so I can wrap my calves around his ass and hold him there.

"I hear charcoal is coming back as a food trend," I whisper, when he breaks away for long enough for me to get use of my tongue back.

"Huh?" Dav asks, kiss-drunk and pillow-eyed.

"Butter. Burning."

"*Coc y gath.*"

It's gotta be a cuss, based on the volume he says it at when he dives for the smoking pan.

# chapter seventeen

T he lineup is so long it's literally down the street.

"Yikes on bikes," I say.

People are selfieing in front of Beanevolence. As we approach, the mention alert on my phone becomes a near constant single note. I switch it to silent, and lordy, I do not want to see what kind of photos people take of us as Dav and I squeeze past the crowd to open.

Within an hour of flipping over the sign, Hadi has had to skim the till twice, Min-soo is relegated to just grinding beans and making fresh pots, I've burned my hand on the steaming wand, and we've stopped making baked goods because there's literally *not enough time* to get into the back to mix dough.

We're slammed until all the out-of-towners who'd made the journey from all over Upper Canada to check out the business-of-the-week have made like a Hobbit, and have gone back again. By mid-afternoon, our espresso machine is *overheating*. I didn't think that was possible.

The bean-roaster may be overheating, too; when I head into the kitchen—which is a *furnace*, why won't he open the back door, the paranoid bastard?—Dav's stripped down to just the tank-top.

Christ on a whole-wheat cracker, he looks tasty.

"Hey handsome," I say while he takes a moment to catch his breath. "You're sweaty."

"I never thought my abs could be sore from *fire*," Dav admits.

"I'll kiss 'em better later," I promise and he sends me a sharp, cheerful leer. "What do you want for lunch? Min-soo's doing a run."

"I can—" he starts, wiping his sweaty forehead.

"Nuh-uh, Mr. Martyr. You're taking a break if I have to shove you outside myself."

"Are you accompanying me?" he asks, eyes dropping to my mouth. How can he say so much without saying anything at all?

"Nah, I can't abandon Hadi yet. But she's started looking at resumes."

"That's good." Dav regards the empty space in the corner pensively.

"You can still take up a table every morning." When I tug on the front of his tank top, Dav bends down and lets me have his mouth for a few long, beautiful minutes. Then I push him toward the back door. "Go cool off."

"I'll miss being in the kitchen," Dav admits as he cracks it. The breeze that churns in feels like a blessing, sweet as a kiss. Though Dav's kisses taste more like smoke and char lately, caramelized like a fine scotch.

"It won't stay busy forever. Eventually the novelty will wear off, the roaster will come in, and I'll be able to sneak you back here for other reasons."

"That sounds promising. If not hygienic." He leans against the doorjamb. I reach out to loop my fingers into his belt, slide my hand over the slinky tilt of his hips, lean up for—

"Colin!" Min-soo shouts from the other side of the kitchen door. "Order!"

"Roasted veggie sandwich with salad!" I shout back.

"How vulgar," Dav says, teasingly. He's genuinely annoyed—his manners are *so* easy to offend—but he doesn't actually care that much. He crosses the room, provides his order in normal tones, and slips a hundred dollar bill into

Min-soo's hand, insisting he pay even though Beanevolence is making more than enough scratch to buy our lunches in return for missing our breaks.

When Min-soo returns, we rotate through who sits out back to eat. I'm just coming back inside when a black woman with wild eyes and a massive grin slams herself against the side of the counter in a skidding slide.

"You cured my allergy," she says, breathlessly. "I drank your coffee and it cured my peanut allergy!" She dances in a gleeful circle, arms thrown wide. The scattering of patrons still in the café all turn to look at her, murmuring and, in one case, recording.

Oh, *great*. More Internet bullshit.

I'd already read a dozen posts from people claiming they slept better, and they felt healthier after partaking at Beanevolence. Which was a whole big pile of malarky because yeah, no, as much as coffee was touted as a miracle cure when it was first introduced to Europe a billion years ago, it's still just caffeine-laden bean-infused hot water.

"I did a study and everything." the woman says. Now that she's not thrashing around in a horrifying victory dance, I recognize her. She's one of the pharmacology grads interning at the drug mart around the corner. She's their afternoon coffee-bitch. "I saw the rumors online and I thought, well, why not try?"

"By risking anaphylaxis?" I ask, horrified. While my food allergy is bad, at least it doesn't make me *stop breathing*.

"This is crazy," Hadi says, leaning on the counter, intrigued.

"Crazy, but plausible. I've had two cups every day since you changed the formula," the young woman says. "And I've been keeping a blog about it. This morning, I had peanut butter for the first time in my life, and look at me!" She turns in a circle again, braids spinning out.

Dav has frozen just this side of the kitchen door. His face is shuttered, his mouth pinched. Something in my gut lurches. Shit. I think we're in trouble.

"Coffee can't cure allergies." I want it to come out casual and self-assured. Instead it sounds like I'm choking on my own teeth. "Trust me, if they did, I'd already be eating chocolate."

"But you are," Hadi cuts in, straightening. "You had that latte."

"That's not—"

"You see!" the young woman says, pointing to me with a finger like a sword—sharp and dangerous. "There's other research, too. I shared it with my journal group—" Dav makes a sound like a kitten that's been stomped on, slumping back against the wall. He's gone so pale, his freckles stand out like gold shavings. "—and everyone's dying to know what you've done differently. Can I have a sample of the beans, before and after roasting?"

"No!" Dav shouts, and then slaps his hands over his mouth, mortified at his ill manners. "I, no," he repeats, at a more civilized volume. "You can't."

"What's your name, hon?" Hadi asks the young woman.

"Pedra," she says, taken aback.

"Pedra," Hadi says. "Min-soo is going to get you a cup of whatever you want. Have a seat and I'll come talk this over with you in a bit."

"Sure," Pedra says, cutting her gaze between Hadi and Dav, finally cluing in that the staff of Beanevolence are not as thrilled with her discovery as she is.

"You two," Hadi snarls, turning to us. "Kitchen. Now."

Dav and I march to her orders like two naughty little boys. Which, you know, we kind of are.

She stomps right over to the fridge and pulls out the box of chocolates that Dav had given me a few nights ago. One of the truffles is gone, but the other one is still nestled in the purple paper grass.

"Eat it," she says, shoving the box under my nose.

"What?" I ask, hands up, *don't shoot.* "No, I—"

"I will shove it down your throat myself if you don't."

"Now wait a moment, here," Dav cuts in but Hadi puts a hand on his chest, halting him on the spot as he recoils from her unexpected touch.

"Eat. The. Chocolate," Hadi snarls.

I don't have to. That's the thing, we all know it. Hadi won't actually hold me down and force it. But I'm curious, and if it does make me sick then all the weird stuff online will pipe down.

I pop it in my mouth.

*Ugh.*

It's everything I can do not to spit it back out. It tastes like hours of stomach aches, things exiting my throat in the wrong direction, and blinding headaches.

Also, a bit of raspberry.

"Colin!" Dav yelps. "You stupid man, what are you—"

I swallow. Dav frets and fetches a glass of water for me. Hadi throws away the packaging. I lean against the fridge, wrap my arms around my stomach, squeeze my eyes shut, and wait. And wait. And wait. After about five minutes, Dav puts his hand on my shoulder, thumb sweeping over my jugular sweetly.

"Colin?"

"I... I'm fine," I admit slowly. I relax from my anticipatory clench. "I've actually never felt better. Never mind the chocolate, I haven't had a middle-of-the-night anxiety attack in..." I check the tracking app Dr. Chen recommended. "Uh," is the only noise I can make when I figure out the day.

"Uh, what?" Hadi prompts.

"Uh, since Dav started roasting."

"No," Dav says, panic crawling across his face. "That can't be happening."

"Just because a dragon is handling the beans does not make my coffee *magic*," Hadi says. "What... *the fuck*... is going on?"

"This *can't* happen," Dav says desperately.

"But it is," I say gently. "Did you know?"

"Of course not!" Dav protests, wringing his hands. "No one has ever... how could I possibly...?"

"Tell me the truth," Hadi says. "Because I'm starting to think Pedra's not full of shit. I'm sleeping better, too."

"No." Dav's fingers go to his hair, clenching. He looks like a trapped wildcat, eyes darting as he turns in panicked circles, with nothing to lash out at and nowhere to run.

But Hadi is relentless. "My insomnia is *gone*. I haven't had heartburn once since you started, and I used to go through a pack of Pepcid a week. Colin had chocolate and didn't get sick. Twice."

Dav looks at me, helpless and pleading.

"I think we should 'fess up. If you want to. It's your secret."

"Explain!" Hadi roars.

"It was meant as a joke, you see," Dav says, wild. "I was only going to do one batch."

"Yeah, but then it was *good*," I cut in.

"*What* have you been doing to my beans?"

Dav checks both the doors are closed before picking up the cauldron of beans he had been preparing before Pedra's shouting pulled him to the front. Hadi opens the chute cap on the manual roaster, but Dav shakes his head, and backs into the corner, as far away from us as he can get.

"What's he doing—" Hadi says, but I interrupt her with a murmured: "Just watch."

My hands are shaky. My heart is kicking hard. I can't seem to get a deep breath. One stupid joke, and suddenly Dav—*my* Dav, *my* dragon—is cowering in a corner.

What have I done?

Dav inhales, purses his lips, and blows. Hadi gasps as Dav swirls the cauldron, making sure each bean is well-coated with flame. After a few minutes, he stops, and holds it out for Hadi to see. The room smells deliciously of fresh roast and warm smoke. Hadi takes a cautious step forward, eyes massive, and peers into the cauldron. One bean cracks loudly in the tense quiet, and she jumps back with a yelp.

"That's the only difference," I whisper. "And you can't tell anyone."

"Why not?" Hadi asks, eyes darting between the two of us. I've accidentally trapped her in the middle, forcing her to turn her head fully to speak to one of us, unable to keep us both in her sights. She looks uncomfortable, like she's remembering, maybe, that Dav isn't *homo sapiens*. Dav moves slowly, lets Hadi back away as he circles around her to put the hot cauldron on the metal worktable.

"Because it's, uh, kinda against some big dragon taboo," I answer.

"So you roasted beans for a joke, but it was good, and now you've been doing them all this way?" Hadi asks, starting to put the pieces together. "Why?"

Dav draws himself up like a soldier preparing for reprimand. "Because I like feeling useful. No, because I *wanted* to," Dav corrects, rueful and cowed. "I truly did not anticipate there would be any side effects. I'll stop immediately."

I shoot him a sharp glance, but he isn't looking at me.

Because he *wanted* to?

More like, *because I asked.*

Shit.

"Wait, hold up, I never said I was mad about it," Hadi says. She sucks in a deep breath, shakes out her shoulders, rolls her head back and forth. "I'm just confused."

"I'm happy to sit down and explain it more thoroughly," Dav says, which surprises me. "But for now, you must send that young lady away empty handed."

He looks pained as he says it, and I inch around Hadi to snag his pinkie finger with mine. The touch of skin-on-skin has an immediate effect on him. He lets out a deep breath and leans into me. I'm happy to be there to hold him up.

*Anytime*, I think, and then swallow hard when that thought is followed by a fervent, *All the time. For the rest of time.*

Dammit. I am in much deeper than I thought. But the honest truth of it is: I wasn't lying when I said that whatever shit Dav is in, I would rather help him wade through it, than to leave him to drown alone. Dav squeezes my finger, pulling my whole arm against his, and it's a staggeringly *intimate* thing for Dav to do in public.

"You can stop looking like I'm about to shoot you." Hadi's back to being the kind, no-bullshit-allowed Hadi again. "I'm not greedy enough to demand that you keep roasting our beans when it's clearly gonna get you in shit."

Next to me, Dav shudders in a breath, and lets it go slowly.

"You wouldn't be disappointed?" he asks slowly. "Your business has never been better."

Hadi shrugs. "Roasts change. We tell everyone we were experimenting with a technique that was ultimately unsustainable, and we move on."

"Or maybe we find a way to replicate the dragonsfire in the machine," I suggest.

"It is too hot. It will melt it," Dav says. "Again."

"We can hash this out later." Hadi gestures at the cauldron. "Finish that one, we'll use it for taste testing. Then I'm kicking you out for the day. Starting tomorrow, you use the machine. Got it?"

Dav nods, relief washing off him in waves so palpable that I can practically feel it.

"Thank you," Dav says.

"For what? You're not my employee."

"For not being angry," Dav says softly.

Hadi scoffs. "Listen, I don't know how dragons see it, but right now, you're the one doing me a favor. And while you didn't do it the way I expected, and the results are not what I was banking on, you've done my business good and I can't be pissed about that. Thank *you* for even being here."

"It's the least I could do, considering," Dav says, some of his teasing humor coming back.

"Yeah, yeah," Hadi says, and heads out to the front.

Before the door has swung closed, Dav and I are already reaching, mouths magnetized. When I let him up for air, Dav ducks down and kisses my shirt over the five round scars on my arm.

"That went better than I thought it might," I say. Dav buries his face in my neck and wraps his arms around me so tight my ribs creak. "Okay, ow a little. Ease up. What's eating you?"

"I don't know," Dav confesses, voice muffled and breath hot. "I thought I would have to leave, or you would hate me or—"

"Why would I hate you?" I cup his face, meet his sunflower eyes. He looks away instead of answering, and I let him get away with it for now. "C'mon—let's get a cup of the good stuff before it's gone. It's limited edition now."

Dav lets me take him by the hand and lead him out into the café. We slide over to the espresso machine just as Hadi shouts: "You *what?*"

Min-soo flinches. "I told her the name of our bean supplier and gave her a take-away cup of the whole roasted beans. Isn't that what you asked me to do?"

"No, I—" Hadi stops, and then scrubs at her face. "Yeah, okay, I could have phrased that better. Shit."

That's when I register it: Pedra's gone.

Dav presses himself back against the wall, hands over his mouth, every part of him trembling.

"They'll never forgive me," Dav whimpers, as he blinks hard, over and over. "I've done it again."

# chapter Eighteen

M in-soo finds Pedra's social media profiles, but they're locked down and there's no way to message her. By the time I get to the pharmacy, Pedra's left for the day, and her employers won't give me her phone number no matter how much I beg. She's in the goddamned wind and we're *screwed*.

Dav is fretting so badly that Hadi tells him to go. We both agree that it wouldn't be wise for Dav to be alone right now, so I take him back to my place. When we get there, a small leather carry-all is waiting on the porch.

"How'd this get here?" I ask as he sets it on the sofa. It's a quaint brown Gladstone bag that could be a hundred years old for all I know.

"I have staff," he says stiffly, as if each word is gagging him.

"Right," I say and leave it at that.

Fine. He'll talk or not, and I'm not going to get my head snapped off for trying to make conversation. We eat cold leftovers in silence, take turns in the shower, and even though it's just approaching sunset, we curl up in my bed. After a few tense minutes, we give in to the urge to hold on to each other.

This is nice.

This is better than snapping. This is physical connection, warmth and safety, but no need to talk. We're facing each other, ankles hooked. Our damp hair leaves wet patches on the pillow we share. Dav's got his pinkie finger wrapped around mine.

I stay still and let him look at me. It's not a gaze of adoration, or even of lust. He looks like there's a math equation written on my forehead, and he's sure he should have the answer but he doesn't know how to get there.

I guess it's got him stumped, because he asks, "Why are you here?"

"This is my bed."

He rolls his eyes, but it makes him smile, so I count it as a point on my scorecard.

"You know what I mean."

With my free hand, I reach out and push his hair back from his face. It clings to my fingers like fine-spun spider silk. "You're hot."

Dav snorts. "Hardly."

"It's my opinion that matters in this case, not yours."

"I'll concede to that."

"I like how you talk as if we're in a historical romance."

The corner of Dav's mouth twitches up. "We can't all speak like incomprehensible meme-masticating machines."

"There, see? Just like that." I shuffle closer, sliding my hand between his shoulder blades, holding him in place. "I like that you give a shit about people."

"That's draconic instinct," Dav says. "Nothing I can help."

"Doesn't mean I can't still like it."

Dav hums, disagreeing with me.

"And, ah, the way you look at me."

Dav scowls. "Creepily?"

"When you just sat at that table and said nothing, yeah. But now, I just... I can tell that you want me."

Dav's frown deepens. "Those are all things about my attraction to you making you feel desirable. Is there nothing about *me* that you like?"

"Ouch. Got me right in the Rules."

He brushes his thumb across my bottom lip. "I've told you why I want you. But that's not the same as you choosing it for yourself. My interest doesn't mean you *must* reciprocate."

"I dunno, I *like* you, okay? Do we have to think that hard about this? You're a decent person, and you give a shit about other people, and you like me. I guess it's... I asked you to read me a love story in the hospital, and you didn't laugh at me. Isn't that a good place to start?"

"Colin," Dav with sudden and urgent intensity. "You have to be sure."

"Why?" I ask, sitting up.

"Because... because I don't know what's coming." He levers himself up, too. "I can't ask you to... to be a *part* of it if you have any doubts."

"Well holy shit, we're just *barely* dating," I splutter. Dav flushes up, but it's not the cute blush—it's mottled and mortified. "You're talking like this is a forever thing."

"Colin—"

"Hold on, *is* this a forever thing? Are we accidentally dragon-married?"

"Don't be absurd," Dav snorts.

"How is it being absurd?" I snap back. "I don't know where you live, I know nothing about your family, I don't know *shit* about you."

Slimy fear drops into my guts. It's mixed with worry and confusion, not just for Dav, but suddenly for me, too. He's rattled, and he won't tell me *why*. I'm just now realizing that I could be collateral damage.

Miserable, Dav lays his hands on my shoulders. "I have been as open as I felt was safe."

"For who?" I challenge. "For you? Or are you trying to protect me, too?"

"Of course."

"How can I be protected if I don't know what it's *from*? You're talking like it's gonna come for me, too, just because we're a thing. But you won't say what it is? Well, fuck that." I crabwalk to the edge of the bed, and clamber to my feet.

"Colin, please," Dav says, reaching for me. I know how fast he is. If he wanted to grab my wrist, he would. He just doesn't care enough to.

*Or he's respecting your right to back away.*

*Shut up,* I tell the little voice in my head. *Who's side are you on, anyway?*

I head for the front door, don't even bother with my shoes, and slam it open. On the porch, I turn in a circle, wipe my palms on my thighs, scrub my hands through my hair, let out a loud, furious growl, and then slump down. The cement is cool under my ass, and now that I've finished my temper tantrum, the late-evening air is uncomfortably bracing.

Dav looked so *hurt.*

Aw, fuck.

*Dipshit,* I think as soon as the first wash of fresh air cycles through my lungs. *Weren't you just vowing that you'd wade through the sewage with him?*

I groan and hide my face in my knees. I hadn't known he would ask me to ride or die, but that doesn't change the fact that we are here because he did something that may get him in deep shit because I *asked* him to.

*I'm an asshole.* And because Dav deserves the chance to agree with me, I go back into the house to tell him so. *Also, I love him, so there's fucking that.*

Dav's jamming the things he had spread across the sofa into his bag.

"I'm an asshole," I tell him. "And I overreacted."

Dav grunts, jaw clenched, agreeing without saying so. He's got such nice *manners* that I want to mess him up. Rip buttons off his shirts, make him drool, throw him to the floor and give him rug burn.

"Hey." I flex my fingers to keep from grabbing him, forcing him to look at me. "You wanted to know if I was in this enough to stand beside you for it?"

"I take the answer is no?" he sneers, eyes resolutely on the clasp twisting shut.

"It's *yes,* you absolute meatloaf!" I shout back. "Jesus fucking Christ on a motherfucking pogo stick. Fuck me sideways on every second Sunday, but the goddamned answer is *yes.*" I throw my hands up to the sky, begging the Lord whose name I'm taking in vain to strike me with lightning if I'm lying. "I don't know what I'm signing up for, but here's my fucking signature. The answer is y—"

Dav's tongue in my mouth jams up the last of that sentence.

"You don't have to." He pulls back to let me breathe, to rearrange myself from the startled flail into something pressed up against his chest, hot and hard. "I wouldn't blame you."

"Don't go trying to talk me out of it now," I protest.

"What about your Rules," Dav says when I start backing him up toward my bedroom.

"You've made your interest explicit, you're not a charming narcissist, as far as I can tell, and three doesn't count because I haven't even got you naked yet and I already lo—" I stop, jerking my head up from where I was working on his belt buckle. "Uh," I finish stupidly.

He presses a lingering kiss on my temple that's so tender that my lungs squeeze. I splay my hands on his waist, gentle. Not possessive, but absolutely sure of my welcome.

"Uuuuuhhhhhnk," I reply, not sure what to say next.

"Rule four?" Dav prompts gently, taking a step back, fingers hooked in my belt loops, tugging me along after him.

"We *are* working it out," I reply, too breathless with the feel of the back of every single one of Dav's fingers pressed against the sensitive skin below my belly button. Every *atom* of my skin feels sensitized. "Five... five and soulmates..."

Dav looks hunted, realizing what he's started. How serious this has gotten, and how quickly. It's a sweet revenge. I shove him back onto the bed, and he lands like a slutty starfish, open and ready.

"Let's leave the last three rules on the other side of the bedroom door for now."

"Let's," Dav agrees, relieved, and reaches for me greedily.

Look, I'm skinny, with a soft stomach, big ears, and hair that will never be tame. But Dav thinks I'm hot, so I shuck my shirt before letting him pull me down into the cradle of his thighs.

I like sex.

I might even be good at it.

And if not good, at least well-educated. I'm *not* super cut or have a massive dick, so I have made it a point to absorb the best the Internet offers: *Oh Joy Sex Toy*, and *Make Love Not Porn*, and *Dr. Nerdlove*. I may have trouble picking up, but once I have someone between my sheets? I make sure that's where they want to stay.

Call me a greedy bisexual, but what I really am is a master of my trades.

Coffee and orgasms: I'll make your eyes roll back with both.

Which is why all the breath is startled out of me when Dav rolls us over. He twists with his knees, and pushes with his thighs, and suddenly his arms are under my back and my head is on the pillow and I am absolutely *dizzy.* Partially because it's a slick move (he's so strong! Holy shit!) And partially because I am suddenly so fucking hard I have no idea how I'm going to get my jeans off.

Dav does, though. He slides to the end of the bed, and pulls his shirt off, leaving his hair standing up. He makes short work of our pants, quick and efficient. He even *folds up my underwear* when he sets it on my desk chair, oh my god, how is he *real*.

Then I get to see him from top to (currently not on display) tail for the first time. His shoulders are dusted with more freckles, and his body hair is so ginger it's like spun copper. I want to lick every millimeter of his soldier-strong thighs. I want to suck him. I want him to fuck me *so bad*.

Part of me wondered what his dick would be like, if it would have scales, or knots, or a pointed head like they show in the kinky draconic porn. But except for his eyes, his tongue, and his absent belly-button, when he's in his human body, he's completely human. His cock is perfect, uncut and proportioned to the rest of him. It looks like it would reach all the good spots *just right.*

"My body is ready," I proclaim.

Dav chuckles and slides one finger up my thigh, behind my balls. "Not *quite* ready. May I?"

"Oh, yes *please*," I blurt. I twist around to get at the bedside drawer, find the little tin box filled with bottles of lube and condoms—are they expired? No. Excellent!—Do dragons get STIs?—Question for later—and Dav takes them out of my hands.

*Nice.*

"Destroy me." I shove a pillow under my ass.

Dav stalks up my body, and presses his chest to mine so he can get at my mouth. He kisses me hot, and possessive, and dirty. I'm not whimpering. I don't whimper.

I totally whimper.

"Allow me to serve you, instead," Dav pants, and my hips snap up to mash against his without any elegance or say-so from me, because you know what?

*That's the fucking sexiest thing I've ever heard in my whole-ass life.*

"Yes, yes, yes," I pant, sex-stupid and unable to think about multisyllabic words. Dav's face is suddenly between my legs, and his *genius* forked tongue is *everywhere* and I have *never* felt so worshiped. Dav is making that growl-purr noise of delight, my own breath is harsh in the sex-thick air, and the gentle click of the lube cap is the perfect counterpoint to our song.

"You're amazing," I whimper, arm thrown over my eyes. "You're incredible."

*I love you.* I'm so worried that the thought is going to climb out of my mouth if I let him do this for me that I chivvy him back and take control of my own prep.

"But I want to—"

"I know, next time, I promise, lay down, hold on," I say, twisting an arm behind me to finish what he started.

Dav's pouting, god help me, but when I swing a leg over his waist, his fingers join mine and do something *so fucking illegal* that I'm suddenly peaking like a rolling tide.

*I love you.*

*I should tell you.*

*Not yet.*

*Soon.*

Dav licks his lips smugly while I shiver down from my orgasm, hands splayed over his heart, and streaked with white.

"Satisfied?" he asks.

"Ngk," I reply, unable to do anything but roll my face up to the ceiling. Dav leans forward and nips along my jugular, and even that's gentle and kind, for all that he's deliberately leaving marks.

Possessive bastard.

I regain enough brain cells to line us up and bear down.

"Best makeup sex ever," I hiss into his ear, and everything is too much, and sloppy, and humid, and *I love him*.

"I'm happy to fight with you every day, if this is how we apologize." Dav moans, smearing the vow into my stomach. The shudder that wrings out of me is obscene.

"I'd rather not," I pant. I circle my hips to encourage him to *get the fuck on with it already*. "Although, I still want to know what you meant by 'I've done it again'."

"Lord above, Colin," Dav hisses, clutching my thighs. "Can we please save that discussion for later?"

"But you *will* tell me?

"Unf."

I clench around him, and Dav yelps.

"Promise?"

"You *filthy* little cheat," Dav growls. I squeeze again. "I promise! You'll be the death of me."

"Most likely."

"You minx, I'm supposed to be serving *you*," Dav says, struggling back up to his elbows.

I grin and pinch his nipple. "Then get on with it."

Dav gets on with it.

You'll be happy to know dragons do not spit fire when they orgasm.

I'm not gonna lie, I was worried.

# Chapter Nineteen

I turn off the alarm, annoyed it's morning already. Everything aches in the best way possible, and I think *I love you* again. I should say it. But then he'll kiss me, and neither of us have brushed our teeth yet.

"I've made a terrible mistake," Dav says, haunted and miserable.

"I will kick you off the side of the bed if you mean the sex." Dav's eyes pop. "Of course not!"

"I figured." I kiss the tip of his nose because it's there.

Dav reels me in, mouth going to the hickey he left on my neck. Someone else is trying to rise to the occasion, but we honestly don't have time. I peel back and try to will away my semi. Shower sex only really works in romance novels, much to my disappointment.

Of course, because this is my stupid life, the brain weasels strike as soon as my feet are on the floor. "Did you roast the beans to make me think I owed you—?"

Dav grabs my hand. "Never that. Hoarding is in my nature, but not by deceitful means."

"Okay." I try to let go of the fear I didn't realize I was holding onto until just then.

Dav scoots out of bed. "I did it because I wanted to make you laugh." He shakes away the haunted look that crosses his face. "I don't regret it, but I–"

"Hey," I say. "It's nothing huge, just some beans, right?"

"Right," he echoes, but I can tell his heart isn't in it.

"Coffee."

"Coffee." He follows me into the kitchen as placidly as a duckling.

Buck-naked coffee can be a thing, right?

Right.

"The problem is, I should have stopped with peacocking for you," he mumbles into my neck, plastering himself to my back as I conscript my French press into service. "I knew it, and I did it anyway."

Turns out I'm not the only one sporting some morning glory. Well. Hadi can't be mad if we're a *little* late. After all, it's Dav's last day. As we wait for the kettle to boil, I turn and push Dav just back far enough to give me room. He grabs the edge of the sink as I kneel.

He reaches down, one hand cupping my cheek.

"It's worth it, though. I love you," Dav says, simple and honest.

Dammit!

The fucker beat me to it.

Hadi is putting in a double batch of scones when Dav and I slink in.

"You don't have to be here." She points at Dav.

He's already rolling up his sleeves to show off his delicious, delicious forearms.

"The roaster hasn't arrived. Until then, someone is required to turn the crank." He's bouncing on his toes, already getting things set up, quick and efficient, like he's been doing it this way the whole time. He's *humming*.

"Turn down the sunshine, Prince Charming," Hadi snipes. "If I didn't know any better I'd say you—" she turns to look at me and squinches her face. "Ugh. Okay, congrats. Yay orgasms."

"I'm gonna go hide in the front now," I say around my own sunshine smile.

I'm most of the way through prep when the door chimes. A group of maybe half a dozen people come inside, and I curse myself for forgetting to lock the door behind us.

"I'm pretty sure the sign says 'closed', folks." I duck around the counter, and smash into some sort of invisible... *something*. The sheer *force* of the people entering the café makes me stumble. You know the way humid air slaps your lungs as soon as you leave an air-conditioned building? It's like that, but in reverse. Every *atom* feels magnetized, like I need to grab the counter to keep from being sucked toward them. There's just so much... *presence*.

*Dragons,* I realize immediately. *A whole goddamn congregation of them.*

They're trying so hard to look harmless, but their effort is laughable. Dav's draconic magnetism feels like subtle charm. This feels like a bludgeon.

They're all wearing bland suits, with some sort of crest embroidered on the front pockets. Each symbol is different, but they're all cupped by what looks like film festival laurels, held together at the bottom with three maple leaves and a stylized lick of fire. The people are equally bland, with varying degrees of brown-to-blonde hair and flame-shaded eyes.

Except for Pedra, standing glumly in the back of the crowd, looking like she wants to say something, but is too scared to speak up.

"Are you the man in these photos?" one of them asks. He's round-faced, aggressively clean-shaven, with the kind of dark, nondescript hair sported by office workers on TV. There's disgust on his face, which is frankly offensive. He's holding up a phone, and it's displaying the pic Hadi took, where I'm looking at Dav like he hung the stars.

*Bitch better not be a homophobe.* I square myself up, doing my best to block their progress into the café. I glance at Pedra, trying to gauge what the fuck is going on, but she won't meet my eye.

"Yeah, that's me but—" The sound of the kitchen door slamming open cuts me off.

"Your Excellency," Dav says from the threshold, and if I didn't know Dav as well as I do, I'd call his tone civil. Now? I'd call it downright frosty.

The man with the phone taps the embroidery on his chest, the emblem of a hand holding a dagger. Dav pulls a lapel pin with a similar design from his waistcoat pocket and pins it on pointedly. The symbol in the middle of Dav's laurels is unmistakably a Tudor Rose.

I've never seen this pin before.

Hadi is standing out behind the counter now, watching with a silent and stony expression. I don't know what Dav told her in the kitchen before he banged out to defend my honor, but it must have been serious. Pedra slides to the side of the group, eyes bouncing between me and Dav.

"Is this him?" what's-his-nuts asks Dav, staring straight through me, as if I haven't already answered.

"I haven't told him a thing," Dav says.

"I don't understand—" I start.

"And let's leave it that way," the guy interrupts.

"Excuse you," I interrupt right back. "You can't talk to my boyfriend like that, buddy. I don't care who you are."

"I am your Lieutenant Governor," he snaps, ember-dark eyes blazing, and yeah, this dude is a *dragon*. Dav seems human, until you realize he isn't. This dude... no way you'd ever mistake him for anything but what he is. "As you fall under my control, I hereby order you to *stay silent*."

I'm such a goddamned idiot. Lieutenant Governor Francis Simcoe. Right. This is who I'm mouthing off to.

So what?

He's made Dav—*my boyfriend*, I'd just called him that out loud and we haven't even *had* the conversation about what we are to one another, so there's me jumping ahead again, *shit*—upset.

"Fuck you!" I snap back. "I don't belong to anyone but me!"

"Oh, don't you?" He offers me an amused, predatory grin. "That's good to hear." He turns a flinty, superior look on Dav.

I expect my dragon to spit fire, or bluster, or come around the corner and dip me in a kiss. Something possessive. Something to prove to everyone in this weird too-polite stand-off, that I do belong to someone, and that someone is *him*.

That, after all my protests, he actually *is* my dragon.

He loves me.

He said so.

"Colin... please. Hush," Dav says instead. He's moving slowly, coming around the counter, but not toward me. He's walking right past the other dragons (holy shit, we're infested with royalty) to stand in front of Pedra.

She cringes and jams her hands into her pockets.

"I didn't know," she says. "I took the beans to a lab and they called—" she gestures to the suits. "I didn't *know*."

"I'm not angry with you," Dav says gently. He turns to face the Lieutenant Governor, standing between Pedra and the other dragon, almost like a... claim.

For the first time, there's a corona of red around Dav's pupils. His hard gaze looks *alien.* And I'm not going to show how much this surprises me, I'm not taking a step back, because that's my motherfucking *boyfriend* right there, who *loves* me, and I am not gonna look scared of him—*be* scared of him—in front of people who've treated him as expendable.

"Stand down, Alva," Simcoe says.

Dav bristles.

"Lord, your *temper*," Simcoe chuckles with a self-satisfied smirk.

I want to punch him. And I'm upset enough not to think about what might happen to me if I *do* manage to punch Lieutenant Governor Francis Simcoe, representative of Elizabeth Regina in her colony and effectively the power behind the human Prime Minister. He'd probably rip my hand off at the wrist and *eat* it for daring to touch him.

"It wasn't supposed to go this far," Dav growls softly.

"You always say that, my friend, and then it always does."

"I've stopped."

"Damn straight you have."

"There's no need for—"

"I say what there is a need for!" Simcoe roars.

Dav snaps to a swift attention, legs together, chin and chest thrust out. The only thing missing is the salute. Silence descends—heavy, fearful, angry, and shamed.

I want to scream.

I want to stand between Dav and these people who are supposed to be his family, but speak to him like he's a criminal. Instead I fidget, sliding my hands into my back pockets, shifting from side to side, filled with energy I can't, I *won't* lash out with. I don't know what the hell is going on. And knowing me and my comedic karmatic butterfingers, anything I do right now will probably make it worse.

"You never *learn*, Alva," Simcoe says at length, like he's talking to a kid with a disappointing report card. "Your foolish idealism has gotten the better of you again."

Dav's chin drops. "You can't compare Colin to her."

"I'm not the one doing so."

Dav sucks in a sharp breath, like he's been slapped.

*What the fuck is happening.*

I wish I could ask. I wish I could take Dav's hand, squeeze it, show him I'm here, beside him in the shit, like I promised. There's a power struggle happening here that I can't fathom, and if Dav wants to make a statement about who we are to each other, I have to let him make the first move.

He raises his head, finally, meeting the impassive, unimpressed gaze of each of the dragons around the room, one by one. Dav looks to Simcoe last. Simcoe clucks his tongue impatiently.

"Colin," Dav says slowly, softly. "I left something in the Murder Basement."

I know an excuse when I hear it, but I'm not stupid enough to say so out loud.

Dav and I make our way to the door, uninterrupted but watched. I get the creepy feeling that someone is about to shoot out a sticky tongue to reel me back and chomp me up.

"What did you leave?" I whisper, when we're in Hadi's office. It's creepy as heck with the lights off. Dav closes the door and we're suddenly in absolutely pitch black. At least to my human eyes.

"It's not something I have left." He crowds me against the desk. "It's something I'd like to leave."

"What?" I ask, following the sound of his voice, the direction of his warmth. The cold worry that has been churning in my guts frosts into my extremities, solidifying into shards of fear in my blood, racing like shrapnel toward my heart. "You said you might be in trouble, but I didn't expect—"

"Nor I," he admits, breathless, harried. "But I ought to have."

"What did you want to leave?" I ask. "Something you think will upset them? Or—"

"This. Colin I—" His hands scoop under my ass and in an impressive show of draconic strength, I'm suddenly sitting on the desktop and he's sliding in between my knees, mouth on mine.

The kiss is...

Holy shit, now *this* is a kiss.

It's wet, and it's filthy.

He's got one hand on my chin and another on the crown of my head, holding my face up, holding me *still* so he can dip his forked tongue into my mouth.

"Mmph!" I say into his own mouth, because he's not letting me up for air.

Honestly, I could get on board with this. There's jerks upstairs and we're totally making out, but you know what? If Dav wants to keep kissing me like this until I pass out from lack of oxygen, I am a-o-fucking-kay with that.

I reach up to tangle my hands in his hair, urge him to kiss harder, deeper. I tilt my head back, make it as clear as I can with lips, and teeth, and tongue, and breath, and heartbeat, and skin, that I'm here for him. That I am all his, no matter what he has to say to the pricks upstairs.

And then, just as I'm getting into the swing of things, he's gone. He's eeled out of my arms and out the door so fast I'm dizzy.

A dull prick against the inside of my wrist makes me jump. When I turn on the light, I can see what's jabbing me. His lapel pin, with its ominous sigil, is stuck under the band of my watch. I must have accidentally skimmed it right off his waistcoat when I reached up.

I wobble up the stairs.

The front of the café is empty, save for Hadi, and she's sitting on one of the sofas looking absolutely wrecked. When I say empty, I mean *empty*. There isn't a single bean in the place. The glass canisters are barren, the mason jars are missing. Even the compost bin is gone.

"What happened?" I pant. I know my mouth is bitten-red, and my hair is mussed, and the front of my jeans isn't sitting exactly flat, but that's not why she's so shaken.

"They're gone."

"Good fucking riddance. Bunch of uptight pricks." I say, then stare in horror at the growing queue of customers. "Shit, though. How are we supposed to make coffee?"

"I think that's literally the least of what they care about."

"We'll ask the customers to come back tomorrow." This is Hadi's livelihood we're talking about. I can be mad at the self-important royal assholes later. Right now we gotta get the beans going so they have enough time to cool. "Come on, we roast more. Is Dav already in the kitchen?"

"Is he...?" Hadi pulls herself to her feet, coming over to me, stumbling like she's seen a ghost.

"Dav! Start up the roaster, babe!"

"Colin," Hadi says, grabbing my elbows. "Colin!"

"What?" I ask, looking over my shoulder for my boyfriend. "Dav!"

"*Colin*!" Hadi shakes me once, hard enough to get my attention, expression grim. "You're not *listening*. They're *gone*."

My heart flops, my stomach flips, and the world under my feet lurches.

"Gone," I repeat, as the smile falls off my face. I take a step away, and Hadi lets me go. Every breath judders behind my ribs, like a knife skidding along bone when someone stabs you sloppily. "That's... I don't..."

"They told him to go with them and he went," Hadi says softly. "There was a limo parked out front, and he got in it, and they drove away."

The pastry cabinet is cool against my back when I slide down onto the floor.

"Oh. *Oh*," I hiss, insides churning. "Oh, *fuck.*"

The thing he wanted to leave behind was *me*.

# chapter Twenty

I t takes us a few moments to have enough brainpower to tell the crowd clogging the sidewalk that Beanevolence isn't opening today. Some dickbag whines that he drove three hours to get there, and Hadi flips him off as she locks up.

My phone vibrates a minute later, and I'm treated to the horror-show of pictures of me gathering likes at the top of the hashtag. In it, I'm sitting with my back against the counter, face dead white, hair a bigger wreck than usual, mouth kiss-chapped and eyes swollen.

I look like I've been crying.

I am crying.

I wipe my face with my sleeve. Stand up. Sway on the spot. Make a fist.

Hurts.

Oh right, the pin.

I shove it in my pocket, because otherwise I'll throw it against the wall.

Go to the kitchen. Look around.
Empty.
Hollow.
My phone beeps a few more times, and my own devastation plays out as the picture of me—posted with the caption "Trouble in paradise?", nosy fucking clueless bastards—is shared around.

"No." Hadi plucks the phone from my hand, turns off the notifications, shoves it in my back pocket. "Hey. Colin? Colin! Hey!"

It takes a few tries to get my eyes to meet hers.

"First, Rule Seven, okay?" I nod stupidly as she cups my shoulders in her hands.

The edge of her finger brushes scars on my bicep and I suck in a hard breath. It doesn't hurt.

It just *hurts*.

"Say it, Colin."

"I'm worthy of love."

"Yes, you are."

Hadi gathers me up in a hug, and I proceed to soak the tail-end of her hijab clean through. When I've exhausted myself, she pulls herself up to sit on the workstation and lets me lean against the wall, giving me space to be sad.

"Sorry," I say at length, scrubbing at my nose on my sleeve.

"You don't have to apologize for crying, duh."

"No, I know. I mean for fucking up your business."

Hadi heaves a sigh. "You didn't fuck it up."

"I'm the one who let Dav into the kitchen in the first place. I'm the one who suggested he try roasting the beans with his breath. I'm the reason he kept doing it. It's all my fault, and now they've taken everything from you—"

"I haven't lost anything but a few day's revenue," Hadi says, the corners of her mouth turned down in a deep scowl. "And I can bounce back."

"I'm such a fuck-up," I heave, the confession like slime crawling up my throat.

"Colin—"

"I'm a disaster."

"Stop—"

"I can't do anything right, I can't—"

I can't breathe.

I swallow around the bile and brutal honesty, bite my bottom lip hard enough to taste blood, and Dav isn't here to kiss it away, to soothe, to squeeze all of the dumbass out of me, and he's gone, he's gone, he's not coming back, they always go away and never come back, and I can't, I *can't*—

"Colin!" Dr. Chen shouts right into my ear, and I jerk on the spot.

My lungs burn, my mouth is dry, my eyes are gritty when I blink.

I swallow hard.

"Doc," I crackle.

Hadi touches my hand, and I jump. I'm on the floor, curled around my knees, fingernails puncturing half-moons into my shins above my socks. She gently uncurls my fingers from around my own leg, presses my phone into my hand, raises it to my head.

"Hey, Colin," Dr. Chen says from the other end of the line. "You back with me?"

Hadi puts a glass of water into my other hand. I take small sips, and when I'm ready, say: "Yeah, Doc."

"Good. You wanna start talking about it?"

"Not really."

"It will be now or later, Colin."

"Later," I decide.

"I'll call you in the morning," Dr. Chen says. "Let's focus on getting grounded and balanced again, okay?" She takes me through the 5-4-3-2-1 exercise, and we talk about triggers and the first time I disassociated, the day after Dad's funeral, how it had lasted for long enough for Gem to start researching professional help.

"Our first date, Doc," I joke weakly, wrung-out. She chuckles.

When I hang up, Hadi sits on the cool tile beside me, presses her back to the fridge door, and shows me an email on her phone. "Guess what's showing up tomorrow?"

It's the big, fancy, industrial-grade bean roaster Dav paid for.

The one he replaced.

The one that will replace him.

I bite the inside of my cheek, and try not to puke.

I'm not gonna succeed.

"I need... sorry," I say, and run to the washroom.

On my way back, I find Dikimbe pressed up against the big window, peering inside. Mauli is kneeling by the door, tongue half-stuck out of their mouth as they try to pick the lock with what looks like a manky old chopstick.

I stalk over to let them in. Mauli lunges at me, dark eyes shining with pity, crushing my ribs in a hug that lifts my feet off the ground.

"Bro," Dike says, phone in hand, flashing that wretched picture. My guts cramp again, but I take a deep breath to keep the panic and tears back.

Or at least, as deep a breath as I can with Mauli still squeezing me.

"Where is that asshole?" Mauli growls. "Dragon or not, I'm gonna kick his ass."

"No, you're not," Hadi says, entering from the kitchen with a tray filled with mugs, milk, and a pot of tea. Ugh. Hot leaf juice.

Mauli walks me over to the sofas and dumps me on my ass, then brandishes their chopstick, ready to stab. "You sure? What happened?"

They both look to me. I shake my head, and let Hadi tell it. Well, as much as she knows, anyway. There are some things Dav asked me to keep secret, and I may be wrecked, but I'm not a disloyal asshole.

"Let's get you wasted," Mauli says when Hadi's finished. "Day drinking solves everything."

The tea pot is empty, and the morning light is giving way to the harsh glare of noon, and I feel gray and hollowed-out. Face-down on the table, my phone vibrates. Someone is trying to call me. I don't feel like answering. I don't want to talk to anyone but—

*Dav.*

I lunge for the phone, flipping it over, and—

"It's Mum," I say, staring at it dumbly. "It's... it's not him... it's..."

I hit 'ignore.'

I can't do that right now.

"He'll come back, you know," Hadi says softly. All casual-like.

The sentiment is echoed by Mauli and Dike.

"Sure," I say. I'm not sure I believe it, though.

The next morning, I stay in bed, stare at the ceiling, and don't let myself squeeze Dav's pillow to my face.

One, because I refuse to be that pathetic.

Two, because it probably doesn't smell like him anymore.

Three, okay, I am that pathetic, but I won't give into it.

24 hours, and nothing.

No phone call. No email. No well-dressed, coiffed dragon on my doorstep with a shame-faced grin, dorky socks, and an explanation.

Nothing.

(Is it 24 hours when it becomes a Missing Persons case? No, that's 48. It's the first 24 hours after a kidnapping that are the most vital. Is it a kidnapping if he just got in the goddamned limo and went with them?)

In the afternoon, Hadi sends me a picture—the roaster is in. It's the sports-car of bean roasters, bigger than the last one, and sleek in a way that makes me wonder if it might actually launch into space if I press the wrong button. As she oversees the installation, we work together to craft the perfect post to explain the emergency closure that's both upbeat enough that it will encourage people to come back, and isn't so abrupt that it reads like Beanevolence failed a health inspection.

Or isn't the kind of honest that makes Lieutenant Governor Asshole come back.

Hadi wants to put him on blast.

I would like her to not get disappeared, too.

Because that's what it is.

*Disappeared.*

I call Dav, and his phone rings out. I text, and there's no read notifications. Dav has no social media I can find, and I never got his home phone number or address. "Dragon estate Canborough Niagara" brings up literally zero results when I search for it.

Nothing should get *zero* hits. There's a puzzle here, and that's a piece of it, but I don't know the shape of the whole thing yet.

On the second day, the grief hits me like a sucker-punch as soon as I wake up.

*Not everybody you love will leave without a goodbye*, Gemma had said.

Ha fucking ha.

I'm glad Katiya's in Europe, because it means I can lay around as long as I want, lunging for my phone when it buzzes, and ignoring every phone call and text that comes from anyone who isn't *him*. On the fifth day, Hadi abuses her spare-key privileges again, and the gang drags me to the Brass Monkey. I drink red wine that wasn't made by Dav, and feel recklessly angry enough to eat a slice of chocolate cake.

I puke in every trashcan between the bar and home.

That night, I clutch my stomach and hate my self-destructive bullshit, and miss Dav so hard it feels like someone has heated a metal cage and wrapped it around my lungs.

Sometimes, on the days when my grief is at its worst, I get these... these flashes of images that sear into my head. Of... of Dad.

Dad as a corpse.

Dad as a *rotting* corpse, in a box, in the ground. I can't stop picturing his flesh gray and sagging off the bones of his skull. His brains and his tongue, liquefying—everything that made my father a *person*, I person I *loved* and who loved me back—putrefying, gone forever, and unable to come back.

And now I can't turn off the thoughts of *Dav* like that.

Dead. Corpse-still, unblinking and pale. Laying in a ditch, or at the bottom of the ocean, or buried in cement, whatever it is they do when dragons disappear someone.

Day six, I have a panic attack in the morning, a call with Dr. Chen from under my sheets in the afternoon, and I spend the night looking at old photos, desperately missing all the people who are supposed to be beside me and aren't. I only have a few pictures of Dav. The two Hadi took, three stupid selfies, and one I snuck of him on the back deck of the café, when he'd turned his face up to the sunset after a long day.

I hyperventilate instead of sleep, so when I get back to the café on day seven—finally open again, Min-Soo on the counter shadowed by some new kid named Rajish, me in the back putting the new roaster through its paces and hating every second of it because it's a machine, it's not *him*—I look like ass-on-a-cracker when I get papped.

Yeah, you heard me.

Fucking *papped*.

As in, some of those princess-killing, celebrity-chasing, danger-creating photogs have caught wind of something, and decided to take five-hundred horrible, unflattering photos of me trying to shoulder my way through the crowd of trend-chasers outside the café when I try to leave the café at noon. I scramble back into Beanevolence, bombarded by lots of noise I can't separate out as individual phrases in my sleep-deprived state, but know aren't polite.

Not a single one of those pictures is anything I'd want my mother to see.

So of course, some chucklefuck tracks down her home address, and shows up on her front doorstep at just after noon, brandishing his camera and asking for a comment. Mum has the good sense to slam the door in his face and draw every curtain.

By the end of the day, my misery has been reduced to a string of pithy hashtags. #Alvalin, #FairyTailEnded, and a few more not fit for print. I'm holed up in the café kitchen, pacing in tight circles while Stu gives me the play-by-play of Gem on the lawn with a shovel, playing whack-a-mole with expensive telephoto lenses.

Hadi and I sneak out the back way, to where Min-soo has her car parked at the bottom of the ravine, and I spend the night on Hadi's sofa. I don't get any sleep.

I just lay there and call Dav. Call again. And again.

The voicemail is full by dawn.

"Just tell me you're okay," I say, in the last message I can leave. "That's all I want. Please."

It isn't until the next morning, stuck in Hadi's apartment with nothing better to do, that I learn why the paps even give a shit about me. It's not the trendy coffee—and thank fuck it hasn't gotten out that it was dragon-roasted, despite all the Influencers complaining about the change in recipe. It's the fact that almost no one in the Royal-Watching community has seen Dav, (who turns out to be the fucking Marquess of Niagara, *what the fuck*) in literal decades. And then he pops up working in some random coffee shop and just as suddenly vanishes again, which is the icing on their invasive cake.

It's on the goddamned *news*.

I turn on the TV to pass the time, and the first thing I see is that photo of Dav and me walking on the sidewalk in the sun.

It's... gross.

They have no right taking those pictures where we're happy, and distorting it into something cruel and selfish. That smile is mine. It was for *me.*

And it's dumb, but you know what upsets me the most? The news tells me his age. I had *enjoyed* our game of guess-and-deflect. I wanted to learn from Dav himself, because he trusted me with the information, because he wanted to celebrate with me. And some newsreader just blurts it out.

Like it isn't a treasure.

Like it isn't something I was trying to *earn.*

*"Our top celebrity story tonight is still the brief appearance of the two-hundred and sixty-seven year old Alva George Tudor, Marquess of Niagara. The Marquess vanished from public life in 1921—"*

Born in 1758.

Two hundred and sixty-seven.

And now I can't unknow it.

That moment of intimate confession was stolen from me.

I hate them. I hate myself, and this worry, and this grief *so fucking much,* that I'm up off the sofa and down at the front door of Hadi's apartment building before I understand what I mean to do.

"He's missing!" I screech at the assembled mass of paps scrambling over the lawn in front of her apartment building. How did they even know I was here? I must look like shit: hair unwashed, scruff no longer artful, bruises under my eyes and tear-tracks on my cheeks. I don't care. The crowd strains forward to jam their phones in my face. "Do you idiots not get that? The Lieutenant Governor came and *took him away!*"

Someone shouts, "Oh sure!" and they explode into uproarious laughter.

"Everyone knows you can't make a dragon *do* anything!"

"Was it you who broke it off?" someone shouts, and I stand there, gawping, as they barrage me with obscene, personal, terrible questions: *What did I do to make Dav leave? Have Dav and I ever fucked while he was in dragonshape? Who takes it up the ass? Why was I forcing Dav to work in a coffee shop?*

"He was a volunteer," I say. "We didn't break up."

Didn't we? I press my hand against my pocket, push the pin into my hip.

He'd been so scared.

"They *kidnapped him*," I shout over the noise. "I haven't heard from him in a week! He would never worry me like this, he must be somewhere, being held against his will, or... or... ordered to... I don't know. Isn't *that* the story, here?"

Laughter again.

Another piece of the puzzle clicks into place.

The media tells us what we're supposed to think about dragons. They share—or don't share—information with the public. And they're not *listening*. They don't believe me. They don't give a shit. I need someone to give a shit.

I run back inside and grab my phone.

**#MarquessNiagara** is a trending topic, so I send out: **#MarquessNiagara was taken by Lt. Gov. Simcoe against his will. He is missing.**

The message takes forever to upload and then... blips out of existence.

"No," I whisper.

**I'm the #MarquessNiagara's boyfriend. We didn't break up. He was forcefully removed from the café by dragons.**

Uploading... gone.

"*No*," I howl, furious.

**Hello new followers! I'm Colin, and I studied Sustainable Tourism and Biodiverse Winemaking. Remember to take only pictures and leave only memories when you visit our beautiful Garden City!**

Uploading... posted.

**I work at @Beanevolence and the #MarquessNiagara was our volunteer bean-roaster while our kitchen was being renovated.**

Uploading. Gone.

**I look forward to sharing how you can promote #SustainableTourism in your own city.**

Posted.

**Help me. They took him, and I don't know where he is, and I'm afraid they'll hurt him. Help me, please.**

Account suspended for 24 hours.

# chapter Twenty-One

I compose a letter. I spend an hour getting the email addresses of every major reporter and newspaper in Upper Canada I can find. Hit send. It lingers in my inbox. Server issues. Won't go. I send a test email to Hadi, some random jumble of bullshit asking how the crowds are at work. It goes through.

"*Fuck*," I sob, hands shaking, as I dial 911.

The operator laughs me off, and when I try to call the non-emergency line, my call won't connect. The robotic voice bleeps obnoxiously and tells me that number is blocked. I try from Hadi's landline, and when I reach an officer, I'm told to stop wasting their time.

All my life I've known that dragons run the world, but in a sort of vague, abstract way. They head Business Associations, they own land that they manage for municipalities, they have parallel parliaments and support human governments, they write policy and invest in charities, they create structure. What I didn't realize is that they don't just run the world... they *control* it.

So much of what I know about dragons has been fed to me by those very dragons themselves. It's the ultimate propaganda machine, and I've been raised inside of it.

I spend the rest of the night trying to reach out to someone, *anyone* who might help, and can't. The news is playing a loop of me looking like hot garbage whispering "We didn't break up", delusional and desperate. The commentators insinuate that Dav's brief blip of a reappearance was just that—a blip. And that I'm a mistake he's retreating from.

*Lies!*

*...aren't they?*

Dav would come back to me if he could.

Right?

He loves me. He said so. Even if I never got to say it back.

After a shitty, nightmare-plagued sleep on Hadi's sofa, I expect to have to elbow my way through a sea of cameras and obscene shouting the next day. But when I leave the building, there's nothing but footprints scoured into the trampled grass. I slink home, hollowed out by the perpetual fear that I'm worth abandoning, and drop into bed, missing the warm comfort of Dav with an ache that's physical. I yearn for the way we curled together, heads sharing a pillow and the small gap between our bodies cupping our world, our future, and all its possibilities.

Mum visits for a few days. She believes what the news says, tells me I'm better off, while I lay on the sofa with my head in her lap. She doesn't say 'I told you so', and I don't try to tell her the truth. What would be the point?

After she goes home, Gem and Stu call every night. They trade off, as if they're on self-harm watch.

Huh.

They're probably on self-harm watch.

Another week passes. Then two.

I talk to Dr. Chen every other day, and on the days it's not her, it's Dike, or Mau, or both "just popping by" with takeout and beer, or new video games to try, or some academic journal article to read aloud and mock.

I try very hard not to resent everyone.

They only want to make sure I'm healthy.

Fuck.

I just want to sleep.

I sleep too much.

With nothing better to do, I go back to work.

Our popularity has remained the same, but now it's not because of the coffee. I don't want to be gawked at, so I stay in the kitchen, hiding in the stainless steel cave like Dav did. I roast. I bake. I call, I post to social media, I email. Letters are returned unopened. Security won't let me get close to government buildings. (Though, even I know better than to rock up to Chorley Park and bang on Lt. Gov. Scumbag's door.)

I reach out fruitlessly, work resentfully, sleep fitfully, and miss Dav terribly.

By the fourth week, I'm mad at myself.

How could I let him mean so much to me, how could we spend so much time together, and I know so goddamned little about him? His home address, his family's names, I don't even know what his dragonshape looks like. Why didn't I push more? Why didn't I *care* more?

It's stupid, but Dav never got to tell me what it is that "I've done it again" meant, and I think that out of everything, that's what pisses me off most. He promised me he would explain, and they wouldn't let him keep that promise.

The sharp pain of missing Dav turns into something else, something resentful and moldy. It feels like giving up. I'm just human, after all. What can I do if the Draconic Powers That Be want to do something horrible to the man that I love? (*Yes, I still love him, and they can choke on it.*) Shit-all. And it's wretched.

And then somehow, it's been five weeks.

Then six.

It takes a few weeks for me to catch on, because I'm so cocooned in misery, but one morning I leave my house, I realize with a sudden-fog-clearing fury that I have a stalker.

There's some goddamned dragon following me around. Or at least, I assume he's *homo draconis* because he's a mountain of muscle with a *vibe* that frazzles my short-hairs when I walk by his vehicle-du-jour. Maybe he thinks he's being inconspicuous, but hanging out in different cars outside of my apartment and my place of work only functions in movies. Especially with a neck like that—you don't get a neck like that just being a driver.

Is he security?

Or am I being tailed to make sure I don't do anything naughty?

*Fuck 'em.*

Fuck every single one of the split-tongued, scaly-assed bastards keeping me and Dav apart.

So I...

I don't know why I do it. Except that I'm angry. I want them to know that no matter where he is and what they're doing to him, Dav is mine. I am his, and he is mine.

So, on the morning of the forty-sixth day, I step out of my apartment, stare the security dude straight in the face, and put on the little rose-and-laurels lapel pin. I stick it right on my Henley, directly over my heart.

The guy's face goes ashen. His car peels out of the parking spot.

And three hours later, Onatah calls me for the first time.

Alright, so you remember what I said about the Inciting Incident? That it's the tripwire that sends the protagonist hurtling towards the first major obstacle in their path? Well, if I can stretch the already thin metaphor, the protagonist then fetches up against the wall of the first landing. Getting their feet under them, they can either head back up the stairs, and the story is over, or they can peek around the corner and see what comes next.

You know, if they haven't already broken their necks.

After that comes something called the "pinch point". At the top of act two, the hero is squeezed, and either they slither out and go home, or stay there while the pressure becomes unbearable, forcing them to make difficult decisions that affect the rest of their lives.

"The Vice," my English professor had called it.

Of course, most protagonists aren't dumbfuck enough to sit in the chompy part of their own volition, let alone reach around the machine to turn the crank themselves.

But hey, whoever said I was smart?

I put on that pin. And okay, I didn't know what it meant at the time, but the thing is... when I found out? I didn't take it off.

I'm getting ahead of myself.

Phone call. Blocked number. I ignore it. I'm at work and I have better things to do than listen to fake-ass shit-stirring 'reporters' asking me invasive questions. It's not until a few hours later, when I'm heading off on my break, that I realize someone left a voicemail.

I schlump to the back deck. There's no shade from the late-August sun. I could stay inside with the air conditioning, but that defeats the purpose of having a break, because I'll just end up puttering. And it's too damn hot to go for a walk. *And*, and I don't want to go to any of the restaurants around us on St. Paul because every single one of them is somewhere Dav and I once had a meal and I *hate* that it's all I can think about.

With nothing better to do, I decide to give the voice mail a listen before deleting it.

"Hey, so, listen," the message says. The speaker sounds like a woman, voice resonant. I can tell English isn't her first language, but her accent is nothing I've heard before. "Man, you gotta knock it off."

Anger flares hard and fast under my skin. *How dare they try to intimidate me!*

There's a silence, and I expect the speaker to hang up. Instead, she sighs. "Dav says I'm supposed to tell you he's sorry and this is bullshit, although we both know he'd never actually use that word, and he's fine, but you gotta knock it off because the wrong people are paying attention and he doesn't want that, okay? He's a noble fuckwit and you're giving him heart attacks on the daily." There's another deep sigh and then, quietly, almost like I wasn't supposed to hear it: "Shit, man. You *had* to don the token."

The message ends and I sit there, wide-eyed and gawp-mouthed.

*Dav's fine.* It's all I can think, the two words crashing around the inside of my skull. *Dav's fine. Dav's fine. He's fine, and he's worried about me.*

Before my brain catches up with my fingers, I've already hit redial. The annoying bleeping reminds me the number is blocked, and I *can't* call her back. Whoever *her* is.

I'm suddenly full of buzzing energy. I need to *do something*. I want to rush off like the heroine in one of my romances, to hail a cab, to tumble out of it at the base of the office tower, race to the elevator, break into the board meeting, confess my love—

I can't.

First, because I don't know where Dav is. Second, because the way this voicemail was phrased, it sounds like maybe he doesn't want to see me. Or maybe he *can't* see me.

We've broken enough rules as it is, and look where it's gotten us. If he's not allowed to contact me himself, if he had to ask a friend to do it for him in secret, then rushing to his side would not only be clichéd, it might be risky.

Third, because *I don't know where Dav is.*

Spinning the pin over my heart, I wrack my brains for a way to not only let the mysterious caller know that I got the message and am dying to hear from them again, but also to let *Dav* know that I've heard him. Message delivered. The only dragon I've seen directly lately was my stalker—and he's vamoosed.

Ah! Someone is curating my social media feed, which means maybe Dav is reading it?

I open the app and type: **It's so nice when friends reach out and slap you upside the head. Even better when you can catch their hand and not let go. Rules 4, 6, and 7 still apply.**

Hit send. Posted.

Mauli immediately replies with a string of question mark emojis. Rebekah replies a few seconds later with heart-eyes face.

Know-it-all.

My phone does not ring.

With five minutes left on my break, I return early. I'm getting a sunburn, and I'm going to go crazy if I just sit here, willing my phone to make noise. I turn the ringer up as loud as it will go, shove the phone into my pocket, then head through the empty kitchen to the cooler front-of-house.

Where Pedra is accepting a coffee from Rajish.

She looks up and freezes like the proverbial deer in the headlights. It's an accurate metaphor, because the second I see her, I careen around the side of the counter toward her like an eighteen wheeler.

I'm not much of a violent person, okay?

Dad taught me how to throw a punch, and I've tussled enough with Stu to more-or-less hold my own. But I've never lashed out in anger, or deliberately sought to hurt somebody. Which means that even I'm surprised when I reach out, grab her coffee out of her hand, and throw it in her face.

I am lucky, *really lucky*, that she ducks and the steaming hot liquid doesn't catch her skin.

But right then, it doesn't feel lucky.

It feels like I've been cheated. I fist my hands in her lab coat and swing her around hard enough that she smashes into the counter.

"Colin!" Hadi snarls, from somewhere behind me.

All around us, people are standing, gasping, shouting at me to let Pedra go. Rajish is leaning across the counter, his hand around one of my wrists, trying to pull me off.

"I'm sorry!" Pedra wails, arms up, protecting her face. "I'm sorry!"

"Damn fucking right you're sorry!" I roar. "They *took* him, and you dare come back—!"

"Colin!" Hadi snarls again.

Rajish manages to break my grip on Pedra. She stumbles away, horrified and wary. A few customers get between us, eyes hard and chests squared.

"I didn't know they would do that!" Pedra says.

"Get out!" I shout, and it feels like vomiting. It feels like hurling every broken and jagged shard of the happiness I'd once had with Dav at her, weaponized shrapnel.

*Dav is fine*. The lady on the phone said so. But that doesn't mean I might never see him again.

"Get out!" I repeat when Pedra looks from Hadi, to Rajish, and back to me.

"Hey!" Hadi says, getting right in my face, blocking my line of sight. "This is my place, not yours!"

"It's her fault they took your beans!"

"We've already talked that out, and she's apologized."

"I can't believe that after all this time she has the balls to—"

"This isn't her first time back."

"What?" I ask, the revelation like a slap to the face, fury crystallizing to shock. "What did you say?"

"I've, uh, been timing my trips to your, um, breaks," Pedra confesses softly.

"Unbelievable," I mutter, fury crystallizing to shock. "And you helped her?" I ask Hadi, who nods. "Unbe-fucking-liev-able."

"You don't get a say in who I allow in," Hadi scolds.

Hadi.

One of my most cherished friends. A great boss, who made sure I ate, and slept, and studied when I was failing because I was still grief-stricken and dealing with Dad's loss. Who teamed up with Gem to bully me into staying regular with Dr. Chen. Who wrote me the Rules because she wants to see me happy.

Hadi.

Standing between me and the person who ruined *every-thing*.

And telling me I get no say on whether I have to see her every day for the rest of... for the rest of my... until—

"Fine then." I sound calm.

Am I calm?

I might be calm.

I might be shrieking.

I can't tell.

My heart is in my throat, my ears rushing with blood, every sinew and muscle pounding with the desire to *fight scream rage hurt lash out.* I do none of those things.

Instead, I strip off my apron, and drape it over the arm Hadi has out to keep Pedra and I separated.

"Fine," I repeat. "Your business. Your decision."

I pull my keys out of my pocket, and wrestle the one for Beanevolence off the ring.

I don't say - *But I've been here since day one.*

I don't say - *You've always relied on me. You've always trusted me.*

I don't say - *This place means as much to me as it does to you.*

I don't say - *I need this to feel wanted and useful. Please. I don't have anything else.*

I do say - "Bye, Hadi."

And put the key in the apron pocket.

# Chapter Twenty-Two

My phone rings as I'm opening my front door. I drop it in my eagerness, cursing and hoping they don't hang up.

"You seriously don't know when to quit, do you?" the voice from earlier asks, when I finally fumble my phone up to my ear.

"Is he really okay?" I ask, instead of answering. Besides, what would I say? *That's what my therapist says?* Yeah, not exactly the first impression I want to make. "Is he *okay?*"

"He's fine."

"Where has he been?" I stalk into the kitchen, find a bottle of whiskey, and pull the cork with my teeth like a TV villain. I don't give a fuck that it's still early afternoon. "Did they hurt him?"

She snorts. "They don't have to beat the shit out of him to hurt him. That's something you should know. If you're serious."

"Of course I'm serious!" I take a swig. "Uh... what am I serious about?"

"Well shit. There's two of you," she groans. "The *pin,* you dipshit."

I set down the whiskey long enough to fumble the pin into my palm. "What about it?"

There's a groan, loud and long, from the other side of the phone. It carries some of the rough growl that only *homo draconis* can make.

"Wait," I say. "Are you... uh... are you..." I rifle through my brain for the name of the only friend that Dav has ever mentioned. "Onatah?"

"Aren't you the clever boy."

"You're the awesome sock lady."

"You know, I'm gonna accept that," Onatah says. "But only because you called me awesome."

"Dav hasn't told me much else about you. Except that your territories touch. Sorry, is that rude to say?"

"Nah, it's fine for a Dragon's Own."

I choke on whiskey. "Sorry?"

"Yeah, you just might be when this is all over. Listen, he's back, and he's sleeping right now. I'm gonna let him keep sleeping because fuck knows he needs it." I try not to think of torture chambers and deprivation pods. "So that gives you some time to sober up."

"Fuck you," I say, but in that heartfelt breathless way that means the opposite. "How did you know?" I set the whiskey back on the counter top, head starting to get light and shame prickling at the back of my neck.

"I know the sound of a cork coming out of a bottle."

"Uh. Okay. I can do that."

"I'll be there at four," Onatah says. "And this is significant, so wear something nice."

"Nice," I repeat. That blazer Rebekah picked out has seen the light more in the last two months than it ever did when we were together. But I don't have anything else. "See you soon," I try to tell Onatah, but she's already hung up.

I save her in my phone as Snap-Dragon.

Onatah shows up on a motherfucking *motorcycle.*

If I wasn't already in love with one dragon, I might have fallen head over heels for this one on the spot. It's all I can do not to swoon when she swings one muscle-thick, denim-clad thigh over the saddle. She pulls off her helmet, and a dark shining braid uncoils down her back. Bone-bead earrings flash gold and cream in the streetlight. The back of her leather jacket has been embroidered with a swirling, interconnected mass of animal motifs, picked out in beads that wink as she moves. I've never seen a dragon who isn't beautiful in their own magnetic, not-quite-human way, and Onatah's eyes are an arresting onyx, pools of deep space and starlight, striking against her bronze skin.

I had no idea that any Indigenous dragons still held Territory, and here's one who is not only Dav's neighbor, but enough of a friend to give him stupid novelty socks.

"Uh," I say. "I don't have a helmet."

She tosses me hers. I catch it on the first bounce.

"I don't need it." She brushes a hand over the top of her head, and what I took for rows of intricate braids turns out to be four thin, twisting horns that wrap from her forehead back across her skull.

That's *so* fucking cool.

I wonder if Dav has horns, and if he's able to manifest them like he does his claws. I've had my hands in his hair enough to know that he doesn't wear them daily, but if they make him look as badass as Onatah...

...right, no.

My Dav is charming, fussy, curated, and kind. He's handsome. When he's upset, he's intimidating and, I'm not gonna lie, *sexy.* But he is not, and will never be, *badass.*

While I was checking her out, she was returning the favor.

"Will I do?" I ask.

"You're good but, yeah, that boy's got a type," Onatah chuckles as I clamber on the bike.

'A type' implies that Dav's dated before. There were people—humans? dragons?—before me. *He's over two hundred years old.* I shove down the bitterness that comes with remembering that Dav wasn't the one who told me so. *Of course he's dated before.*

Before I can indulge my curiosity about Dav's 'taste', we're speeding off into the sticky afternoon.

The ride is smooth, which I appreciate like whoa. Onatah doesn't seem like she needs to prove how macho she is with crazy stunts. Or maybe it's that she knows Dav will kill her if something happens.

A knot of emotion makes it hard to swallow—old grief, and giddy relief, anticipatory joy, and a simmering resentment I hadn't realized was still on low-heat in my veins. Dav had kissed me *like that* in the Murder Basement, and then gone upstairs and *left me* there, literally in the dark, knowing full well that he intended to walk out of the door with Lt. Gov. Jerkface. Onatah made it sound like he hadn't had a choice in staying away, but the point is: he went in the first place.

Calm and docile. Like a lamb to slaughter. *Or a soldier obeying orders.*

*Marquess*, I had learned in my panicked scan of Wikipedia, was a title given to those who presided over border territories on behalf of a monarch. Military leaders granted land and titles, responsible for the safety of their March and tasked with being the first line of defense. Dav had told me he was insignificant. But Marches are important. And Marquessate of Niagara encompasses the whole *peninsula.*

Including where I live.

Including, that means, *me.*

And he'd never said.

He'd never *used* it.

He could have. He had every right to. I realize that now.

And he *hadn't*.

That's the important part.

He sat in that corner, nervous and patient, and hadn't been pushy or selfish. Granted, I don't think either of us could have predicted a kitchen fire is what would have brought us together. But I think we were already two proto-planets, just starting the slow dance of gravity that would lead to our inevitable fusion. The fact that I had been excited, thinking that I'd run into Dav at the bar the night before the fire was proof that I had *already* been thinking about him that way.

The sudden, gut-dropping reminder that I'm in *way* over my head makes me tighten my grip on Onatah's waist. Man, I don't even know who *Onatah* is. Do I have my arms currently wrapped around the waist of a princess? Do her people ascribe to the colonizer hierarchy of royalty? Is she a chieftain or a... fuck, should I bow or something when we get off the bike? Fuck.

Lost in my introspection, torn between excitement and lingering resentment, I miss when Onatah exits the highway. Suddenly we're bordered by fenced-in pastures, and hedges planted along the roadside to protect the delicate grape vines in the fields beyond them from the wind and exhaust. That smokey-warm scent that follows dragons like expensive cologne fills the helmet, but I can imagine the scent of the countryside in the glowing, humid late afternoon—barnyard, foliage, and the pungent scent of fallen fruit.

That's when we start skimming by the walls.

They're about three meters high, I'd guess, made of local golden sandstone, and heavily wreathed in trailing vines with bright trumpet-shaped orange flowers or little purple blossoms. There's no barbed wire, or spikes. There's no need. The sheer solid gravity of the wall is a pretty solid 'go away' sign.

We stop in front of an ornate, art-nouveau style wrought-iron gate. It wouldn't look out of place on the cover of a gothic romance novel. I imagine leaning back against the iron to gasp for breath as I flee into a star-lit night, clad only in a windblown white nightgown. I giggle as Onatah drops the kickstand.

"Nerves," I lie when she cuts me a funny look.

Close-up, the swirls of the gate resolve themselves into grape vines and bunches of fruit, and a slit-eyed, content dragon winding his way bodily through the plants. There are flowers around his ears, and his wings arch up to form peaked arches, the fingers of each wing descending to create the bars of the gate.

I wonder if it's an accurate portrait.

"How true are the stories?" I ask as I take off the helmet. I move to hand it back to Onatah, and she points at the seat, so I set it down there.

"What stories?" Onatah tilts her head to the side, earrings swaying, and it's the first time I've seen her move in a particularly reptilian way. It makes something in my chest quiver.

While Dav tries so hard to move, and blink, and breathe like a human, Onatah isn't even bothering. She's wearing skin, yeah, but she moves like a lizard. I can tell just by being near her that she's *homo draconis*. Like I could with Lt. Gov. Fuckstick.

How small does Dav crunch himself down every day, to suck that all in?

"I mean... the fairy tales, right? Shouldn't I have an enchanted sword if I'm going to break into a dragon's lair?"

"Going into battle, are you?" She's smirking.

"You know how he is. Shuts down. Shuts up."

"Stands at attention."

I shoot her a pair of finger-guns. "Exactly. Maybe I need a can-opener, instead."

Onatah laughs, hissingly sibilant and delighted. "Yeah, you'll be fine."

"I'm serious, though. Have you ever managed to get Dav to listen instead of just deciding what's best for everyone around him? This might be—I mean, he really is okay?"

"Yeah." Her face softens for a second, and then twists back into that amused sneer. "And to be clear, you're not the knight in this little drama."

"Oh, I'm not?"

"Honey, you're the princess."

"Fuck off."

"Gladly," she says, and mounts up.

"Whoa, no wait," I yelp and reach for her hand.

Onatah jerks away from my touch like its acid. There's no skin-to-skin contact, but she's still staring wide-eyed at my fingers. "That's a big no-no, princess."

"What?"

"Dav'll explain."

"Come with me," I say again. "I don't... I'm not scared, okay, I just don't know what I'm... please."

"I'm not going in," Onatah explains patiently. "Not without an explicit invitation to cross into his nesting grounds. Which he's never given."

"Fuck, man. Dragons," I blow out a sigh and shove my hands into my back pockets. "Why do you make everything so complicated?"

"It's you humans who make it hard to know where you stand with each other. You're weird."

I feel like sticking out my tongue at her, so I do.

She laughs. I take it as a good sign. "Go on. House is at the end of the walk."

She's roaring off down the road before I can say thank you.

# chapter Twenty-Three

The walk is deceptively named. It's long enough to be a *hike*.

I was expecting a nice country path with a romantic avenue of trees, leaning in to gossip over my head. There are trees, but they're regimented, evenly-spaced, canopy-shy maples. They border a darkly-paved drive wide enough for two vehicles to pass, marching toward a house hidden beyond a high wall of shrubs with a second arching gateway.

It's nice, but there's no *personality*.

There's nothing to suggest, beyond the whimsy of the front gate, that it's Dav who lives here. My Dav, who is proud of his wine, and secretly loves silly socks, and drinks his coffee with a hit of espresso. My Dav, who is tactile and comforting, and tries hard to please. My Dav, would be a hedonist, it's so clear in the way he makes meals, and makes love, but is not *allowed* to be.

That's what this walk looks like: Dav being denied.

Again.

In the ten minutes it takes me to get to the house, I oscillate between sorrow, fuming anger on his behalf, and curiosity. There are more walls inside the estate, low enough I have a view of the outbuildings and vineyards they section off. What would I find if I walked across the manicured lawn, risking the wrath of a security detail or gardener to crush the grass and hop the nearest boundary? The sustainability-nerd in me is desperate to see if the original watering systems are still in place, if the equipment is run on gas, or solar, or literal-horse-power. I want to poke through every shed, analyze a real working farm that has been at it for centuries.

I don't because that can wait.

I'm going to see Dav.

I pass through the ivy-heavy wall—*an inner bailey*, my brain screams, *a fortress prepared for a siege*—and the house that's revealed looks like something out of Jane Austen. (*Dav was seventeen years old when Jane Austen was born*, I recall with a jolt.) The house is two and a half stories, topped with a pitched roof and dormers, built of the same sandstone as the walls, and overflowing with fussy classical detailing. The windows and front door are surrounded by stonework that looks like Greek pillars. The front door is topped with a little stone roof trimmed with ornate scrollwork, and a modern front door in a cheeky wine-red. I bet Onatah put him up to that.

The whole building is so quintessentially Loyalist it might as well be on a postcard.

But this isn't a museum. People live here: housekeepers, farmers, winemakers. And I'm standing like a dumbass in the middle of the inner courtyard, surrounded on both sides with a riot of barely-controlled rose bushes. I wonder how many pairs of eyes are watching me through the regimented rows of rectangular windows. The thought of being judged by the people who know Dav's private life better than I do gives me goosebumps.

The front door opens before I'm halfway up the three shallow steps.

"Hi," the woman holding the door open says. She's shorter than me, white, probably in her mid-thirties, with funky glasses and plump cheeks that betray a ready smile. Right now she looks serious, but not the *bad* kind of serious. Her gaze drops to the pin on my lapel, then bounces up to my face, politely bland.

"Uh. Hello. I'm, uh, I'm Colin."

"Yes, I know." She waves her hand to invite me into a narrow, well-lit foyer.

"Um, Onatah dropped me off."

"I know that, too," the woman says, and nods to a small screen beside the door, where a video feed streams a view of the front gate. It flicks to the walkway, the inner courtyard, and a terraced stone patio. Yikes, she watched my whole walk-of-not-shame. Awkward.

She thrusts out her hand, business-like and confident. "Sarah Appleby." We shake. "I'm the P.A."

"Colin Levesque," I say, like an idiot, because she knows who I am. "I'm the, er, boyfriend. I think? I hope."

She shoots a reassuring, if slightly pitying smile at me, and I follow her out of the narrow, wood-paneled front hall. We head through a pair of double doors with an elaborate stained-glass transom into what looks like a formal sitting room done up in powder blue and daisy yellow.

Okay, so maybe this place *is* part museum. I tuck my elbows in as we weave through spindly sofas and tables, which someone clearly stole off the *Downton Abbey* set, terrified of knocking over some precious family knickknack.

Christ, this room doesn't feel much like Dav, either.

Is *any* part of his life his own?

Sarah bustles through a side door—green baize and everything—and suddenly we're in an ultra-modern industrial kitchen. It's easily as big as my whole apartment, bisected by a massive worktop lined with stools.

One side is all chefy stainless steel, and the other is a wall of pantry cupboards, as elaborately and classically wrought as the exterior of the house, but in expensive gleaming wood, and likely just as old. There's a big bay window framing a spectacular view of the vineyards, ringed on the outside by the limestone patio I'd seen on the security feed.

And sitting at the window, curled up on their knees to reach coloring books on a much-loved family-sized dining table, is the last thing I expected to see in Dav's house: kids.

Two of 'em. And the little girl, maybe seven years old, is ginger.

I feel all the blood drain from my face.

Both kids bolt up from the table with delighted "Mom!"s.

"They're not his," Sarah says, smirking as she hugs the younger boy to her thigh.

I hope my relief isn't too obvious. "Well... okay."

I'd have been annoyed if Dav had children and he'd never mentioned them. But the deal-breaker would have been that he'd *hidden* them from me, not their existence. I'm suddenly wondering how a child with Dav's hair and my ears would look. Besides it being a biological impossibility because, *hello, we are both dudes*, that is very much not what I should be thinking about right now.

*You're mad at him, remember?* I remind myself, tearing my eyes away from the kids before my staring gets creepy. *You're worried about him, and scared for him, and you should not be thinking about how baby dragons are born. You are getting lightyears ahead of yourself, Colin. How about you figure out where the two of you stand before you start thinking about spawn. Spawn that, may I remind me, you did not want with Rebeckah, which is what tanked your proposal before it even began.*

I'm starting to think that Dav's PA is some kind of mind reader, because she says: "He's in the library. Third door on the right." She jerks her chin at a hallway off the back of the kitchen.

"Thanks. Uh, bye small humans."

They chorus a jumbled "bye!" at me.

It's another wood-paneled affair that has seen some modernization, but not too recently. 1970s, I'd say, by the carpets.

"Of course there's a library," I mutter to myself, peering into each of the rooms I pass: a pokey, plasticky '80s bathroom, and a meticulously tidy and '60s era office complete with black leather club chairs and crystal bar set.

The third door is a heavy beast of a thing polished to a high shine and probably original to the house. I ease it open.

This isn't a library. Libraries are tidy, carefully curated, with shelves that have been dusted, and lamps with stained glass shades. Libraries are neat gardens of literature.

*This* is a jungle. These books tower, they weave, they fill the space, climb to the ceiling, tilt. There must be shelves under all of the books somewhere, but I don't see any as I pick my way around a tumble of leather-bound tomes that surround the door.

"Hello? Dav?" The books swallow my words.

"Over here." Dav's voice floats out from behind one of the groves of paper and ink.

There's a narrow path cleared through the mess, and I follow that around a corner. Dav is standing in a shaft of syrupy late-afternoon sunlight, and I know enough about the bastard that it's clear he planned it that way. More of his Old Hollywood Charm nonsense. He slides his gaze, glowing gold in the dramatic lighting, to my feet. This surprises me, until this gaze skims all the way up to meet mine, and I realize he's disquieted.

This isn't a slow, sexy eyefuck.

He's checking, piece-by-piece, that I'm all there.

Guilt springs across his face when his eyes land on the pin, then camps in a furrow between his eyes. I've never seen that furrow before. He's always been a sort of perpetually youthful late-twenties, but now he looks old and exhausted in a way I've never seen him before. It's not just the way the chiaroscuro of the sun carves heavy lines in the corners of his eyes, or the bruises under them. It's something more. The not-quite-a-dimple is so deep.

I want to kiss the frown away.

I don't move. I don't know how welcome I am.

To be honest, I *hadn't* imagined what it would be like to reunite. I think a part of me genuinely believed we never would. That Dav would stay away—either because he'd been made to, or because he wanted to—and I would get old, and be forgotten, and die. He's a dragon. He could ignore a human until he simply outlives them easily, if he wanted to. He's already outlived every human he's ever known. Multiple times.

Yet here he is, standing in a shaft of light that's slowly inching away, dropping him into the cool evening darkness. He's right *there*.

But also... not.

This Dav isn't the *right* one.

He's worn. He's weary. He's heavy with silence. He's wearing plain black pants, and a plain white shirt, with a plain black waistcoat. He looks *boring*. He's not even wearing fun socks, just a pair of worn-in, period-drama slippers. He matches his house.

I hate it.

He looks desperately unhappy. I thought he'd at *least* be pleased to see *me*. That feeling twists up inside me again, the one that's squirmy and acidic. The one that's kind of rage (but I'm not sure who it's directed at) and kind of misery (but I don't know what for), and kind of like a scream that's just waiting for me to breathe deep enough to give it life.

"Hullo, Colin," he says softly, when we've both looked our fill.

Dav's voice is, at least, still as wonderfully rich, his accent as strange and comforting. I half expected his voice to be thin and reedy, aged a century in the time he's been away, to match his eyes.

"Hello, Dav."

I reach into my blazer pocket and pull out a gift. It's a paper bag of his dragon-roasted coffee beans, crumpled and mostly-empty, with just enough left in it for one pot.

Dav steps forward, slowly, to take it. The sensitive insides of our index fingers brush, and I don't repress the shudder at the touch of his dragon-warm skin. His nostrils flare. It feels so good to be close to him again.

I want to be closer.

I don't think I should have to be the one to close the gap, though.

After all, *he* left *me*.

Dav rests the packet on a stack of books. "You shouldn't have this."

"I don't care. You made those for me. I saved them. So we can... it's stupid, never mind, I... I just... I thought, the first morning, after you come back, I wanted to make coffee for you. Our last batch. Symbolic. *Fuck*."

Dav's fingertips linger on the bag. "I know."

Another long stretch of wrongish silence, like a bath that's just too hot. You can't relax into it, just yet.

"You didn't come back," is how I finally break it. Dav winces. "I was worried," I add. It's true. It's not the whole truth, but it's true. Dav curls in on himself more, shame etched on every curve of his limbs. "There were paparazzi!" I force a laugh, but it's fake and weak. "They gave us a celebrity couple name—Alvalin. Sounds like a medieval weapon."

"I'm so sorry," Dav whispers into his own chest.

I'm close enough to touch him. Close enough to reach out. It's clear now he won't reach first. Doesn't feel he has the right to. Okay.

I can work with that. So I do. Cup my hand, extend my arm, aim for his cheek.

Dav flinches and hisses like a terrified kitten.

I gasp, horrified. Not because he cringed away, but that he cringed away from *me*.

He's always been weird about people touching him. But never me. Not when he saw it was coming. When was the last time anyone touched Dav in a way that wasn't meant to hurt him?

How do dragons punish one another?

"Okay." I take a step away, give him space. "I'll let you do the deciding about—" Something warm and dry coils around my ankle. I look down, expecting a cat. Instead, it's a vividly red snake. I swallow back a scream, and quash the instinct to kick.

Because it's not a snake.

It's a *tail.*

# chapter Twenty-Four

"Don't..." Dav starts, but then chokes on whatever it was he was going to say. The smooth lines of his waistcoat are rucked up, golden freckles shining along his hip.

*Don't go?*

*Don't scream?*

The scales are softer than I expected, sliding along the skin above my sock. There's a row of wine-red shark-fin spurs along what I assume is the top of his... spine? But they're not touching me. The arrow-head spike folds in like an umbrella against my shoe. It's not at all the hard weapon I expected it to be, when I tried to guess what Dav's other form might look like.

"I don't know if this is the right time to say this," I whisper, staring down at the appendage slowly coiling around my leg, to the same tempo as Dav's anxious hand-wringing. "But your tail?"

He cringes back further. "Yes?"

"It's adorable."

His mouth drops open.

I crouch and get my hand under his tail. It's no wider than my arm, about as long again as Dav is tall, and tapers into a point about the circumference of my little finger. He lets me lift it. It's heavy. And expressive. He curls it around my forearm, the arrowed tip sliding over my palm.

I press my lips against the fire-warm scales.

It smells like Dav, that smoke-and-cologne smell. And carpet dust. Bleh.

"I missed you," Dav hiccups miserably.

"Then why didn't you answer my calls?" The resentment that's been simmering begins to boil.

His tail drops away, retreating behind him, swaying once, twice, and then is gone between one blink and the next. "At first, I had no phone. And then because..." he smooths his waistcoat nervously. "It's unseemly to have humans in your Nesting Grounds when they are not, ah, yours."

"I'm pretty fucking sure I made it clear I was yours," I snap, and, oops, *there's* the anger. "Had a few magical nights about it, too."

"Sex doesn't make you mine," Dav says, but the dimple beside his mouth is curling upward. I'm glad he's amused. That makes one of us. "Any more than it makes me *yours*."

"I am so fucking angry with you," I tell him.

"I know," he says, but it's not condescending. It's a bland statement of fact. *I see you. I acknowledge what you're feeling.*

"You walked out the door with them."

"Yes."

"Dav, you—" Something in the fury freezes, cracks. "You *left*."

"I had no choice."

The frozen thing shatters. It turns to shards, pierces the knot of anxiety at the top of my stomach, drives into the back of my eyes. I make a noise that I haven't heard come out of my mouth since Dad's funeral.

"You *left*," I accuse. "I thought that it was the last time I was ever going to... to touch you. That you were dying somewhere and I wouldn't be able to hold you and—and I can't *do* that again!"

"I never meant to hurt you," Dav says, all in a rush. "It was better—"

"You don't get to decide what's better for me."

"Colin, please, there's so much you don't understand."

"Because you won't explain it to me!" I thump his chest in frustration. He lets me. "You were *gone.*"

"I know, and I—"

"You *don't* know!" I shout, glaring up into his face, not caring that my own is wet with tears and snot. "My Dad... he was fine, and then he wasn't, and we weren't allowed... I had to watch through a window. All I could do was press my face against the glass and beg him to breathe, to keep breathing, and then he... he *stopped*, and I couldn't... I wasn't even allowed to *touch* him. He's gone *forever*... and I *wasn't—*"

"Colin, shhhh."

Somehow, we're on the floor, now. He's petting my hair, and I'm tumbled into his lap.

"You left on *purpose.*" Everything inside of me is cracking open, escaping as ugly, horrible sobs. I'm choking back bile and fury, the root of my tongue burns, my heart squeezes, my hands feel numb even as I claw at his sleeves to make sure he can never escape, can never run away from me again.

"I had no choice—"

"You could have fought! There were people with cameras on the sidewalk, they—you could have *fought* for me!"

"I did," he whispers, cheek against mine. "Believe me, Colin, in all the ways I could, I did."

"What did they do to you?" I ask, trying to pull away, but Dav is strong, holds me in place. I struggle for a second, and then try the opposite tack. I melt into him, tilt my chin up to whisper in his ear. "What happened?"

"Later," he breathes, ruffling my hair. "Let me... I want to... you smell so good, I've never explained how much I..." His forked tongue flickers out, touches the skin behind my ear.

I push back enough to frame his face with my hands.

"Were you trying to protect me by staying away?" His gaze drops down to where his hands knead my waist. "Answer."

"I complained about the media. Said it wasn't right, their hounding you, when you and I had never... reached an arrangement. He put a stop to it."

"The paps?"

Dav's eyes rise to meet mine, slow as molasses. "And us."

"Was that the punishment?"

"I explained, before, about draconic instinct?"

"Yeah."

Dav dries my cheeks gently with the silk cuff of his boring shirt. "I want you very badly, Colin." His eyes drop to my mouth, and he licks his lips. "I want to *keep* you."

"You can," I tell him, leaning forward, offering up that kiss he clearly wants, but he holds me away.

"I can't. That we were, ah, on friendly terms at all was a gross violation of an edict that had been passed on me a hundred years ago. But His Excellency was willing to overlook it. It was fine so long as it wasn't *serious*. But I had also violated a second rule."

"The beans," I say, desperate to ask him about what he had done that was so bad that it meant he had to be lonely, for a whole century.

"The beans," Dav confirms gravely. "So I was to be kept from you. And you from me."

"For how long?"

He avoids answering by giving me that kiss I wanted.

It's a great kiss. Confident, warm, comfortable.

It's also not an answer.

(*Forever*, the kiss says. *For the rest of your life.*)

"Oh Colin," he says gently, when we finally part. He reaches up to rub his thumb over the pin. "You don't know what you've done."

"I *never* know what I've goddamn done," I snap, weeks worth of panic and fear and hurt bubbling hard in my throat. "That's the problem with you."

Dav flinches again.

I don't feel sorry for it.

I feel a little sorry for it.

I grab his nipple through his waistcoat and twist it.

"Ow, ow!" Dav whines, cringing away. "Colin!"

"That's for saying 'I love you' before I could say it first," I snarl, letting go. "And this," I add, pressing a biting kiss to his mouth. "Is because I love you too, you dumbass."

"Even still?" He asks cautiously, dipping his pinkie fingers into the dimples on either side of my tailbone, where my shirt has ridden up.

"Yeah. I love you—" I let him kiss me again, possessive and hot. "—even though I don't much like you right now."

He wuffs out a laugh, startled. "I more than deserve your ire."

"More than," I agree.

He runs his thumb over the pin again. "You shouldn't have put it on."

"I can take it off. I don't know why everyone's so upset."

"It's too late. You asked me why we're allowed to be together now? It's this." He ducks his head, mouths up my neck from my collar to the base of my ear, wet and wonderful. "I find I'm *quite* satisfied, though."

I tip my head back, give him room.

No, wait.

I'm mad at him.

"Cut that out when I'm pissed off."

Dav noses up into my hair, presses his thumb against the pin hard enough that the backing is a delicious little point of pain in counterpoint to the pleasure of him reacquainting himself with me.

I twist his other nipple.

He yelps and falls back, catching himself on the book-shelves.

"You have to explain."

"Colin." He straightens, rubbing his chest to soothe the bruises. I wonder what they'll look like. Does he get mottled the way a human would or is there too much scale under his skin? "It's not... I just—"

"Nuh-uh. We're not playing that game this time. Answers. Clear ones. Now. Or I'm leaving. And I'm staying gone."

His face drains of color. "You wouldn't."

"I would." It's not an empty threat, either. I'm fed up.

"You love me," Dav says, confused and small.

"I do."

"So you won't leave."

"I abso-fucking-lutely will," I correct. "*Because* I love you. So let's start with this." I tap the pin. "Why did you leave it with me if you didn't want me to wear it?"

"I didn't," Dav says, but I can't figure out who he's trying to convince. He's twitchy all of a sudden. I slide off his lap to sit cross-legged on the floor in front of him. "It fell off. You picked it up. I didn't... it wasn't..."

"Is that what you've been telling Simcoe? That it 'fell off'?"

His eyes cut away. "Yes?"

*Coward*, I think.

Then I say it out loud: "Coward."

He snaps his gaze back up to mine, mouth dropping open so prettily that I just have to stick my tongue in it. We lose the thread for a few minutes as I crowd him back against the shelf.

"Tell me," I smear into his mouth, and he pants, and whines, and scrunches up his eyes.

"I didn't give it to you because I wasn't allowed to!" Dav blurts. "And even if I wanted to, to, to *do* it—"

*Do what? Just say it!*

"—it was too soon. Months. Years!"

"So it means something? Like, *really* means something?"

"Yes."

"What?"

He whines again, distressed, and I press my cheek to his chest, wrap my arms around him tight, think calming, weighted-blanket thoughts.

"It means you're mine," Dav says, but it's not romantic, or heartfelt. "...*legally*."

"I'm sorry," I say, jerking back and pushing the palm of my hand hard against his forehead to force him to look at me. "Fucking *what*?"

"Do you understand?" Dav whispers, distraught. "You're now my *property*."

"Kinky," I croak, trying to make a joke even as it feels like the world has dropped out from under me.

*Owned,* my brain screams. I resist the urge to use the hand already on his forehead to bounce his skull off the shelving behind him and scurry to my feet. The instinct to flee, run, *get away* coils like a serpent in my guts, but instead I take a deep breath and try to breathe through the urge, because I already knew this. This isn't news. Everyone knows what a hoard is. Everyone knows that dragons own all the land and rule all the people and resources on that land.

This isn't... this isn't *fresh* information.

It's just, ah, more *detailed* than it was before.

That doesn't make one iota of difference to the small, terrified, snarling bit of me that lives in terror of confinement, who finds uncomfortable situations claustrophobic, and has recurring nightmares about being locked in a glass fishbowl and suffocating under soulless plastic piles of medical tubing. To the part of me that wanted to shove Dav away and make a run for it, no matter how irrational that was, and how little difference it would make to our situation.

But to hear it put so *bluntly...*
*Hoarded.*
The only difference is that I, one specific human, have now—in accordance with draconic law—made myself the chattels of one specific dragon.
*Enslaved.*
I let Dav go, and try to calm the twanging fear racing across every nerve in my body. My hands are trembling so hard it takes two tries to jam them into my pockets. My chest feels like Dav's wrapped his tail around it and is pulling tight.
*I will not have a panic attack about this*, I tell myself firmly, huffing on the little distressed sounds that are fighting their way up my throat. *Breathe.*
"Kinky?" Dav echoes, confused before he catches the look on my face, the cadence of my heartbeat.
"Yeah, it's—" I start but choke on the joke I'm trying to make.
"Oh, Colin, you needn't attempt to be flippant about it," Dav rushes to assure me, sitting up from where he'd been draped on the shelf. "It's wretched. I didn't even get to *ask* you."
"Ask me?" I say, grasping for some sort of even footing. Telegraphing his every gesture, and moving slow enough that I could wave him off or push him away if I wanted to, Dav wraps his hands around my elbows, holding tight to help me stay upright. "Ask me if I would like to make myself some sort of indentured servant? Jesus *fuck*."
"Ask you if you would care to spend the rest of our lives together," Dav corrects, eyes darkening.

# chapter Twenty-Five

I t sounds so fucking romantic the way he says it.

Especially with the last of the golden sunlight pooling on the floor around us, the long honey-amber shadows cast by the tumbles and towers of books. It was almost like being on the ramparts of a castle, the stone spires and high walls sheltering a pair of lovers from the hateful gaze of the enemy far below, held back by their passion, and the moat.

It *is* romantic.

It *would* be romantic, under literally any other context.

Because he still looks desperately unhappy. That's what I keep circling back to.

*It's like he's playacting. He's putting on a show of what is expected of him, not what he wants.*

I'd had the thought while clocking his plain boring pro-scribed landscaping, his plain boring proscribed house. And now here he was, too terrified or ashamed to look me in the eyes, plain and boring, and proscribed in his terrible, bland suit. Wearing the uniform of a good, professional, genteel man of society instead of just getting to *be* one. He's playing a part thrust on him, when the real Dav is wild, and unfettered, hedonistic and passionate. He loves hugely, so much so that it spills out into every interaction with everyone around him, translates into his joyful desire and cell-deep need to ensure that everything he does pleases and brings joy to whomever happens to enter his orbit. He enjoys things with an immensity of satisfaction that I've never seen before, savoring each bite of food, each sip of coffee, each heady kiss. He takes pleasure in the simplicity of a clear blue sky, or the comforting tap of rain against the glass, the softness of a gorgeous fabric, or the warmth of my pinkie finger curled around his own.

And *this* is what Lt. Gov. Fucknuts is trying to squash. To regiment. To *rule*.

To keep me away from.

Well, screw that guy.

I free my hands from my pockets and reach up to cup Dav's face. My whole body is quivering, but not from anxiety this time.

Dav licks his bottom lip, leaving it plump and shiny and so very fucking tempting. His tongue is split and purple. Usually when Dav loses control of the shift, and some of his more serpentine traits slip out, it's the precursor to funtimes. Right now, though, I think it's the possessiveness, his desperate draconic need to hold, and protect, and *please* coming to the fore. His ears have elongated a little, the pointed ends sticking out of hair that has turned into a golden-red halo by the last of the sunset. Tiny, ruby scales freckle his hairline. When he shifts his grip on my arm, his nails are sharp and the beds dark, but not quite talons.

"Please let me keep you," Dav whimpers. "Colin, I couldn't bare it if you came all this way, and didn't want--"

I kiss him.

Partially, because it's all I've been thinking about since I saw him standing there in that pool of light like something out of a cinematographer's wet dream. But partially because I don't know if I can answer his request the way he wants me to. I don't know if I'm capable of just... being his. Like that. With no information, no clarification, no understanding of what it is that he's actually asking for, or telling me.

And this is easier.

Falling into bed with him is *so* easy.

And I missed him. *Fuck*, I missed him.

Missed his warmth, the taste of his skin, the smoky-amber scent of his happiness filling my nose, the weight of his body on top of mine, the rumble of his purrs under my cheek as we laze together in the afterglow.

We've been away from each other so long, I can only imagine how hard he must be fighting the urge to shove me down onto the floor and pin me there for a few hours.

Actually, that sounds like the perfect way to deal with both of our nerves.

*Sex doesn't make you mine, any more than it makes me yours*, he'd said. But it would go an awful long way toward settling the nerves that were making our words stilted and our touches tentative. It would bring us back to where we were before we were forced apart, forced to hurt one another, forced to have to start over.

Look at me, being all introspective and shit. Dr. Chen would be proud.

Decision made, I ball my hands in the fabric of his horrible boring vest, and tip us backward. Dav realizes what's happening quickly enough to get his hand behind my head, toppling a small stack of tomes to make room for us on the carpet. He digs his fingers into my hair immediately, tugging my chin up so he can get a good look at my face.

"Colin, darling, what are you--"

"I missed you," I tell him, because it's true, because it's echoing through the chambers of my heart with every pump of my blood, and because he deserves to hear it. "You left me behind, and I'm still really fucking mad about that, but you're here now, and I want you to be *here*."

"I want you very badly, Colin," Dav groans, sliding forward until his knees are on either side of my hips, propping himself up on one elbow and sinking down into a filthy, filthy kiss.

"You can have me," I pant back into his mouth, when he leans back so we can breathe a small eternity later.

"I want to *keep* you," he adds. When I don't answer immediately, he pulls back to check my expression, eyes roving over my face. "Colin?"

"We'll talk about that later," is what I finally settle on.

"Are you sure that is wise? Should we not... *before* we—"

"*Later*," I insist, and punctuate the decision by cupping the distracting bulge in his terrible, boring black trousers.

"Cheat!" Dav makes an obscene sound, grinding down into my grip and dropping his head to press the blunt flats of his teeth against my neck, just shy of actually nipping. "Tease. *Minx.*"

"Fuck me," is how I reply.

It's not teasing if I mean it.

Dav sucks in a breath, startled and incredibly turned-on sounding. Or at least, I assume he is, because I definitely am. Then he drops his body down on top of mine—*finally*—slotting us together from knees to nose. His thighs are a hot brand along the outside of mine, stomachs and chests pressed together, arms cradling my shoulders, hands carding hair made wild by his own explorations off my face.

"I have nothing to ease the way," Dav whispers hotly in my ear. "Unless you were very optimistic about our reunion and have stashed something in your pockets?"

"What, no extra bottle of lube hiding between the stacks?" I ask, chuckling, and grabbing a double handful of his arse to make it clear that I have no intention of letting him go long enough to check.

"If I have hidden some in the library, it would have been so many decades ago that even if I could remember where the bottle was, it would have dried up by now. It has been..." he hesitates, then huffs and finishes with a soft: "Many, many years."

"Plan B, then," I say, wriggling a hand between us to get at his fly, then mine.

He gets with the change of plan fast. While I'm working on our pants, he leans up just enough to strip off first his waistcoat, then his shirt, only undoing enough buttons to allow him to escape inelegantly, before wrestling me out of my Henly. Neither of us bother with our shoes, just bunch our pants down to our knees and call that good enough.

I play my hand over Dav's bare chest. He winces a bit as my fingers brush his abused nipples. Not feeling contrite exactly, but sorry that they hurt, I lean up to mouth apologetic kisses over both. Dav groans and arches his back, pressing into the sensation, hands scrabbling at the carpet as if he's still afraid to touch me. Afraid to hold me close, to covet and to *keep* me, the way I've already told him he can.

Well, that won't do.

I have no illusions that I am anywhere near strong enough to manhandle Dav, but he reads my intent well enough from the tense and flex of my arms, and lets me flip us over. I shove myself into vee of his thighs as best I can with the fabric between us, grab his hands, and press them firmly to the meat of my ass. His talons prick deliciously, but don't break skin.

"Hold on," I warn him, and then make a filthy show and get my hand as wet as possible with my tongue.

"*Annwyl dduw*," he groans, a verbal keysmash of a sound, pupils growing round and consuming the gold of his iris as he stares up at me. The look on his face is... it's worshipful, captivated, besotted, it's...

It's too *much*.

I look away, my own face burning, his expression somehow far more intimate than the fact that we're both nude from the knees up with our cocks out.

My mouth goes dry, tongue sticking to the roof, throat clicking when I try to swallow enough to produce spit to say something about the way he's looking at me. I croak, very unsexily, and decide instead to apply myself to another mode of responding instead.

I take both of us in my wet hand, both relieved and a little shamed at my own emotional cowardice when that look on Dav's face shatters, his eyes roll back, and he thunks his head back against the floor. The long, pale column of his throat is far too tempting, so I give in and curl down to suck a love-bite into the peachy flesh. If I have to wear his token, he can damn well wear mine right back.

Dav doesn't even wait for me to start stroking before he's lifting his hips, rolling into the hot wet grip around us, kneading my ass like a kitten and making those sweet little dragony noises I love so much.

The rumble of his happiness vibrates through his chest, sinking deep into my bones in all the places where we're touching. Which is a lot of places.

"Colin, Colin!" he moans around the purrs. "*Fy nhrysor, please.*"

I do as he begs and speed up my pulls, adding a little thumb flick to his dewy slit with every upstroke. He shivers and shakes, holding himself back, and I am struck with the revelation that this powerful and handsome creature is laying back because I *want* him to. That he's letting me touch him, *fuck* him with my fist, because *I* desire it.

He is obeying me. He is submissive to *me.* Not because I'm demanding it of him, not because I'm *imposing* it on him like all the other dragons who think they can control him through fear and terror, but because he wants to *please* me.

Me.

A funny-eared, overly-anxious, directionless dreamer like *me.*

That's enough to tip me over the edge.

The hot splash of my spend sliding between my fingers and all over his velvety length sends him straight over after me.

It takes a few long, panting, wonderful moments for me to come back to myself. I'm laying smooshed against his shoulder, our softening pricks and my messy hand trapped between our warm bellies. Dav is nuzzling at the hair behind my ear like an affectionate kitten.

"I'm gonna get sticky soon. Don't you usually have a hanky somewhere in that posh outfit of yours?"

"No. Pocket squares are apparently out of fashion." Dav frowns, that moue of distaste putting a furrow between his eyebrows. "And I have been informed that my usual mode of dress is perhaps a bit flam—"

"I love it," I interrupt, already seeing that I'm going to have to spend some time undoing whatever fucking bullshit has been shoved at him since he was taken away from me. "I love your colour coordinating hankies, and your stupid fucking cartoon socks, and how you make a suit that should only look good on a runway look even better, because it's on you. You have the right to dress as joyfully as you want, and fuck whoever told you otherwise."

Dav's sweaty face flushes an adorable pink as he buries it shyly between my clavicles.

"No lube," I chuckle, to distract him from whatever turmoil is rolling through that pretty head of his. "And now no hanky. What are we supposed to clean up with?"

"Allow me," Dav whispers, his voice a deep growl. He pulls my hand up to his mouth.

Jesus Christ, that split tongue of his!

I will never get tired of it.

Once Dav has finished his indulgences, we hike our pants back up, but don't make any move toward the rest. Dav seems too clingy right now to want to let me go, and to be fair, while the floor isn't as comfortable now as it was in the throes of passion, I'm not in any hurry to abandon it for the world outside just yet.

"So now what?" I venture, running my hand through his sparse chest hair, and grimacing at the gray smear of book-dust clinging to the cooled sweat there.

The sun had well and truly set, and the magic of the pooling sunlight had vanished, leaving the room bathed in a night-cool hush.

"Hmm," Dav says, considering the question. He turns his head, presses his temple to the carpet to meet my eyes. His pupils are still fat with desire, leaving a golden ring around the outside, glimmering with satisfaction. A deep thrum rumbles under my palm, nearly inaudible unless one is straining for it. He licks his kiss-bruised lips, and the fire in my own belly flares up as I watch the pink tip trace the peaks of his cupid's bow. "Now, I suppose, we try to figure out how we make this work. For *us*."

"For us," I agree, still unsure, but at least hollowed out of the simmering anger that had taken root when he'd walked out the door. "But I was thinking more about the immediate future."

"Immediate?" Dav asked.

My stomach growled in lieu of my response, and Dav chuckles.

"Dinner it is," Dav says, and curls up onto his feet so swiftly and easily I barely have time to realize he's upright before he's offering me his hand.

"Dinner," I agree, and let him pull me up onto my feet and into his arms, like it's where I was always supposed to be.

Maybe it was.

"Dinner," I say again. "And then you can tell me exactly what 'your property' means.

# chapter Twenty-six

Dav has a cook, and apparently she leaves lots of little easy-to-reheat dishes stacked in the freezer. Dav chooses a roast meal for himself. I pick the lasagna. Once they've heated through, we sit at the table by the window, watching the moon rise over the vineyard while we both struggle to find something to say.

"I was placed on house arrest," Dav ventures at last, the first thing he's said since we cleaned up that wasn't about food. "I asked Onatah to watch you."

"Lt. Gov. Asshole had a stooge, too."

Dav cuts me a sardonic smirk over his potatoes. "Please don't ever let him hear you call him that."

"It's not like I'll ever spend any time around him," I say around a mouthful of what is, honestly, the best pasta I've ever had in my life.

Dav's ears flush.

"No." I set down my fork. "I refuse."

"You *cannot* refuse," Dav says patiently. "You are legally my Favorite. You may be commanded by any dragon above me in rank, or in family."

"Okay, so, one." I hold up a single finger. "I'm not forgetting about the house arrest thing, so don't think you've changed the subject, and two," I hold up a second finger. "Could the queen snap her talons and I'd have to hop-to?"

Dav sets down his own fork. "One, there is nothing to discuss. Part of my punishment was to remain within the walls of my nesting grounds for a decade. Donning my token—voluntarily and without my interference—has invalidated that. Whether I leave the property or not, *you* may now be here, as you are mine, with every freedom and obligation that entails. Including the demands of my protection, my shelter, my coffers, my table, and, should we both desire it, my bed. Two, in exchange for those demands, you are a vassal of her majesty, so yes."

"One, that's cruel. And me just a ten-minute drive away? *Cruel.*" I reach out and link our pinkies. "And two, a what?"

"One, that was the point. It was a punishment, after all. And two, as I am gifted with land in return for military service, you are likewise now promised."

"Service," I say flatly.

"*Not* sexual," Dav says quickly, blushing again. "Not *always* sexual."

"Could Simcoe—"

"Never!" Dav gasps, horrified. "It is quite one thing to be a vassal to a dragon. It's another entirely to be Favorite of a titled peer. No one would *dare.*"

"Yeah, let's talk about that title thing." I twist my wrist to pinch the back of his hand playfully. "*Marquess Niagara.*"

"Would it have impressed you?" Dav asks.

"Probably the opposite."

"And so you see why I did not mention it." His eyes drift to the pin, and his expression gets soppy. "For which I am immensely thankful."

"What if I forget to wear it?" I ask, knowing what a disaster I am. "What if I *lose* it?"

"Many wear the emblem stitched into their clothing. Others, as a motif or cameo in a piece of jewelry. In some cultures, tattoos are given to honored Favorites. Though that has never quite caught on amid the courts of my cousins. I could, ah, have a signet ring commissioned for you, should you like?"

"A ring," I echo, the connotations of the *other* symbolic meaning of a ring clanging in my brain. "Or a tattoo? Man, I don't know if I'm ready to be that permanent."

Dav looks at me with slowly dawning worry. "Colin. It *is* permanent. You do understand that, don't you?"

I shove a giant piece of pasta in my face.

Dav uses his napkin to wipe sauce off my chin, and takes both of my hands in his. "Look at me, Mine Own."

I look at him, chewing morosely. I've done it again. I've gone and ruined everything by being impulsive and...

"Best you swallow *before* you have the panic attack," Dav says, effectively cutting off my growing anxiety with annoyance.

I swallow. "So what is this, then? Like... marriage?"

"No," Dav says, far too quickly for my liking. "A spouse is not the same as a Favorite. You may marry elsewhere. Should you choose it. Though I would not prefer that. I *do* love you." He says it simply, like it's a fact of the universe.

"So, Sarah. Is she, like, an Own?"

"Oh no, only of my hoard. Her whole family has been, since her great-grandfather was Collected into my service as a batman during the Great War."

"So they're... *yours*." I sit back. I'm not sure what my expression is doing, but I can't imagine it's reassuring.

"Yes."

"I... sorry." I spring up from my chair, filled with more frenetic energy than I know what to do with. "Let me get this straight. Once a human enters your... your vassal-dom, or whatever, they can't leave. Ever?"

"Why would any want to?" He shrugs.

"You own the kids, too?" I ask, mouth twisted in distaste.

"Obviously."

"Explain to me how this is any different from slavery!" I shout, and we're both startled by the way my voice bounces around the kitchen.

"My hoard are not slaves." Dav stands. "They're not mistreated, they're not abused, and they are never forced to do that which they would find distasteful. I pay them, and very handsomely, for their expertise!"

"And will you pay me, too?" I ask. "For my 'expertise'?"

"Colin!"

"Answer me!"

He squirms. "You will live on my largesse. The estate is comfortable. I can keep you in whatever—"

"*Keep* me," I spit.

"You can still work, if you want! Only, you don't *have* to."

"And what would I do all day?"

"Whatever you like!" Dav says, reaching for me desperately, but I duck out of the way.

"And what if I want to leave?"

Dav stops, arms dropping. "That, you may not do. You donned my token, Colin. In full view of Simcoe's enforcers. There were telephoto lenses across the street. The media have *photos* of it. This is not like a human engagement you can call off." Right, that fucking hits like a wrecking ball. Asshole. "There's no, no... takesie-backsies!"

"But I didn't know that when I did it."

"That doesn't make it any less binding," Dav says, in the pedantic, soothing tone that's starting to piss me off.

I gesture between us with a sharp finger. "And what if we, I don't know, we don't work out? What if we break up? What then?"

"Then I will..." Dav swallows audibly. "I will provide you with all you need to live as independent a life as my instincts and our laws allow. A separate residence, an allowance, permission to marry if you so desire. Though I would be... terribly heartbroken."

And he's back to being small and crushed-in on himself again.

*Fuck*.

"I'm not breaking up with you right now, okay? To be clear." I abandon dinner and burrow my way into his arms as he curls over me, clinging.

Red wings suddenly close us off from the world. Peering up at them, the kitchen light through the membrane of the wing-leather highlights a delta of blue veins. I trace one fingertip along one, amazed.

"Tickles," Dav complains.

It's as easy as that to be kissing him, again.

"Today has been shit," I say when the kiss drifts to a natural stop. I squeeze him hard before he can tense up. "Not because I finally got to see you again, but because there's lots of complicated bullshit that neither of us want, and we're both frustrated, and hurt."

"I owe Dr. Chen a case of wine," Dav says softly.

"Har-fucking-har. Look, all I'm saying is there's lots to talk about. We're gonna get upset and shout. But that doesn't mean I don't love you, okay? I'm really fucking happy you're back, and I don't regret tokening myself or whatever, because it means I get to be with you again. And the rest of it, we'll figure out."

"You are?" Dav asks. "You mean it? Happy?"

"Right now, yeah, I am."

We lose a few more minutes to another sweet kiss. His wings loosen around us, letting in fresh air.

"Will you stay the night?" Dav asks sweetly.

"Are you kidding me? I finally got to see your place. Of course I'm spending the night."

Watching Dav undress is like watching an endangered species of wildflower bloom. I'm sure my face is filled with stupefied wonder, each inch of precious skin setting my heart juddering.

He's stripping less because we're totally about to have amazing reunion sex, and more because his wings tore up his clothes. (But also, yes, reunion sex please.) Even though they're probably beyond repair, he folds them up anyway, as if some valet is going to come and put them away in the morning.

Each inch of precious skin has my heart juddering. My fingers itch to help, but Dav has asked me to sit in the big wingback chair by the fireplace in his bedroom—the *fireplace in his bedroom*, I need to stress that—and wait. The fire is banked, in deference to the warm August evening, and the crackling is the only sound as Dav disrobes.

It's not a show. It's methodical, the actions of a man used to wearing much more complicated clothing in a bygone era. Clothing that needed to be cared for in a certain way. It's beautiful and frustrating all at once. I want to *touch*, but he's just out of range, the smug bastard. So instead I squeeze my own knees tightly.

*No underwear*, I realize, when he's finally backlit by the glow of the fireplace, nude and comfortable in his human skin. Which, *duh, of course not. He couldn't have done the tail thing if he'd had any gitch on.*

With the world dark outside of his window, the ember-red firelight gilds the edges of him. He's incandescent. I want desperately to kiss him, and then it hits me again that he's *right* here. He's back. He's real.

I can do just that.

"Please." I lean forward, and Dav obligingly drops to his knees close enough for me to drape my arms over his shoulders, and open my mouth to him. I'm perfectly happy to be plundered, held close and treasured.

"I want you," Dav says, with all the heat and honesty of a confession.

"You can have me," I promise.

It's true. Whatever Dav wants, he can have.

We'll work out the details later.

I slide my hands down to cup his shoulder blades and... *What the fuck is that?*

"Wait a sec," I smear the word against his teeth. "Back up."

Dav waits a sec and backs up.

"Turn around," I say.

His posture goes stiff. "Colin..."

"Let me see them."

He turns.

The lash marks are closed, at least. That's something. I lean forward and press a kiss to the biggest welt, angry pink and still inflamed, right along his spine.

"Barbaric," I say into his skin.

Dav hangs his head and wraps his fingers around my ankles, holds on like his life depends on it. Maybe it did. Does. I don't know. I don't even know what I don't know about dragons, as Dav keeps reminding me.

"There's little that can be done to hurt a dragon," Dav says quietly. "Take away their hoard, isolate them. But they will go mad of grief and loneliness in short order, and likely destroy their prison and kill many people—including themselves—in the desperate attempt to be reunited with those he calls his own."

"Fuck," I whisper, and shuck my shirt. I press my chest against his back, carefully, watching for any cues that I'm hurting him. When he sinks against me, I wrap my arms around his torso, press my mouth to the little ducktail where his hair touches the vulnerable knobs of his spine.

"Corporal punishment is..." he trails off. He pulls off my socks, curls his hands so his fingertips are pressed to the pulse in the arch of each foot. "It is a lesser horror to inflict."

"You didn't do anything worth punishing."

"That's not for you to say, Colin."

"It's for *you* to say, though, and clearly you only feel guilty that you got caught."

He winces. "It doesn't matter what I want."

"It matters to me."

"You're not a dragon."

"No, just a Favorite, whatever that means."

He lifts one of my hands, kisses the palm. Kisses my bare wrist. Then he turns to kiss the inner bend of my elbow, my bicep, my neck. He arches over me as he works my fly.

"It means you are mine," Dav says into my temple. "Mine to undress. Mine to protect. Mine to bed. Mine to love."

"Yours to serve?" I ask, and Dav jerks back, startled, kiss-chapped and flushed. "Babe. I know what a service top is."

"Brat," Dav says fondly, and whips my belt out of its loops with a swish of his wrist.

"I'm not calling you 'Daddy'." I shift so he can yank my pants down. Every accidental brush of skin as Dav undresses me leaves electricity in its wake. "It's weird."

"Agreed," Dav says, mouth latching to my inner thigh, sucking a hickey that I'll feel for days.

Nice.

I lean down and whisper: "How do you want me?"

His answer is to heft me up into his arms with a devilish grin. I whoop as he tosses me onto the obscenely luxurious four-poster bed.

Can dragons actually glow? Is that where the word "afterglow" comes from? Because if they can, Dav is just lousy with smug light. It's probably just the bedside lamps sparkling off his damp skin.

"Prideful," I accuse, wiping the sweat off my forehead. I kick away the covers he's trying to wrap me in, the possessive lump. The room is humid with sex. I don't want blankets.

"Satisfied," he corrects, sliding up to worry a bruise onto my collarbone.

"You mean your dragon-instincts are satisfied," I protest, and it's no less impressive for the fact that I have to stop to yawn in the middle of it. "You're taking care of me. You fed me, you gave me a spectacular orgasm, and now we're going to cuddle and sleep."

"Cuddle," he scoffs playfully.

"Cuddle," I insist, and burrow into his chest. His heartbeat is right under my ear, a slow three-chamber waltz I assume all dragon hearts dance to.

Dav *sighs*. So quietly. So contentedly. So... earnestly. It strikes like lightning, somewhere behind my eyes, pouring brightly down my throat, pooling warmly behind my heart. Is this what it means to be a Favorite? Is there something in the claiming that changes my own instincts, the way that it satisfies Dav's?

"Hmm," Dav says and I love the way Dav's happiness makes me all bubbly and stupid in a good way. "I finally get to be the big spoon."

"Only because you're being cute and kinky about it."

After that everything becomes a blur of skin, and heat, and kiss after kiss after kiss, as Dav gets his second wind, and applies himself like it's his mission in life to taste every last bit of my skin. He's making purring squeaky noises, which I assume is what all happy dragons sound like.

By the second orgasm, I'm flying high.

By the third, I'm ready to pledge my life to Dav, so long as he doesn't make me get out of this bed. I'm too noodle-limbed to even reach for the carafe of water on the side table. Dav catches my longing glance, and pours me a glass, holds it gently and tenderly to my lips.

It's sweet. It's service-toppy. It's perfect.

I am *so gone* on this guy.

Hydrated and content, I tuck up under his arm, my leg thrown over one of those glorious thighs. There's something intimate and trusting about the way he's letting me rest my soft dick on his bare hip. "Will you tell me now? What 'I did it again' means?"

"Tell you, hmm?" he asks, voice heavy with bliss.

He's asleep before I can elaborate.

Never mind.

I'll ask again tomorrow.

# chapter Twenty-seven

I quit. I had thrown five years of friendship in Hadi's face, like a complete fuckhead. I have no job to go to. And no reason to be awake.

So why am I awake?

There's no alarm. No one is knocking on the door. Dav closed the curtains. And yet there's light, right beside my face. Warm, golden light and the soft, gentle sound of birds chirping, and—

"You *asshole*—" I laugh, bolting up and whacking him with a pillow. "You got a sunrise alarm clock?"

Dav giggles. It's free and unfettered, and *thank god*. Watching the way his eyes squinch and that furrow between his eyes disappear sends desire unspooling down my spine. When I wind up for another whack, he yanks away the pillow and somehow gets me under him all in the same move and, fuck, *yeah*. I trap his waist between my thighs, and leer.

"Are you chafed?" he asks. Wow. A word like *chafed* should not be sexy. And yet.

"Bit sore," I admit. "But I could go again."

"Best not," Mr. Bossypants Top decides.

His fingers brush idly through the short hair of my nape. I need a haircut. I didn't mind it shaggy before, when it helped hide my face from the paps. But now, laying in this meticulous room, with my carefully groomed boyfriend, (owner? *boyfriend*) I feel unkempt.

"How's this instead?" I ask, getting a hand wrapped around both of us. His eyelids flutter. He scrabbles for the lube he'd shoved between the mattress and the headboard last night.

"You're being pretty fucking smug," I point out, neck straining as I lean up to keep my eyes on the prize. Not that he doesn't deserve to be smug.

Dav slips a pillow under my head so my neck won't cramp. "I have everything I've wanted for months. Years, if I'm honest."

One of his hands joins mine, slick fingers twining around us. "Years?"

"How long have I been coming into Beanevolence?"

The name of the café pierces the bubble of joy around my heart like a poisoned dart.

Dav twists his wrist *just so* when I don't answer. "Five hundred and thirty seven days."

I snort. "Not like you're counting."

"They weren't all in a row," he protests gently. "That was spread out over, hm, three years? Your schedule changed every semester, and—"

"Stop talking and kiss me, you dork," I groan.

He kisses me. "You started it."

"I know, and, hnnn, I'm regretting it. Just. Yes, like that. *Please* Dav, like that!"

*Like that* he does, and pretty soon he's rooting around for something to clean us up with.

It turns out to be a nice soft towel—one of a stack—in his night stand.

"Optimistic, much?" I ask him.

"Prepared," he counters, and reaches across me to turn off the fucking chirping clock.

When he moves to get out of bed, I octopus around him.

"Darling, I do have things to do today," he protests with a laugh.

"I already told you, I'm not a *thing*," I joke.

Dav sucks in a breath, clearly not taking it as one.

"It doesn't have to be like they say it is," Dav ventures slowly, sinking back into the mattress.

"What doesn't?"

Dav presses his other hand briefly over the side of my chest, right above my nipple, where the lapel pin would be if I were wearing my blazer. "We can let them think it, but we'd know differently."

"The point isn't that we know differently." I roll over to blanket his body, covering him from knees to nose, twining my fingers between his. He lets me stretch his arms above his head, kiss his chin, each bicep, the little hollow at the notch of his throat. "The thing that I take exception to is that *anyone at all*, including one of us in this bed, can, in the goddamned motherfucking twenty-first century, be considered an object to be *owned*."

"According to dragons, you are."

"No. That's not what we have, okay?"

"Okay," Dav agrees. I don't know how that will look outside of this bed—will he stand up to other dragons if they call me his property?—but this feels like a good first step.

"Can I at least tell people that I stole you?" Dav asks with a smirk.

"Stole?"

"Your mother is Scottish, your father was Quebecois. Lower Canada, at least in language, remains the domain of Louis-Charles Roi. Your parents immigrated into Elizabeth Regina's territory and I am the victor as a result. "

I snort. "Collecting humans is not a competitive sport."

"Says you." He rolls me over, bites playfully at my cheek. "Victory for the British over the French once again! Huzzah, lads!"

"I think Mum would protest the 'again'," I laugh.

"Would she?" he asks, and then sits back on his heels. He's got such a contented look on his face that I can't help but reach out for his hand. Warmth blooms in the hollow of my throat, and I swallow hard against the tears that threaten. I've cried enough lately. Even if they're happy tears, I'm not in the mood. "Will your Mum be upset that I'm British?"

"You're Canadian now, Marquess Niagara," I remind him. But his question is like a blow to the gut.

Will Mum like Dav?

Yes, I think she'll like the person he is.

Will she be alright with him being a dragon...?

That, I can't answer.

My family has been tentatively happy for me. But I can still hear it, in every phone call, over every text—*Are you sure? A dragon? He hasn't been back in weeks, mo leanbh, who's to say with someone like him? They're so different. They're not like us.*

Dav cares what my family will think. Before, it always seemed like the wrong time to introduce them. I was being greedy. I wanted to keep Dav to myself, for just a little longer.

And now.

*Now it doesn't matter what they think*, I realize. There's something both comforting and horrifying about that realization. *Liking him won't change the fact that this is a forever thing.*

*Doesn't matter what you think, either,* a dark little voice says, but I push it aside.

We're not doing this today. Today is going to be good. Just me and Dav reconnecting, and as much sex as I can get him to agree to.

"It'll be okay," I finally answer Dav.

*Eventually*, I don't add. He might hear it anyway, though.

He flips his hair out of his eyes, and slaps my butt playfully.

"Up, up, come on! The dawn breaks and the world awaits."

"Oh no," I groan and reach for the pillow to block out his sunny cheer. "Mornings suck, I don't care how nice a good morning grind is. No."

"Stay here until I'm out of the shower, then, lazybones," Dav says, and springs toward the extremely self-indulgent, and extremely fancy en suite.

I don't blame the guy. This place was built back when outhouses were still a thing. If I were him, I'd have converted the whole bedroom beside the master suite to a palatial bathroom, too.

Too trained by my morning shifts at Beanevolence to slide back into a doze, I decide I might as well try to get my clothes in order while I wait for my turn. I didn't fold mine like Dav did, and hope I didn't fling my shirt into the fire by accident.

I reach for my phone, still on silent, then I change my mind and leave it on the nightstand. I'm sure Hadi left me a scolding in my texts, and I'm not in the right headspace to deal with it. The rest will just be Mum and the twins checking in.

*Nobody knows yet*, I realize.

I let a strange dragon whisk me away on her motorcycle, because I was desperate to see Dav. In retrospect, it was pretty stupid. Good thing it actually worked out and I'm not dead in a ditch. Or chained to a wall in her own nest, or something. God only knows what would happen if one dragon decided to take someone that belonged to someone else.

Is that something dragons might do?

Try to take me away? For... reasons? Politics? Petty disagreements? Power plays?

Dav had seemed horrified when I suggested another dragon might try to horn in on his territory in the bedroom. Maybe that goes for the whole thing?

I have no idea what I've gotten myself into.

Right. Clothes. Focus on that.

I find *no* clothes on the floor, though.

What I do find is a bathrobe on the back of the door. Dav took his into the bathroom. I saw it. It's red. This one is hunter green. Which is a color Dav has told me I look good in.

Suspicion niggling, I open the closet. It's a walk-in, which doesn't surprise me, given the number of outfit combinations I've seen on Dav. What *does* surprise me is the section at the front. It's filled with dark-wash jeans, long-sleeve tee-shirts, a few dress shirts and V-neck sweaters, all in my size and colors.

I mean...

It's... thoughtful, right?

But also, just a little bit creepy?

Not up there with the worst gothic romance stuff I've read but... yeah, okay, I'm gonna decide to be flattered by it. It means he was living in hope. He'd been told we were never supposed to see each other again, but he laid in supplies anyway—clothes, lube, fussy little towels, and I bet my favorite shave gel is in the bathroom. I don't know when he *got* these clothes (did Sarah have to go shopping for them? God, there's fresh packs of *underwear* on the built-in shelf next to the hangers) but the fact he didn't throw them away means he had hope.

Hope that we wouldn't be separated forever.

Okay.

It's overstepping.

But it's also sweet.

*Overstepping for a human*, I remind myself. *Not for a toppy, possessive, service-kinky dragon. I guess? It's not like I have any other Favorites to compare notes with.*

Will I meet other Favorites? I hope so.

It would be nice to have someone who *gets it*.

If any of them *get* it.

*Stop thinking about it*, I scold myself. Today will not be ruined by me being grumpy about a few teeny tiny legal technicalities. *You woke up happy. Stay that way.*

*Just think of the look on Gem's face when you tell her the sunrise alarm clock worked.*

As our plans for the day apparently include tromping all over the farm, Dav is in honest-to-god blue jeans with a lumberjack plaid shirt. His ass in those pants makes my mouth so dry I need to drink two glasses of water before we go downstairs.

Breakfast, Dav tells me, is usually a spread for everyone on the estate. But because he's *crazy*, we're too early for it, and we'll have to fend for ourselves. And because Dav's PA is clearly as insane as he is, Sarah beat us down, and the kids—Nathaniel and Martha, both good Loyalist names—are stirring up a pot of porridge. Dav and I both accept a bowl, topped with maple syrup and cream, and join them at the table as the real sunrise crawls above the horizon. It paints the vineyard gold. I want to know everything about the way Dav runs the agricultural part of his estate, but my brain is nowhere near online enough to ask.

"It's too early," I complain theatrically. "Don't wanna."

"Master Tudor is always up earlier'n this," Martha tells me, and I bite my tongue.

No.

She doesn't mean it like that.

'Master' is just a polite way to refer to a... a young, unmarried man.

Fuck.

Dav looks both startled that the kids noticed, and ashamed. "I was up early so I could spend the mornings with Master Levesque," Dav says carefully.

"Then he stopped gettin' up at all an' sleeped all day," Nathaniel adds.

"Master Tudor was feeling ill," Sarah tells the boy, in a tone that says *We talked about this*. "But he's better now."

*Sleeping too much is a sign of depression,* the voice in my head that sounds like Dr. Chen reminds me. *But sleeping a lot is also probably a way to heal from being whipped.*

"Master Levesque," Martha starts, "I think you—"

"No," I blurt, interrupting her. "I want to hear what you think, but, no, decidedly *not* Master anything. Just Colin."

Martha looks to Dav, dumbfounded. Then to her mother. Both give her a look that says 'humor him.'

"Colin..." When I don't interrupt, she goes on: "You left your token in the kitchen. I polished it for you." She retrieves the pin from the front pocket of her overalls.

My blazer isn't on the chair, where I left it last night. I wonder if it will reappear in the closet next to all of those new shirts. This is not a habit I want to get into. I don't like the idea of making people clean up after me.

Oh, god, is some poor housekeeper going to have to put away the lube and change the sheets on the bed Dav and I thoroughly befouled? *Mortifying*.

"You should get a necklace, like me," Martha says, as I'm trying to decide the least stupid place to put the pin on my tee-shirt. She pulls a delicate golden chain out from under her own shirt and shows me the cameo-style pendant adorned with the laurels, rose, maple leaves, and flames. "It was grannie's."

"She's too young to wear it," Sarah says, watching my internal panic rising. "But she saw the necklace in mom's wedding photos and fell in love."

"And I'm really careful!" Martha says. "Even when I take it outside?"

"Ha! That's a big fat no." Sarah holds out her hand. Martha sighs, unclasps the necklace, and pools it in her mother's palm.

If Martha is too young, then Nathaniel is, too. But when I glance over, Sarah oh-so-casually lays her right hand on the table, showing off a golden bangle.

A wash of raw dread shivers up my spine. When I look at Dav, his expression is introspective. Is he plotting jewelry for me? He'd mentioned a signet ring. It could easily be a leather cuff. Or a dog collar.

*Shit.*

Yesterday, I had thought it would be nice, knowing that there's nothing and no one who could get between Dav and I for the rest of my life. That this was it. Endgame.

But this is the result.

Branded jewelry, and five generations of indentured servitude, casually dressed up like a cute little family having breakfast together. And this would *be* it—me, Dav, Sarah, the kids, whatever other servants were close enough to us to be afforded this casual relationship—forever.

"Don't you like porridge?" Martha asks, breaking into my panic. "We made the maple syrup with my class. Did we do it wrong?"

"No, it's fine," I reassure her, and shove a glob in my face.

It's *all* fine.

I'll make sure of it.

# chapter Twenty-Eight

When the vineyard caretaker Luiz Mendoza calls me "Master Levesque", I just say, "Colin's fine," and remind myself of Rule Four. This isn't exactly the kind of hard work I thought relationships would be, but I'm already in for the pound; might as well be in for the penny.

And Dav, joyful under the August sunshine, he shines like a new penny, too. He watches proudly as Luiz and I chat hectolitres and acreages, aphids and natural pest deterrents, and the virtues of grafting. We yap long enough that Luiz tuts and waggles a finger at Dav.

"Master Tudor, your nose."

"I'm fine," Dav says, childish petulance creeping into his tone. "Dragons don't get skin cancer."

"But a red nose will not be appealing to your young man." He winks at me. "Help me, Mast—Colin. He's a bad influence on the children."

The playful banter is endearing, and puts some of my worries about Dav's attitude toward the human beings his 'owns' to rest. This man, decades his junior, mother-hens Dav. And Dav is okay with it.

"There's nothing sexy about blisters," I play along.

"Dash it, I'll get the bloody hat!" Dav throws his hands in the air.

He turns toward a chicken coop that's hidden from view of the back patio by the natural rolling curve of the land—nothing in Niagara is ever *flat*—and before he can get a few steps, Luiz adds: "Since you're headed that way, take the feed with you, boss."

Dav spins on his heel, and eyes up a massive sack leaning against the end of a privacy hedge.

"That's too heavy—" I protest.

"Draconic strength," he reminds me, hefting it effortlessly onto his shoulder, and, okay, *yes*, more of this please.

"Nice," I comment as I enjoy the sight of Dav walking away. "You didn't engineer it so we're alone so you can give me a shovel talk, did you? Because like, Sarah already did that with her eyes over breakfast."

Luiz sticks his hands in his pockets, and offers up a shit-eating grin. "Tell me more about these Green Farming grants?"

"Very subtle subject change," I praise, and I proceed to do just that.

The crunch of boots on gravel gives me enough warning to face Dav as he approaches, and boy am I glad I did because it is a *sight*.

"There," Dav says, holding his arms wide. He's wearing a ratty wide-brimmed straw hat, like something from *Far from the Madding Crowd*. He looks so *stupid*. I love it immediately.

A lifetime of stupid, happy moments like this spool out before us; busy days filled with farmyard chores, and early morning porridge, and grapes. All of it meaning ultimately nothing, but at the same time are the fabric from which the *everything* of a contented life is woven.

Content.

Yes.

That's what I feel.

Aside from owing Hadi an apology, and my family an explanation, I'm content.

*Can I be content with being owned?*

Dammit.

The hazy golden bubble deflates.

No. I am *happy*, goddammit.

And I am going to stay that way.

Dav plops a similar hat, though newer, on my head. "You don't have the advantage of scales."

Luiz tugs a bottle of sunscreen from his chest pocket, and I attack the back of my neck, my pokey-outey ears, and my nose.

"If you had that, why did you...?" Dav starts, but then realizes he's been played. "Shall we start with the chickens, Mine Own? Seeing as I've just delivered their breakfast."

"Sure." I toss the sunscreen and a goodbye over my shoulder to Luiz. "I thought you weren't allowed to labor in front of humans."

"It's different when it's my own farm," Dav says. "It's not for them, it's for *me*."

"Sounds like splitting hairs bullshit to me."

"Hmm," Dav agrees, without agreeing.

We spend an hour at the coop, watching the calculated head bobs of the feathered menaces. The way they move reminds me that birds were once dinosaurs.

Some people think that the first dragons were actually dinosaurs, but like the way that some species will always evolve toward *crab*, it's been proven that humans and dragons evolved separately from some common ancestor millions of years ago. Us towards furry and mammalian, them towards scaly and reptilian, but in such a way that we became compatible enough again that, like *homo sapiens* and *homo erectus*, we can interbreed.

Although, like, *how exactly* dragons make babies—eggs?—is a guarded royal secret.

*Maybe it's ugly,* I think, imagining a big-ass egg squeezing out of a human-sized vagina. Ouch. I try not to imagine what it would feel like if a contraction shattered a shell.

Thinking about eggs makes me wonder if Dav has siblings. And baby photos. Or... baby *portraits*, I guess, seeing as he was born before cameras.

What did my forever-person look like before me?

Putting it like that, it seems immediately and vitally important that I've never seen his dragonshape. I try to recapture the sense-memory of his wings stretched over my head, his tail wrapped around my ankle, even the stab of his claws in my arm; every moment I glimpsed the other half of my other half. I've gotten into what amounts to a marriage without even having the important pre-cuffing conversations like if Dav wants to combine finances, or have kids, or whether he has horns.

We meander to the barn, where I'm distracted by Dav's gentleman landowner menagerie: a couple of grand old Clydesdales who still work the plows in the areas the electric tractor can't reach, a fat old sow, and a small gaggle of geese with a horrible leader who tries to steal my new hat. Dav lets half a dozen goats out of the barn to do their duty keeping the weeds and grass around the base of the vines cropped, and the low-hanging fruit eaten so the upper grapes develop sweeter. They also provide excellent fertilizer. We follow the goats down the path toward the back patch, dodging examples.

"I'm so impressed you do the thing with the goats. I love the thing with the goats."

"I know," Dav says gently.

The back lane is idyllic, bordered on either side with wild-flowers and the chest-height sand-stone walls that intrigued me yesterday.

(Did I only arrive yesterday?)

A field of vibrantly green grain waves gently in the mid-morning breeze. The world smells of evaporating dew and fresh country air. It's filled with the soft bleats of the goats and the tinkle of the antique bells strung around their necks, the hum of bugs whose names I don't know, but I bet Dav does, and the distant white-noise of the traffic beyond Dav's insulating walls.

It's romantic as fuck, so I reach out and snag Dav's pinkie finger with mine.

His answering smile is like the bright crescent of the sun during an eclipse.

Dav explains the terroir of the grapes, and how land has always been worked the same way here, mostly because he's a stick-in-the-mud. The exception being only the stuff that made it easier on his workers themselves, like introducing machinery as it was invented. Although, he admits, he has made some sweeping alterations of late to take advantage of the new understandings in sustainability.

The goats are left to their own devices, trained to wander home when it's milking time. Our ramble eventually leads us back to the house, where this mysterious cook has left a buffet on the kitchen counters. I meet more farmhands (I'm never gonna remember all these names) filling their plates and taking them outside to enjoy.

And through all of this, I can't get the thought of scales and tails out of my head. And yeah, okay, some of the thoughts are kinky—hello, I read draconic historical romances like they're going out of style—but mostly I just wonder what Dav *looks* like. By the time we've had lunch, and we've taken a wagon ride out to the middle of the vineyard with Luiz and his teenaged son Diego to tie off the new growth, I'm a man obsessed.

The second Diego and Luiz are out of hearing range, I blurt out: "Hey, can I see you? Is that a weird thing to ask?" I tack on at the last second, because I remember how strongly he reacted to my request to even visit this place.

"You do see me," Dav says as he ties a vine to the guide-wire.

"No, I mean the..." I don't say *real you*, because the human-shape version of Dav is just as real as the draconic one. "The scaly you."

It takes Dav a second to process what I'm asking. When he gets it, his whole face does the complicated wriggle I can't interpret, and the sides of his face flush red with little scales.

"Not now!" I hiss.

"Oh, no, certainly not," Dav says in a low gravelly rumble, and he cuts his eyes over at the others. I've asked for something sexier than I realize, according to the expression that finally settles on his face.

"But it's okay? To ask?" I check in.

"For you? Yes."

"And it's okay to show me?"

"Yes," Dav husks. The smolder he levels at me would keep him employed as a romance book cover model for years.

I swallow hard, and my throat is so dry it clicks. I reach for the water bottle Luiz had tossed at our feet and take a few strong pulls, trying to ignore the feel of Dav's eyes on my neck, the line of my arms. He takes his turn with the bottle and I turn away from the others to adjust the lay of my jeans as subtly as I can.

"Hey, slackers!" Diego calls. "Stop whispering sweet nothings! We want to get back in before the sun sets, eh?"

Dav and I hop to like naughty teenagers caught beneath the bleachers with their hands down each other's pants.

"After dinner," Dav says softly.

"Okay." Excitement, anticipation, and a small, hard ball of fear churn in my guts. Fear of what, I'm not sure. That maybe this will change everything? That maybe Mum was right, and I'll realize that we're too different, too late? That maybe it will change *nothing*?

I've never seen a dragon in the flesh. I have no idea how it will make me feel. What I do know is that I love Dav, no matter which skin he's in, and no matter what stupid rules his culture imposes on our relationship. I love him. And he loves me.

And goddammit, that's going to be enough.

When we get in from the field, Sarah informs us that our supper is waiting for us in the formal dining room.

"That's not necessary—" Dav starts, and I'm relieved to see that Sarah's comfortable interrupting him.

"It's getting cold. Go on, sir. Quick-time."

And just like that, we're being near-to blinded by the sparkle of an obscene amount of candle light reflecting off of mirrored crystal. Clearly, the mysterious and unseen Cook (whom I am starting to believe may be some sort of fairy-tale gnome) is a *romantic*. I'd be pleased with how into Dav-and-I-as-a-thing everyone is, if I wasn't having such a hard time with it myself.

"This is... nice." I try not to laugh as Dav grimaces at the flower petals strewn on the table cloth, the massive silver candelabras, and the excessive amount of silverware.

Dav walks stiffly into the room, clearly uncomfortable with the ostentation. Personally, I like that his staff feel comfortable enough to be silly. Nobody runs roughshod over him, I've noticed. His opinions are considered, and his authority respected. But Diego will tell him when he's doing something wrong, and Sarah manages him the same way she manages his schedule, and this Cook isn't afraid to make my first proper dinner here look like St. Valentine puked all over the room.

"At least they have us seated beside one another," Dav says, holding out the chair to the left of the head of the table. I let him tuck me into place only because he seems to be too preoccupied by the over-the-top display to realize he's being old fashioned.

And it's kind of cute, too.

"It'd be a bummer if I were too far away to be able to do this," I agree, as soon as he's seated, and reach out to tip his chin toward me for a kiss. "I meant it when I said it was nice."

"It's garish."

"It's funny," I correct. "They're teasing us."

"It's not necessary."

"It means they like me," I say, and wow, when did I become the emotionally intelligent one? "I'm glad they like me."

Dav softens. "Me too."

He starts pulling lids off of plates and the amazing aroma of roasted meat, savory potatoes, and buttered veggies fill my senses.

"This is all from the farm." Dav mutters. "Show off."

"Thoughtful," I correct. "Let's see how good you are at your job."

Dav says he rarely changes skins in his bedroom, but he thought I would feel more comfortable where we could be alone. It's not a strip-tease, but it's not a rush, either. It's sensual, back-lit by the fire, and it highlights each lean muscle and soft curve. I want to interrupt him, to kneel, press my mouth on the swell of his hip, cup his ankle in my hands, to kiss the spot where his belly button should be. Instead, filled with a wonderful dinner and half a bottle of Dav's delicious wine, I grab onto the side of the mattress to keep myself still.

"Are you watching?" Dav asks, hushed and shaky.

"Yes," I whisper back.

"Don't look away."

I'm worried it's a warning. That what's about to happen is going to be gruesome, like those werewolf movies, where you can hear joints breaking, the actor's face pulled back in a rictus of pain.

And then I realize it's only because if I looked away, I'd miss it. It's fast. And it's smooth, like a time-lapse of an ice sphere rolling around in warm water, smooth as glass and trickling into nothingness in an instant.

Silently, but with all the kinetic force of a weathervane suddenly pausing, swinging around, and whirring in the other direction, red scales appear on Dav's shoulders. They don't look like they're breaking through his skin so much as they're flipping over to reveal the ruby shine. The red starts on his back, washes around the edges of his hips, up over his ribs and shoulders, to end over his heart. Dav lowers his head, and suddenly he's on four legs, his chest powerful and proud, with a bright copper underbelly. His tail lengthens out from his spine, capped in that fleshy arrow, and topped with the sharks-tooth triangles of dark bone. His knees and elbows point in the opposite direction, and as he rises from a crouch, they grow spurs I can imagine would be excellent at keeping off challengers in battle. His hands and feet are now thick paws, and an articulated, backward-facing thumb. Each is capped with the curving black talons my arm had become so intimately acquainted with.

He shivers once all over, and two massive red wings rise up out of his shoulder blades. The sail of the membrane glows crimson with the firelight behind them, eight fingers—spines?—to each wing, and the apex topped with another bone spike.

His mouth elongates, becoming a short muzzle. His nose comes to an almost beak-like point, with another hard, dark spur rising up to protect the fine, vulnerable scales along the bridge of his nose and forehead. Unlike Onatah, there are no horns arching back from his forehead, but a pair of surprisingly mobile ears. Not quite like a rabbit's, but not quite like a dog's, they flex and swivel toward me, covered in an incongruous bit of fuzz which must be to protect them in cold wet weather. The edges of his jaw stretch into more of the hardened scale armor, tipped with tiny prickles. His tongue, when he flicks it out, is thin, split, and dark purple.

And his eyes.

They're still sunflower yellow, but now the iris has grown to take over the whole orb, the rim of his slit pupil dancing with a dark umber that flickers, as if the fire inside him is shining out. They remain more-or-less human-shaped, pointed forward, with a thick overhang of muscle and scales standing in for eyebrows.

I'm giving you the impression that this is a process made up of individual parts, that it was slow and I could catalog the changes one by one. But it's not. Everything happens all at once, and it is over in seconds.

Dav was standing before me, human and nude. Then he tips forward, and he's before me in all his draconic glory. Fast as a sneeze.

In humanshape, Dav is classically handsome, if lean.

In dragonshape, he's powerfully magnificent, the top of his flank easily level with my ribs, and his neck long enough that I would still have to look up to meet his gaze.

And speaking of those eyes, I was afraid that they would be beast-like, empty. But no, that's still my Dav in there. Still intelligent, still aware, and looking at me with trepidation and no small amount of shame. He ducks his head, and the wing closest to me droops, as if to cover himself.

"No, no." I stand, reach out.

Can I touch him like this?

Am I allowed?

Do I actually *want* to?

I freeze where I am, two steps from the bed, hands raised. Unsure of my welcome.

"You're lovely," I say, with as much feeling as I can muster. "Don't hide. I'm not scared." Okay, so my heart is beating like a jackhammer and my breath is bottling up in the hollow of my throat, but so what?

The gaze Dav levels at me asks, *Really?*

"Really." It hits me, all at once, that *this* is what I've promised my life to. And it isn't the actual dragon before me that leaves me feeling like I've been punched in the gut, so much as the heavy reality of what I'd unknowingly tethered to finally smashing into me after a day of *not thinking about it.*

This is it for me.

This is my everything, for the rest of my life.

And there's *no getting out of it.*

"Dav? I can't," I choke, reaching out for him. "I can't breathe–"

# chapter Twenty-Nine

When I come to, we're in a different room. A glance out the night-darkened window makes it clear it's been a bit since I...

Since I what?

Swooned like a fucking maiden.

Onatah was right: I *am* the princess.

My throat tightens again, and I—

Five things I can see: the back of a light brown, worn-out leather sofa to one side of me. A hideous popcorn ceiling, yellowed with age and tobacco. A brass-and-amber glass lamp hung in the corner. Orange shag-carpeting that has been worn flat. Wood-panel walls that I think are original, and very lived in.

The leather is buttery under my hand, well-cared for despite its age. My hair, when I run my hands through it, is sweat-dampened. My toes, when I wiggle them, are wrapped in hands, on a lap. There's a knit blanket, heavy across my belly, anchoring me to the world.

I hear soft music, something slow and jazzy. The soft, cautious cadence of breathing that's not my own. The creak of the house settling around us as the night cools off.

I can smell the cedar chest that the blanket must have come out of, and a faint whiff of smoky-amber of a dragon in human form. When I reach out, brace myself on the arm of the sofa, grab for the back of his neck, it's Dav I taste when he submits to my kiss.

"How are you?" Dav asks, when we part. He tugs at me until I'm leaned up against him.

I'm fragile in a way that I can't name. I want to burrow into Dav, live between his heartbeats, safe and unseen. Unjudged. I want what we have. But I don't want it the *way* that we have it. And I don't know how to tell him that, because he's so *happy*.

He showed me something beautiful, and breath-taking, and incredible. And the sheer scope of the truth that I was the one who got to see it, the meaning behind my access to his most intimate confidences, it scares the *fuck* outta me.

But isn't that what Dad used to say?

*"I loved your mother so much it scared me shitless, Colin. She walked up that aisle and I swear to god, it was the most terrifying thing I'd ever seen in my life, Helen in that white dress."*

*"Then why did you go through with it?"*

*"You know how there's good pain, and there's bad pain? Like a massage, and dropping a hammer on your foot?"*

*"Yeah."*

*"This was good scared. I didn't know what was coming, but I knew that we'd do it together, and that made it worth it."*

"I'm fine," I tell Dav.

"I thought—when you fainted... that I—"

"I'm *not* afraid of you. Okay?" I crane my head up to meet his eyes.

He looks unconvinced. "Then what was it?"

I squeeze the hand in mine. "Don't worry about it." Dav makes a noise that I haven't heard in a while, the annoyed click-growl. "Can't we just...not do this? Please. Just for tonight."

"Very well," Dav says, but doesn't sound happy about it.

This room is nothing like the museum-quality drawing room downstairs. This one is filled with old leather furniture and worn-out pillows. There's a jumble of remotes in a bucket on a glass coffee table. There's also a stack of romance novels—the exact same line of historical draconic romances that I'm not ashamed to say I have a delivery subscription to. I'd guess Dav got them specifically for me, except the spines are all cracked. Someone's been reading them.

At the top of the pile is the book form the hospital: *The Azure Ariki's Royal Bride*. Below that are books set during the failed American Revolution, the retaking of New Amsterdam by the Dutch, the Mexican conquest of California and Texas. All books set right around the same time Dav came to Canada to helm the Loyalist efforts against the fractured American forces.

"Shall I read to you?" Dav asks, when I pick up *The Scottish Duke's Reluctant Wife*.

"Isn't this treasonous?" I waggle the book at him. "An English dragon reading a romance about a Scot?"

"I'm Canadian, remember," Dav says playfully. "Besides, Raibeart Rìgh and Elizabeth Regina are mostly friendly, at this point. They meet once a year for tea on the Wall, you know. He's getting on, for a dragon, and David Beithir is by all accounts quite smitten with Anne Coronam Reginae.. So that bodes well for continued good relations."

"And a union of the British Isle via their heirs?"

"Heavens, no—two draconic monarchs marrying? Never. Anne shall have her Wales and England, David shall have his Scotland, Mann, and Iceland. And nothing short of a bloody coup would unite them at this point. And never for a moment suggest that Domnhall Mór-rí the Third ever succeed Ireland to British rule to his face, or he will take his great-great grandfather's sword off the wall to threaten you. I have witnessed it."

"Do they each have, um, an Own?" I ask, picking nervously at the book's spine. I figure if all this royalty nonsense is going to be a part of my life now, I should get it figured out, right?

Dav blinks down at me, neck adorably scrunched. "I forget that what is common knowledge among my family is not amongst yours. Elizabeth Regina's most favored is, of course, Robert Dudley, the Earl of Leicester."

"Oh, of course," I say, wracking my brains, but I'm coming up blank. It's not like I *read* the royalty gossip magazines I've been splashed across.

"Anne has her Grey Brydges. There was Castlehaven, for a time, terrible fellow, and none of us were surprised when she bit his fool head off. David is rarely without his own Elizabeth, and Raibeart's is, ah... Isabelle? Isabella? I've forgotten. And I regret I have never been close enough to the Irish court to be introduced to their king's Favorite."

Putting aside the part where the heir to the English throne *bit someone's fucking head off,* a sinking feeling grows in my stomach. "Are... is *everyone* in the royal family straight?"

"Heirs must be got."

"But... it's okay, right? This isn't going to be a *thing*?" I gesture at the invisible connection binding us together.

"It's different among dragons," Dav says softly. "It's less, oh, defined, shall we say?"

"But you *are* gay, right?" I ask, leveraging myself up on his chest so I can meet his gaze dead on.

"I'm in love with *you*," he says, which isn't an answer at all.

"So pan, then? Or bi?"

Dav draws me in for a sweet kiss that I let him have. "I'm yours."

*No,* the grumpy thunder cloud in my head corrects. *You're his.*

"Shall we read, Mine Own?" he asks, reaching for the hospital novel.

Labels aren't for everyone, anyway.

I let myself be coddled because he so clearly wants to be coddling me. As he reads, I wonder if he's going to dodge this question too or—

"Oh," Dav says softly, breaking stride. "That sounds lovely, doesn't it?"

"What?" I ask, realizing that I hadn't been listening at all.

"The Ariki's choice of token. He gave her a hair-bead. Though not quite in keeping with your fashion sense," he teases. "I think something more traditional for you, yes? How about a golden cuff?"

"A cuff," I echo, brain finally catching up to what he means. He's talking about something to replace the pin. Something to mark me as his.

*Owned.*

"No. Not a cuff."

*Too much like manacles.*

"A Favorite may wear a ring, but—"

"Too soon," I croak, struck by the other connotations of a ring.

"Right. As you say," Dav concedes, and if he's sad to hear it, he's turned his face away so I can't tell.

Over morning coffee on the patio, Dav takes something out of his pocket and puts it on the table between us. For a wild, gut-clenching second, I think it's a ring box. A tiny blip of rage follows because we had literally *just talked* about this and—

It's a phone.

It's *my* phone.

"Uh." I take a sip of my coffee. It's not *bad*, but it's certainly not dragon-roasted.

"Call your Mum."

I stare at him for a moment. "I know we're kinda working on the together-forever-thing, but I didn't think you'd start nagging me this quick."

Dav rolls his eyes at me, fond and exasperated. "You have hundreds of texts, Colin. Talk to everyone. Tell them you're okay."

I pick up my phone, frowning now. "You snooped?"

"You have lock-screen alerts on, and I only picked it up because I thought you'd left it on the nightstand by accident."

"Sure." I thumb it open. The easy morning calm crumbles into a shameful sinking in my chest when I see how many calls I've missed.

"It wasn't an accident, then?" Dav asks gently.

"Maybe," I twist out, flipping the phone over in my hands, fiddling. "I don't know what to tell them."

"The truth. I'm back, and you're spending some time with me to reconnect."

"I barely understand how I feel about all the paps stuff, how do I explain when I—Christ, Dav, I just... There's gotta be like, I dunno, Royal Watcher social media bullshit—"

"Tell them it's all bullshit, then." I look up at him, eyes on his mouth, loving the sound of curses in his old-fashioned accent. "Tell them the news has it wrong," he adds.

"Even if the news has it right?"

"The news *never* has it right," Dav says gravely. "Call them. It's a fine thing, to have a family who loves you."

I inhale at that, try to make it sound like a non-committal sound, when it was really a gasp of horror. Of course. I'm a selfish prick.

My family may pester, but Dav's literally whips him.

"Fine." I stand up to put some space between my... lover? Fiancé? Boyfriend? I have no idea what I should be calling Dav now. To him, I'm his Favorite. For me, he's my... there's gotta be a dragonish word for what he is to me now. Dav watches from the patio, and I know his ears are sharper than human ones. Walking away from him is really only giving *me* a sense of privacy, but I can live with that.

The first person I call is Dr. Chen's receptionist.

My therapist gave me a lot of great stuff to prepare for if I saw Dav again, but I need to resupply. Figure out what it is I'm actually *feeling*, and how to articulate it. I book an appointment for tomorrow morning, then hang up, and start scrolling through the endless pages of messages in the family group chat. They all basically amount to: **What did you do? Where are you? Are you okay? Answer! What's going on?** And, from Stuart, one of the last messages:

**If you don't answer in the next two hours I'm driving down there and kicking your dipshit ass.**

I run my free hand through my hair, turn my face up to the sky, wish I had remembered to put on sunscreen, and hit 'call'.

"The *fuck* is wrong with you!" is how Stu answers.

"I'm fine," I deadpan back at him. "By the way."

"I know you're fine, you're calling me. But Mum is *losing it*. Some photographer caught you leaving your apartment, and now you're in *Hello!* You're in *People!* Christ, Colin, you're on the goddamned *news*. And not like Entertainment Tonight. *Real* news."

"Oh," I say softly. "I didn't think they'd call out a manhunt for a missing person that soon."

"Manhu—Colin, the CBC is losing its shit about a royal wedding! Mum is boycotting Entertainment Tonight on principle."

"You know the celebrity gossip shows, Stu-pid. Mountains out of molehills. Besides, Dav's just a peer."

"Still a Tudor, though!" Dav calls from the patio. I flip him off and deliberately walk down toward the barns.

"Wait, what, *is* he in line for the throne?"

I groan, and scrub at my face, and explain that Dav is so distant a cousin that most of the British Royal Family would have to die for him to get anywhere near that crown. And thank god for it, too. But the thought that my family only knows the man that I will be spending the rest of my life with through shitty grocery store magazines curdles my breakfast.

"Hey, how about we set up a video chat soon, huh?" I ask. "You can meet Dav properly?"

"We could drive Mum down this weekend?"

"Uh. Maybe, um, maybe not just yet," I hedge. "Let me, um, talk to Dav about it."

"What are you hiding?" Stu asks, voice soft. He sounds like Dad.

Royal weddings. My forever person. And Dad's not here for any of it.

He'll never be here for any of it.

Fuck.

"Nothing! Just... we're getting caught up, okay? At his place. I've been..." *Acclimating to the reality that my boyfriend's people are going to see me as little more than a glorified pet.* "...hiding from the press. He's got a farm, with these tall walls. It's nice—"

"Yeah, I know," Stu snarls. "They keep replaying a clip shot through the *bars on the gate* of you standing in some second floor window looking wistful and shit."

"Say what?" I ask, head swiveling around to see if I can spot the glint of sunlight off of a telephoto lens. I can't see Dav's expression from here, but the line of his shoulders as he stands and marches into the house makes me think his hearing is better than he let on. Also, that somebody in security's about to get a strip torn off them. "Wait, is there like, a media circus parked outside of our front door?"

" 'Our'? " Stu echoes. He's been talking on speakerphone as he drives, but now he's pulled over. He cuts the engine of his pickup and the world goes strangely quiet and echoey.

"I... it's complicated," I say miserably. "Dragons."

"Yeah," Stu says. "I'm getting that. Hey... do you need me to come down there, *mo leanbh?*" He's trying to make light, but behind that I can hear the big-brother offer to beat up someone on my behalf.

"I'm fine." I mostly mean it. I can't imagine what might happen if Stu did take a swing at Dav. Dav would probably let him, in all honesty. And I do mean *let* him—Dav'd be able to block or duck away, before Stu had even finished swinging at my boyfriend.

Boyfriend?

Husband?

Keeper?

"And you do still love him? Even after the disappearing act? And all this media bullshit?"

I look back up at the patio, at our abandoned coffee cups and the side plates scattered with croissant crumbs. Then at the other wrought iron tables gathered around the kitchen door, where Dav eats beside—lives beside—the people he's hoarded, the humans who run his life, but who don't live their own subservient to his.

For a brief second, I wish Dav wasn't inside so he could hear me when I say: "Yeah, Stu. I still love him. Like, a gross amount."

"Okay. Fine." He blows out a sigh. "Call Mum. And if there's a next time, don't leave us hanging so long."

We say our goodbyes, I promise three more times to actually respond to the group chat, and then I repeat the song-and-dance all over again with Gem. Same accusations, same admonitions, same apologies, same promises. Same parting blow: "Call Mum."

Well, with my siblings building it up so much, now I'm *nervous*.

To buy myself time, I make Hadi the next stop on my Apology Tour.

"What," Hadi answers flatly.

"I'm a prick."

"Yes, you are."

"Am I still welcome at Beanevolence, or will you throw a pot of coffee at my head?"

"Are you going to come to apologize?"

"Yes."

"Then you're welcome. Dav too."

"Thank you."

"Should I have an apron ready for you?"

I look back up at the house. Dav is at our table again, sipping a fresh mug of coffee and staring off over the vineyards, pretending like he doesn't have his ear angled right at me.

"Not yet?"

" 'Not yet' implies a 'maybe soon'. Or is the Marquess Niagara hoarding you like a Kept Man?"

I swallow hard, the jibe hitting closer to home than I like. Dav hunches down in his seat. "That's a conversation for... for later. I'll text you when I know we're coming, okay?"

"Okay."

"I'm sorry, again."

"... me too," Hadi says softly. "For... for not stopping Pedra from taking the beans."

"That was a miscommunication."

"Min-soo is wrecked over it. And I should have talked about Pedra coming in with you—"

"It's your café, you can do what you want."

"It was still shitty to go behind your back."

"It was. But I forgive you."

"Thanks."

"Okay."

"Hey... you're safe, right?"

"I'm safe. I'm okay. I'm... fuck, I'm even kinda happy?"

"Okay. Shit. Wow. Okay. Talk to you later. Bye."

"Bye."

The call with Mum is harder, filled with tears and grovelling on my part, because I'm not the only one still suffering the trauma and grief of losing dad suddenly. The worry in her voice, the way she describes her desperation to get in contact with me, makes every organ I possess twist with guilt and nausea roil in my gut. I promise to never vanish on her like that again, and when she hangs up, I feel only marginally less like the shittiest son on planet Earth.

A few minutes later, Dav finds me leaning on the fence of the coop, watching the chickens and wiping my face dry.

"I like your farm." His arms wrap around my waist, his chin rests on my shoulder. I don't want to talk about the calls, and he lets me change the subject. "I like what you've done. The aquaculture is fascinating. I read an article about..." I trail off, clear my throat. "Sorry."

"Why sorry?"

"Uh, I get ranty about my hyperfocuses?"

"Colin—you don't think I know that?" Dav presses a kiss into my hair. "I've been going to the café long enough to be there while you were still studying. "

"Oh god—" I groan, letting my head drop forward both because of the way Dav's mouth is playing at the back of my ear, and also because I am mortified. "All those times I read my thesis to Hadi while we were slow."

"It was fascinating. You've got a flair for word-crafting."

"It's all the romance novels. Sorry."

"It was a delight." Dav says, and pulls the lobe of my ear between his teeth, gently. "I wouldn't have come back if I hadn't enjoyed it."

I turn in his arms, slide my own hands through his hair, and kiss him quiet. Or at least, I try to.

"The thing you said in the first chapter, about serving the community by serving the world—"

"You kinky motherfucker," I laugh.

"It's noble," Dav protests, but he's leering.

"I don't think there's a lot noble about basically shouting for three hundred pages straight—"

"I do," Dav interrupts. "And Luiz agreed."

"That's flattering but—*wait*, hold on." I push him back to meet his eyes. "Say *what?*"

"I did my best to remember everything you said," Dav explains, as if he's talking about the mundanities of reporting a boring office meeting and not *reciting my thesis to an actual winemaker*. "But I made rather a hash of it. Too much staring and not enough active listening. Luckily, I was able to obtain a copy after the university published it. Luiz was quite impressed with your diagrams for an aquaculture bed for... what's wrong?"

*Jesus.*

*Fucking.*

*Christ.*

No wonder I find his farm fascinating.

It's a living, breathing, *working* model of what I had laid out in my goddamn *thesis.*

Well, as much as it could be, when imposed on top of a pre-existing geography and... and... "Wait, wait, so like, all of this? You what, you did all this because...?"

"Because it was clever. And it sounded like it would work."

"You do the goat thing *because* I love the goat thing?"

"Precisely."

"This isn't just to get into my pants?"

"That was part of it," Dav says, and slides said hands down the back of said pants, giving me a healthy squeeze. "But I never could quite figure out how to broach the topic. 'Oh, pardon, Colin—I've barely spoken a paragraph to you, but would you like to come to my farm, which I've redesigned wholesale to fulfill your designs for an eco-conscious utopia?' That's a step beyond 'creepy regular'."

"Yeah, maybe." I scan the horizon, taking in all the vegetation, the smell of the barnyard, the sounds of the goats tinkling their way to the back fields, the soft cluck of the chickens, the warmth of the growing heat of the day on my face. "But, man. This is..."

"Is it a grand enough romantic gesture for you, Colin Levesque?"

"What?"

"Remodeling my farm is not quite the same as saving your sister from ruin, but if it's not enough, I am willing to go jump into the duckpond in only my linen shirt."

I laugh at the thought and cling to him. "This is *so much*."

I feel breathless.

"I wasn't lying when I said I had hoped, Colin. That I had... *wanted*." He pulls me tight against him, the long, lean line of him. I'm feeling overwhelmed, if I'm honest, and I'm learning that the grounding force of this embrace is a hundred times better at keeping me connected to myself than any weighted blanket. "Dragons play the long game."

"I'm getting that."

"*Without* any expectation of reward," he adds, making sure I meet his eye, that I understand that he did all of this knowing that I might say *no thanks*, and he would respect that.

But Christ, how could anyone ever honestly believe that I wouldn't...

I had spoken.

And he had *listened*.

I had dreamed.

And he had made it a *reality*.

"You know, I think this is the sexiest shit I've ever seen." I push him, gently, around the fence and back against the wall of the chicken coop, where we'd definitely be hidden from any lingering paparazzi. "I should thank you. Hm. I think I owe you a few."

Dav groans. "If we start keeping score, I'll—"

I don't know what he'll do, because I yank his jeans and underwear down all in one go, and kneel in the grass.

After, we're both flushed and panting, sitting in the lee of the coup. Dav is eying the empty upper windows of the house with mortification and no small amount of suspicion. I link our pinkie fingers and say, simply, honestly: "Thank you."

Dav gifts me with one of those sunrise smiles. "No, thank you. My land is what makes me a Marquess, as much as my military service. And when you saw it all yesterday, and called it good, and innovative, and clever, without realizing I did it all to your specification, it was the first time I've been proud of it in a very long time."

"What's not to be proud of?"

"It employs hundreds, and feeds a community, I see all that. But I also see... what it used to be. Who it used to belong to. This should be Onatah's."

"Your estate?"

"And beyond—the Dutchies of Windsor and of Toronto, Lord Hamilton's holdings, the lot. The whole peninsula, really. From the Grand River in Upper Canada to Glenwood Lake in Dutch North America. Before... before *us*, before this terrible, all-consuming need to subjugate the world, this was the territory of Hinon the Great Thunderer, the Serpent Behind the Falls."

"What, like the Maid of the Mist?"

Dav does laugh, now. "Onatah tells me that the colonialist interpretation of Lelawala is, ah, shall we say 'sensationalized'?"

"So, what, Simcoe stole all this and gave it to you?"

"The polite term is 'to annex'," he sneers. "The fighting with the Americans wiped out or pushed off the Indigenous dragons, and the elder Simcoe was... opportunistic. I was gifted this piece of it and charged with the protection of a vitally important location against Jefferson's 'mere matter of a march'," Dav says. He scoffs an unimpressed lick of flame. "For spearheading the Presidential Mansion incident."

I goggle at the thought of Dav being the one who set the match to the former American capitol building to solidify the Canadian victory. Or, probably, being the actual match himself.

Who knows what would have happened if he hadn't been there, and the Americans had won the war, or even if there'd been a stalemate. Maybe big chunks of the country would be American, now. Though I can't imagine New England or, like Pennsylvania, or any of the bits of Regina and Alberta that border the Mexican Empire as being *American*. To me, America will always be rippling wisteria, mint juleps and sweet tea, peach orchards, and that thick drawl.

"I could have declined..." He stops, stares out wistfully towards the Falls.

"Why didn't you?"

"It was offered in such a way that I was put in a rather difficult position, and could not say no. I thought I could manage the territory *in absentia*, but... no dragon may hold more than a single territory, per Elizabeth Regina's law."

"And you chose Canada over an ancestral estate back home?" I guess.

Dav wriggles, uncomfortable. "My word means something to me, even if Simcoe's did not to him. I signed that treaty on the battlefield. I promised to protect the interests of our allies—" he breaks off with a frustrated draconic hiss. "I just didn't realize that I would need to do so after the war's end, and against my own side. I accepted protection of a March, but it was not *this one* that needed safeguarding. Onatah's territory would have been stolen if I was not here to act as a stopper."

"You don't know that."

"Believe me, Mine Own, I do." He squeezes me tight against his ribs. "I think worst of everything, what I despise most is that they forced me to become some sort of archetypal white savior. It's distasteful. Although, there is one benefit."

"Which is?"

"If I had gone home to St. Ffagan's, I would never have met you." He sends me a sloe-eyed look.

"You romantic goober."

"I gave back as much as I could before Francis protested. Everything from the Escarpment to the riverbank remains mine, regrettably."

"The Falls themselves?"

"No. It would be abhorrent to control her grandfather's Nest. Onatah's territory starts at the river. But it's less than half of what it was." He snorts. "The government, they say she should not have it, because she doesn't know how to use it. That because she declines to *urbanize*, and factory farm, she is *wasting* the land." He spits out 'wasting' like it's acid. "They do not see her natural agriculture, or the sustainability of their lifestyle. The deep community they have. All they see is what I *lost*."

"Sounds frustrating."

"They speak about it as if I'm weak. As if it's a matter of will, or physical strength, or wealth. Just because I'm strong enough to take it doesn't mean I *should*. I barely have any contact with the general public supposedly under my care as it is. What would I do with *more*? A dragon oughtn't have everything simply because they *can*." He juts out his chin, stubborn, jaw clenched. "This is what rots empires. Rome fell to ruin because there's simply a limit to how far from the home nest a dragon's influence—both good and bad—can reach."

I think back to our book. "Is that why the Dutch couldn't get a foothold in Aotearoa?"

"Part of it," Dav says airily. He's doing that thing where he tells the truth, but not all of it.

"Your, uh, your opinion on this stuff... is that the thing?" I ask softly, resting my cheek on his shoulder. "The thing that they're mad about? The 'I did it again', thing?"

Dav kisses the tip of my nose. "No. I promise, I will tell you when I'm ready. But no. This is just something *else* that has not made me popular."

"Then why'd you do it?"

"We Welsh dragons have long memories, and we recall what it means to be conquered and stripped of one's language and culture. England colonized Wales long before they built their ships and left the island to steal an Empire."

"But your last name is *Tudor*," I point out, a deliberate dig at his earlier jibe.

"Ah, well, one can't choose one's patronym."

And then Diego comes and kicks the bottoms of our shoes and tells us to quit being such lazy Draconic Overlord stereotypes, and get to work.

# chapter Thirty

"**S**o, theoretically, if one was to want to get from, say, this house to, I don't know, Beanevolence, how would one go about doing that?" I ask as we're finishing up lunch.

Dav cuts me a funny look. "I do have a car."

"Oh? You didn't strip naked and fly to the café every morning? Clothes clutched in a talon, dressing furtively in an alleyway?"

"Of course not!" Dav gasps.

Sarah, who joined us for the meal to review upcoming picker hires with Dav, laughs up a storm.

"Rats." I snap my fingers. "There goes that fantasy."

"I can have the car brought up," Sarah says.

"The way you say ... oh my god, do you not know how to drive?" I twist in my chair to face Dav.

"It's... unseemly," Dav says, with that same wince he gets when he talks about draconic taboos.

"And not necessary," Sarah breezes out, focused on her tablet. "We have a driver."

"What if you want privacy?" I ask. Dav squirms instead of answering. I can tell by the way his eyelashes move that he's flicking looks at Sarah and doesn't want her to see.

"Wait, every morning, someone drove you to the café? Someone *always* drives you? They picked you up from my house? You did the backseat ride of shame? Was the rideshare from the hospital actually *your* car?"

Dav squirms more, and cuts me a pleading look that begs for me to stop. It hits me, all of a sudden, that Dav, the Master of the Estate, has to ask someone to take him places.

Like a child.

Just another way Lt. Gov. Dickface can control him.

"What happens if you say no?" I ask, facing Sarah.

"Why would I?" She finally looks up at me. "I don't control where Master Tudor goes."

"Unless I'm meant to be elsewhere," Dav adds softly, with that unhappy throat-click.

Sarah chuckles. "Yes, of course, sir. You did put me in charge of your calendar."

"So you *can* tell him he's not allowed to go," I clarify.

Sarah finally seems to hook onto my mood. "If he's meant to be somewhere—"

"—even if it's somewhere he doesn't want to be?"

"—I'm going to..." Sarah trails off, eyes bouncing between us, growing wider behind today's bright purple frames. "Sir?"

"Never mind Master Levesque," Dav says, standing. "Yes, we'll have the car please."

"No, not 'never mind' me. We'll have the car, but not the driver."

"Colin—!"

"I'm 'Master Levesque', but I don't get to issue orders?"

"The car will be around the front, sirs." Sarah says, disgruntled, and types into her tablet. Probably texting the driver. "Keys will be in the ignition tray."

"Thank you. And the next time Master Tudor asks to go somewhere and your schedule says he's not allowed, consult me before you say no. Come on," I say, head high and determination set, tugging Dav to the door. "I'm teaching you how to drive."

Dav twists around to say something to Sarah—probably an apology, I don't catch it—but lets me pull him out the door.

"Colin, that wasn't—"

"What kind of car do you have?" I ask, as we jam on our shoes. "Vintage Bentley? A Tin Lizzy?"

Dav huffs and the dimple makes a brief appearance. "Why not the new solar one?"

"The Helios? I didn't figure you for a gadget guy."

"Why would I not have an interest in environmental sustainability? I have generations to live on this planet yet."

A pang of sadness echoes behind my heart. That's a long time to be alone. After me, I mean.

*I hope he finds someone.* Maybe it should make me jealous, the idea that after I'm buried, Dav will kiss someone else, tell someone else that he loves them. Instead, I'm just wistful. *I hope he does. And I hope he's bigger in his own skin by then.*

And one way that's going to happen is by teaching him how to drive his own damn self.

Trying to hide the sudden gravity of my train of thought, I tease: "Oh, I see. Then pursuing me was calculated—you caught yourself a pet expert."

Dav rolls his eyes. "You're not my pet."

And then he Vanna Whites, and I follow his gesture to the sleek, discreet silver car crouched on the gravel drive.

"Holy shit, it *is* the Helios." I skip down the steps to run my palms across the solar-panel roof.

"Are you sure you don't want the driver?"

"I want you to learn."

"I understand," Dav says. "But this is her job."

"She can do something else."

"She wants to do *this*. This is what she requested when she came of age."

"The dragons bully you. I'm not letting you get 'managed' by your staff either."

"They're not staff, they're..."

"Hoard?"

"Yes. More like... family."

"Family that you own and order around."

"When have you seen me ordering any of them around?" Dav asks, taken aback. "You're the one who was issuing orders just now. You were rude!"

We glower at each other over the roof of the car, at an impasse.

"Fine," I relent. "I'll apologize when we get back, but you still need driving lessons. You can let the chauffeur drive you, if you want, but I'd feel better..." *About you getting cornered or trapped*, I think but don't say. "If you could drive in emergencies."

"Very well. If it will make you happy, Mine Own."

"It will."

I slide into the driver's seat, and run my hands over the dash. So many shiny buttons! The key fob, like Sarah said they would be, is in the ignition tray. I put it in my pocket right away, knowing I'll lock us out when I park if I don't. A passenger side door opens, but it's in the back.

"Absolutely not! Front seat, mister!"

Dav hesitates, closes the door, opens the front one, and folds himself inside next to me.

"Ignition, gas, speed gauge, rear view mirror, side mirrors, steering wheel," I point out as we buckle up.

Dav offers up an exasperated eye roll. "I'm not *that* helpless."

"Well, I don't know how long they've kept you in the back seat."

I turn on the car, reveling in the barely-audible purr. Gorgeous. I take us down the drive, nice and slow, talking Dav through it. He's surprised you have to micro-adjust the wheel as you go, that you can't lock your arms in place.

"Quite different from a horse," Dav says, as we wait for the gates to open. "They steer themselves, more or less. It was convenient after a long night. I had a lovely mare, oh, around the turn of the last century. I could tell the horse to go home, and nap in the saddle."

"And that worked?"

"Every time. She was spoiled by the groom and knew on which side her bread was buttered."

"So you were allowed to ride a horse around alone, but you can't drive yourself places."

Dav leans back, away from where he was watching my feet. He stares out the window for a few minutes, and then, softy, says: "You recall, what I said, about doing it again?"

*Finally.*

An electric thrill runs up my spine and I concentrate on the highway on-ramp, so we don't swerve into one of the deep grassy ditches. I want to take his hand. But I'm also supposed to be demonstrating good driving behavior, which means hands at Ten and Two. "Yes."

"In the aftermath of... that mistake... concessions had to be made. Rules had to be..."

"Obeyed?"

"*Established.*"

"Rules that include you being babysat literally every hour of every day?"

He shrugs. "Save for when I am in public."

"Like when it was just you and me at Beanevolence."

"Yes."

"Is it to keep you from something? Or to keep something from you?"

"The latter. Though..." he brushes my cheek with the back of his fingers slowly, so as not to startle me as I'm driving. "... it seems to have found me anyway."

*Jesus wept.*

"That's a lot to unpack, so either I'm pulling over, or we're scheduling this for later."

"Later," Dav says. "You have my word."

Dav's never broken a promise to me of his own volition, so I relax into the drive, relieved and satisfied that I'll have my answers soon.

The first thing Hadi does is hug me. Then she punches my shoulder. Hard. And then she hugs me again. Min-soo and Rajish linger behind the counter, and Dav makes small talk with them to give Hadi and I as much privacy as the front of the café affords.

"I'm an asshole," I say softly.

Hadi shakes her head. "We don't need to rehash it. I'm just glad you're okay."

Every tense muscle I have unwinds with relief. I didn't realize how much I relied on her to talk me out of my brain-weasel and steel-wool days, until I didn't have her to call up and ask if she had the bandwidth to listen. As much as I love hanging out with Dikimbe and Mauli, Hadi is, in all ways, my best friend.

"You looking for your job back?" Hadi asks, waving at Min-Soo, who starts making what I assume is a round of coffees for us. Hadi nudges me toward the black leather chairs.

"Do you need me?"

Beanevolence is a third full, about a dozen people read-ing textbooks or tapping away at laptops. It's not bad for a weekday morning during the school year, but nowhere near as jammed as it was when Dav was in the back. I glance over my shoulder—no, even Dav's regular table is empty, too.

Hadi shrugs. "It's nice to have experience on the floor, but if your sugar daddy—"

"He's not—!"

Hadi interrupts me with a cackle.

I huff and drop down into the chair. "Internet fame fleet-ing?"

"Isn't it always?" Hadi asks. "At least it was enough of a boost to the business that I got the last of the loans paid off. This is about our usual crowd, now."

"Hey, congrats," I say. "That's great."

"Thanks. So. Job—yes? No?"

"Job?" Dav asks as he slides into the chair beside me, grace-fully placing three mugs on the table. A tobio, a regular for Hadi, and a thickly frothed, caramel-drizzled monstrosity for me. Nice.

"What, Colin didn't tell you about his dramatic, apron-throwing tantrum?" Hadi teases. If her opinion of Dav has changed since he was taken away, she's not letting on.

"I didn't throw it!" I protest as I settle back with the mug cupped between my hands. "I placed it in your hands."

"Forcefully."

"Either way, you still quit," Hadi points out.

"But you're so good at this job," Dav says.

"Keep your kinks in the bedroom, darling," I laugh, patting his thigh. Dav huffs, a sort of hissy not-human thing that's partially a laugh. He lays his arm along the back of my chair and I lean back until my neck is resting on the inside of his elbow.

Hadi rolls her eyes, and I waggle my eyebrows, like, *Jealous that my man is awesomest? You should be.*

"Not gonna lie, it may be nice to have some, er, reason to leave the house, you know?"

"Hey, if you don't actually need it, Rajish wants the hours," Hadi points out.

"Oh, yeah," I say, suddenly glum. "That would be sucky of me."

"And your expertise is appreciated on the farm," Dav says. He and Hadi share a look over my head that reminds me of when my parents would talk me into accepting a decision they had already made.

Hadi may be the mom-friend but, *heck* no, this is not happening. I get bossed around enough by the twins. I'm not letting my best friends haggle for my time without any input from yours truly. "Hold up. I don't like where this is headed."

"So you *do* want to come back?" Hadi asks.

Dav frowns. "Surely you're not looking for the media circus to restart?"

"No, but—"

"And appearing in public with my token, there will be speculation."

"I won't wear it on shift."

"Colin," Dav chides gently. "You know that will cause more problems than it will solve."

"To be honest," Hadi cuts in, "I don't know if I could sustain another employee—"

"Okay! I get it! I'm not wanted!"

Hadi gives me the stink-eye. "Who said anything about 'not wanted'?"

"Aren't I?"

"You're not *needed*, Colin," she says patiently. "There's a difference."

"I'm not really needed back at the farm, either, am I?"

"Not precisely," Dav says. "Though Luiz would appreciate a paper copy of your thesis—"

A pit of horror yawns wide inside me. "Oh my god, I've turned into you."

Dav does that affronted-pigeon thing. "What do you mean?"

"I'm going to come here, and sit in that corner, and do nothing because I'm not *allowed* to."

"You're twisting my words," Dav says sharply, frown growing. "Don't exaggerate."

"But I'm not wrong. You're a... a gentleman of leisure who only came in to fill your days, and now that I'm... I'm *yours*, I'm the same?"

"Sarah fills her days just fine. Janet did as well, until you declared her superfluous."

"Who?"

"My driver."

Now I feel like an asshole.

Hadi pats my knee softly. "Hey. Listen, you've spent a whole year bitching that you don't know what to do with your life."

"Not a *whole* year," I mutter. Hadi and Dav share another conspiratorial look that makes it clear that they both take umbrage to that claim.

"And now you got what you wanted. Time, and space to explore your potential. And money—forgive me for saying so Dav—to take care of the rest while you do."

"No, by all means, you're correct," Dav allows. "The state of my coffers is such that Colin need not take employment for the rest of his life, should he so choose."

"But I don't want to be *useless*."

*I don't want to be a pet, to be coddled, and fed, and played with. But that's what a Favorite is, isn't it? They're just a living, breathing ornament.*

"If you want employment, a job title, a schedule, we'll arrange it," Dav says. "If you want none of those things, my income will provide for you. You don't have to decide immediately."

"Enjoy the honeymoon period," Hadi says, and I look up sharply, because, okay, how much does she know? Is she aware Dav and I are kind of dragon-married now? Or is she just talking about the nice part of the relationship where everything is a golden bubble and you can't keep your hands off each other?

I mean. Dav and I *can't* keep our hands off each other.

"Why don't you just come in every morning, and we'll see how it goes from there." Hadi says.

"Colin?" Dav asks me.

"If you think the paps'll leave off, then yeah, okay. Yeah."

"They'll leave off," Dav says, with a dangerous finality.

# chapter Thirty-One

We settle into a routine. Mornings we go to Beanevolence, surrounded by my friends, and sometimes come home to more blurry #Alvalin photos on the news or social feeds. Invasive as it is, at least we'll never have the problem of never having any photos together. Jeeze. In the afternoon, we work on the farm, surrounded by Dav's beloved hoard. In the evening, we play cards with the field hands, where Dav loses a small fortune in dimes (on purpose, I sometimes think), or the kids teach us the latest board game, or we tuck up in the hideous orange lounge, surrounded by one another.

He tells me stories about people whose famous names have become streets and parks: Jarvis, Brock, Pierpoint, and the other heroes of the wars he's fought in. I tell him stories about chem labs, and getting tipsy at tastings, and hijinks at the minigolf course on Lundy's Lane, which now stands on the place he'd once made camp and given orders.

For good or bad, it gives me a lot of time to think.

While Janet teaches Dav how to handle the car, I look out the window and think about territory, and colonies, and wars. When I pop back to my apartment for spare clothes and to pick up the mail, I think about property taxes, and how a small part of my rent had been landing in Dav's pocket, and I'd had no idea. While we sit in the front window of the café, and I pour over a freshly-printed version of my thesis and the freshest academic publications so I can update it, I think about sustainability, and a dragon's life span, and what it means to modernize so much that you slide into the past.

When I meet up with Dikimbe and Mauli at the bar, I think about how everyone can see my pin, and how my behavior will forever be the yardstick by which Dav is measured. When Stu laughs about some weird telephoto shot of me, I think about privacy, and the performative nature of social media, and what it means to be owned by the public. When I walk past the pharmacy and catch a glimpse of Pedra, I think about food allergies, and taboos.

When we get silly videos or photos of sunsets over the lakes from Onatah, I think about how beautiful the cities on her territory are, like something out of a solarpunk futurist's wet dream. I think about how her architects build up, not out, preserving the land and serving the people, all at once. I think about how much urban planners here could learn from her; how much I, personally, could learn.

Mostly I think about how dragons are so firmly interwoven into the fabric of human lives, and none of us understand how *much*.

**Never thanked you for driving me to Dav's,** I text Onatah in the middle of the night.

**You did,** Onatah texts back, which means, like me, she's probably having a bout of insomnia. **But I take your text in the spirit of searching for an opener. What's up?**

Glancing quickly at Dav, asleep beside me, I roll out of bed and pad down the hall to the hideous orange lounge, where my screen light won't disturb him. **? 4 U.**

**Ask.**

**Why r drgns so separate? Have feelin Dav wld rather not live behind walls. He LIKES humans.**

**He really does.**

I sink lower, glancing over my shoulder to make sure Dav hasn't come looking. Even though it's only texting, it feels like I'm cheating on Dav a little. But I want dirt on him that only a friend can shovel.

**Dav hates walls**, I agree.

**First, you gotta know that Dav's young, okay?**

**?! He's 263!**

**Young. Which means he's enthusiastic about humans. Hatchlings love you guys.**

**Like kids like puppies?**

**No**

Well, at least Onatah isn't into the pet analogy. Thank god.

**So...?**

**We do best when we have a person. We're creatures of the air, and fire, and water. We're all over the place until we find a human to be our ground.**

*So less like a love match, and more like a compulsion?* Dav called it his 'stupid draconic instincts' and I'm wondering how much they had to do with us falling for each other. I asked Dav once why he liked me, and he'd given me the pretty line about caring, but it might also have been just because I was available to be the target of this instinct.

I'm okay with that. Humans have stupid instincts that want them to hook up at the biological level, too. Doesn't mean the relationship that grows out of it isn't as real.

**Do you have a person of your own? Can I meet them?**

**No.**

**No, you don't have one, or no, I can't meet them?**

**Dav's British.**

*Nice dodge.* **???**

**They all have sticks up their asses. They live in impenetrable mansions, separate and utterly unknown to the humans in their territory. Get me?**

Something... something is so close to clicking...

**0 I C,** I text.

But I don't.

I wake to Dav draping the sofa-blanket over me. "You can sleep longer. You were up late."

"Couldn't shut off my brain," I confess, scrubbing my eyes. "Lots to think about."

"You have been quiet, lately." Dav runs the backs of his fingers down my prickly cheek.

"Lots to think about," I repeat and sit up.

"There's no plans today."

"Kinda is, if you want this to be our 'later'."

He sits on the coffee table so we can meet eye to eye.

"I'm not letting you off the hook," I say softly. "But if you're uncomfortable, maybe you could write it down?" Dr. Chen had suggested this method, to help me lay out my feelings to Stu in a way he couldn't interrupt or derail.

"No, no," Dav says. "I've stalled long enough. I want to tell you, but... I'm struggling to find the words. I wish I could..."

"What?"

"It's selfish." He nudges forward, down onto his knees, and mashing his face against my chest. Hiding. "I wish I could ask you to promise to not be afraid. But that's not fair."

"I'm not afraid of you. Your scales, the fire, none of it scares me."

"No, not..." he says softly. "It's...other things."

I pet his hair back from his temples. It's still damp. He hasn't done his flippy-flappy morning hair-drying routine. It's ballet and porn, all at once. God, his hands. The way they carry, and lift, and touch. Styling hair. Petting goats. Sifting coffee beans. Pulling espresso. Even when he's accidentally lightly stabbing me, I love them. I lift one of his hands to my mouth.

"Colin." He breathes my name softly, like a benediction.

"I fucking love your hands," I tell him, because he deserves to hear it.

"You may not want me to touch you again, after I explain."

Moments like this one, where we were both still sleep-muzzy and warm, it feels like I might overflow, like there's no way I'll ever find room for all of this... all of *this*. But maybe I'll expand, somehow, to hold it all under my skin, close to my heart. I'm Dav's ground, and his gravity, and his center. And he's my air, and my laughter, and my heat.

"So explain, and maybe let me decide for myself?"

But he's not meeting my eyes. I know how sometimes it's easier to say big things when you don't have to watch people's faces as you do, so I don't mind. He shudders, inhales, takes the offering for what it is. "I don't want to lose... Our lives are so... our home is..."

"'Our' home," I repeat, and I meant for it to sound sarcastic, but instead, wrung out on overthinking and sleeplessness, surrounded by the smoky-amber scent of happy dragon, it comes out more awestruck and quiet.

"Of course, 'our', Colin. Everything mine is yours now, too." I nip his ear. "So, this *is* a marriage."

"You are determined to apply human terms to everything that we are, Mine Own," he says, but it's not unkind.

"Just trying to understand."

"Has Onatah been a good instructor?"

"What?"

"She is my best friend," Dav says, looking up at me. After a beat, he adds: "After you. She was worried you were tying yourself into knots. Of course she texted me."

"Gossipy lizards. Does she have a Favorite?"

"Yes."

"I asked if I could meet them and she said no." I offer up the most theatrical pout I can manage.

"One day," Dav promises. "Perhaps we can... host an event. To celebrate your taking my token."

"Babe, we call those weddings."

"Ha ha ha," Dav says.

Strangely, forever with a dragon doesn't sound as terrifyingly permanent this morning as it did a few days ago.

"But, uh, before we start auditioning bands and sampling cake, maybe we could do something smaller?"

"What are you thinking?"

"I'd like to have some people over. Just my posse-Dike, Mau, Hadi, maybe Min-soo? All people you already know."

Dav makes that thoughtful *prrrowt* noise. "I suppose... perhaps, an evening thing? Out among the grapes?"

"Not in the house?" I watch him carefully. He did say it was uncouth to let humans that aren't his into his nesting grounds, but if we're going to be even in this, if we're going to be equal, I want my friends to be able to visit.

Of course, he *knows* I'm gauging his reaction, so his face goes blank.

"Okay, not in the house," I concede.

He lets out a breath. "I am sorry," he starts.

"Whatever makes you comfortable," I interrupt, and it's true.

"It must seem wretchedly unfair—"

"No, actually. I get it. Small steps. Between the two of us, who has the therapist?"

Dav winces. "The more I hear of Dr. Chen, the more I wonder if I should make an appointment."

"Would you?" I ask, trying not to sound too enthusiastic.

I mean.

I love him.

But my dragon needs someone to talk to, STAT.

"Perhaps a draconic therapist," he concedes. "I'll have Sarah look into it."

"That's all I ask."

Dav squeezes me close. "You ask a great deal more than that."

"Like an informal get together among the grapes," I tease.

Dav squirms, which does interesting things where he's pressed against my thighs.

"Why so insistent?"

"I want to show you off. Rebekah is dying to meet you."

"The ex with the excellent sartorial taste?"

I kiss that beautiful multisyllabic word out of his mouth, leaving a dimpled smile behind.

"Don't be jelly, babe."

"I'm not... jelly."

"Good."

"And perhaps she can give our shopper advice," Dav says. "Your taste is wretchedly hard to pin down."

"Ah!" I laugh. "Can't name what doesn't exist."

"Your taste?"

"Bingo."

"What about inviting your family?" Dav ventures coyly.

"Friends first. The horror of the Levesques, second."

"Horror?"

"On my part," I clarify. "Mum'll bring baby photos, and Stu will tell you it was not his fault the dock came unmoored, and he is full of shit so don't you believe him for one second, and Gem's gonna eat you alive."

"Sounds delightful," Dav says, with a dopey, dreamy look on his face.

He's asked tons about my family, but I've never heard a thing about his, except passing mentions of distant cousins, or far-off ancestors.

"So, uh, hey," I say, trying for casual and sounding the exact opposite. "What about, um, your family?"

Dav goes still again. "They're in Wales."

"I don't mind long flights."

"I don't know if..." he trails off, cornered. "Father has had to take on so much, recently. Perhaps nearer to the holidays, when they'll have the extra staff in. We'd be less of an imposition."

"It wasn't a demand," I say gently. I take his hand and kiss the tips of his fingers. "I'm in no rush."

"And mother is..."

"Passed?" I ask, heart seizing for him, that he can't say it. That I know how he feels.

"Brooding. I'm to have a sibling."

"Oh! When?"

"Anytime in the next decade," Dav says, casual-as-you-please, and *fuck me.*

He could be a big brother, like, tomorrow, or... or when I'm in my mid-thirties.

"Well," I say shakily. "Um. Yay? And that's normal, then? One, uh... baby?"

"Egg," Dav confirms.

"One egg at a time?"

"Generally. I am an only child. For now."

"Looking forward to it?"

"I believe so." He cups my ass playfully. "Though I ought to ask Stuart and Gemma for advice on being an older sibling."

"Please. Don't."

"So, it's not in good taste to unmoor a dock—"

"It wasn't me!" I protest.

We laugh and tussle, and it's not until we're downstairs, partaking of the workers' breakfast that I realize how neatly he had talked his way out of answering the "done it again" question.

Damn, he's good.

# chapter Thirty-Two

"This isn't a Halloween costume," I complain, as Dav ties my neck-cloth for me. I love period romances, but I have no idea how to get into the dandy clothes. Luckily, Dav has lots of practice. "Halloween costumes are supposed to be bloody, and scary, and stupid."

"It's not a Halloween party," Dav reminds me, eyes on what his fingers are doing. I haven't seen any difference in the three other ways he's constructed the knot every time he's stepped back to assess my reflection in the mirror, but he is now on his fourth go-round. "It's an All Hallows Eve Masque, which is entirely different."

"I want to stay and hand out candy."

"We don't get trick-or-treaters."

"Then let's go to Beanevolence—"

Dav looks at me sharply. "You know why we can't. I don't want to do this any more than you do, darling, but we have no good reason to decline the invitation."

"Sure we do. His Excellency is a prick."

He pecks a kiss off the tip of my nose. "True. But as that's not a new development, we cannot use it as an excuse."

I grumble, but sucking up to Lt. Gov. Bossypants is part of the game.

"There now. What do you think?" Dav asks, turning us to the mirror.

He looks delicious. He's in bleach-white stockings, and delicate black shoes with a slight heel. His waistcoat is as red as his scales, which he's let out a little so that ruby fire reflects around the edges of his face, and the back of his hands. His breeches and cutaway tailcoat are cloth-of-gold brocade, the same shade of deep shimmering yellow as his eyes.

I am, of course, dressed to complement Dav, because that's my role in life now.

Ugh.

And yeah, okay, it's flattering, I guess. But if it were me, instead of a cobalt blue tailcoat embroidered with Tudor Ros-es, and a dusty yellow waistcoat, I'd be going for something a lot more *Nightmare on Elm Street*. That's how I prefer my Halloween: fake blood, glitter, glow-in-the-dark-shots, pumping music, strobe lights, candy and condom bowls in every shadowed corner.

Not Regency recreations and delicate gold wire-work masks that perch artistically over half our faces. The crafts-manship is impressive, especially the way Dav's mask seems to highlight the scales along his forehead. But *fire and water* isn't a costume, it's a concept.

Apparently, it doesn't have to make sense. It just has to be pretty.

We leave after an early dinner to make it to York, and the Lt. Governor's summer mansion at Castle Frank, for sunset. Yes, Simcoe's mansion is called *Castle Frank*. To be fair, his father named it.

"You know he picked this theme because I hate it, right?" I grumble as I try to get comfortable in the back of the car. It'll be two hours and I am already not enjoying the way the waistband is cutting into my ribs.

"Shockingly, Mine Own," Dav says as he hangs his coat from the peg above the car door. "Not everything is about you. Last year the theme was the Twenties. I'm sure the party-planner meant Gatsby, but more than a few people dressed as plague doctors."

"Were you one of them?" I ask, as Dav leans over to help me struggle out of my coat, too. I should have done it before getting in the car.

The twinkle in Dav's eye is answer enough.

I'm feeling more relaxed by the time we get through urban Toronto and into York proper. Janet is wicked funny and tells the most elaborate, ridiculous stories about her amateur dirt bike circuit. By the time we're at Castle Frank, my stomach hurts more from laughing than it does from the breeches.

I know better to expect an actual castle. But to drive up a gravel road through a regimented pine forest, slowly winding up little hills to the highest point, and find what is basically a glorified log cabin is a disappointment. Sure, it's shaped like an ancient Greek temple, columns and all, but it's still a log cabin. I expected it to be showy.

"While his Excellency is a nagging stickler, he's not a nouveau riche boor," Dav mutters to me when I make this observation. We're standing on the drive and he's helping me back into my coat, which is too damn tight for me to manage on my own. Of course, he can put his coat on alone, but this shit was the height of fashion when he was young. He's got practice.

"Not a boor. Just a Family Compact snob."

"Mine Own," Dav huffs. Then he comes around the front of me to adjust the lay of my lapels. "Peace. We're here to appease, not challenge."

"Yeah, yeah," I grumble.

"Here," Dav says, handing Janet a black credit card through the window. "Take yourself somewhere lovely for dinner. We'll text when we're ready."

Janet grins. "Thanks, sir."

As she pulls away, another limo comes up the drive. It would be weird if we were still dawdling on the steps when they pull up. So I square my shoulders, screw up my courage, and let him lead me on.

Favorites don't *have* to stand a few steps behind a dragon, but Dav thinks it would give the old-fashioned dragons in the room a favorable impression if I did so, at least when we enter. I hate the idea that I'm supposed to behave as if I'm grateful to be able to toddle along in his wake, but we *are* here to appease.

Not to challenge.

Not yet, at least.

At the top of the stairs, we're met with grandly carved wooden doors depicting scenes of early 1800s post-war bucolic bliss. In the bias relief, farmers trade swords for plowshares; the Failed Rebellion of 1837 is put down; shackles fall away from the wrists of grateful enslaved Africans; Indigenous humans lead settlers to happier lands; and glorified portraits of the ten Fathers of the Family Compact, the dragons who came up with our system of government, and guide it all benevolently. The dragon's names are inscribed into their hides so the observer knows who each is. As if any kid who went to school in Upper Canada wouldn't.

The scene is a mix of things I consider genuinely celebratory, and things that anger me now that I'm in the middle of the game, and have a better understanding of draconic politics.

The door reminds me of the front gate at the farm. Is this a thing all dragons do—lay out their accomplishments in figures and façades, so anyone entering their nesting ground knows who they are, and what they've accomplished?

If so, it's telling that Dav's is devoid of any depiction of violence. The thing he is proudest of, the thing he wishes to show the world, are his accomplishments in wine-making and farming. All the human figures on his gate are fat and cheerful, and the dragon's wings are outstretched to protect them.

In the center of this door, the dragon depicted is more cat-faced than Dav, with prominent nostrils and ghoulish eyes. The body is serpentine, but the legs and tail are lion-esque, with a sharp-spined sail down the back. According to the little name carved into the scales, this is Simcoe the elder.

I wonder how much it burns Francis to walk through his father's doors. I bet Chorley Park's are bigger and more elaborate. Francis strikes me as the kind who needs to one-up his dead dad.

When we reach the top of the steps, two honest-to-god-footmen pull the doors open for us. We're greeted with a blast of warm air, and the sounds of a live orchestra playing somewhere in the depths of the building. We step into the vestibule, filled with tastefully spoopy flower arrangements on pedestals. We take a moment to smooth out each other's jackets, and adjust our masks.

"Now, Mine Own, when you're introduced, no handshakes. You may not touch the skin of another dragon. It's—"

"Onatah's already told me."

"She has?" Dav asks, startled. "I'm grateful, it's—"

The next set of doors, opened by another pair of footmen—oh my god, their jobs must be so boring—depriving us of privacy. Whatever Dav is grateful for, I don't know. But as long as I don't touch anyone, I won't break any more dragony taboos. That's all that matters.

The vestibule deposits us in a room that looks more like a large drawing room than the sort of grand affair I assumed Lt. Gov. Poshbritches would go in for. The floors are gleaming dark wood, the walls paneled in the same, and there's an absolutely massive fireplace taking up most of the far wall. There are two doors, one on either side of the open hearth, and I can see right through the fire to the ballroom beyond.

The front room itself is dotted with spindly, fancy conversation sofas and delicate tea tables, antique and uncomfortable. Despite that, there are a few people taking advantage of them, sipping from fancy glasses, dressed in their own colorful versions of the masquerade historical attire from every century. The decorations here match the room—tasteful wire-work bats, orange glitter gourds piled like a television decorating hostess herself had fairy-godmothered each one, and a galaxy of paper lanterns in the shapes of stars and all the phases of the moon hanging from the ceiling. The fire is burning green from some additive, and it's a cooler effect than I expected to find in Simcoe's party cabin.

Dav enters first, and immediately what I had assumed was just a large group of people chilling by the entrance rearranges itself into a receiving line. Dragons in front, humans lined up just behind them—some in the same livery as the door guys, some in costumes, and one holding a big silver tray of champagne flutes I don't want anywhere near me in case the trashfire part of my personality flares up. That's a lot of breakables.

Around the room, several people lift their faces, not exactly as if they're sniffing the air, but more like someone had strung a wire between them and Dav, and then plucked it. They're all dragons. I can tell because they've got that deeply magnetic air about them. That, and a smattering of their scales are out, too.

They all incline their heads politely, adding a flourish with their hands beside their faces that evokes a lick of flame. Dav returns the gesture, grave and performative.

"What was that?" I whisper.

"Just a hello."

"Oh. Should, I, uh, do the same?"

"No. When you've been presented formally, bow at the waist, with a fist over your heart."

"Ugh," I reply.

Dav cuts his twinkling grin at me. "Indeed."

The lamplight shines over his scales, cute wee ones running up the shell of his now-slightly-pointed-ear, winking like garnets. Here's another way Dav's different. Everyone else's scales are all shades of blue, green, and brown. I don't see any other red. Is it because Dav's descended from that important Welsh guy?

Now's not the time to ask, though, because suddenly we're standing in front of Simcoe.

*You whipped him*, I think suddenly, the intrusive black thought pressing hard against the inside of my skull. Something about my vibe must change, because Dav rests his hand on my elbow, a soothing, gentle message: *He's not worth it.*

I school my expression as best I can. I may hate the man, but it's not a good look.

Simcoe is at the head of the receiving line, dressed in a resplendent cloth-of-silver outfit absolutely sagging with military braiding, and a silver mask worked up to look like the moon. The woman next to him, also a dragon, is in copper and red, evoking the sun.

"Ah, and here are our men of the hour. Everyone is dying to meet your little conquest, Alva," Simcoe says, without even looking at me.

"I'm honored to be in your presence again, Your Excellency," Dav says, formally. He bows deep, at the waist. I follow with what is probably the awkwardest bow in this history of awkward bows, to a man I truly despise. It's made harder by the fact that I'm not used to heeled shoes, and I tip forward more than I thought I would and have to shuffle to catch myself.

Ugh.

"Oh, none of that, now," Simcoe says, with a joviality loud enough that it's clear he's speaking at volume deliberately. He wants to be overheard. "Old Etonians like us, chum. No need for such formalities."

Of fucking course they went to fucking Eton together.

"Very well, Frank," Dav says. "Lieutenant Governor of Upper Canada Francis Simcoe, may I make known to you Mine Own Favorite, Colin Fergus Levesque, son of Helen MacTavish of Edinburgh and Jean-Francois Levesque of Laval. He bears proudly the insignia of my clan, and enjoys the hospitality of my home, my bed, and my protection."

*Oh, sure, just tell everybody in the room that we fuck on the regular. No, no, that's not even remotely mortifying.* I can feel my ears getting redder and choose one of the buttons on Simcoe's waistcoat to stare at so I don't have to meet the eyes of anyone who may be wondering what kind of a lay I might be.

"Welcome, Mister Levesque," Simcoe responds, as if butter wouldn't melt.

"Uh, yeah, thanks," I mutter.

"My wife, Georgiana," Simcoe says, gesturing, and I raise my eyes to the elegantly attired woman standing beside him. She's speckled with scales in shades of forest-green, and so are the dragons dressed as constellations in the receiving line after her. "And my daughters Florence, and Anna."

Just behind each of them stands someone I assume is human, in various shades of skin tones and genders. They're staring with blatant curiosity, and inclining their heads as their dragons are introduced. Simcoe didn't even mention their names.

*Snob*, I decide, making a point of meeting each of their eyes.

"John?" Dav asks, nodding attentively with that little finger flick to each of the ladies. I return their nods with shallower bows, hand over my heart, and it seems like that's the right thing to do because nobody comments.

"Ah, my son couldn't get away from Ottawa," Simcoe says congenially, and pats Dav on the shoulder, like it's a tough break. I've never heard Dav mention John Simcoe the younger before, so I can't imagine they're close. "You know him. Up to his ear tufts in politics, as always. We've now got airplanes that go so fast he could be here in an hour, but no, he won't leave that Bytown cabinet for love or money."

Dav chuckles, as he's expected to do, at what's clearly a worn-out family joke.

And then Simcoe refocuses his gaze on me. "Speaking of devotion to one's scholarly pursuits, how are you finding Fynyth?"

"Oh, uh, just fine," I lie as convincingly as I'm able, shooting Dav a puzzled look.

*The farm*, he mouths back.

Oh.

Oh, of *course* his cute little farm has a fancy name like 'Pemberley.' I'd pinch him for keeping me at a disadvantage, except that Lt. Gov. Shitface is pleased I'm on the backfoot.

"Perhaps we can get you from 'fine' to 'happy' tonight." He makes a sort of absent-minded flapping motion over his shoulder. "I've asked my Favorite to take special care of you this evening."

A woman steps out of his shadow, and I realize I am a terrible person. I had been ignoring her exactly as everyone else had been ignoring me while acknowledging Dav.

She's white, cutely plump, shorter than me, with a mess of dark hair pinned up in an elaborate cloud of curls. 'Cloud' is an apt description, because she's dressed to match the Simcoe family—as a tinkling raincloud. Sapphires drip from her dress, sparkling as she moves.

She steps around Simcoe and offers me her hand to shake. I cut a look at Dav, and he nods encouragingly, so I take it.

"It's permitted between Favorites," the woman says, dark eyes amused by my hesitation. "That's why everyone's scales are out this evening."

"Uh, that's thoughtful, I guess," I say, and place my palm in hers.

"A pleasure to meet you, Colin Levesque." She pumps my arm once, firm and self-assured. "I'm Laura Secord."

# chapter Thirty-Three

"**S**orry?" I ask, freezing. "Did you say Laura Secord?" I let her hand go, feeling like a complete tit, and wipe my now-sweating palms on my thighs as discreetly as possible. Which is to say, not at all discreetly. "As in, the chocolate?"

She tilts her head impishly. "Mr. O'Connor named his company in my honor, yes."

"I hope they pay you your imaging license fees in chocolate, at least," I say, which is a stupid thing to say. My whole brain has been thrown for a loop and all that's coming out is my Mum's small-talk platitudes. I try to reboot, but my mouth keeps running. "I, uh, just tried it for the first time, you know. S'good."

Dav winces. He usually finds my mumble-mouth charming, but we're supposed to be trying to make an impression. A good one.

I don't even want to look at Simcoe's face.

"Oh?" Laura-war-hero-of-the-nation-Secord says. "Why just now?"

"Um, I'm allergic to chocolate. Or, at least, I was," I start, and then bite my tongue. Shit. I shouldn't be talking about the benefits of dragon-roasted coffee.

Instead of looking surprised, Laura nods knowingly. "Ah, The Gift."

That...

That's not what I expected her to say.

Dav's eyes go wide. The bastard's realized something, and he can't share because Simcoe is still watching us like a rapt bird of prey.

Dav swallows hard, cornered. "I was working up to telling him."

"Tell me what?" I ask, annoyed at Dav for putting me in this position. He looks as thrown as I feel, though, so at least we're idiots together.

Yup. We're totally charming everyone. Absolutely according to plan. Uh-huh.

"Naughty naughty, Alva," Laura tuts at him. "You're usually so eloquent. I've no fear that you'll frighten him off."

"You flatter me, Laura," Dav says. They cup one another's clothed elbows, kindly and comforting. With Laura's head tilted back like that so she can look up at him, it's sort of cute. "But then, you always have."

"Nonsense," Laura laughs, beaming up at him. "I only ever say what you are too humble to put words to, dear."

A frisson of jealousy spikes, but quickly evaporates. Dav's looking at Laura the same way he looks at the kids—there's affection here, but it's nothing I need to worry about. The band strikes a flourish, and Dav and Laura startle apart. Dav immediately reaches for me, crooking his arm. I've read enough historical romances to get swoony as I take it, and let him lead me further inside.

The ballroom is 1930s jade-and-gold art deco, more modern than I expected. A few dozen couples are lingering by the high-top tables sprinkled with candy bowls, while a handful more square up on the dance floor.

"How's your cotillion?" Laura asks me, falling into step with us.

"Non-existent," I admit.

"Tsk tsk, Alva," Laura teases Dav again, and he ducks his head, like *aw shucks*.

"Show me how it's done, babe." I say. A little audacity never hurt anyone, so I grab Laura's hand and press it against Dav's shoulder. "Go on, wow me."

"Thank you, Mr. Levesque," Laura says, startled but happy. She dons a pair of gloves from her reticule. "How kind."

"It's just Colin," I tell her. "Now shoo."

Dav nudges the side of my head affectionately with his nose, and then promenades Laura onto the floor.

"Alva has been neglecting your education," Simcoe says from behind me, and I jerk around, because *fuck* that guy is good at sneaking. Somebody oughta put a goat bell on him.

"Uh." I wish I had pockets. I don't know what to do with my hands. "We haven't been going to ballroom classes, if that's what you're getting at."

Simcoe smiles meanly. "If you'd been raised in a coterie, as proper Favorites are, it would have been part of your upbring-ing."

Oh. Okay. That's the game we're playing? Fine.

"Laura's doing okay." I gesture at where she and Dav are swoosh-hopping back and forth. "Wasn't she born in Ameri-can New England before it was annexed? No fancy education there, I bet."

"I make her practice," Simcoe sneers. "She's come a long way from the colonial boor who first attended our parties."

"Aren't you colonial, too?"

"I was born in England." The scales around his hairline encroach a little more on his flesh.

Ha.

Score one for me.

Simcoe relieves a passing waiter of two frail glasses of sparkling wine, and presses one at me. I hold it still when he chimes his flute off mine, and take a sip because he's *watching*.

"What do you think?" he asks.

"It's fine."

"It's *French*," he corrects.

Snob.

"Niagara produces sparkling wines just as good as the Champagne region," I defend.

"Ah yes," he simpers. "I had forgotten Alva had captured himself a pet winemaker."

"Biodiverse viniculturist," I correct. "Two different jobs. Though I don't expect you to know that. I don't imagine you spend a lot of time mucking in with your hoard."

Simcoe sniffs. "Certainly not."

*Fucking* snob.

"I couldn't help but notice the front door," I venture. "Your father was very accomplished."

Simcoe's knuckles whiten on the stem of the flute. "He was. It is a shame illness took him so soon. As I believe your father was also taken?"

Grief stabs at my heart, and I gulp the wine. That was low. Well, what did I expect? I was the one to bring up dead dads first. I deserved that.

I'm about to offer another volley, try to get my own back, when Laura whoops with laughter. Dav's facing the wrong direction in the line of dancers. Laura tugs him playfully to catch up. It's sweet. I like seeing Dav with someone he's comfortable with. Those almost-dimples are on full display as he laughs at himself.

A plume of smoke escapes the corner of Simcoe's mouth.

*He's jealous*, I realize. *He's seeing the exact same thing I am, yet he totally thinks that Laura's, what, cheating on him?* I don't see it. *How insecure is this prick? Whipping Dav for making people happy, curating a night so fancy that half his guests look hella uncomfortable, bragging about the wine to someone he barely tolerates, and now this.*

"They look like they're good *friends*," I say, trying to diffuse the rage radiating off Simcoe.

"In*deed*," he snarls.

"If you and Dav are such good old chums and all, you can probably trust him to—" I bite my tongue when Simcoe swings around to blaze a glare at me. "Sorry. Guess it's not my place to comment."

"And you would do well to remember it," Simcoe snarls. "You, Mr. Levesque, have a great deal to learn about the expectations of our society. If Alva fails in his duty to bring you to heel, do not doubt for a moment that I will *gladly* step in."

Holy *fuck*, is that a threat?

I think it's a threat.

Because I am not completely suicidal, I lower my eyes as demurely as I can manage, a good little romance heroine pretending to be cowed by the villain.

"Alva may have the peninsula, and his little coffee fan club, but he will not have—"

"Frank," Laura laughs, sliding up to us breathlessly, red-cheeked and windblown. "Come, Frank, you simply must fetch Mrs. Simcoe and—oh my." She darts a curious glance between us. "Are you well? You look... peaked."

"Quite well, Mine Own," Simcoe lies badly, struggling to pull himself together.

"Come, come," Laura says, and bustles him away. "You oughtn't let yourself get so affected..."

Dav, who had detoured to the bar, rejoins me and hands me a red wine.

"That is some serious jealousy." I whisper.

Dav makes a little serpenty hissing noise. A glance out at the crowd—more than tripled in size since we arrived—shows Simcoe glaring daggers at his back from across the room.

"He has nothing to fear. What little there was between Laura and I is quite over."

"Oh my god! Did you two used to...?"

"It was a very long time ago, Mine Own."

"That's not a no."

"She was widowed and without protection. I had just come into my majority. It was... mutually beneficial, until she was established in society."

"Oh my god!" I repeat, delighted. "I've been dicked down by the dick that dicked down Laura Secord!"

It takes Dav a second to parse what I mean, and then he laughs. "Nothing so crass! We simply... held a deep affection for one another. But I was too young for a Favorite."

"So how...?"

Dav's face puckers. "Laura was much admired among the Draconic set. If I was unwilling to, ah, offer for her, there were many others who were."

"And she chose *that.* Do you think she's happy?"

"It's no longer my place to work for her happiness," Dav says diplomatically.

"That's not what I asked."

"I know, Mine Own." He lifts my hand to kiss the palm.

"Simcoe hates me."

"Of course he doesn't," Dav says. "He deeply dislikes not being in control, and the coffee phenomenon put us outside of his censure and into the limelight."

"For which he *whipped* you."

Dav shrugs, as if those weeks when he was gone weren't the worst of my life since Dad died.

"Frank is arrogant and selfish," Dav allows. "But we are old school friends. My happiness is his happiness."

"Especially if you're too busy with me to go sniffing around Laura."

"It's a grave thing, to trifle with another's Favorite," Dav says. "Besides, why would I ever throw you over?"

"Romantic asshole," I accuse.

"I learned it all from your delightful books—ouch! Colin, that's my foot!"

"Oh, is it?" I bat my eyelashes at him.

"You're a menace."

"And you love it."

"Lord help me, I do." He kisses my hand again.

I drag Dav over to a table and help myself to a fun-size chocolate bar from a candy bowl, because I can.

"Are you going to tell me what The Gift is," I ask, holding it up demonstratively before I snap the chocolate in half with my teeth. "Or am I going to have to corner Laura?"

"I'm so foolish," Dav says with a groan, and nips the other half of the candy out of my fingers without even asking. "Laid out so plainly, I don't know why I didn't see the correlation. There is no biological reason why The Gift should be reserved solely for Favorites."

I'm tempted to step on his foot again. "Explain."

"Favorites in close proximity to a dragon experience a strengthening of their constitution. Disease does not touch them, the afflictions of age pass them by. Just as drinking the dragonsfire coffee did for your allergy, and Hadi's insomnia, Laura's aging has been retarded. However, it is also not a guarantee," Dav says. "It's been unevenly successful, historically."

"Well, if it's all down to the infectious rate of dragon spit, there'd have to be some serious hanky-panky if you're not breathing all over the food. And if every relationship isn't sexual...?"

"They're not," Dav agrees.

"Then the platonic Favorites don't get the literal benefits of their friendship?"

"Quite," Dav says. "I am beginning to wish we'd paid greater attention to Pedra."

"No kidding." I let that sit between us for a moment. Then, softly, I ask: "Why didn't you tell me?"

"I suppose I wanted to see if it would take, before I—"

"Before you what?"

Dav pushes the mask up my face, and leans down for a soft, gentling kiss. For all his talk of no PDAs, he's being awfully handsy. And tongue-y. Still, illicit dark-corner smoochies *are* on the list of my fave Halloween activities.

Dav backs me up against the wall, into the pool of shadow cast by a nearby pile of jack-o-lanterns, and whispers: "Before I told you that you have every reason to expect to live for exactly as long as I do."

# chapter Thirty-Four

"Let me get this straight. We fuck," I hiss, pushing him back with my hands balled in his fancy lapels, forcing him to meet my eyes. "And it cures *death*?"

"Aging," Dav corrects, glancing around cagily. If he tells me to keep it down I'm *really* gonna stomp on his foot. "And when I pass—"

"Babe, I am *not* ready for the discussing-funeral-arrangements stage of the relationship—"

"When I pass, and you're no longer, ah, being serviced, you'll pass, too."

That slaps into my solar plexus. It takes me a few tries to get enough air to ask: "I'll die when you die?"

Dav cups my face, eyes skimming over my features, memorizing this moment. "Yes. Within a few months, your lost time will catch up to you. Most Favorites simply go to sleep and never wake up."

"And until then, I'll be twenty-four forever?"

"You'll age, but slowly." A fond look steals across his face, and he brushes the hair that's come loose from the mask behind my ear. "I look forward to seeing how handsome you are with some gray here, in a century or so."

A century.

Fuck.

"And, uh... how many of these centuries will I... enjoy?"

"I don't expect to be in my dotage for at least another four or five hundred years."

"Five hundred," I repeat, suddenly feeling floppy. I prop myself against the wall, wine sloshing through my veins. "Dav, sweetie, honey bunch, cutie claws... I'm not mad, but I'm over this thing where you don't tell me big, important, fundamental truths until I stumble into them. It's not awesome and it makes me feel like you think I'm stupid."

"No," Dav says quickly. "You're one of the most clever people I know. But... I suppose I'm afraid."

"Of?"

"That you'll leave."

My first instinct is to deny it. But to be fair, every big life-change he's sprung on me, I *have* reacted badly. Maybe it would be different if he told me in a calm, rational discussion, instead of after I've fucked something up. But then again, yeah, maybe not.

He looks sad, so I kiss him until the expression is replaced with dozy contentment. He tastes like champagne and those sticky molasses candies that always stick in my molars.

"Does it scare you?" he asks when we come up for air.

"Yes? No? Only, it's kinda hitting me that..." I take a deep breath. It punches out as a shuddery kind of thing. "I'm going to have to watch Hadi, and Stu, and Gem get old and die, and man, I *do not* like that. At the same time, science-wise, it tracks. So, yeah, happy Halloween, eh? Helluva trick."

"I was hoping you'd consider it a treat," Dav says wistfully. There's an expression curling in the corner of Dav's mouth that I want to lick.

It's a...

Holy shit.

It's a Peter Pan kiss.

I cup his face in my hands, and run my thumb along the edge of his mouth.

"Colin?"

"You have a kiss," I whisper. "Right here."

"I'm sorry?"

"Like Mrs. Darling."

"Ah," Dav says, catching on. "Are you sure it's not a thimble?"

"May I have it?"

"Always." Dav tilts the side of his face to me. "Forever. It's yours, my boy who will never grow old."

"At least not for a long time, I hear." The gooey, hopeless romantic center of me burbles with delight at this happy, sociable Dav. This Dav who is... is filling out his skin. *Uncrunched.*

"Shall we dance?" Dav whispers.

Oooh, he has good timing. Waiting until I'm all compliant and kiss-drunk to ask. Cheater.

"I don't know what I'm doing," I protest.

"Please," Dav begs, sending an honest-to-god *pout* my way. I let him pull me into the paired-off line up. "I do so love a dance."

"We never used to get Niagara off the floor," an older dragon to his left says. "And a good thing, too, for he kept all the Favorites well amused. Let us old codgers catch our breath. Glad to have you back, Niagara."

"Glad to be welcomed back, my Lord Toronto," Dav says, shaking his hand gregariously. But he's tense around his eyes.

*Ha!* I think sourly. *"Glad to be allowed off his territory finally, more like.*

Skulking by the bar, Simcoe glares like he could knife Dav in the back with the power of his disapproval alone. Laura's petting his hair back from his cheek gently. They don't look like they're lovers—ew, I do *not* want to think about that. Their body language is more like a mother, gently soothing her son. Yuck.

I'm lost in my thoughts when the Lord Toronto's partner, a handsome middle-aged dragon who is as comfortably rotund as the Lord Toronto, leans in conspiratorially to me and says, "We're glad to have you too, son. Wonderful that Niagara has overcome his little difficulty."

"Little difficulty?"

"Wretched tragedy, what happened to Miss Woodley," she says. "All the same, you needn't fear, he knows better now."

*What?*

"Watch my shoulders, Mine Own, rather than my feet," Dav says, and that's a tight Customer Service Smile if I've ever seen one.

"Right, uh, sure," I mumble, blindsided by the dance starting. Lord Toronto bumps into my arm. "Sorry!"

"Quick, to the right," Dav chokes.

"Right, right," I mutter, and trip along to follow the line. Dav holds out his hands, and leads me through the patterns. When we come together for a turn, our arms curled around one another's waists. "What are they talking about?"

"Oh!" Lord Toronto says, when we collide again. Not my fault this time, I don't think. The asshole is trying to eavesdrop. "Has Niagara not given you his full name yet?"

"My Lord," Dav warbles. "Now is really not the time."

"Nonsense," Lord Toronto laughs. "If one can't gossip on the dance floor, then where?"

"No, I know his middle name," I say, earning a startled, hurt look from Dav. "It was on the news. What does it matter?"

"A dragon's middle name is not given at birth, Mine Own," Dav says. "It is earned."

"So? What's so special about George?"

"I don't suppose I could expect you to know your draconic histories," Lady Toronto says, as we weave in a circle. "But even you must know of Georgius of Lydda."

"Yeah, the Dragonslayer."

"The vicious soldier who used his faith to betray Christian dragons to the Romans. A murderer of his own," the insensitive cow sniffs.

I turn to Dav in horror. "Murderer of his own?"

*Poor Dav*, I think as the dance brings us back into orbit. My sweet, kind, generous man, with his heart large enough to hold the whole world... and *this* is what they tell him he's worth? And the news had used his full name like it was *nothing*. Like it wasn't a shard of hate stuck into Dav's heart.

"And this is just something people *banter* about? Like common gossip?" I grit out.

"It *is* common gossip, Mine Own," Dav says, valiantly attempting to keep calm.

I'm overwhelmed with a righteous, unselfish rage on Dav's behalf. They talk about this injustice so *easily*, so cruelly. "That's not fair! You were a *soldier*—"

"Oh, no, not on the battlefield," Lord Toronto corrects me. I despise him. "His first Favorite."

I stop.

Step out of line.

Dav lets me.

"*First* Favorite?" I echo dumbly.

I feel like I've been concussed. Everything around me has stopped making sense.

And then, all of a sudden, it *does*.

This is what he meant by *I've done it again.*

# chapter Thirty-Five

Laura catches up to me as I'm stalking out of the ballroom.

"And how are you enjoying your first Draconic fete?" she asks, trying to manners-away the scene that turning on my heel and storming away is causing.

"You mean, now that I'm aware that I'm immortal because Dav and I get freaky?" I snarl, grim, and sweaty. "I can't believe I was so starstruck that I missed the part where you should be *dead*."

"Ah," Laura says, keeping pace.

I crane around just once to meet Dav's eyes. He's standing in the middle of the dance floor, still and bereft, surrounded by chatting little sycophants. I can hear them all laughing about our hashtag—"Alvalin! How modern!"—utterly missing how tight and miserable he is.

I want him to come after me, to soothe, to explain.

I don't want him to touch me.

I don't know *what* my feels are doing.

And I'm not sure where I'm going, just that I know it has to be somewhere Dav is not right now.

"Oh, *and* that I just found out what his middle name means," I add, slaloming around a glittering rainbow of brocade-clad gawkers. "*And* that he had a Favorite before me? Who is *dead*? Oh, no, I'm fine. Totally peachy keen!"

"Perhaps we should have a word in private," Laura suggests a bit desperately.

She corrals me into the cool, refined quiet of a library. And just like that, I am alone in a room with Laura-McFreaking-Secord, heroine of the Battle of Beaver Dams, the woman who walked all night to warn Dav and the other British officers of a planned American attack after they'd occupied and used her house as a secret base. A woman I should, by all right, respect like crazy, and right now just *hate* a little bit.

I want to scream. I want to break something. Instead, I cross to the window, shove up the sash, stick my overheated head out into the cool night air, and do Gem's stupid fucking yoga breaths.

The Don Valley spreads out below me, wild and wooded, the moonlight glimmering on the rushing river. Obviously, I like that there's a forest in the middle of the city, with just a bridge connecting Old York to the rest of Greater Toronto Area through the undeveloped greenery. Entering the historic capital of Upper Canada feels like you're stepping back through time.

I just hate that the attitudes of everyone here are still stuck in that era, too.

Laura sits in one of the artful magazine-spread-perfect chairs by the fireplace and patiently waits for me to get my shit back under control. When I feel like I can talk without hurling, I join her, perched on the edge of the chair, too revved up to relax. She matches my posture as if we were Regency romance heroines in each other's confidence. Which, in a way, we kind of are?

"Don't be upset with Alva," Laura says. "He's always kept his secrets close."

"I'm not," I choke out. I'm mad at the fuckheads around Dav who think his personal tragedies are titillating *bon mots*.

Laura chuckles, and I'm struck with the impression that she's quick-witted in a calculating way, hidden under biddable charm. I hate to admit it, but I can see how it would work with Simcoe's Father Knows Best bullshit. I bet she rides herd on him and he doesn't even notice. I wonder how that works, when Simcoe has a wife. The fact Laura is alive means she and Simcoe have to swap spit at least semi-regularly. Eugh.

"I'm sure you've noticed that there's a, hm, let's call it an aversion to transparency, among dragons."

I snort. "That's a polite way to say it."

"It's uncouth to discuss such things as The Gift openly, in much the same way humans tend not to explicitly discuss the sexual part of their marriages when they declare love for their spouse."

"Then how does anyone... I mean, you, how do you make a decision of whether you want to be a Favorite? How can there be informed consent if there's no *information?*"

Laura chuckles again. "'Informed consent.' How modern."

"It's only fair to know what you're getting into before you get into it." I point to the black velvet ribbon around her throat, with the Flame-Laurel-Maple Leaves-Hand-with-Dagger motif set in a cameo at the hollow of her throat. "Did you know what that meant before you put it on?"

"Of course," Laura says.

"I didn't."

Her expression softens. "Alva grew up in the heart of the British court, did you know that?"

I had once chided myself for wanting to make out with someone who, for all I knew, might actually be a Prince. It makes my stomach lurch to hear Laura lay out that whatever his position is in the puddle of blue blood, it means that he's important enough to basically grow up in a palace.

Damn.

Oblivious to my inner turmoil, Laura goes on: "His Excellency was raised on the periphery of nobility, so his manners are much more forthright. When he offered me the position of Favorite in return for the service I rendered to the crown, he explained what it meant, what I would gain from the position in terms of support, wealth, and health. My husband James had died in the Battle of Queenston Heights. I had my children to think of. I accepted. But Alva... in the world of his childhood, one didn't speak of such things because everyone around them already knew."

"Nobody, like, sits them down and explains the birds and the bees, uh, or the tokens and the gifts, because everybody just grows up with it?"

"Yes, exactly. Well put."

It feels so dumb to preen under her praise simply because she's like a national icon, but I puff up all the same. "So Dav hasn't explained, not because he's hiding, but because he just forgets he has to tell me."

"If it makes you feel any better, Alva's first Favorite reacted much like—" Laura stops guiltily.

"*First* Favorite," I echo. "You're the second person to mention that tonight."

Laura slows to a quiet, contemplative pause. "You didn't know."

*Whoever they are, they're dead*, I remember, all in a rush. *Or they'd still be here. They'd have The Gift and they... I won't be jealous of a dead person. I refuse. Whatever happened, Dav doesn't talk about it and it must have been awful. I won't let this fuck anything up. I can't, I won't believe that he killed her. That's not who he... oh god.*

"Why... why would Dav keep that from me?" I ask, feeling the tenuous grip on my temper slipping.

Only, only he hadn't, had he?

*I've done it again*, he'd said.

"Wretched tragedy, what happened to Miss Woodley," she ventures evenly, neutrally. The cadence and tone are the exact same as the way the lady dragon on the dance floor had said it. By rote. Like it's something said often, around here. "I dislike that Alva will carry it for the rest of his life."

I don't think she means it as a warning.

Still sounds like one, though.

The crown princess bit the head off of her abusive Favorite. Dav could have—

"Did he kill her?" I ask, voice trembling.

"No," Laura says, gently. "And yet, yes." Her mouth does a complicated thing and I get the sense that there's a lot she wishes she could be saying, and isn't. "It was... an accident. You've met Alva's neighbor? Miss Hino'Hawank?"

"Onatah? Yeah."

*Oh, no, please, don't say she had anything to do with it.*

"Miss Woodley... Charlotte," Laura corrects herself sadly. "Was adventurous. Curious. She and Alva travelled widely, visited many territories, and one day there was an accident. A cliff."

I press a hand to my chest, relief splashing hard into my veins. *Dav isn't a murderer. Thank god.* It's followed swiftly with a deep grief for a woman I've never met, but was loved by the man I love. "How come they blame Dav, then?"

"The unnatural death of any Favorite is a cause of the deepest shame for a dragon. A Favorite is a dragon's greatest treasure. They must be guarded as such. For Charlotte to have died as she did is already a terrible stain on his name. But that she died on the territory of another dragon—a non-British dragon—is the ultimate dishonor."

"So they branded him a murderer?" I gasp. "All because she, what, she *fell?* How is that on him?"

"Oh no," Laura murmurs. "Much worse."

"What's *worse?* Do you mean the whipping, 'cause that's—"

Laura glances at me shrewdly. "Do you know what it was, exactly, he was whipped *for?*"

I'm startled by her casual acceptance of such a brutal act.

*A different era*, I remind myself. *She was born centuries ago, and she's lived with the dragons long enough that beating the shit out of someone seems acceptable.*

"For... breaking taboos, um, about labor?" I hedge, still not sure how much she knows about... all that.

"You mean roasting the coffee beans? No," Laura says, sweeping aside all cautious tip-toeing around the topic. "It was you."

"Me?"

"Part of his punishment for Charlotte's death was that Alva was forbidden from taking another Favorite for a century. Yet, here you are, a decade too early."

"But... but that's not fair! *I* kissed *him*—"

"It doesn't matter, Mr. Levesque. He shouldn't have put himself in the position where it was possible."

"But... but you can't *punish* love! That's ridiculous!"

"It's already happened," Laura says. "Frank was furious. But the Draconic Parliament conceded when Alva pleaded his heart. He swore you were in love, swore that despite not being of titled family or without the proper education in a coterie, you were loyal, and clever, and devoted to him. That it would be cruel to deny you."

"We'd only dated for like, a month," I warble.

*My god. The promises he's made. And there's no way he could have been sure. I wasn't even sure myself, not then.*

"But you looked for him," Laura says. "Calling. Sending letters. Posting on the Internet. You looked for him, and that was what changed Parliament's mind. You appeared to be equally invested."

Holy shit.

What I did actually made a difference.

It *mattered*.

"That's why I was being followed? Because they were checking to see if I was in love enough for them to stop *torturing my boyfriend?*"

"And to protect you from the worst of the gossip mongers."

*Fuck.*

"You're new to this world," Laura says, taking my shoulders in her hands, trying to soothe. "You can't understand—"

I don't want to be soothed. I shrug her off and she lets go, thankfully. Good. I didn't want to have to punch a war hero. "This is all *completely* fucked up."

"And yet," a voice by the door sneers, and Laura and I both whip around to find Simcoe leaning against the closed door, smirking. Just how long has that jackass been there, listening in on a private conversation? I hadn't even heard him come in. Asshole. "You accepted Alva's token."

"I didn't *know*," I snarl at him.

"That's hardly my problem," Simcoe jeers.

"Frank," Laura tuts. "There's no need to *scare* the boy."

"Colin!" I hear Dav shout from the other side of the door. There's a thump, and I realize it's locked. I'm trapped with people who are trying to convince me that my lover is a *murderer.* "Let me in, or I swear I'll—"

"You'll do nothing but stand there and wait!" Simcoe hollers back. "Know your place!"

Dav doesn't reply, doesn't thump on the door again, or break the lock, or any of the things he's strong enough to do. Simcoe waits a few seconds, to confirm he's cowed Dav, and then turns back to me with a smirk.

"Will you give us the room, Mine Own?"

Laura cuts a glance at me—*no, don't leave me alone with him!*—but curtsies and heads for the door. I want to beg her to stay, because I can't... I'm scared.

"I'll soothe the Marquess," she tells him as she passes Simcoe. "And assure him of his Favorite's safety?" She says it like a challenge, and when he doesn't answer, she cocks an eyebrow at him. "Frank?"

"Of course, my pet," Simcoe simpers. "More than assured."

"See that it is," she bites out politely.

Holy shit.

She's *mad*.

When she opens the door, I expect Dav to barge in. But he stands on the other side of the threshold like a forcefield is keeping him out. His hands are balled into fists at his side and he's significantly more draconic looking now than an artful splatter of scales. His tail lashes back and forth behind him with a graceful fury that warms my heart.

*I'm fine,* I mouth at him, even though I have no idea if it's true.

*I'm here*, he mouths back.

Which does, actually, make me feel better.

"She's not a pet, she's a person," I grind out, once the door has swung closed again and Laura's out of hearing range. She may be complicit with this pseudo-slavery; it doesn't mean I have to *like* it.

"Good lord, you sound like Alva," Simcoe scoffs.

"I'll take that as a compliment."

"Of course you will. Listen well to me, boy. It is time you also learned your place. Humans domesticated wolves, and now you have dogs," Simcoe sneers. "And dragons domesticated humans."

"Fuck you," I snap. "I'm not a dog!"

"And still you snarl at me."

I bite back the rest of what I want to say and just bare my teeth at him.

"You can come in now, Alva," Simcoe says softly, once he's sure I've been leashed.

There was no reason to keep him out. It was just Simcoe proving that he's the one in power. Dav opens the door, the clicking door handle loud as a gunshot in the tense, thick air. Dav enters, makes a small bow to Simcoe, and walks to my side slowly, elegantly. His tail winds around my ankle.

"You are both too young to know this, but if you continue to rock the boat, you will capsize us all," Simcoe sighs.

The tight, horrible feeling of being caged rushes back, settling like permafrost in my bones.

"The Gift," Dav says. Simcoe nods like a melodramatic stage villain. "All this time I was told that it was... it was exclusive. But that's not true."

"Of course not. Do you really think we didn't already know everything your little friend discovered in that lab?"

"It's mutually beneficial symbiosis," I say.

"It surpassed *mutually beneficial* centuries ago," Simcoe snaps. "Humans breed fast enough that they'll overwhelm the world if we let them."

"I thought the more humans the better, right? That's what all this Empire-building bullshit is about."

"There is being wealthy," Simcoe allows. "And then there is being greedy to the point of endangering society. Just as the human One Percent is taxed heavily on their excess money, dragons must also pay for excesses."

Dav scoffs. "So we're taxed by being denied our natural desire to serve and uplift, for the greater good?"

"Just so," Simcoe says. "We voluntarily deny ourselves in order to protect our territories, and our rule."

"I see," Dav chokes out.

"I don't!"

"Humans live for a long time in our care," Simcoe explains patiently, as if I'm the village idiot. "It is our duty to ensure that it is the *right* humans. And not so many of them that they endanger the management of the climate and environment."

I don't like this second revelation of the evening any more than I liked the first.

They're *letting* humans get sick.

They're letting us *die*.

It's not concentration and labor camps. But they have the means, the ability, and the instinct to help and heal. And they are *deliberately choosing not to*. They are dividing the world into the desirables and the undesirables, and letting the latter category, the larger category, suffer needlessly. It's...

*...it's so goddamned stupid.*

"And what are the right humans?" I sneer. "White, upper-class, attractive?"

"Preferably," Simcoe agrees. He looks me up and down like a show pony. "At least you're white, and... Alva certainly seems to consider you attractive. We can work on the rest. We have decades."

I'm going to puke.

I'm going to puke up champagne and candy-corn hors d'oeuvres, and I'm going to aim for his *face*.

"Don't speak to my Favorite like that!" Dav snarls.

"Your temper, Alva," Simcoe singsongs, and Dav immediately draws himself in, crunches up. "Now, I have other guests to see to. Avail yourselves of the library and calm down before you rejoin the party. Welcome to The Great Confidence. You *will* keep it."

Dav, seething, only offers Simcoe a low, slow bow. Not knowing what else to do, I follow suit, hand fisted over my heart, loathing every microsecond.

By the time we look up, he's gone.

"I find," Dav growls, "That I am no longer in the mood for dancing."

# chapter Thirty-Six

One of the advantages that film has over books is the 'smash cut'.

This is a kind of editing technique used by the filmmaker to deliberately juxtapose the tone or information of the previous scene with the next. Sometimes it happens mid-sentence for a character, or comes accompanied by a record scratch sound effect, or some sort of audible music sting to really make sure the audience is jarred by the harsh, quick transition.

You can't 'smash cut' in a book. But if I could, this is where it would happen. Imagine the obnoxiously over-decorated, stiff and stuffily-crowded, loud party of Castle Frank and then, *bam*, Dav and I, in our PJs. Dav is buttoned all the way to the neck, and we're staring at one another over the expanse of the bed, in the tense and miserable quiet of his bedroom.

"*Did* you kill her?" I ask.

Dav shudders, stricken. "It was my fault."

"That's not what I asked. Was it homicide? Was it premeditated?"

Dav gasps in horror. "Of course not!"

"Then why have you never talked about her before?"

Dav scrubs the heels of his hands into his eyes. "How could I? I never wanted you to feel as if you were second best, and she—" He shudders again, curling in on himself, back heaving.

"Okay, hey." I scramble over the mattress to wrap him in my arms. "I don't feel second-best. I'm just sad that you felt that you had to hide her from me. You loved her. She matters to you. That means she matters to me, too."

"Oh, Mine Own," Dav sobs, and I navigate us down into the blankets.

I pet through his hair, loosening the ridiculous gel he'd put in it to slick it back for his mask, as he hides his face in my neck and mourns. When he's cried himself out, I say: "Can I ask, if you want to talk about it... if it's not like they say it was... then how did she...?"

"We met..." his voice crackles. "In France. During, uh, the war."

*Which one?* I wonder. *Simcoe sent you to all of them.*

"She was English, a front-line nurse. In the trenches. She was..." the hand wrapped around my middle squeezes. "Brilliant. No-nonsense. Caring. Thoughtful. Beautiful." He cranes his head around and brushes his nose against mine. "Rather like you."

"Onatah said you had a type," I joke, trying to lighten the mood, instead of telling him he's utterly wrong—I'm not beautiful or brilliant, and I'm a selfish little prick some days.

"She agreed to return to Canada with me, to become my Favorite, and we... I loved her very much," he says, like a protest. Like a confession.

"I know. That's good."

He's quiet for a moment, chewing on his thoughts. "I would never have met you, never have wanted you, if she hadn't died. I regret her death, and yet I take joy in loving you. All the same, I wish she was here to—she'd like you."

"Yeah?"

"Charlotte was interested in all the ways we can improve the world."

"See? A type."

Dav chuckles. "She formed a strong friendship with Onatah."

Okay, maybe I'm a *little* envious of a dead woman. "Wait, hold up. Did Charlotte get to meet Onatah's Favorite?"

"Colin," Dav scolds.

"Right, fine, whatever. Continue, please."

"We developed something of a habit of visiting Onatah on Sundays." He pauses to wipe his nose on his cuff, which is the least gentlemanly thing I've ever seen him do. It makes me love him just that little bit more. "We'd go to church, the cook would pack us a picnic, and Onatah would show us all the lovely little lakes she safeguards. She was teaching Charlotte the traditional medicines and—" Dav trails off into a wet whimper. "There was an outcropping, over one of the rivers, high up, had a good view. It became our preferred picnic spot."

My heart seizes. *How awful.*

"The rock was perfectly solid the week before, but that Sunday it just... Maybe our continued presence dislodged something, wore away at... or perhaps there had been a storm and the run-off..." He takes a deep, stuttering breath. "I went down first. Charlotte tried to catch my hand and..."

Beneath my hand, the waltz of his heart jackhammers.

"Breathe, babe."

He takes a deep breath. Lets it go. Takes another. "She didn't survive."

"I'm sorry." I kiss his shoulder again. "I'm so sorry."

"It was my fault."

"It wasn't."

"I pulled her over."

"You didn't mean to."

"I took her there, I put her in that danger. I made the wrong choice, I took her into another dragon's territory, and she paid for it. How could I have been so reckless? And then I did it again, with you, with the coffee, when I knew it was wrong..."

"I don't think that's fair," I point out.

"I regret, Mine Own, that the others don't care what your opinion is."

"See, that's the part that I can't pretend isn't fucking *weird.*" I try not to tense up or lash out. "That they all treat me like I'm not..." *Go on, you coward. You can't bottle it up forever.* "Like I lost all ability to think or reason or speak for myself now that I've basically become your *slave.*"

"Colin, it's not—" Dav gasps, sitting up.

"I know it's not, I *know* that," I say, hands out, *stop*. Dav stops, sits back against the headboard, small.

"You regret putting on the pin," Dav says.

Even his voice is tiny, and this isn't what I—*fuck*.

"No," I insist. "But I... you have to see this from my point of view, okay, like, I didn't grow up with any of the dragon shit, I didn't—"

"Shit?" Dav interrupts, eyebrows pulling down.

"—I don't mean it like *that*, I just mean..." What *do* I mean? Maybe I should throw myself out of the window and save us both this agony. Ugh. Feelings suck.

"Do you fear that I'll kill you next?" Dav asks, bristling. He clambers to his feet, so I do too. I stay on the opposite side of the bed, not because I'm afraid of him but because I don't know what *I'll do*, how *I'm* feeling, and I don't think I'm ready for him to touch me, not with my skin tingling like I'm licking a live wire.

"Of course not! But—"

"But what?"

"I love you, but I can't... I can't *leave*, Dav. There's all these secret rules I didn't know about, and now I'm gonna live for *centuries*, and I'm expected to maintain this fucking conspiracy, and I—don't you get how terrifying that is?"

"You put the pin on yourself—"

"You never told me what it meant!"

"And so easily, we're back to it being my fault."

"No!" I shout, and stomp my foot because he's not *listening*. Because I can't find the *words*. Because even I don't understand what I'm trying to say. "I just need *time*, okay? And *space*, I need... I don't know what I need. I have to wrap my head around this. If I'm not your slave, I'm your, what, your trophy husband? Is that it? I don't... I don't know what I am to you, Dav, and I don't know what you are to me, and that *scares the ever-loving fuck* outta me, because all I want is to be *with* you."

"You are with me." Dav seizes on the opening, reaches across the bed, snags my pinkie finger with his.

"No, I'm here *for* you. Do you see the difference?"

"No."

"*Dav*." I wrap his whole hand in mine. "I'm struggling. I am really trying to be okay with this, but if I'm going to find a way to be happy about being... Your Own, or however it is that I'm supposed to refer to myself—do *not* even *think* of interrupting me to tell me the right term right now, I will scream, I swear—then you can't do this flat refusal bullshit. You have all the power here and if you just... if you just *use* it, then it's not like we talked about. It's not *us*, it's *you*, and me under you."

"I don't think of you like that."

"But you're *acting* like it. Every human at that party was *branded*, don't you see that? Rings, and embroidery, and... you might as well use a leash! How are the other dragons going to talk about me? Look at me? Treat me? You say 'Favorite' but what does that *mean*? How can I..." My whole body is quaking like I'm coming down with hypothermia. My tongue feels heavy and numb. "When being with you means everything that I am is going to *change*, right down to the DNA?"

Dav crawls over the bed, and then it's his turn to wrap me in his arms. It feels good. *Nice*. Warm. We're trading off, tonight. And I want it. I want it *so bad*. I want everything that this is, and *nothing* about what it means to everyone who isn't us.

"Howm'I supposed to love you when I don't have the choice?" I mumble.

"I don't know," Dav says gently, pets down the back of my head. It's soothing and nothing at all like what you'd do to a dog, and yet it's still *petting*. Just like Simcoe said. I tuck his hand between us, hold it against my heart. "I don't know how to help you with this."

"What," I ask, chuckling, but snottily, drowning in my worry and fear. "No etiquette book to follow? 'How to Collar A Human in Ten Easy Steps'."

Dav uses his other hand to tip my chin up so I can meet his eyes. He's as miserable about this as I am.

That makes me feel a bit better.

But just a bit.

"Usually it's not so abrupt," Dav says. "We've only known each other *months*, Colin. It's normally *years*. Decades, sometimes."

"Fucked everything up again, did I?"

"No," Dav assures me, and places a long, chaste kiss in the center of my forehead. "I hoped for this very thing. But you are impetuous, Mine Own. We've barely had time to learn how we work together. Now you've thrown us into something else entirely."

"You came into the café and you *picked me*. Why?"

"It wasn't so calculated. I didn't come in for a coffee one day and thought, 'ah, yes, there's the one. I shall make him mine and lock him in my nest forever.'"

"You could lock me in?" I yelp, leaning back to meet his eyes, knowing my own must be bugging.

"Of course not," Dav rushes to reassure. "You can leave."

"I just can't *leave*."

Dav hesitates.

"If you wanted to..." he starts slowly. "If you *really* wanted to. I would... I could... no one would be happy about it, but I could... bear it."

The way he says it makes it sound like it would be the same as me dying.

"Would they...?" I reach around, slide my hands under his loose shirt, trace the welts there with my palms. "Would they do this to you again?"

Instead of answering, Dav slides his face against my neck, tucks in close, inhales.

We shuffle off the bed. He wraps his arms around my waist. I wrap mine over his shoulders.

Someone starts swaying and somehow, ridiculously, we're dancing in slow circles, swaying in our bare feet to the memory of tonight's band.

Miserable and desperate.

"Doesn't matter," Dav says. "I'd make them leave you alone. That's what's important. When you go."

"*If* I go," I correct with a pinch to that beautiful bum of his.

"If you go," he says, but he makes it sound like it's inevitable. "Hey, can you look at me?"

Dav lifts his head slowly. At first I think he's going to lean back, but he simply slides up until our foreheads are touching. Eyes closed, he inhales again, gentle, and then leans down and finds my mouth on the first, blind try. We kiss, a slow slide, like how we dance. I imagine Dav asking me, with each soft kiss, if I'm alright, if I'm happy, if I'm still his. I reply with teeth and tongue that I'm *annoyed, and shaken up, and absolutely don't want to think about the fact that the act of kissing him is actually mutating my DNA right this very moment, so keep me distracted with making out, thank you*. Only then does he pull back and meet my gaze.

"I'm not going," I tell him, and it's true. "I may never go. But I also don't know how to stay yet."

"I've waited this long. I can be patient," Dav insists. "Until you're ready."

"Ready to be owned by you?" I ask, and yeah, it sounds bitter.

"Ready to find a way to be equals in a dynamic that's trying to prevent us from doing so. Ready to... to fight, if we have to."

"Ever the soldier?"

"You're mine, Colin," Dav says fiercely, cupping my head in his hands. "And in all the ways that matter, I am *yours*. And if I have to tear down everything so they understand that, I will."

"You hopeless romantic." I won't lie, it's swoon-worthy.

"No," Dav says, and suddenly the determined expression on his face curls up into something predatory and dangerous. In a good way. "You're the romantic. And it's not hopeless."

His strong fingers slide down my throat, and in one quick push, I'm up against the wall. There are hands on my thighs, the sound of his knees hitting the carpet, and then everything stutters and the rest of the world beyond his hot mouth ceases to matter. I get my hands into Dav's hair, knuckles tight.

"Stay," he moans, before he opens his mouth and does his best to take away my ability to ever walk anywhere ever again.

One of the nice things about having staff is that you don't have to yank on your pants and careen towards the door whenever the bell rings. But it also means that you can't dramatically slam said door in an unwanted visitor's face, either.

I wonder if dragons have the ability to sense each other's presence. Because when we're fetched downstairs mid-morning grind by Sarah, Dav isn't surprised to see Lt. Gov. Dipshit sitting on the antique sofa in the fussy parlor, sipping tea. Simcoe's in another black suit, white shirt, subtle lapel stitching. Dignified. Boring.

For all that he's just sitting there, elegant and patient, the sight of Simcoe under this roof feels like a hard punch right against my sternum, knocking the air out of me. It feels... wrong, somehow. Violating. Challenging.

Just plain bitchy.

Dav had pulled on dress pants and a button down, and now I realize what had looked off about them. He's drab, too.

Also dignified. Also boring. I stop in the doorway, and flatten my hair, trying to make it look like my boyfriend (husband? Owner?) wasn't in the middle of railing me into the mattress when Simcoe arrived.

"Alva," Simcoe says, setting aside the cup and saucer, but not rising to his feet.

*Bitchy.*

"Your Excellency." Dav nods formally.

Simcoe's eyes cut to me, and I only offer Simcoe an unimpressed grin —as sassy as I dare right now—as I stride into the room, and flop into one of the chairs. This man got in the way of an orgasm. I'm not bowing.

Listen, I'm a half-ass student when it comes to things that bore me, like math and history. But stuff I give a shit about? I read like crazy. And in the time Dav was missing, I did a lot of reading about the dragon who took him away from me.

The Simcoes were Family Compact hoity-toities, who believed that their name and status meant that they were *more* equal and *more* important than everyone around them. Simcoe the elder had already been centuries older than Dav was now when he was asked to take on the leadership of Elizabeth Regina's Canadian interests. He conquered French Canada for Britain, abolished slavery in the colonies, made deals and purchased land from the Indigenous dragons, founded York, laid out order of rule, and established the legal system.

That's good stuff, if you're a white British dude. (Less so if you're one of those Indigenous dragons he screwed, and whose human children were scooped into residential schools. Bastard.)

And all that time, Francis was at school in England, learning how to be a good little soldier and statesman. Then Napoleon got too big for his britches. Francis, like many young patriotic men, joined Wellington to trounce him.

Then Francis was shot in Spain.

That he lived at all, apparently, was due to his draconic nature. The action had been fierce enough to kill every human in his unit. While Francis recovered, the war spilled over into North America, so the elder Simcoe recruited Dav from that same school to take what should have been his son's place at his side.

After the war, Simcoe the elder returned to England to get treatment for a mysterious nerve illness, and Francis took custody of Upper Canada in his absence. And when it became clear his father wouldn't recover, Francis made his good-byes, and took over his father's Canadian territories full time. Sounds noble, right?

But by every interview I'd watched on YouTube, and every newspaper profile I could get my hands on about the guy, he's obsessed with procedure, precedence, and the superiority of dragons—specifically *European* dragons.

The ultimate colonizer, he waltzed in and was all "hey, the way we do stuff is better than the way you do stuff, so do it the way we do it or else," and that's some bullshit right there. Now I see how his control-freak crap extends to the dragons of Upper Canada—and the humans they own (slavery is only bad when humans are doing it to each other, I guess).

I help myself to a cookie from a tiered tray on the little table in front of Simcoe. Simcoe makes a face like he'd *like* to make a sour face, but thinks it would be impolite. He's proper, and it rankles the hell out of him that I'm not.

Fucking *good.*

"I've come to apologize for the... unseemly display last night," Simcoe says, when it's clear neither Dav nor I have anything to say to him. "It is such a shame a commotion was caused."

*Excellent use of the passive tense to shift agency and blame away from you.*

Dav waves it away, as if the traumas of yesterday were nothing more than a minor inconvenience. I crunch through the cookie, glaring.

Simcoe does a double take, appalled. "Alva, surely there are more appropriate—"

"He doesn't want appropriate," I interrupt, shocking him. "He wants me."

Simcoe looks to Dav for permission. For something. Dav, with a head bob, grants it. Shit.

I sit up, feet flat on the floor, ready to... ready to what? Duck a backhand? Jump away from a jet of flame? No, Dav wouldn't let Simcoe hurt me. But then, he'd let himself be flogged, so who knows what dragons think is acceptable.

But Simcoe only folds his hands on his knees, meets my eyes—his are darkly orange compared to Dav's—and says, "And you want *this?*"

Oh good. It was only permission to talk to me. Maybe after this incredibly uncomfortable conversation, I can get Dav to revoke it so I never have to listen to the self-important asshole again.

"I want *him*," I correct, brushing away crumbs. "And if that means it has to come with..." I gesture around us. "Well, then that's what I deal with."

"How magnanimous," Dav says softly, the amusement clear in his eyes, if not his tone.

Simcoe cuts a narrow look between us and I get the feeling that we're playing with fire. I don't care. I'm not spending the rest of my very long life scraping and kowtowing to the man who is, as far as I can tell, single-handedly responsible for making Dav crunched.

Begin as you mean to go on, Mum would say.

Simcoe narrows a calculating gaze at me. "Do you understand the honor of your position? Your responsibilities as a Favorite? Especially in the house of Tudor?"

"*Barely* within the house, please," Dav says gently.

My boy's got his hands folded behind his back, his shoulders loose but his fingernails digging into his palms. No, not fingernails—the tips are black, hard. Talons. Maybe Dav's feeling it too, the way there's something off about Simcoe being here. Like a whole-ass thunderstorm has been boxed in between these four walls and has nowhere to go but through our skin, into our cells, to make our insides crackle.

Now Simcoe stands. "His impertinence is wearing off on you."

"Or perhaps I am less inclined to be ruled by traditions that are of no benefit," Dav says, and I choke back a gasp because *fuck* that's bold. I'm being a little shit on purpose. But Dav's taking it a bit far.

I stand, partially because they're already talking over my head, and it doesn't need to be literal. But also because I want to literally be standing in solidarity with Dav. *I'll be in the shit with you.* I'm not going back on that. Not now that we're fighting to be happy, when everyone and everything around us is determined to force us into some definition of a relationship that fits like a flea-infested suit, three sizes too small.

I lay my hand on the small of Dav's back, and he twists his talon, unseen by Simcoe, to hook our pinkies together. Lt. Gov. Jerkface doesn't do anything so uncouth as look back and forth between us, but his eyes narrow further, and then land on the lapel pin hanging heavily and awkwardly on the collar of my wash-thinned shirt.

"Tradition matters," Simcoe hisses. At the corner of his jaw, the skin becomes dark brown scales.

"Not in the way it used to," Dav counters, just as forcefully. "Now it's all just celebrity gossip and tabloids."

"You think my work, the work of my family—"

"And what work is that? Your father created a beautiful colony, but a *colony* nonetheless." Dav cuts his free hand at the window, palm up, indicating the tightly manicured façade of control and opulence the world gets to glimpse through iron bars, never knowing the charm of the higgledy-piggledy working mess of barns and baby animals out the back. "There are different ways... better ways."

"Your idea of what this place was before we made it right is a *fantasy*," Simcoe snaps. "With the privilege of your birth comes expectations."

"And what contributions have been allowed?" Dav sneers.

"*Ef yw'r dewis anghywir*," Simcoe replies.

Okay.

What the fuck language was that?

# Chapter Thirty-Seven

D av's whole arm flushes with scale.

*I'm not scared of him*, I remind myself. *He'd never hurt me. Again.*

"*Nid eich dewis chi yw gwneud*," Dav replies.

Is it a dragon language?

Simcoe's pupils slit, his teeth growing larger in a mouth that's stretching to accommodate them. "*Nid wyf yn caniatáu hynny!*"

This is getting rude. "It's not fair to—"

Dav's ears start pulling back. "*Nid oes angen eich caniatâd arnaf.*"

"You will *respect* me!" Simcoe thunders, and suddenly his whole face is dappled with forest-coloured scales, hands hardening into claws, and okay, alright.

I'm a *little* scared.

Dav pushes me behind him. I stumble, and go down hard on my ass. A red tail whips around my shoulders, steadying. My palms sting with carpet-burn. I lean sideways. I can't see. I don't know where the threat is—

"You've done nothing to earn it," Dav's shoulders drop forward, heavy with sudden muscle that tears through his button-down as his wings unfurl. He makes that hiss-click noise that features in the rare nightmares I have about Beanevolence burning.

"No!" I shout, and with nothing else I can do, I tug on his tail.

Hard.

Dav stumbles back and yowls like an affronted cat. I get myself on my feet and between the two dragons. Dav tries to push me aside, and I hold my ground, hands planted flat against his chest.

"Cut it out!" I shout. "You're not setting him on fire!"

"Colin—!" Dav says, my name squealing through his elongating mouth like the screech from a rusty pulley.

"Move," Simcoe snarls. "It would only burn my clothes."

"Then you can't spit fire in here because I have no desire to see your junk!"

Both dragons pause. Dav chokes back a surprised chuckle. Simcoe snorts smoke out his nose.

"Go cool off." I shove Dav at the door toward the kitchen.

"I am not leaving you—!"

"I will be on my best behavior," Simcoe says placidly, scale melting back into flesh, smiling like the Cheshire Cat.

*Biiiiiitch.*

Fuck it. Simcoe wants to treat me like I'm the little wifey? Fine, I'll act like it.

God, getting between those two for the rest of my life is going to be like refereeing for the twins.

"Colin—" Dav tries again, even as he's letting me shove him into the hall that separates this formal public space from the privacy of the house.

"Out. Chill." I close the door in his face.

When I turn around, Simcoe is entirely human again, smugly patting his hair into place.

"Well that was certainly a visit, wasn't it? I'll walk you out," I say, diving for my best imitation of Mum. It's a good trick—most people are too polite to tell you that they want to stay and fight more without sounding like a complete twat.

Luckily, it's a trick that works on dragons. Or at least, dragons as obsessed with poshness as Lt. Gov. Fuckface. He only looks mildly shocked to be railroaded to the door so politely.

Simcoe follows me to the modest foyer, and we shuffle awkwardly as he waits for me to open the door for him.

"Well. Thanks for stopping by," I say, when he hesitates on the front step. "See ya."

"Wait," Simcoe says, hand on the door to keep me from shutting this one in his face, too. "I hope that display hasn't put you off a life amongst dragons."

"But you'd be fine if it has?" I ask.

Simcoe blinks, not expecting to be called out. "You said it," he simpers, recovering quickly.

"And you could make it happen?" I shove my hands in my back pockets, unimpressed. "I was told there were no take-sie-backsies."

Simcoe gestures after Dav. "He is the one who says it's all just gossip rags and celebrity television. I suppose it would not be too much of a scandal, were I to exert a modicum of, shall we say, influence?"

He's saying he's willing to threaten journalists? No surprise there. He's already had my socials shadowbanned.

"Nah. I'm good."

Irritation crosses Simcoe's face, but leaves quickly. "If that's your choice."

*Wasn't aware you thought I was worthy of getting to choose.*

"Not just mine," I remind him.

"Then I want us to be friends," Simcoe says, and the way he delivers it sounds and looks genuine. Which gets my hackles up, because I don't know how much friendship I want from a man who thinks corporal punishment is peachy. "You are to be family in a way, son."

"I'm not your son," I blurt.

It's the second time he's called me that.

There won't be a third.

"Ah, yes, of course not," Simcoe says. "I would never presume to replace Jean-François Levesque."

I blink hard, because otherwise I might shout *how do you know his name?* I don't because it's a stupid question–Dav told him last night. Besides, the minute I blipped onto his radar, Simcoe was probably handed a file of all my personal information, and like, I dunno, my grades and shoe size and copies of every piece of macaroni art I'd ever done in kindergarten.

"But if I may presume at least a sliver of a paternal relationship, you must forgive me," Simcoe presses. "Alva was sent to us so young, you understand. He was beloved of my father., and I have done my best to serve him after. As his Favorite, you will be as valued in my heart."

*So, not at all?*

Simcoe holds out his hand, clearly looking for a friendly parting hand-shake and, sulkily, I take it. He covers my offered hand with his other one, pressing our palms together, sliding the tips of his fingers across my pulse point. It's weird.

"Thank you." When he finally lets go, I resist the urge to wipe my hand on my jeans. He raises his eyebrows expectantly. I force myself to add: "Your Excellency."

He wasn't expecting that, and his eyes widen slightly. "Hmm," he hums to himself, and finally heads to the waiting town car.

Good riddance.

I expect to find Dav in our room, but he's not there. I'm antsy, so I decide to use that nervous energy to screw up my courage and take another flying leap off a different cliff.

I've made it clear to Dav's people that this is happening.

Now to do the same with mine.

**Fam vidcall now pls?,** I text the group chat, before I can chicken out.

A rhythmic thump catches my attention, and I move to the window. Dav is in the back, tucked around the side of the house, barely visible. He's swinging an axe with ferocious anger, plowing through a swiftly-dwindling pile of firewood, the remaining shreds of his shirt hanging off his arms. At least he's getting his frustration out in a productive—and very hot—way. Much better than burning the reception room.

I throw open the window and stick my head out.

"Hey! Sexy!" I call. Laughter floats up from the patio below me. I look down. Luiz and Sarah wave. When I look back up, Dav has the axe buried in a log and his hands on his hips, watching me. "He's gone."

"Am I allowed in?" Dav shouts back, aggrieved but not angry. "Or will you slam the door in my face again?"

"Come in, drama queen." I duck back inside before the peanut gallery can add their nickel.

My phone chimes, and I have just enough time to sit in one of the chairs by the fireplace before the video call starts.

"*Mo leanbh*!" Mum says. "Hello!" She's in her back garden, by the look of it. Stu's in his own living room, and Gem is taking the call from somewhere by the water.

"Hi fam."

Gem sets down what looks like an iced coffee and says: "What's the emergency?"

"None, really. I just... um..." I fiddle with the pin on my shirt. "Uh, wanted to tell you that—"

"What's that?" Gem shrills, pointing over my shoulder. I crane my head around, to find Dav crawling in through the bedroom window like a fucking gargoyle.

"What, the stairs were too much?"

Dav leers at me. "I thought I was a drama queen." He steps down onto the carpet, brushing the tattered button down off his arms, and tucking his wings away. His naked torso is on full display. "Who are you talking to?"

"Uh," I say, pressing my phone to my chest, which only partially muffles the laughing. "You... you may want to grab a shirt, babe. And then, um... come say hi to my family?"

Dav flushes up and dives for the wardrobe.

As first meetings go, this could have gone worse.

Once he's decent, Dav wiggles his way behind me on the chair, his thighs bracketing mine, so he can hook his chin over my shoulder. He looks so *cute*, his hair slicked back with sweat, smelling of rough labor, and pressed right up against my ass, and it is *so not fair*.

This dragon is going to be the death of me.

"Pleased to meet you all," Dav says, charming as fuck and smiling as if his arms weren't cinched around my waist.

I'm guessing he's feeling possessive after that *display* downstairs. It's fine that he's re-grounding himself in my presence. According to Onatah, that's literally what I'm here for. What's less fine is him octopussing in front of my siblings.

"Oh, pleased to meet you, as well, er, your Lordship," Mum says, blushing and giggling, and jeez Mum. I didn't expect her to be the kind of woman who titters about royalty and peerages. Especially when Dav is so far down in the pecking order.

"Dav, please, Mrs. Levesque," my dragon corrects.

"Then it's Helen to you, dear."

"So polite!" Gem says. "See if you can get your manners to rub off on Colin."

"I'm sure there's other things they rub off."

"Stuart!" Mum scolds, while my blush goes nuclear.

Dav grins wider, evidently delighted to be tortured by my brother.

"I'm so glad you called," Mum says. "*Despite* Stuart. We've been wanting to meet you."

"And I you," Dav says smoothly. Out of frame, Dav slides his hand down my free arm, to brush his fingers along my pulse point. I try not to shiver.

Bastard.

"So, where were you when you vanished?" Gem asks, looking innocent. "Because, like, it *wrecked* Colin. You know that, right?"

And that's my big sister.

Straight for the kill.

"I am aware," Dav says seriously. His hand tightens around my wrist, warm and reassuring. "And I regret that I cannot say."

"But Colin knows?" Stu asks.

"Hey, I'm right here," I protest. "Also, I can fight my own battles."

"Colin knows," Dav confirms. "And it will not happen again."

"That's why I called you," I break in. "We're, uh... shacking up."

"Shacking up?" Mum repeats, and Dav echoes it in the exact same incredulous tone.

"There's formal dragonish words for it and everything," I rush to say, before Dav can add anything. "But basically it amounts to me and Dav, living together."

"I see," Mum says, clearly not seeing at all.

"What about your apartment?" Stu asks.

"Uhhh..."

"Colin is paid out until the end of the year," Dav says. "At which time his roommate should be back with her fiancé, and they will assume full control of the lease."

I'd be mad at him for arranging that behind my back, except that was sorta the plan with Katiya all along.

"Do you need me to come down with Dad's van?" Stu offers.

"I thank you, no," Dav says. "My people will arrange for Colin's things to be packed. I doubt we'll elect to move, ah, the furniture."

"Yeah, no, it's crap," Stu agrees.

"You're the one who helped me move that sofa into the apartment," I remind him.

"After the previous tenant had already left it on the curb. It was already garbage when we moved it *back in*."

"It was free."

"Doesn't make it any less garbage," Gem says.

"We can make a weekend of it!" Mum suggests, and yeah, *no*, I'm not ready to have that conversation yet. The one where I have to explain the walled compound, and the privacy hedges, and the staff, and Dav being weird about people on his patch.

"Er," Dav says, and thank god, he's on the same page.

"Maybe we'll come to Orillia," I suggest.

"How about Friday?" Mum asks. "Colin doesn't work at the café on the weekends. Dav, is that fine with your work schedule, dear?"

I have *so much* explaining to do.

And I cannot *think* with the way Dav's other hand has moved to my thigh.

"Uh, we'll talk about it and I'll text you," I say. "Uh, sorry, there's a thing that... Dav's gotta do now... so, we gotta go."

"Oh," Mum says, disappointed. "Thank you for finally introducing us."

"Yeah, love you lots, bye," I say, reaching for the disconnect button.

I get to it just as Gem is chuckling: "Don't call yourself a *thing—*"

As soon as it's off, Dav pulls my phone from my hand and drops it onto the table beside the chair. He lifts my wrist to his mouth. His tongue is hot and wet, and damn that feels nice, so I wriggle around until I'm straddling his lap.

"Hello," I say, as he noses up the path of a vein, pressing a ticklish kiss into the bend of my elbow, then nipping all the way up to the corner of my jaw. He worries at the skin under my ear. "What's this?"

"You smell..." I assume he means in a good way because he sucks in another deep lungful, pressing his face against my neck, then my wrist, then my neck again. Then he sticks his tongue in my mouth, so, you know, I'm figuring he's not going to finish that sentence.

A little prick at my collar surprises me, but only because I wasn't expecting it.

Dav's got one sharp talon hooked into the neck of my Henley.

"Don't move," he whispers, and pulls downward slowly.

The shirt stretches, and I hold my breath, forehead pressed against Dav's, the anticipation delicious. I groan and arch my back as the fabric gives way. Five stinging points of warning pressure prickle around my belly button. I freeze. "I said, be still."

"Go faster, then."

"Impatient," Dav growls. "*Impertinent.*"

One hand goes to my fly, shredding, but they're not my favorite jeans, so I don't care. Those sharp claws don't break my skin; knowing that they could, though, that Dav could scrape me to ribbons if he wanted to, gets me horny. All that power under me, and he's controlling it. His other hand pulls the tatters of my shirt away before lifting that same wrist to his mouth. Fuck, the things his tongue can *do.*

"The scent here," he says in a strangled hiss. When he pulls back, though, his face has *changed.* Dav's eyes, which have always looked human except in color, suddenly seem alien. His pupils have elongated, opening wider like some eldritch orifice, deep and consuming and magnetic. He leans close, nose twitching, lips redder than kissing would make them, forked tongue flickering. I flinch when it flutters along the side of my temple, tasting the sweat there.

He's never slipped his skin in bed before.

Something's wrong.

# Chapter Thirty-Eight

My breath catches in a burning ball at the hollow of my throat. Part of me shouts *Predator, run away*! Another part shouts, *Teeth! Stay still*! And another, the deeply human part of me, the part that was my ancestors who had grown up with dragons, lived alongside them for uncountable generations, says *Be still, he'd never hurt you.*

"Dav," I whine. My voice is squeaky and tangled. My heart kicks like a rabbit in a shoebox. "Hey, hold up."

Instead of holding up, he surges to his feet, wings snapping open with a bullwhip crack. In a second I'm on my back on the bed. Claws prick along the soft flesh of my inner arms, where he's got them pinned above my head.

"Dav, please," I try again, chest hitching. He snuffles behind my ear, god, are his teeth pointed? Are they right above my jugular? "What's wrong?"

"Mine Own," he hisses. Goosebumps ripple across my flesh. He burns like a star, and where his cheekbone drags across my throat it's slick with scales. "*Mine.*"

"Yes," I choke desperately. "I'm yours, okay, but—"

"Stay sssssstill," he hisses, and hunches his shoulders, visibly shudders as he pulls away from my soft underbelly.

*What the fuck is happening,* I think frantically, *He's usually so together, what—*

"You stink," he growls, hands flexing gently, ankles tangling with mine, pushing outward so he can settle into the cradle of my hips.

Usually I like it when he manhandles me a bit. It's sexy, the way he can move me so effortlessly. *Would* be sexy if we were playing, if we'd negotiated any of this in advance. But we hadn't.

*I'm not scared of Dav, I can't be. I won't let him make me.*

"I'll take a shower," I say.

I can't see his expression now. His hair has flopped down in front of his face, his features screwed small, as if he's concentrating with all his might. I don't know what he's thinking. Christ, I don't *know* what he's thinking.

"Let me up, love," I say, a tiny, breathy plea. "Come on, I can shower."

"No!" he snarls again, dropping the whole weight of his body on top of mine, punching the breath out of my lungs in surprise.

"Sssssstay sssssstill." His body rolls against mine, once, a high whining keen escaping. "Please. Help me, Mine Own. Stay still."

"I'm staying still," I say. "Okay? I'm here. I'm yours. I'm not going anywhere."

He's fighting something. It's in the way his muscles flex and roll, the way he shudders, letting his mouth get close to my face, my hair, but never touch, never kiss.

"Please," he sobs, miserable. "Don't fight me."

"I'm not," I protest gently, and I take as deep a breath as his weight on my ribcage allows, then force my muscles to let go. Legs limp, hands soft, uncurled from their fists, head back, chin raised.

Exposed.

Vulnerable.

He exhales, relief in the noise. He presses his mouth against my leaping pulse, tastes the flop-sweat gathered on my collarbones.

I focus on my breathing. Slow in, slow out.

Gentle.

Calm.

I *am* scared.

Scared as *fuck.*

Dav's nose smushes against my cheek, breathing in the air straight from my lungs, chin resting on mine as if he's desperately weary, can't even hold his head up. Or like he can't let himself have any more than this awkward press of face-to-face.

"That whoreson," Dav says, smearing the words against my mouth. "That *thief.*"

"Who?"

"He *touched* you."

What?

*What?*

And then it slams home—Onatah refusing skin-to-skin contact, Laura's dancing gloves, the way Lt. Gov. Fuckface offered his hand at the door, held on too long. The way his finger had brushed along the underside of my wrist. My brain lights up like a Tesla coil, arc lighting jumping from vertebrae to vertebrae up my spine until it tingles out the top of my head: *revelation.*

I'd thought the handshake was weird.

I hadn't realized it was *deliberate.*

"That's right," I say hastily. "He touched me."

"You *let* him," he accuses, wounded, and now he pulls back. He lifts my arm, sneers at it as if he could see the stain Simcoe imprinted on my flesh.

Now I can see him, too. Somehow his eyes have gotten too big for his face, red scales gathering around their tender rims.

"It was a handshake. To mend fences." I'm careful to keep my body language open, accessible, all his. "He wants to break us apart, but I won't let him. It was just a handshake, because it's good manners. Because he cares about manners. I did it to keep us safe."

Dav growls, a rolling, menacing sound that shakes my bones. "*I* keep you safe."

"But you weren't there, and I—ah! Dav!" I whine and wriggle. "You're hurting me!"

He stops moving, eyes flickering down to where his claws have punctured flesh. They're just a small constellation of blood spots, no worse than a prick with a pin.

"*Fy Nhrysor*," he says in that language I don't know but I am starting to suspect is Welsh. He sounds wounded and terrified. He hasn't snapped out of whatever this is, he's still holding me down, but his eyes are his again, fearful and wet. "I'm sorry,... I don't know how to..."

"Mark me," I say suddenly, before my sense can catch up with my mouth. "Give me a hickey. On my wrist, right here. Bite it."

I push the arm he's holding up in front of his face.

"Colin—"

"Go ahead." I try to infuse more confidence into it than I'm feeling. "You won't hurt me."

"I might."

"You *won't*."

He runs his tongue first over each of the pinpricks, lapping away the blood and soothing the little stings. His mouth is wet and wide on my arm, his saliva washing away whatever trace of Simcoe might be left. By the time he's sucked a livid purple mark into the skin, he's shuddering and heaving like he's just run a marathon.

"Hey," I say softly, when he's sprinkling little kisses around the hickey. I reach up, brushing his lank, damp hair back from his forehead. "Hey. Look at me."

I'm still fucking terrified. But Dav is clearly more scared than me.

"I'm sorry," he sniffles, raw. "It's been so long since I've had a Favorite, and I—no, it's not an excuse, I'm *so* sorry—"

He retreats to huddle against the footboard.

"If I leave, will you jump me?" I ask, feet tingling with the itch to run, lungs tight. I take deliberate, slow breath after deliberate, slow breath, keeping up the illusion of calm surrender.

"No," Dav grinds out, curling in on himself. His knuckles are white as he grips his own bare ankles. I want to kiss them. I want to scream. "Just... move slow."

I sit up as slowly as I can, abdomen trembling with the effort.

"Don't look me in the eye." His whole body shudders. The tendons of his neck stand out, ropes under his flesh. "Don't challenge me. But don't turn your back."

I slide as slowly as possible to the side of the bed, eyes firmly on his feet. I've never studied them before. The vulnerable sweep of the arch. The knobbly way his pinkie toe sticks out. I back toward the door, slip my phone off the table. His big toe has sparse ginger-gold hair on the knuckle. His toenails are as fussily manicured as his fingernails.

Yesterday's jeans and shirt are still laying on the floor by the door, and I scoop them up. I bump into the door frame, shuffle to the side, and back into the hall. One step to the left, and his head shoots up, pupils slit again as he struggles to restrain himself.

Another step, and I'm cut off from his eyeline.

He lets out a desperate, terrible wail.

I tear toward the front door. I'm in the shirt before I hit the landing, and I swap the jeans in the foyer. I jam my feet into my shoes, and don't stop running until I am all the way to the front gates. I wrench them open, and eel through the gap. I wriggle into the space between the twisting trunk of a cedar hedge and the wall, slide down, press my bruised wrist against my mouth, and start to cry.

My phone tells me it's only been an hour. Feels longer. It's felt like an entire fucking geolithic era: an ice age, and a thaw. My eyes and nose are raw from rubbing them on my shirt and the hickey on my wrist *throbs*.

*What do I do?* My mind is starting to rev back up. *Holy shit, what was that? Do I go back inside? Do I... I don't know what to do.*

Dav hasn't come to find me.

I can't decide if I'm relieved or hurt.

What if he's still out of his head? But what if he's just Dav again? What if he's sorry, and he's back to normal?

My hands are shaking. I don't know what to do.

It's quiet. There's no search party calling my name. There's no Sarah peering around the bush, asking if I'm alright. There's no Diego shouting "found him!"

There's nothing.
Dav hasn't told anyone.
Or he *has* told them, and they don't care.
What do I do?
Do I go back inside?
Do I leave?
Dav said to walk away, to get out of his sight.
He didn't mean forever.
*Did* he mean forever?
I think about texting Dr. Chen, but she doesn't know dragons. I type out a text to Hadi, **What defines an abusive relationship?** Then I delete it, because that's not right. Dav isn't abusive. He was... *changed*. Hadi wouldn't know why.

That leaves just one other person. I text her: **I need you to come get me.**

Another hour later, the gentle roar of a motorcycle wakes me from a miserable, dehydrated doze. I lift my head from where I had it resting on my knees, the monster hickey cradled against my stomach. The motor cuts off right in front of my bush. There's the crunch of a kickstand on gravel. How does she know where I am?

I must stink.
Stink of Simcoe.
Stink of what Dav did.
Onatah parts the bushes far enough to get a good eyeful.
"You look like shit," is what she says.
"You got gloves on?"
"Yeah."
"Help me up?"
Onatah levers me to my feet, pulls me through the branches. She lifts my wrist, turns it over and sniffs at it. It's flaked over with gross dried saliva. The bruise itself is huge, three wobbly circles overlapping one another, already angry red around the edges and purpling in the center, a thin cut oozing a sluggish bead of drying blood. It's horrifying. It hurts like crazy.

*It was my idea.*
She circles around me, looking for other hurts. My neck burns when I turn it. It's rough with another massive suck bruise. Onatah comes back around to stare at my face, which I'm sure is puffy and lined with tear-tracks. My eyes feel swollen.

"Fucking colonizer bullshit." She yanks me in for a warm, firm hug.

"Don't touch me!"

"Over the clothes," she says gently. She smells dragon-smoky, and like the wind, and leather, and that's good, right now. It's *safe.* Then she adds in a slightly louder voice: "You're not going back in there. Not before you clean up, and we have the conversation someone else clearly wormed out of."

A rustling on the other side of the gate catches my attention. "Who was...?"

"Never mind. Get on the bike. Helmet's in the saddlebag."

We're already off down the road before I realize that the sound on the other side of the wall had probably been Dav. Standing right *there*.

Probably had been there the whole time.

And not saying a goddamned thing.

# chapter Thirty-Nine

For those of you following along at home, this is the climax of Act Two, the part of the story where the clues are supposed to all come together and a revelation occurs. The main and subplots merge, and you realize what was happening over *there* was part of what's happening over *here* all along. Surprise! Here's the thing though: this is real life, and not a story. So all the small, important clues? I wasn't fucking clocking them.

By the time Onatah parks the bike on St. Paul Street, Beanevolence is closed. The lights are still on, though, and Hadi lets us in when I bang on the glass.

Without so much as a hello, I make a bee-line for the bathroom. Through the closed door and the rush of water in the sink, I can hear the murmur of voices but can't make out the words. I strip off my shirt. In the harsh light of the bathroom, I look sallow. Well, more sallow than usual. My hair is a wreck, my face smeared with tear tracks and road dust. The burst capillaries on my neck are a horror show. There are fine red lines and prick-marks from Dav's teeth and claws all over my chest and belly.

I look savaged.

And it hurts.

Fuck, it all *hurts*.

I've been scratched up by lovers before, but this wasn't pleasurable. I didn't want it. Dav didn't want it either. He fought it, and he fought it hard, shuddering and telling me how to get away from him.

This isn't something Dav did *to* me.

This was...

This was bullshit.

I scrub every bit of skin I can reach—and I am angry now. So angry I have to flex my fists to fight the urge to punch the mirror, which won't make me feel better and would mean I'd have to buy Hadi a new one. I shove my way back into my shirt, seething, the scrape of fabric making it worse, and good, good, I *want* to feel it. The anger. The pain. Because... how dare, how *dare* Simcoe do that to Dav?

I'm mad about what happened to me, too. I'm filled with terror at the memory of how effortlessly Dav proved he could overpower me, how quickly it had all happened and how... how *helpless* I'd been.

But worse is that Simcoe shook my hand and he *knew* what would come of it.

I hate the bastard so goddamned much right now. I try to imagine the hate as a physical thing, a black sludge I can expel from my body. Dr. Chen taught me this one, visualizing an emotion you want to purge. I cough, hork up the hate, spit into the sink, imagine it swirling down the drain, gone. It works, sort of. Leaves me feeling hollowed-out.

When I shut the taps, it's just in time to catch Onatah's "Got anything stronger?" through the door.

When I emerge, damp around the edges but feeling slightly more human, there are coffee cups, a carafe, and a bottle of whiskey on the table in the conversation area. The black leather sofas are occupied with Onatah, Hadi... and Pedra.

"Hi," she says softly, when I stop to glare at her.

"Colin," Hadi says, and it's not a scold so much as a warning.

"Hi," I say back, feeling small and shamed. "I'm an asshole and I'm sorry?"

"Is that a question?" Hadi hands me a mug and chivvies me into a chair.

"No. I'm really sorry."

"Emotions were high," Pedra says. "No one was thinking clearly."

"And we are now?" I take a gulp of what turns out to be more booze than bean juice. "Whoa, that burns."

"Yes," Pedra says darkly. She pulls a folder out of the bag at her feet, and hands it over.

I flip it open, skimming the text. **Evolutionary Biology and Ensured Mutual Survival,** jumps out at me. **Still just a theory pending a wide-scale investigation into the macronutrient breakdown of the enzymes in dragons-fire... what saliva does to human blood cells... to cancerous cells... Like an mRNA vaccine, dragonsfire provides human bodies with proteins to block genetic coding for common illnesses... what if all of their bodily fluids... blood, saliva, semen—**

*I've swallowed.* That's what I think first. *I've sucked Dav off, and now I'm not allergic to chocolate. Jeez. This is a scientific study on the medicinal benefits of dragon-fucking.*

"Have you read this?" I ask.

Hadi nods. Onatah holds out her hand. I don't know how legible the diagrams will be to her, don't know what kind of science education she has, but the way her eyebrows are slowly pulling down as she flips through, I'd bet the answer is 'pretty damn legible.'

Pedra is clearly proud of it. I don't have the heart to tell her that the dragons already know all this... and don't care.

"What do you plan to do with this?" I ask, trying to figure out how best to rain on her parade.

"You know about Onatah's controlled urbanization and food forests?" Pedra asks.

"No."

"Cultivated wilderness," Onatah explains. "Planting food-bearing plants that work harmoniously with wooded areas, instead of strip-clearing for farming, and ruining the topsoil."

"It's aspirational," Pedra goes on breathlessly, sounding like the biggest fangirl I've ever met, and Onatah shoots her a flattered look. "It's the way North America was before the European dragons started spreading their Empires, and hoarding as many people as they could."

"People they've never even met. People they've never even touched," Onatah growls.

The way she says that gives me a shiver and I set down my mug to wrap my arms around my stomach. My wrist throbs.

"I understand that the dragon-controlled territories to the West, in the Mexican Empire, are even more vibrant and natural. The trade route systems that colonization disrupted alone would—Let me put it this way," Pedra interrupts herself. "What's the average lifespan of a human in Canada?"

I shrug. "Eighty-something?"

"Eighty-three," Pedra plows ahead. "But the data's skewed. It's eighty in British territories, and ninety-seven in Indigenous ones. And in Aotearoa *and* Nippon, it's around a hundred and twenty! I was right about the food allergies, and the beans. I put it out there—"

"And got Dav arrested because of it," I hiss. *And whipped*, I think, but don't add. I know better than to share that. I have no illusions about how long Lt. Gov. Sadist's arms are.

Pedra stutters to a stop. "I am sorry for that. It wasn't my intention. But there are people out there reading it, secretly, in the dark corners of the internet. It's growing. There's more than they're telling all of us."

I exchange a guilty glance with Onatah. Hadi, of course, catches it immediately.

*Don't tell anyone*, Simcoe had commanded us. Me.

But he hadn't explicitly told us to *shut down* anyone else, either. Or that I had to deny anything when directly confronted.

Malicious compliance it is, then.

"You already knew this," Hadi says.

"I just learned it like, fuck, twenty-four hours ago but... yeah."

"The dragons know?" Pedra gasps. "And they're not...?"

"Of course they'd hide that they're the greatest pharmaceutical miracle in existence," I scoff. "Of course they'd make a big conspiracy out of it, make themselves feel *important*."

"Makes sense," Hadi says. "Humans outnumber dragons. It could get ugly if there was a push to just *take* it, to kidnap dragons, strip them down to parts for medicine—"

Onatah makes one of the serpent-noises of disgust I'm used to hearing from Dav. "This wouldn't be a problem if—uhg. European dragons are the speciesist jerks, and Simcoe is one of the worst." She holds up Pedra's paper. "This isn't the way I do it. The way any of the rest of us do it. This knowledge is shared freely everywhere but in the European kingdoms."

"The dragons don't have that much control over our lives," Pedra laughs. "They can't censor the whole Internet!"

"Yes," I say softly. "They can."

Across from me, Hadi swallows hard. Pedra turns a queasy sort of gray.

"Explain how you do it, then," I say eventually, wheels grinding. "There's seven billion people on Earth, and maybe only about a million of them are dragons. You can't possibly cook for every single person every day."

Onatah rolls her eyes. "It's tune-ups, not daily sessions. It's touchpoints. It's barbeques and festivals, and making food that stores. Smoked meats, or dehydrated fruit. My people are getting ready for one right now, which is why Nîcimos isn't here. It's a lot of hot, hard work, but it's worth it."

*Ha! Nîcimos! Finally got a name!*

"I see," Pedra says slowly. "I assume the efforts are... appreciated?"

"Very much so. My people are happy. And very healthy."

"It must be lovely, to be able to gather everyone together to celebrate," I muse. "Dav must be envious."

Onatah gives me a meaningful look: *Of course he is.*

"And *nobody* around here knows about this?" Pedra says.

"Some have to," Hadi says. "Or humans wouldn't join hoards, right?"

"Only Favorites get The Gift," I say, which I probably shouldn't but... fuck it. Let Lt. Gov. Fuckface whip me too, if he wants. I'm not lying to my friends. "Dav doesn't cook the daily breakfast. He just pays for it."

"Then why would any of them stick around this many years later?"

"Their great-grandparents had special skills the dragons wanted, like winemaking, or they needed security, shelter, jobs and they were ... annexed, for want of a better term. Then that's it," I say. "For you and for your descendants. You're set for life, but you're also Collected for life, too."

"So they're *picked*," Hadi clarifies, nose wrinkling in disgust. "It has nothing to do with where you're born?"

"You can apply, too," Onatah corrects. "But the ones who live and work with Dav now? They're the children and grand-children of the 'right sort of people' who were hand-picked for him when his territory was established."

"*For* him," I repeat with disgust. I bet I know who by, too.

"And what does that mean, exactly? The right sort of peo-ple," Hadi scoffs, looking around at everyone crowded around the coffee table, cataloging each face. "Wait, hold on. How many of Dav's staff are people of color?"

"What?" It takes me a second to figure out what she's driving at. This room, this group, this rainbow of faces... this is what Canada looks like. This is the Canada that Dav fought for, bled for. So why doesn't Dav's hoard reflect that?

"Oh, like maybe a third of them?" I guess. "Um, but, uh, now that I think about it, not many of the legacy families."

"But the settlers in this area, at the time his household was set up—"

"No, of course they weren't all White," Onatah says. "There were my people, before they were driven off by bullshit bro-ken treaties, then a large community of Africans, who had escaped enslavement. Dav was told they weren't respectable."

"Told by who?" Pedra asks.

"Guess," I sneer.

Onatah scoffs. "This is new territory to them, at least. Your boy is the first Marquis, and he'd never established anything before, didn't have the benefit of family close by to help him make his selections. John Simcoe, he... took Dav under his wing. Fatherly. Bossy. Didn't sit well with Frank, when he found out that his dad had given a prime piece of real estate to an unrelated upstart who already had territory to inherit in Wales."

I tuck my fouled hand under my armpit.

"What happened?" Hadi asks.

"The way Dav tells it, Frankie boy was supposed to be sent home from Wellington's regiment when the fighting got serious with the Americans, but he got shot before he could. They weren't sure if he would live, so Dav was recruited to take his place and..." she shrugs.

"He won the Battle of Lundy's Lane and burnt down the Presidential Mansion," I fill in. "And was gifted a march as a result."

Onatah snorts a plume of smoke at the inadequate descrip-tion of the injustice done to her grandfather.

"And the people of color who *are* part of the hoard, who chose them?" Hadi presses.

"Dav did," Onatah says. "Later. When he had someone to help him make better decisions."

*Charlotte*, I realize. *Oh, fuck. That'll be my job. Dav will expect me to help him... pick people to Collect. To entrap.*

Hadi makes a frustrated noise and blurts: "So, what, the gift of long life and good health is just for white folks? After they took over half the world and killed all of *our* dragons? That's bullshit!" Hadi scowls. "Whites as a deliberately cultivated invasive species."

"Exactly," Pedra says, voice hitching. She's shaking. We're all shaking. Right down to our bones. "It's population control. It's *selective breeding*."

Revulsion shakes up my spine, and my mug judders so hard I slosh all over my thighs.

That's what Simcoe meant.

That's what he...

Oh, god, I'm gonna puke.

I swallow more coffee instead to keep my gorge down. "And what, I'm supposed to go back there and help Dav with that? After... after what happened today? No way."

"No, you don't have to. Dav doesn't want—he's never wanted... fuck." Onatah shakes out her shoulders, releasing her frustration.

"What do you mean, *what happened today*?" Hadi asks.

I lift my arm, turn it outwards, so everyone can see the horrible bruise I've been hiding. "Touching another dragon is a no-no."

"The fuck is that," Hadi snarls, jumping to her feet and grabbing my arm. "First he stabs you and now, what's this, did he try to eat you?"

"It wasn't his fault." I drag my arm back, tuck it against my pooch, skooch down in the chair, feeling exposed.

"If you make a single joke about walking into a doorknob I'm going to kick his ass myself."

"When another dragon touches a Favorite, leaves their scent on them, a dragon goes... feral," Onatah says. "Or, they do if they're touch-starved idiot settlers."

"So your favorite, Nîcimos, they're not out of bounds?" I guess.

"Why would they be?" Onatah asks. "My beloved is an extension of me, and I of my beloved. And we are all Wahkohtowin. This—" she sneers, gesturing at the ruin of my neck. "—only happens when you lock a Favorite away like a jewel in a vault."

Hadi turns a horrified expression to Onatah. "Why would you touch him, then?"

"It wasn't me," Onatah says.

"It was that fucker Simcoe," I explain. "I shook his hand when he left the house—"

"Why was he at your house?"

"It's not *mine*. He came to try and talk Dav out of me, and then they fought and I made Simcoe leave and—"

"On purpose?" Hadi demands. "And he knew Dav would react like that?"

"He knew," Onatah says softly. "Because it's happened before."

# chapter forty

Onatah splashes another tot of whiskey into everyone's cups but Hadi's.

Okay.

This is going to be *that* kind of story.

"Charlotte was Dav's first Favorite," Onatah starts gently. Hadi shoots a startled look at me. I slump lower. "She's the one who gave him that nickname. She gave him front gates. She loved to dance as much as him. Can you imagine Alva-draig Tudor doing the Charleston? It was hilarious."

"How did they meet?" Pedra asks.

I'm glad she does, because my tongue has shriveled.

"Ypres, 1915. She was a nurse. She was kind, but angry at the pain the war inflicted. He was the Lieutenant Colonel in charge of a battalion."

I may find real-life history class boring AF, but even I knew that Ypres was both a Canadian triumph, and a slaughter. It's where John McCrae wrote *In Flander's Fields*: poppies, black birds wheeling across a gun-smoke sky, and crosses, row on row on row.

"Dav wouldn't allow the doctors to treat him until his men were seen to. To hear Charlie tell it, he was the most stubborn cuss to bleed all over her tent. Dav says he was helping the nurses with first aid. Charlie said he was fluttering around like a moth, leaving slipping hazards in his wake. She stuck him with an anesthetic and apparently he went down like a sack of potatoes," Onatah chuckles.

*Charlie.* Of course Dav would fall for a strong-willed, devious woman, who served people through healing, and called herself *Charlie.*

Still not jealous.

"When he came to, she was dressing his shoulder. He said she was glowing. Charlie said it was the light hanging above her head. But Dav spun it out that it was like she was a *twyleth twyg,* come to snatch him into the fairy realm."

Okay, maybe a bit jealous.

Has Dav ever talked with Onatah about the first time he saw me? Did he compare me to a bog witch?

"Charlie was an incomparable goddess, okay? I get it," I grump. Onatah kicks me under the chair. "Ow!"

"Don't be like that," she tuts.

"I'm not," I protest.

Hadi snorts.

"By the time the Great War was over, Dav had won Charlie over, too. She agreed to move to Canada, to become Dav's Favorite. But the life was... restrictive." Onatah shakes her head. "Dav... he doesn't pick humans that acquiesce or kowtow. He never has, not even for his casual lovers. You're so much like her, Colin. You're both bold, and blunt, and clever as fuck. And you give a shit about people, you know? Parties, and diamonds, and whatever else royal Favorites get themselves all worked up about, that doesn't matter to you. You're pretty in the same way, too—big eyes and stupid hair."

"Hey!"

"Charlie scandalized the county when she arrived with a bob."

"I feel like I should protest more." But the compliments, however backhanded they are, fill the hollow place today's other revelations carved out in my chest.

"You're also good for each other in the same way. He smiles more, he's grounded, he's focused. And you, kid, you're calmer, too."

"How do you know that?"

"Do you think I'd let my BFF moon over a human and not scope you out?"

"You were here before?" Hadi asks.

"Multiple times."

"Shit," I say. "I never noticed." I point to her horns.

"I wear a hat, dumbass. And it's not like you ever paid attention to anyone but Dav, anyway. The way you stared at him when you thought nobody was looking..."

I groan and cover my rising blush with my hand. "Don't."

"You know he added the chapter about PDAs to the book just for you?" She laughs. "He noticed that you're handsy."

"What book?"

It takes Onatah a second to realize I have no idea what she's talking about. "Fuck's sake. He had a book made for Charlie, with all the rules and stuff. He didn't give it to you?"

"That sounds horrific," I snort. "'Here's a textbook listing everything you're allowed to do for the rest of your life. Study up!' No thanks."

Onatah wipes at her face. "So not exactly like Charlie. She didn't resent having staff, like you seem to. Living the high life, she liked that. But she wanted something meaningful. Useful."

"But Favorites aren't useful," I say softly, as Hadi scowls. "They're ornamental."

"Becoming a Favorite is a reward for a victory well-earned, or a talent well-honed, or a blood-line well established. You have to have been born right, or you distinguished yourself," Onatah agrees.

(I had done none of those things.)

"At least in the British court?" Hadi asks, perceptive as always.

Onatah smirks.

"I don't want to rest." Despite my full-ass post-graduation year of spinning my wheels, I'm too hungry to rest. I *want* to do stuff. I just don't know what that looks like yet.

"Neither did Charlie. She gave a shit about Dav's hoard. Charlie was the one who set up the communal breakfast, so no one went into the field or to our offices hungry. She established charities. She was on local committees for schools, and veteran housing. She was determined to make a difference."

"She sounds amazing." I take another petulant sip of my coffeeish whiskey.

"She was," Onatah agrees.

I try not to take it personally. Just because Dav's first Favorite was incredible doesn't mean that he's traded down. Even though it feels like it.

*Does Dav only love me because I'm the male version of Charlie?* I could spin myself in circles second guessing him, but Dr. Chen would call that fawning behavior, and put a stop to it.

*Let what he shows you be what you believe*, she'd say. *Don't look for hidden meanings or subtext or tricks. People will tell you who they are—pay attention and accept it for what it is unless they prove otherwise.*

Dav loves me.

Dav loves *me*.

*Loves me so much he...* I press the heel of my hand against the hickey sharply. The pain brings me back into my body, into the present.

"So. How?" I don't need to elaborate.

Onatah knows what I mean.

"Dav and I, our lives, our cultures, our way of managing our hoards is... Charlie wanted to learn everything about how I do it, see what they could improve. They'd visit a lot. Sunday picnics, on this outcropping, above a river." Onatah's shoulders roll inwards in misery. I know this next part, but it doesn't make it any easier to hear. "Dav was... so young, and so cavalier, and..." She gestures helplessly, rumbling to clear away the wet thickness in her words. "He went down. Charlie reached out too far for him and... Dav caught himself. And I caught her."

Onatah looks at me, meaningfully. Hadi sucks in a hissing breath of horror, understanding right away what it means.

"Charlie swung back against the rock and, and there was so much blood—" Onatah's voice crackles. "I couldn't get past him. He was crouched over her, snarling, and she was bleeding and... he thought he was protecting her, you see?"

"Oh my god," Pedra whispers. She reaches over, offers Onatah the comfort I can't, lays a hand on her knee. Onatah clutches it. "That must have been awful."

Onatah takes a few, sucking breaths. "He was out of his fucking head. By the time Nîcimos came back with help—" she bites off the confession with a hard grunt, teeth clenched.

"It was no one's fault. But they blame Dav. His Favorite died in the territory of a 'heathen savage'." A prickle of foreboding crawls up my spine. "Because I touched her. And he let me."

"But you couldn't let her fall!" Hadi protests.

"According to them, I should have," Onatah snarls. "Better a dead Favorite, than a violated one."

That word—*violated*—slams into my chest like a baseball bat. What little calm I'd managed to cultivate shatters. The shrapnel stabs at my lungs. I half expect to cough up blood.

I must make a wounded noise, because everyone's eyes swing to me.

"He did it on purpose," I manage to shake out. "Dav's history, his past, Simcoe *knew* and he touched me anyway."

"That sadistic motherfucker," Hadi hisses. Suddenly she's on her knees in front of me, arms wrapped around my shoulders, my face in the tail of her hijab, clinging.

"But Dav stopped." I lay my forehead hard against her shoulder, grounding myself. "Dav stood in the bushes and let me cry, he didn't crowd me, didn't—"

My hands start clenching into fists of their own volition, and I press them against my heart in an effort to control both.

"Colin! Hey... breathe!"

"I am! I am breathing. I... oh god!"

Hands on the side of my face, fingers on my temple.

Five.... Five... five things I can see... I can't... I can't see... anything.

*Anything.*

"Colin!"

"I'm here."

"No, you're not, come on, look at me... Deep breaths."

That's something I can do.

In. Hold. Out.

The black spots at the edge of my vision recede.

When I look up, Hadi's eyes widen, and I can tell it's bad.

"Fuck. *Fuck.* I *knew* he hadn't told me everything," I hiss. The coffee threatens to make a reappearance. I bite down hard on the inside of my cheek to keep that from happening.

Hadi looks desperate and lost. "What can I do to help?"

"I can't... I don't think I can go back there." My insides cramp up, my breath clogging in my throat. The tears are already rolling down my face, my vision sliding. I grab Hadi's arms, fingernails digging in.

"Favorites don't get to change their minds," Onatah says softly.

"You can't seriously think we're going to let him go back there if Dav is going to maul him!" Hadi snarls.

"Hey, I don't make their rules!" Onatah protests. "But I can tell you this—if you run away, if you leave, they will find you and they will bring you back."

"Fuuuuuck," I whine.

"If it's any help, I do genuinely believe Dav will never hurt you."

"The thing on Colin's wrist begs to fucking differ!" Hadi says.

"That was my idea," I tell her. "I thought if he could mark me a different way—"

"Next time use soap," Onatah says.

"Well I know that *now*," I snark back.

"Yes. Now you do. And he'll work on it if you make him. He'll do better, too."

"You're starting to sound an awful lot like an abuse apologist," Hadi warns.

"No, just a dragon who knows how Dav thinks. Listen, Colin... do you know how suicidal dragons kill themselves?"

"*What*," I screech.

Hadi backs off to round on Onatah. "What the fuck is wrong with you?"

Onatah looks up at us both placidly. "Do you?"

"No!" My skin tightens in horror. "Of course not!"

"They cut themselves off," Onatah says. "They build walls, and they hide behind them."

Jesus fucking Christ.

She's not subtle. I knew Dav was unhappy before we got together. But I didn't realize he was *this* unhappy.

"They wait for the next war," Onatah adds, leaning back, eyes soft.

"Oh god." I was not prepared for this conversation. "Why would he...?"

"He thinks it's right that he wither away. Whether or not you or I, or anyone else who knows the full story agrees, *Dav* thinks it was his fault."

"But he's surrounded by humans." I point out.

"Servants," Onatah says, nose wrinkling. "Not a community, not the way it's supposed to be. He doesn't..." she groans, and tries again. "Dragons aren't supposed to be so isolated that another dragon leaving a scent on a Favorite makes that happen." She gestures at my wrist. "You follow me? Dragons need humans, the same way humans need dragons. We're as one species, Colin. The European dragons, they've... I don't know, forgotten it. Or are willfully ignoring it." Frustrated, she scratches at the base of a horn. "They're idiots."

"At least that's something we agree on."

"Let me explain it another way. What if you had a dog—"

"Not a pet," I snap.

"Dav is the dog. So, let's say you leave a dog in a room with a high-pitched whistle, and it howls and scratches, and you don't let it out. And after hours, you go into the room, and it's backed into the corner, teeth out. You pet it, like nothing's wrong. What's gonna happen?"

"It's stressed out and uncomfortable," Pedra says. "It's gonna bite."

We all look at the cut in the center of the hickeys on my wrist.

"Dav's trapped and stressed out?" Hadi asks. "Since Charlotte."

"Yeah," Onatah says. "And Simcoe's punishment made it worse. No Favorite for a *century*, no community engagement, no going into other's territories. Practically had him on house arrest."

"I am liking this guy less and less," Hadi growls.

Pedra squeezes Onatah's hand pensively. "Do you think it's deliberate? Simcoe deliberately stressing him out, isolating him, siccing him on Colin. Do you think that he...?" She turns her gaze up at Onatah, questioning.

"In my opinion?" Onatah says. "Yeah."

"What, so the Lieutenant Governor is what, trying to scare Colin away?" Hadi splutters. "Maybe get him *killed?*"

"Frank's always been envious of Dav," Onatah says. "His territory, his military victories, his father's admiration, his easy charm."

"You should have seen the way he glared at Dav last night," I tell them, instead of letting myself think about what Hadi is proposing. It's too big, right now. "And he's *totally* uncool about Dav and Laura being friends."

"Laura?" Pedra asks.

"Simcoe's Favorite. Laura Secord."

Hadi goggles at me. "When were you gonna tell me you met *Laura fucking Secord?*"

"I just did."

Pedra hums again, brain still whirring, and then, slowly, like her words are wild creatures she's afraid of letting loose, says: "Are we sure Charlotte's death *was* an accident?"

"She fell off a cliff, she wasn't shot by an assassin," Hadi says.

Onatah and Pedra exchange a glance, but neither says anything.

It's a minute before I can work up the spit and the courage to ask: "Do you think... Do you think he's a danger to himself? Will he—"

"No," Onatah cuts in. "Draconic instincts don't work like that. Sarah, the kids, the farm, he can't abandon them. Do you understand? He physically *could not* do that to himself. None of us could."

I'm relieved to hear it in a small, shamefully selfish way.

If he... if he dies.

If he does, then... Then it isn't my fault.

Hopefully.

"But if there was a barn fire, or another war, or something?" Onatah goes on. "Then before you, I might have said that I think he wouldn't be... as careful as he should be."

"Fuck," I say. My heart is beating too fast, I'm lightheaded and tingly with the drive to *runscreampunch* that has nowhere to go.

"You can't ask Colin to go back into a potentially dangerous situation because Dav might off himself," Hadi says, angry and blunt. "Dav's choices are not on Colin."

"No," I agree. "But I put on the pin. And that has responsibilities attached to it. And nothing will change that."

I'm trapped.

Doesn't matter if Dav hurts me again or not—he wouldn't, not on purpose, any more than that stressed dog can help biting—but nothing will change the fact that this is where I am. Now. Forever. This is *what* I am.

I am... Nothing.

Whatever shrapnel was in my lungs melts, liquifies, slides away.

And is replaced with...

Nothing.

Outside of Beanevolence, a car horn sounds.

It's a Helios. Gray. Tasteful. Patient.

I stand. Wipe my face. "That's my ride."

"Colin," Hadi says, tight. "I'll check on you, okay? I'll—"

"I'm fine."
I head for the door.
What else can I do?
Nothing.
Onatah walks me outside.
"Thank you," I say.
"For?"
"Dropping everything to help me."
She sticks her hands in her back pockets, all cocky swagger. "Maybe I'm helping Dav." She smirks at me and I let her push away my gratitude.

Doesn't mean I don't feel it though.

"Thank you for helping him, too. I get now that you're kinda the only one who does."

Whatever infinitesimal respect Onatah may have for British draconic propriety goes out the window, and she clutches me close in a firm hug.

"You guys don't deserve to spend the rest of your lives being bullied," she whispers in my ear as she lets go.

Janet gets out of the car, and opens the rear door.

"Master Levesque?" Janet says softly.

I stand on the sidewalk, hands shoved in my pockets. "What if I asked you to drive me to Orillia? To my family?"

Janet is too stoic to squirm. "I'd do it. But I would stay. I couldn't leave you there."

"What if I asked you to drive me to the airport?"

For a split second, anguish crawls over her face, but is quickly doused. "Please," she says. "Please *don't*, sir."

"No. Of course not," I say, and climb into the car, because what else can I do?

Nothing.

# chapter Forty-One

"You're back," Dav says cautiously as I enter his—our—*his* bedroom. He's seated by the fire, a half-drunk bottle of wine already beside his elbow. I assume the rest is inside him. He stands. Fidgets. Takes a step toward me. "I'm so sorry—"

"Don't," I hiss.

He stops.

It's one thing to know it's not the dog's fault it bit you. It's something else entirely to let it get close enough to do it again.

The nothingness I'd been stewing in since I left Beanevolence dissipates in the wake of... some emotion. Big. Choking.

"Are you alright?"

"Of course not."

"When you said Onatah told you about touching, I assumed—"

I'm humiliated, exhausted, frightened, worried for my safety, and he thinks he can tell me it's *my* fault for not understanding? As if nothing had happened, still didn't have bruises

319

on my wrist from his mouth, as if I hadn't been *this close* to being another Charlotte?

Like the song about the merry murderesses says, Dav has it coming. I throw a punch straight at his nose.

The thing with dragons, though, is that they're fast. Especially the ones with military training. Before my fist can connect, I'm on my back. Dav has one hand balled up in my shirt, holding me flat against the carpet. The air woofs out of my lungs as my internal organs catch up with the rest of me. My head doesn't hurt. It never hit the ground. He's got the back of my skull cradled in his hand.

He put me down as easily as manhandling a sleepy toddler. And he'd done it so gently.

I don't want his gentleness.

"I hate you so much right now," I snarl, pushing his shoulders. "Get off."

Dav stays where he is, oblong pupils blown wide, knees braced on either side of my ribs, hand in my hair like a lover. His fist flattens slowly over my heart, as if he could reach through my flesh and calm its frantic jumping.

Icy terror splashes over me.

Shit.

*Fuck.*

Did Onatah accidentally touch my skin when we hugged? Is Dav going to…?

He lifts my mangled wrist to his mouth to… to kiss it better? *Ha!* Too little, too late. Then he buries his face against my neck. He takes a long, slow inhale, his stomach expanding against mine, and drops his weight onto me by degrees. He's hard, but he doesn't grind down, for which I'm grateful. And then I'm mad all over again, because I shouldn't be grateful when I've already told him to let me go.

"Fuck off!"

"Please, stay still," Dav says. "I need to—"

"Off!" I kick at his calves.

Dav manages to overcome his bullshit draconic instincts, and scrambles back to sit on his heels. "Colin?"

"Don't you ever do that again!" I pant, my voice coming out high and thin, reedy with fear.

"You tried to punch me—"

I crabwalk back until I'm out of grabbing range. I use one of the posts of the bed to lever myself to my feet. "Don't you ever fucking hold me down again, do you hear me?"

"Colin, please—" He stands.

"*Do you hear me?*"

"I hear you!" He backs into the dresser, hands up in surrender.

"Fucking right you do!" I scream, and I jab my finger through the air like a sword. I'm sweating, panting. "You don't touch me again until I invite you to, got it?"

Dav's eyes grow wide in horrified understanding. "Of course. No question."

I want Dav to be the safe option again.

I want my agency back.

He waits for me to say something. *Do* something. He's always been so polite. Waiting for me to notice his regard. Waiting for me to make the first move. Waiting for me to hold his hand, tell him we're in it together, waiting for me to be the one to kiss him. Waiting for me to invite him in.

The only thing he never let me do first was to use the 'L' word.

"Are you really well? Your wrist?" he finally asks, when I'm calmer.

He gestures at the bruise, and it elicits a small kick of fear.

I don't want to be scared of Dav!

And I absolutely don't want to resent him.

This isn't fair.

How dare Simcoe do this to us? My heart is so broken right now. But I don't need to break his, too.

"Nothing permanent," I finally admit.

"I'm relieved to hear it."

More waiting.

"Will that happen every time?"

He huffs smoke out his nose. "It will never happen again, because he will never touch you again."

"That's not what I mean, and you know it."

"You must think me so ill-tempered—"

"I *really* don't," I protest. "I understand that it's a biological urge or whatever. I mean, I don't *understand* why it has to be like this *at all*, but I understand... it's not *fine*, but... it's fine."

"Then why do you reek of fear?" he asks, in a small voice.

I don't know what to say to that, so I don't say anything.

"It frightened me," Dav confesses. "I don't blame you if it frightened you, too."

"Babe, it scared the ever-loving *fuck* outta me. But not because—"

"We can work on it. Maybe I can—"

This isn't fair, making him contort himself like this, like I don't already know what scares him most. "Onatah told me about Charlie."

He makes a sharp noise. "You must hate me—"

"Don't put words in my mouth." He stops short, startled. "I'm angry about it, yeah, but not with you. I'm sorry, I shouldn't have taken that swing at you."

"There's no need to apologize, Mine Own, I—"

"Please let me finish." And then I take a deep breath, screw my eyes closed, and blurt out the rest of what I've been rehearsing in my own head since Janet picked me up. "I *am* terrified. But not of you. Not of the dragony bits of you. What scares me is how... how wrong this could all go. How easily. Do you understand? Accidents happen, so fast... and someone you love can be gone like th-that."

My chest burns, my chin wobbles and *fuck*, memories of Dad have slammed down so hard on the 'grief button' in my heart that I can barely breathe.

"Oh, Colin..." Dav says slowly.

"I can't lose someone I love again, not like that. I couldn't bear it if they did something to you, because of me. Or if something happened and I... I know it doesn't make any sense, I know it's *stupid*, but I love you too much to... to *do* this. Do you get me?"

Without moving at all, Dav *crumples*.

The next thing costs me a lot to say. It hurts. I feel like I should be spitting up blood as I tell him: "I love you. And I want you to be safe so I'm *staying*. But I... I'm not ready to do this. And I don't know... I don't know if I ever will be."

"I'm so sorry—"

"It's not your fault! It's not you. Okay? It's not *you*... it's just everything around you."

Dav makes that awful keening noise again.

The rest of what I was going to say turns to ash on my tongue.

And then I leave the room, because what else can I do? Nothing.

Are you paying attention? We are now in the transition between Acts Two and Three, and that means it's time for what
writers call The Dark Night of the Soul. Tension thickens, and
the final conflict looms on the horizon. We need to shake
things up by pushing the protagonist to their breaking point.

You see, throughout the story, the protagonist has harbored
a core flaw or fear, which causes them to believe or react a
specific way to either a truth of the world around them, or a lie
that they perceive as a truth. It's what made them—me—hesitate to jump feet-first into the action back in Act One.

Like refusing to meekly acquiesce to becoming a *thing*, a
pet, a kept man. Valued and loved, sure, but under the control
of someone bigger and stronger than me, simply because they
are bigger and stronger.

No.

Not Dav.

But also.

Yes, also Dav.

So, despite the positive strides your protagonist has made
post-midpoint of the story, they've yet to address this core
flaw or fear when Act Three begins.

Their greatest weakness. And they do have to face it. They
can't ignore it anymore. Because ignoring it in the first place
is what caused the problem.

Dav is thoughtful, and romantic, and so acquiescent. He
makes it so easy to pretend that all of this is sweet rom-com
nonsense and not at all about the effective, if accidental,
enslavement of the meet-cute love interest.

But we *have* been pretending, I can't ignore that any more.

The Dark Night of the Soul blindsides your protagonist,
pushing them to their breaking point. They must confront the
weakness inside them, or give up everything they've worked
so hard to achieve.

Turns out, giving up is easier than I thought it would be.

Opposite the hideous orange lounge is what Dav called the Consort's Room, when he'd first given me the tour. I had grabbed his ass and told him I fully intended to sleep next to him every night, no need for a whole separate suite for me.

(For Charlotte?)

I'm glad of it now.

I shower, draw the heavy velvet curtains, crawl into the bed and just... lay there. Hadi texts, asks if I'm okay. I tell her I am. Don't know if I'm lying. The blip of rage has faded away again, become that same white-noise *nothingness*.

I can't leave—both Dav and Onatah have made that clear. And if I did, god knows what Simcoe would do.

But I don't know if I can stay.

I want Dav. That I'm sure of. But I don't want any of *this*. Something I'm also sure of. I don't know what to *feel*, and so I'm so overwhelmed with feeling *all of it* that I'm feeling *none* of it.

I roll over and stare at the low bookshelf and a desk under the window. Someone has lovingly shelved all of my books, and the sentimental knickknacks I'd accumulated in my time at the estate, as if they expect this room to be photographed for a magazine spread.

Fuck, maybe it will be.

Some style editor may show up to do a profile of the happy couple—they're still calling us *Alvalin* in the press, *gross*—and we'll have to pretend that this is just my office, and not where I live, now. Letting my eyes drift across the spines of the books, it dawns on me that there are some titles there that hadn't been in the bags I'd brought here. I slide off the bed to my knees, crawling over. My textbooks, my thesis notes binder, my much-abused copy of the nightmare that is *The Canterbury Tales* in Olde English, it's all fucking there.

It's all the shit from my apartment.

Someone has moved me in.

I can see it, now, the places where someone has tried to integrate my shoddy student shit into the decor. A film poster on the back of the door that once hung in my living room. The discontinued Beanevolence mug that was in my desk drawer, now holding expensive wooden-handled pens on the top of the dresser. My piece-of-shit-laptop resting on a sleek mahogany desk.

I feel...

*Violated.*

Like I'm a new rescue cat they need to introduce to a house, so they've taken something familiar—the equivalent of an old tee-shirt—and jammed it into my cage.

I feel...

Nothing.

The next morning, I can hear people moving around below me in the house.

I don't get out of bed.

See? Easy choice.

Because... what's the point?

The world is going to keep going on around me, no matter what I say, or what I want, or what I fight for. This is it. This is my reality. For the rest of my life. Forever.

I don't matter.

I will never matter again.

My phone is filled with messages I don't want to deal with, so I turn it off, bury my head under the pillow, and close my eyes. I can't say I properly sleep. Time passes, I doze, nothing changes. The room stays dark, because I'd drawn the heavy hunter-green velvet curtains. My stomach rumbles, but I ignore it. My bladder complains, so I shuffle to the ensuite with my eyes closed, and then go right back to the bed.

Someone knocks.

"Colin," Dav calls through the door. "Are you awake, darling? No one has seen you yet this morning. Aren't you hungry?"

I stare at the ceiling. Take a deep breath. Let it out again. It only bubbles and shakes a little.

Doesn't matter.

*So what.*

"Love?"

I don't answer.

"Okay, then. You just rest. I'll come back at dinner."

He comes back, but I still don't want to see him any more than I did at lunch.

It's his house. He has the key to this room. He can get in if he wants.

Clearly he doesn't want to.

I can't tell if I'm angry or relieved. If he wants something, he should come in and take it, right? If I have to be here, the least he could do is *want* me. On the other hand, as long as he stays on one side of the locked door, I can live on this one, in my fragile and illusionary bubble of agency. Ha! Everything under this roof belongs to him, including this room. Including me.

Loathing myself, loathing him, I pull the covers over my head, ignore my belly, and close my eyes.

It's very early morning when I get up again, full of jumping, prickling energy. When I throw back the curtains, the sky is bright with the kind of starscape you don't get in the city.

It's romantic.

It's hateful.

I yank the curtains shut, pace the room, clenching and unclenching my fists, trying to decide if I would feel better if I punched something. No, I'd just hurt my hand. What if I screamed? No, that would make people come running. I hate feeling impotent and useless.

Filled with... with *so much* I can't do anything with. Anxious energy, fury, and... and... dreams, and hopes, and potential and—and—I fist my hands in my hair, jump up and down on the spot, try to get this frog-hooked-up-to-a-battery feeling out from under my skin. I drop to the floor and do as many push-ups as I can manage, until I'm wet with sweat.

It doesn't do anything for the anger, but at least I don't feel like a lit stick of dynamite anymore. The tight, hard feeling of wanting to scream presses against the hollow of my throat, and when I go into the bathroom to shower, it comes out as a hot, disgusting spew of vomit. I choke, and cough, and make the quietest noises of hurt and frustration that can be disguised by the running water, and kick the tile wall, and then, then...

All the fight in me evaporates. It feels like a herculean effort to even turn off the water and pull a towel down from the rack. I wrap it around my hips, not bothering to dry my hair, not caring.

Doesn't matter.

Who's gonna see me anyway?

Nobody, that's who.

The next time he knocks and wakes me, he says: "Pedra's dropped off a copy of her research. It explains so much. There's something about symbiotic biology and side-by-side evolution. I don't understand all of it, Mine Own. I need you to explain it to me. Please. I want to understand it."

I'm not hungry. I'm starving. I want him to go away. I miss him. I'm sick of sleeping. I'm exhausted. He waits for me to say something.

"I've called Dr. Chen," he adds. "She's going to call you. Please pick up?"

I haven't turned on my phone in days.

"You can't stay in here forever," Sarah says, barging in to throw open the curtains, letting in the sun.

I hiss at her like a movie vampire. "Just watch."

"I am." She picks up a pair of jeans I'd thrown against the wall days and days ago, and stuffs them into the tasteful laundry basket by the wardrobe. "It's pathetic."

I snort. "Easy for you to say. You're here by choice."

"Oh, am I?" She sits on the hunter-green velvet armchair in the corner of the room. "The Applebys are legacy hoard. I've never known anything else. When I went away to school, I made the conscious choice to pick something that would be useful for Master Tudor. I'm as happily employed here as I would be anywhere else." She shrugs. "And here I get room and board taken care of. We have a cute little house out the back of the vineyard."

"But—" I bolt upright, not giving a shit about my greasy hair or week-old beard. "But you're a *thing*. You're owned. Your kids, too!"

"So is every single human being on this planet. The only difference is that we know it."

She means dragons, and the way they've divvied up every person on earth, but my brain flashes to minimum-wage workers living at the poverty line, and the way capitalism has endangered lives as well as the environment. Sarah is more right than she's saying.

"I wish I could go back to ignorant bliss."

"To be frank? I kind of wish you could, too," she huffs. I gawp at her. "You're being a massive pain in the ass. The cleaners are stressed out, Cook is beside herself, and I've never seen the boss so—"

"Oh, of course!" I interrupt. "Yes, *he's* having a hard time. The boss is so inconvenienced! Dav, Dav, *Dav* is clearly the only person whose feelings matter here!" I throw my arms and let them drop on the covers with a feeble, impotent *fwump*.

Yes, I am being childish.

No, I don't care.

Sarah lets that hang between us. Then she asks, softly: "And you think that yours don't? You're his Favorite."

"Again, back to the part where I *belong* to him!"

"There's a lot that's not ideal..." she starts, and then stops, rubbing her fingertips on her palms, contemplative. "Someone else more or less rules your life, that's true. But you have options. Your opinions matter. Dragons are happiest when they're surrounded by their greatest treasures, when those treasures are happy in turn. It's not... master and slave. This isn't America."

"Africans were enslaved in Canada, too."

Sarah quirks a smirk at me. "And Master Tudor helped enslaved mothers smuggle their babies onto British ships so they'd be raised free."

"Oh, he... he never told me that," I admit softly.

"There's a lot you don't know yet." She huffs out a sigh. "Our relationship is more like family, like I'm working for my uncle's business."

"But the kids—"

"Can be anything they want," Sarah says firmly. "Whatever it is they want to do, Master Tudor will make space. He'll make up jobs here if he has to—or he'll help them find something off the estate. And I never have to worry whether they'll ever go hungry, or go into debt for their education, or if they'll die alone in some state care home, because they'll be looked after, *always*."

"What about their father?"

Sarah looks away for a moment, hand on her cheek, thoughtful. "He was like you. He didn't see the advantages of life in a hoard."

"What happened?" I ask, dread crawling up my throat.

Sarah chuckles. "Master Tudor didn't roast and eat him, if that's what you're imagining. He left."

That piques my interest. "How do you mean?"

"He asked to go, and Master Tudor said he could." She stands. "The price was that he would never see his children again, but that was fine with all of us, frankly. The boss has been a better father to Martha and Nate than that dipshit ever was. You look surprised."

"I didn't think..." Sarah leaves me space to finish the thought, but I haven't formed it yet. So I repeat: "I don't want to be owned."

"No. But you do want to be loved. And so does the boss."

# chapter Forty-Two

There's a tray of food in the hall. The scent of it whirls into the room as Sarah exits. I'm suddenly starving. Under a cloche, I find roasted potatoes and an omelet made of vegetables from the kitchen garden, still warm. I eat, and then shower. While I'm in there, thinking-not-too-seriously about whether it's worth shampooing my beard when I plan on shaving it all off in a few minutes (don't picture Dav with beard burn around his mouth) (okay, picture it a little) I also *think* think.

See the thing is... I've been pretty directionless. No secret there.

It's been well over a year since I graduated, and if I'm honest with myself (which, hey, I don't tend to do a lot. GenZ Gallows Humor, it's a thing,) I can admit that I wasn't trying all that hard.

The pressure to go from Degree to Career to Marriage to Home Ownership to Happy Little Reproducing and Consuming Member of Society is late-stage capitalist nonsense, we all know that. But it's so pervasive. It gets its hooks into you. It feels like it's natural to want, to *need* those things.

And maybe I've been resisting it, as much as my queer ass can. I didn't really *want* the picket fence, kid, and 2.5 dogs. Rebekah and I had made *plans,* and the minute they stopped matching up, they melted like candy floss in the rain. But that's not what kept me working a job that, while enjoyable, isn't what I want to do with my life. It's not the reason I kept slogging through a tedious string of one-night stands.

It was apathy.

It was aimlessness.

It was, to be honest, grief.

I wanted my father to be grinning up at me from the audience when I was awarded my degree, and when he wasn't?

It knocked the stuffing outta me.

I've been drifting because things didn't happen the way I expected, and I... I wasn't being proactive, or thoughtful, or even concerned about my own choices. I was just letting life happen to me, *around* me. Even Dav. I let him just *happen.*

Thank god he just happened.

Where would I be if he hadn't? Not standing in a shower, wondering if I could reconcile my own moral values with the reality of my situation, that's for sure.

But also, not being adored by one of the most emotionally available and kind men I've ever met. Dav's charming, and thoughtful, and gives a shit what I think. He doesn't want to change anything about me. (Even though he keeps trying to get me to dress better. He's not the first.) He doesn't make fun of me for the romance novel thing. He gets it about Dad. He's felt the same kind of devastating grief that comes of losing someone so quickly, so unexpectedly, and so permanently.

He has terrible jokes, and terrible socks, and he tries so damn hard to be what everyone needs him to be. He's so fucking selfless, and he's really good in bed.

He doesn't rush me. He understands the choices I need to make, and he's not trying to make them for me.

He meets me where I am.

I don't get what he sees in me. There are hundreds of humans like me out there. He could have picked any of them. I was just convenient.

But then again, people don't completely overhaul the way they run their farms for convenience.

It's a fuck of a Grand Romantic Gesture.

My friends, my family, my roommate, my goddamned *therapist* keep asking me: "What do you want, Colin?"

I want...

I want a partner who wants me. Romantically, and intellectually, and emotionally, and physically. I want a purpose, and a career I'm invested in, and passionate about. I want to change the world for the better. I want comfort, and financial security. I want to be surrounded by people who care about me, and are invested in my well-being and happiness, as much as I am in theirs.

That's what I want.

And I...

That's...

...that's what I have.

I slide to the floor, legs tented, forehead resting on my knees, as the soap drifts down my back and the revelation sinks in.

I *have* everything I want.

The partner who wants me enough to fight for me, to defy his culture and his traditions to have me. The purpose, in his farm—my thesis come to life, my passion played out on a grand scale, and if it works, the clout to roll it out to other wineries, to literally change the industry. I have a roof over my head, good food, a warm bed, and the security knowing my every need will be met. I will never have to ration my meds, or skip sessions with Dr. Chen because funds are tight. And I *am* surrounded by people I love, who love me in return. Family, and friends, and... and hoard.

I have *everything* I want.

All I have to do is get up off the goddamned floor and figure out how to make it work.

So I get up off the goddamned floor.

When I find Dav, with the silent chin-jerks and eyebrow waggles of three staff members whose names I really should learn, he's in the stuffy wood-paneled study on the ground floor.

"Heya," I say, sticking my head around the frame.

I startle him so badly that the papers he'd been reading flap across the desk, and his mouth sparks.

Right.

Must not sneak up on a concentrating dragon.

His hair is a mess, and his waistcoat discarded. He's wearing a white button-down so fine that it's almost see-through and, yeah, okay, despite everything I am absolutely still thirsty for this man. He's got his shirtsleeves all bunched up at the elbows, not even properly cuffed, and yes please and thank you, *forearms*.

It's not my fault that I get distracted for a second, okay?

"Colin! I didn't know you were—"

*Down. Out of your room. Over being a cranky bitch. Alive,* my brain supplies for him.

"Feeling more the thing," he finishes lamely.

"Kinda." While I am feeling better, nobody gets over a week-long depressive episode in an hour.

"I checked in on you."

"I know." I step into the office and close the door behind me. There are ears in the hall, even if I can't see the bodies they're attached to. "I appreciate it."

"I'm sorry you're so unhappy," Dav says. "And I'm sorry for my part in it."

"I'm, uh, scared of what happened. And I'm angry as hell at Lt. Gov. Shitstain." Dav blinks hard at the crass nickname, a smile threatening to break through his shock at how abrasive it is. "But I... I don't think I'm *unhappy*."

Relief rushes out of me on the same breath as the confession.

"Truly?" Dav asks, hopeful. He steps around the desk, tentative and unsure of his welcome.

Feeling a thousand pounds lighter, I lean against the door jamb, cock my hip out, and grin. *Come and get it, big boy.* "We still gotta talk through some stuff, and we definitely have to figure out how to handle Lt. Gov. Fuckface, but more-or-less on-the-whole kinda-sorta... yeah? I've had time to think—"

"—wallow," Dav snorts, almost giddy. He prances a few steps closer, skittish.

"—*think*, you ass," I correct. "Sarah helped, but I've realized—"

"I didn't ask Sarah to—"

"—I know." I hook my fingers into his belt loops, pulling his pelvis flush against mine, closing the gap.

Slouched against the closed door, the height difference between us is more pronounced, and I raise my chin as Dav lowers his. This is an echo of what it was like when he held me down. But there's no menace here. There is patience. There is respect.

This isn't *that.*

It will never be that again.

We won't *let* it.

Dav's gaze flicks to my mouth, but he waits for me. Waits for me to take the first step. Waits for me to be ready. Waits for me to invite him, just like I told him he had to. Just like he always *has.*

Dav may have just happened to me, but I invited it.

I *let* him happen.

*Willing to stand in it with him*, I remind myself.

"Let me apologize," he whispers, his breath smelling of campfire.

"You don't—"

"*Let* me," he says. "Onatah warned you about skin-to-skin contact, but I should have told you *why*. That's my fault."

"When you say it like that, yes, it is," I say, mulishly.

"I don't blame you for how you reacted when you returned."

"Good."

"And I appreciate your boundaries."

He does. Those delicious, freckly forearms are planted on the door on either side of my head. No part of him is touching me that I didn't reach out and grab for myself.

"Thank you."

"I respect you, I want you to know that."

"I do."

"My love. My darling," he says, and after a quick consent check—*this okay? Yeah, it's okay*—presses his lips to my cheeks and eyelids, the underside of my chin. "My treasure."

I giggle, giddy with joy and relief. I slide my arms around his neck, smear my words against the skin next to his ear: "If you call me 'my precious', I'm gonna kick you."

"My prec—"

"Shut up and kiss me."

Dav slides his hands up to cup my face. Slowly, tortuously, keeping eye contact determinedly, he leans forward and brushes his lips over mine once, twice, an exploratory, questioning touch, eyes open wide and watching, making sure I'm still okay.

Fuck, that's hot.

My head is spinning. I feel like I'm falling. I'm braced for the inevitable shock of hitting the ground, and I don't want it to ever come. When you love a dragon, maybe it never does.

Maybe you just fly.

"A *horse?*" I splutter, curled up with Dav on one of the club chairs by his desk, bare-ass naked and covered in sweat. His thumb sweeps back and forth over the five round scars on my bicep. "You said Charlotte was a fairy, and you think I'm a *horse?*"

"A kelpie!" Dav defends. "Long legs and graceful dark lines."

"That drowns people!"

"You did take my breath away the first time I came into the café and—"

"Shut up, oh my god, you *loser.*"

It devolves into a tickle fight. I pinch the flesh above his knee playfully and he flinches, so I smooth my hand over the hurt. "Sorry."

"No, I... it's alright, if you want to."

I cup his chin and turn his face to mine. "Do you not like it? I'm only doing it to tease."

"I know, so it's fine—"

"Nuh-uh, answer the question. Do you *like* it?"

He flinches again. "Not particularly, no. I had a governess who pinched."

"Ugh, governesses," I say theatrically, so it's clear that I'm making fun of the pretentiousness, not him. "Alright. No more pinching. If there's anything else you don't like, you'll tell me, right?"

He nods, and turns his head to press a kiss into my palm.

My sweet dozy boy. Sex always tuckers him out.

"Don't let your parents hire that same governess for your... eggling? Clutchmate?"

Dav snickers. "Sibling will do. And there's no worry on that score. That governess was human and long dead."

"Good. Serves her right." Fuck not speaking ill of the dead. Assholes are assholes, no matter their state of being.

We're quiet for a moment, and then Dav lifts my wrist to his mouth for a kiss, giving away exactly what he's thinking about.

"Why would he do it? Touch me like that?" I ask. "After what happened with Charlotte?"

Dav stiffens under me, and I don't mean in a sexy way.

Yeah, I think this conversation requires underwear. I slide off his lap to go in search of mine. His is folded neatly on the desk, of course. Mine are hanging from a lamp.

When we're decent-ish, I scoot the second chair around so we're face to face, and put my hands on his knees, comforting and serious. "Despite what's probably running through your squirrelly head right now," I tell him. "I *still* think it was an accident. You were trying to protect her."

"No. I wouldn't let anyone help and she died as a result."

"Be honest with me. How bad was it? The hit she took?"

"... very bad."

"Would she have survived it otherwise? In nineteen twenty-whatever it was, if you'd gotten her to a hospital in time, would she have lived?"

He stares a hole into the carpet, clenches his jaw. "Not likely."

"And if Onatah hadn't caught her, and she fell into the river, would she have lived?"

"... no."

"So she would have died either way." I feel like the most callous bitch alive, watching the agony play out on his face.

"... yes."

I cup his jaw, lift his eyes to mine.

"Then how is it your fault?"

"I took her into another dragon's territory, it wasn't safe—"

"That's Simcoe talking. You don't really think that or you wouldn't have gone there to start with. Are you going to let me go through someone else's territory to go back to Orillia to see the fam?"

"Of course."

"No different, then." Something about all of this is still not sitting right for me, but I can't put my finger on it. "Next question: why would Simcoe touch *me*? What *reason* could he have?"

"None whatsoever," Dav says. "Trifling with someone else's Favorite is a very serious offense. There's a court."

"So he threw you into this frenzy on *purpose*."

"He can't have meant to," Dav says with a shudder. "It was my fault, somehow. It always is. But I promise, I've been working on my temper. I contacted your Dr. Chen when you wouldn't come out of your room. She's been helping me with anger management."

"I see."

Nothing about Dav makes me think that he *needs* anger management.

"I will never hurt you, Colin. I won't ever do that to anyone again. I'm dangerous," he insists, talking over me when I try to interrupt. "I'm so dangerous that I'm only allowed to ever go to war. My temper—"

"Which, hey, reminder, you've never taken out on me—"

"I laid you flat on the floor!"

"After I took a swing at you, and only to *end* the fight."

"The only thing I'm good at is killing."

"Bullshit."

"I—"

"*Bullshit.*" I gesture grandly at everything around us. "Exhibit A." Then I point at the people and farm framed in the window behind him. "Exhibit B." I hold up our linked hands. "Exhibit C."

Dav shudders out a breath. "It's so much, love. It was easier with Charlotte."

"It was also before social media and entertainment news. Can you honestly tell me that if it wasn't for the paparazzi anyone would give a flying whatever about us being together?"

"Likely not. Simcoe wouldn't have known until I filed the paperwork, and by then it would have been too late."

"And yet the person I am wouldn't be different. I'm still too outspoken, too opinionated, too ugly for Lt. Gov. Longnose. I am still the person who encouraged you to break a massive dragon taboo for shits and giggles."

"And I still would have been the dragon who did it, because I wanted to make you laugh. And then kept going because it made people happy."

"Your kink is showing."

"Hush."

I'm relieved that both of us seem to have calmed down enough to tease. "So, the only difference is he wouldn't have seen me coming. Am I wrong?"

"No. Simcoe—"

"Is a controlling jackass. Do you know what Onatah asked me, after she told me about Charlotte? She asked if I knew what happened to dragons who lock themselves away. Apparently, they wither."

"Yes," Dav says. "Like Rome. They weren't connected to the people they stole. It's uncomfortable to be on someone else's territory. Itches."

"Is that what happened in Aotearoa?" I ask, letting him sidetrack me for the moment. "The Dutch got itchy?"

Dav chuckles. "It's so far away from Europe. I can't imagine what it must have felt like. Certainly the land wouldn't call to Dutch dragons there the way it does to a Māori one. It wouldn't feel like it was worth fighting for. And without William Koning there to command his armies..."

"They withered. They lost, and died."

Dav kisses me again, desperate and clinging. I let him take anything he wants. Everything. I want him to live. I want him to *thrive*.

*Onatah*, I think, all of a sudden. *The broken treaties. Her people lost so much—and Simcoe, man, if his father hadn't died when he did, Frank wouldn't have territory either. They would have nothing to cling into, nowhere to dig in their roots, no way to flourish in new soil.*

"Next question, then," I say, when Dav is soothed. "Why would Lt. Gov Asshat make *that* your punishment? A century of house arrest, no Favorite, no contact with humans except those in your nest, no way to serve your people. Was it a death sentence on purpose?"

"No." He frowns. "No, surely not."

"One last question," I say softly, heart sinking, because I already know the answer to this one, and I don't like it one bit. "What does Simcoe stand to gain if you die?"

"That's easy. I have no heirs at present. The marquessate would revert to him." Dav sits back and, gently, puts one hand over his mouth. "*Oh.*"

Man, do I love a great Romance Novel Revelatory 'Oh'™.

# chapter Forty-Three

And here we are at the top of Act Three. These events are generally the most important parts of the story, since the entire plot depends on them to set up that oh-so-important final confrontation. Gotta seed all that stuff, gotta start bringing together the team, gotta start laying out the plan of action for the big confrontation, or revelation, or in the case of romances, love confession. Lots to do. Not a lot of time to do it in. Just like real life—it always seems like every essay is due on the same day, or a rush of customers all come in at the same time.

It can't just be in dribs and drabs, nooooo....

And after all that set up?

After that comes the crisis point, leading up to a climactic confrontation in which our protagonist faces a point of no return: they must either prevail or perish. Win the love interest, or be forever doomed to live as a thornback aunt, alone and bitterly unloved.

Or thornback uncle.

Whatever.

But let's not get ahead of ourselves, okay?

The problem with devastating revelations is that, unless you have proof, there's no way to confirm your assumptions are true. The more Dav and I talk about it, the more it's clear Lt. Gov. Envybritches has *not* been a fan of my man since Frankie-boy arrived from Spain all shot up, and too late to win the glory. School friends though they may have been, this has created a rift of resentment Dav only now understands Simcoe is actively nurturing.

But who could we go to with this?

Nobody. Simcoe is the top of the pops in Upper Canada, and beyond that the matter would have to go all the way to England to the courts. And we have no *proof.*

So what do we do?

We *plan*. Dav is a tactician by training, and a cautious man by nature. He rarely acts without considering all angles. We haven't said much to each other since this morning. Dav's processing. His brilliant soldier's mind is going back over conversations, piecing things together, and I let him have his space for it. I try to give him his physical space too, but he's not letting me more than an arm's length away for the whole day, and I get it. I'm okay with it.

His draconic instincts need to know that I'm near, and safe, and be assured that he doesn't have to worry about me. That way he can tune his heightened senses to me, use me as his baseline. Calm himself with the sound of my heartbeat.

He is my air and my joy. I am his ground and his stability.

But.

Living with an old Loyalist soldier means that when he's morose, he breaks out the old Loyalist comfort foods. Which apparently means drinking something that's stirred with a *red-hot poker.*

Seriously.

Tall heavy-glass mug, egg, ale, rum, spices, stir with fire—it's like eggnog on speed. Dav calls it a Hot Ale Flip and says everyone used to drink them when he was my age.

"Has anyone died from the mug exploding?" I ask from the other side of the hideous leather sofa. I'm hiding in case of superheated shrapnel.

"There were some deaths," Dav says as he wipes down and replaces the poker in the stand by the hearth. "But no more than usual for a rowdy bar fight."

"Except there were *hot pokers*."

"True."

He hands me my mug, and I stop hiding so we can curl up together.

The drink is... thick. But good? Ish? I tell myself it's like a boozy milkshake and decide to at least enjoy the warmth of the mug in my hands. Dav looks like he's genuinely relishing his, and yeah, okay, all power to you then, lover. Maybe if I sip slowly enough he'll finish my leftovers.

Eugh.

Later, in bed, I am side-swiped by the beauty of the man tangled in the sheets, awe-struck by the literal embodiment of everything I've finally chosen.

The curtains are open just enough that a sliver of late August moonlight has snuck its way in, slicing across the room and highlighting all the best parts of Dav. He's wearing just the bottoms of his fussy old-fashioned pajamas, and they're incredibly low on his hips. He looks warm, and boneless, and I want to kiss the relaxed, sleepy line of his mouth, bite along the dramatic curve of his hip bone, and count his lashes.

I take in the feast that is the planes of his chest and shoulders, the elegant lines of his stomach. His hair is covering his face, drawing attention to his parted lips, to the uncompromising line of his jaw. His ginger-pale skin is pearly, greedily soaking up the silvery glow. Stretched out like this, I'm struck by how vulnerable he seems. Almost fragile. A surge of my own possessive protectiveness fills me.

He's music become flesh—the metronome of breath, the pizzicato of his eyelids flickering as he dreams, the subtle movements of his fingers. I have a sudden, urgent desire to shake Dav awake and demand he play me something schmaltzy on a spinet. I don't even know what the fuck a spinet is, but I bet he does.

And yet, the persistent whisper of muscles beneath his skin and the suppleness of his sleeping body gives off the sense of tightly coiled power. Both threatening, and thrilling. I share a bed with something wonderfully, beautifully dangerous, and it would never hurt me, because it loves me.

Dav is a study in contrasts.

He always has been.

Soldier, but gentle. Master, but willing to be overruled by other's expertise. Possessive, but generous and thoughtful. A man from a dynasty of thieves of land, and culture, and resources, but trying to figure out how to give back, if it would even be welcome. A man benefited by every system in existence, and yet willing to deconstruct them, because it would make *other* people's lives better.

*And Francis Simcoe wants him dead. He'll probably back off for a while, but he'll never stop coveting Dav's territory... Onatah's territory, too, I bet.*

*I won't let that happen,* I tell myself, laying down to rest my ear against his heartbeat, letting the waltz lull me into sleep. *I know his world now, and I love him anyway. Rule Four: Relationships are work. I am staying, and I am protecting him, and that's all there is to it.*

Dav wakes up with a plan.

A plan, he claims, that requires a dress rehearsal. As soon as the morning rush is over, Beanevolence is closed to customers, because the group of us—Hadi, Pedra, Min-soo, Mauli and Dikembe, Dav and me—sit in the harsh noon sunlight watching Onatah pace around the café, absolutely losing her shit.

She's currently losing her shit because Dav has just deliberately and utterly betrayed the Great Confidence.

"But what if the planet really can't sustain us?" Dikembe asks.

"What a load of pretentious colonialist horseshit!" Onatah snarls.

"Here here!" Hadi says, and around her, the humans raise our mugs. Min-soo is in the back crafting some sort of breakfast tray for the hungry rebels—her words, not mine—but she can clearly still hear us because she shouts "Huzzah!" as she emerges from the kitchen with nibbles.

"It can sustain us, though! Did you know that if you turned just a third of Canada's grass lawns into food gardens, we could provide free produce to every school in the country?"

Dav chuckles. "I did not know that, Mine Own, but I adore that you do."

"Not to mention the fact that the way Onatah stewards her territory can be replicated," Pedra says, jumping to her feet, energized now. "I can only guess how many dragon societies work just like that! What about all the traditional practices and knowledge the Europeans wiped out? We could talk to... to the Aztecs! And the Māori! What if—"

"Slow down," Mauli says gently. They rub her shoulder soothingly. "You're getting ahead of yourself."

"Besides, the point is... this isn't news to them. They know," Dike mutters. "And instead of using The Gift to make humanity stronger and better, instead of using the evolutionary power they've *developed specifically to do that helping*, they... well, they hoard it."

"Greedy," Onatah sneers. "Selfish, and self-important, and self-righteous, and *greedy*."

"Why can't they ... come out and be honest?" Mauli asks. "Why not 'fess up?"

"That every fluid in our bodies has the ability to heal almost every disease suffered by humans? Including age?" Dav asks calmly. He slides his hand down to my leg, grounding himself in touch, and I cup my hand over his. "Can you imagine the horror show?"

"Riots," Onatah says. "Everywhere European Empires have touched—this will be *news*. Look at how upset you all are, and you're not the kind of people prone to grabbing a gun and shooting up a public place."

"Jesus Fucking Christ," Hadi breathes, as we all envision the outcome of a world full of angry humans deciding that they don't want to be ruled by dragons any more.

All at once.

En masse.

No discussions, or diplomatic talks.

Just... violence.

"And that's not to say what may happen if some humans get it into their heads that they're *owed* this Gift," Dav says. "All it would take is a few enterprising people with no morals, and dragons could start disappearing. The children—the eggs—"

"You don't know that," Dike says softly. "You don't know that's the choice humanity will make."

"But you can't promise otherwise," Dav says softly.

Pedra turns imploring eyes to Dav. "So what now?"

"The problem is, it's *already* out there," I explain. A frisson of urgent understanding ripples through the room. "Pedra's already shared it on her research boards. We *can't* take it back."

Onatah snarls, her throat clicking.

"Watch it!" Hadi says. "I can't afford to have another dragon burn down my place."

Dav chuckles with strained self-deprecation. Onatah snorts out a plume of blue-black smoke with a smirk.

"Unlikely," Dav says. "Onatah's Favorite would never stand for her being careless."

But all of this banter and joviality is strained. An act.

"If we can't take it back, and we can't tell everyone, what *can* we do?" Pedra asks, when the silence goes on too long.

"We get ahead of it," Dav says, sitting forward.

See, here's the thing about Dav. I never forget that he was a career soldier—*is* a soldier, could be called up to serve at any time—but sometimes I need reminding that his medals were earned in tents, and bunkers, and secret meeting rooms, rather than on the field. Sure, he fired guns, stormed strongholds, went over the top, set fire to the Presidential Mansion with his own breath.

But he's really the *plans* guy.

"What's the best way to negate the power of a blackmailer?" he asks us, his Peter Pan kiss curling deviously into his almost-dimple.

"Don't do shady shit?" Mauli asks.

"Besides that," Dav asks. When no one answers, he says: "Expose the terrible truth yourself."

"But you just said you *can't*," Dike protests.

"Not to the humans," Dav agrees. "But we can to the dragons. They have kept this secret for centuries, devoted fortunes to its upholding, believe firmly that it benefits them. But what if we convince them that it's *not* a benefit to us any longer? That the old ways are harming our greatest resource—humans? What if we can show them that there are *other* ways, ways that preserve the planet, and our people, *and* their selfish wealth? And what if we get someone powerful on side, someone who can change laws, implement them slowly, thoughtfully, and world wide. So if the research becomes widely known, it will be old news, even if some of it is shocking."

"Think of it like my thesis," I explain. "But not viniculture—for, I dunno, call it sapiensculture, I guess." I spread my arms wide.

Hadi snorts. "As if dragons are factory farming humans when we should be free-range organic?"

"Sorta, yeah!" I laugh. "But we can't just go in and blow up the factories. We gotta convince them to convert. One by one, bit by bit, you know?"

Mauli makes a noise pretty similar to Onatah's frustrated click. "Right, but where are you gonna find someone with that kind of power?"

Because I have never once in my queer little life passed up the opportunity to be a dramatic bitch, I pull a dollar coin out of my pocket. I hold it up, face-side out. It takes everyone a second to get it.

"The fucking *queen*?" Hadi says. "Are you serious?"

Dike plucks the Loonie from my hand and stares at the embossed profile. "You can do that?"

"Apparently," I say, patting Dav's thigh showily. "This guy right here used to hang out at court when he was a snot-nosed shit."

"I was never a *shit*," Dav protests gamely.

"I'll just have to ask Elizabeth Regina to verify that," I snark back.

"You're crazy, princess," Onatah says. "It might actually work, but I also think you're *crazy*."

"I am not content to spend the rest of my life with my head down hoping Simcoe will let us both not only live in peace, but just live in general. He wants your territories—and Dav being all happily shacked up is a distraction he could try to use to his advantage."

Dav grumbles, a low serpenty noise of displeasure, but doesn't disagree.

"Come with us," Dav says, low and imploring. "Show them what the world could be—"

"No," Onatah says.

"What? No, you know I can't speak on your behalf—"

"Nuh-uh. You saw how well that went for Matoaka. Man, she's *buried* over there. I'm not letting Simcoe have the satisfaction," Onatah says using the same Big Sister Voice I've heard from Gem. "You have to do this on your own, and we both know it."

"I don't—!" Dav starts, stricken, but then he squeezes his eyes shut, frowning hard. "I need you," he says, soft and small.

"I know you do," Onatah says, just as small, just as soft. "But what you're asking me to do, Dav, that's not fair to me. Besides, if you go, one of us needs to stay to protect both our territories."

"*Your* territory," Dav insists.

"Onatah's?" I ask. Dav flushes, realizing that we've got an audience of interested humans. "No, hey, it's cool, honestly, the size of your patch is not anything I give a shit about. But like, are you talking about giving it *all* back?"

Dav heaves a frustrated sigh. "As much as I can."

"The Europeans, they ate away at the whole continent, bite by bite," Onatah explains when Dav doesn't elaborate. "There are so few pockets of protected territory left. 'Reserved' for us, as if this Continent was a goddamned restaurant and we'd been rude and forgotten to book our table in advance. My people sided with the British during the war, and they promised our payment for fighting on their side would be their retreat up the peninsula."

"But Simcoe lied," Dav explains. "He never returned it."

"No. He put him in charge of it, instead." She jerks her thumb at Dav.

"What a fuckhead!" Mauli blurts.

"When I realized the settler propaganda was nothing but falsehoods," Dav picks up the narrative, "That the land wasn't underused, or underpopulated, I tried to return it and go back to Wales. But I had already been trapped into it—Simcoe had the queen's ear and I was commanded to stay. I could have defied it, but that would have meant—" he gives Onatah a significant look.

*It would have exposed her to Frank.*

Panic shoots through me as I realize what he's saying. If we're successful, if he moves home, I *have* to go with him. I don't know if I want to move to the other side of the ocean!

He must hear my heartbeat kick into overdrive because he says, "Don't worry, Mine Own. I'll be keeping Fynyth. Onatah and I sorted this out decades ago."

"More like you came to me and sobbed 'tell me what you need'," Onatah chuckles.

"I won't deny it," Dav allows. "It was unseemly for me to make the decisions when all of yours had been ignored."

"Which is why I'm cool with you staying. I know what it's like to have your home taken away."

"I love it dearly, and I don't need more than the farm," Dav sighs. "I grew up where dragon's territories are small, dense, and contained. No more than an estate, a village or two, a dozen farms. No more people than they can speak to once a week, no more land than they can walk in a few days. It is what I prefer."

And instead he'd been forced to take on a sprawling area, still wet with the blood of the people slain defending it from the Americans, cutting the Onguiaahra territory in half.

Surely there must have been more Onguiaahra dragons who had been stewarding that parcel. Everything I'm learning tells me that Onatah can't oversee it all on her own. She must have cousins, siblings, a community. Not an empire, not the way Elizabeth Regina commands the far-flung territories of the world from the top down, but a *family*. And those dragons in her family were denied, squished into a smaller space with fewer humans, while greedier dragons took more than they could ever need, more than they could ever guide, and let the humans under their care suffer for it simply because they wanted more. They're so remote, so distant, it's like they don't even exist.

I mean, I didn't even know who Dav *was*.

Even now, I have no idea who commands Orillia, where I grew up.

"I've already been fucked in as many ways as they can fuck me," Onatah says. "Which means I have to stay, princess."

"I understand," I say.

Onatah's phone pings in her pocket, and she ambles over to the window to track a motorcycle coasting up the street.

"And that's my time up," she says. "I wish you both the best of luck. Let me know if I can send you anything."

"Of course," Dav says, and we follow her out to the street.

I offer Onatah the bow with my fist over my heart, and she snorts and gives me a careful hug—moving slowly when Dav tenses—with no skin-to-skin contact.

"He's your problem now," she whispers in my ear.

"He sure is."

"Take care of him, eh?"

The bike parks right beside the café, and Onatah swings her leg over the seat to nestle in close behind someone wearing a face-obscuring helmet. "Let's go home, Nîcimos," she tells the driver, and they're off before I can shout after them:

"Hey! Wait, no! Hold on, I want to meet—! Aw, fuck."

"Our own ride is coming, Mine Own," Dav says, putting away his phone.

"That was—!"

"I'm aware."

I point a sharp finger at his nose. "I'm gonna meet them one day," I threaten. "I'm gonna *befriend* them and there's nothing you jelly sneks can do about it."

Dav laughs. "If you say so."

"Now you're just humoring me."

Hadi steps outside to join us, unsettled by everything that's been confessed. She's flipping her keys in her hand, over and over, *click click click*, a metronome keeping time with her discomfort.

*Don't think about having to attend Hadi's funeral in half a century. Don't think about her getting old, and sick, while you stay the same. Don't think of her dying so soon when she doesn't have to. Don't... don't...*

Without warning, Hadi cups my face in my hands, squishes my cheeks. "Congrats, Colin."

"Hadi—" I start sadly. She sniffles once, but forces a bright smile. "Hey, you okay?"

"I'm fine. I'm fucking happy for you, you jerk. He *loves* you and he's trying to change the whole stupid world for you. He loves your stupid clothes—"

"He doesn't, actually."

"—and your self-deprecating humor, and your drive, and that thing you do with your tongue—"

"You can't possibly know about that!" I squawk.

"What, you don't think that Rebekah didn't kiss and tell, do you?"

"Oh my god! You're never meeting anyone I date ever again!"

"I've already met Dav. Tough shit."

"And he's making you cry!"

"It's *romantic*, you fuck."

We're both quiet for a moment.

"I guess... see you when you get back?"

"Yeah," I promise. "Make sure our usual spot is open."

I hug her, holding on for as long as the prickly bitch will let me. I'm acutely aware that there's now a time limit on how long I'll be able to do this.

The car pulls up, and Janet tell Dav she's "packed everything he asked for" through the window.

"Packed?" I ask, as Dav opens the door for me.

"Get in, Mine Own. We're going to the airport, before Frank can stop us. Right now."

# chapter forty-four

I'm not gonna lie, part of me expected we'd travel on an old-fashioned sailing ship. Not a private jet. Okay, well, not *private*, but when you fly super-luxurious-first-dragon-class, it feels like it. There's an actual door between us and the rest of the plane, and just two seats in our tiny cabin, which turn into beds. We hadn't even bought the tickets in advance, just strolled up to the counter with Dav's black credit card. So we're feeling pretty confident that Lt. Gov. Dipshit didn't have enough time to mobilize his spies, or bug this compartment, or whatever else he might try to do to keep us from leaving Canada. (Doesn't mean we don't check under every cushion, though.)

Dav started sending a flurry of emails back to Wales while we were waiting to board, outlining his desire to introduce his parents to his Favorite, and to check up on his sibling's egg. As far as anyone hacking our phones or tracking Dav's spending would know, we're simply heading over for a surprise family reunion. Immediately.

While Dav sets up our digital paper trail, I'm doing some phone-time of my own, telling my family the same things about the trip, but also re-reading some of the research I'd saved on Simcoe.

Specifically, I want to know what *his* middle name is.

"What if this goes tits up?" I ask, as we're taxiing along the runway. "What's the worst case scenario?"

Without looking at me, Dav says: "My titles and lands are stripped from me, you are severed from my hoard, I'm sent to Wales in disgrace if not outright executed, and Simcoe finds a way to take over Onatah's territory, possibly killing her and all of her family in the process."

I suck in a sharp breath. "Shit. So, like, you've thought about it."

"A tactician must always face the worst outcome in order to avoid it." Now he does look at me. He links our pinkies, and lifts them for a quick kiss. "But that will not happen. Because I will not let it."

"Neither will I."

"So we're in agreement," he grins, eyes crinkling. "Nothing horrible will happen, so there's nothing to worry about."

"Okay," I say, trying to leave my anxiety behind as the ground through the window falls away. "Nothing to worry about."

It hits me, just as the seatbelt light blinks off, that I'm about to meet the parents.

Oh my god. That's a *big* worry. I haven't met the parents since... since Rebekah's cop dad. He'd found my verbal spewing charming, thank god, but Dav's parents are...

They're going to be fancy, aren't they?

They'll be dragons, for a start.

And nobility.

And British.

Dav's lived in Canada longer than he ever lived in Wales, but his parents are going to be *properly* British, with scones and clotted cream, and the right way to hold your teacup (is pinkies out a thing? I don't actually know), dry humor and, oh god, they're going to *eat me alive*.

"I can feel you panicking from here," Dav says gently, lifting the arm between our extremely plush chairs to turn it into a loveseat.

I snuggle into Dav's side, and take as many deep, slow breaths as required for my heart to stop racing. As the flight attendant wheels in a cart to dole out hot towels, alcohol, and a snack, I explain what has me worried. If she's a spy, it'd be good for her to hear me talking about meeting the fam. It'll solidify our alibi.

Dav rubs my back. "You'll survive whatever disaster comes, I expect."

"What, no reassurances that I'll charm them, and everything will go smoothly, and I have nothing to worry about?"

Dav snorts. "I've met you."

I blow a raspberry.

"So long as you don't harm the egg, there's little you could do that would actually make my parents dislike you," Dav says gently, once we're alone again. "They're pleased I have a Favorite to introduce to them at all. After Charlie, there was worry I would never, ah..." He swallows hard. "At any rate, they know I love you, and that will be sufficient for them to do the same."

"Will they still love me when they learn we're coming to upend their way of life?"

Dav shoots a glance at the tasteful briefcase of notes that Pedra dropped off during my Long Dark Night, stowed by his foot.

"We still have to figure out what we're actually gonna propose in that thing," I remind him. "Handing the Parliament a jumble of papers without an actual plan isn't smart."

"Agreed. How did you work out your thesis presentation?"

"Working backwards. The desired end game is a decentralization of governance, and breaking up of the oversized, unwieldy territories, right?"

"And a return of land to Indigenous dragons wherever possible. We want dragons encouraged to—no, *enthusiastically participating* in the daily lives of those humans on their territories," Dav says, warming to the topic. "Moreover, they *ought* to be laboring alongside and in service of those humans. And, importantly, using their fire to cook, without punishment or derision."

"Yes, yes," I say, already falling down the essay rabbit-hole. "Gimmie my laptop, babe. I'm gonna start outlining."

I stop, and slap my hand over my mouth.

"What, Mine Own?"

"Oh my god. I actually *like* writing essays when it's not for school."

"You're surprised?" Dav kisses my temple. "When you've got a topic between your teeth, I've heard you *speak* in essays. It's charming." He presses another kiss to my check, then a more insistent one to my neck.

"Okay, okay," I relent. "Joining the mile-high club now, outlining later. Lock the door."

I'm not gonna lie about this, either.

I was kinda expecting something a little more... castley.

When your boyfriend-husband-whatever-the-hell-we-are tells you his parents live in *St. Ffagan's Castle*, you expect turrets and a moat, right? At the very least, it should be up on a craggy cliff. Instead, it's a quick half-hour drive from Cardiff Airport, and the house itself is kind of like a charming cottage on steroids. It's three stories high, with white-washed walls and regimented rectangular windows, the gray-slate roof is lined with wickedly pointed dormers and red-brick chimneys. The castle-iest thing about the place is the saw-toothed medieval wall and the neat round well in the centre of the drive ringed in rose bushes.

"I see where you get your modesty."

"It's not *modest*," Dav protests. "The frontage is public. Mother would much rather spend her attention on the back gardens—"

"I'm winding you up," I reassure him. "Deep breaths, babe."

Dav follows my suggestion, shoulders unwinching only slightly.

He's been tense since we landed.

It's been two years since he's been back, and he'd said he's anxious to see the egg. But he'd said it while staring out the window at the gray November mist, and squeezing my hand for dear life.

He's as nervous about introducing me as I am to be introduced.

Doesn't help that we're coming here with ulterior motives.

"You were supposed to inherit this?" I ask, trying to get his mind off his nerves.

"Yes." He glances around wistfully as the car stops and we get out.

"But this place is amazing." I turn in a circle to take it all in. "Why would you give it up?"

Dav laughs. "Now you sound like a dragon yourself. Are you so keen to move here?"

"Honestly? Not really."

"The truth is, I didn't know what it would mean, to accept the march. I was young, a feted war hero, the pride of society, and I wanted... I very much enjoyed being *wanted*. And John Simcoe, he was steady, and honest. He was so convincing. So *flattering*. But all he wanted was a warm body to fill the space. I didn't know I would have to forfeit the right to my mother's title and the ancestral nesting grounds."

"Babe."

"Don't pity me, *Fy Nhrysor*. It brought you to me, so I cannot regret it. My sibling will inherit St. Ffagan's instead, thank goodness."

As soon as the driver has our suitcases unloaded, he whisks them away to a side entrance with a quick "*Croeso adref, syr.*"

"He's saying, 'welcome home'," Dav translates before I can ask.

*Shit, I'm going to have to learn Welsh, aren't I?*

And then the front door opens. A man with flamingly ginger hair barrels out, down the steps, and slams into Dav. Startled, I jump out of the way.

"My baby boy!" the man bellows, slapping him heartily on the back and lifting him in a bear-hug. I expect Dav to squawk and protest, but he hugs back, grin massive and eyes sparkling.

Yeah. This is not a version of Dav that I'm used to seeing.

I like it.

"Father!" Dav bellows back, when his feet are back on the ground, and takes his turn lifting the man in a crushing hug of his own.

"Yes, *now*, child—Oof!" Dav's father laughs. "Gently! Still human, you know."

A lightning bolt of confusion zaps through me.

Dav's father's human?

Dav sets him down and they go through a clearly beloved slapstick routine of tidying each other's hair and smoothing down the rumples in their suits, only to make it worse. When Dav spins on his heel to face me, his cheeks are flushed with delight and hair drooping with Welsh mist and his father's attention.

Seeing them side by side, Dav's dad is closer in height to me than to his son. There's a handsome dash of silver at his temples, the laughter lines bracketing his mouth and eyes are deeper than Dav's, and he has genuine dimples on both cheeks. His eyes are the color of winter ice, his pupils are as round as my own.

Otherwise, they're practically identical.

"Father," Dav says, puffing up. He takes one of my hands in both of his and presses a kiss to the back of it, showy and lingering. Embarrassment surges, but I don't let myself fidget. "It gives me great pleasure to introduce you to Colin Fergus Levesque, son of Helen and Jean-Francois Levesque of Orillia, in Upper Canada. *Fy Nhrysor.*"

Dav's dad offers his hand. I wipe the kiss off on my jeans before I take it. He laughs, that boisterous, joyful thing that I've only heard my own dragon loose on very rare occasions.

"Colin, meet Owain ap Rhys Tudor, Earl of Plymouth."

He's a Favorite too. And a Favorite who...

"Ah-ha! So I *am* going to have to take your last name!" I say, as Dav's dad pumps my hand jovially. He's got a grip like a rugby player.

"Only if we marry in the human way," Dav corrects me offhandedly. "Father, please don't pull his arm off."

"Right, right, too used to hanging about with dragons, I am." He lets go. His accent is thickly Welsh, and if I didn't watch as much BBC science fiction as I do, I might have a harder time understanding him.

Do I call him the Earl? Do I call him my Lord or... Father? I never called my own Dad that.

"Call me Owain, son," the man in question says, as if reading my mind. When he uses that word, it doesn't grate the way it does when Lt. Gov. SelfImportant does. "If you don't mind me calling you Colin."

"Suits me."

"For goodness sake, *Fy Nhrysor*, don't keep them out in the wet!" calls another voice from the doorway. "It's spitting down!"

"Right. This way, lads." Owain ushers us up the stairs.

We surrender our damp coats to a pop-up servant, and stroll into a richly carpeted foyer. The centerpiece is the wide staircase, leading up to a second-floor open gallery. The room is paneled in luxuriously dark wood, dotted with a grandfather clock that I suspect might be older than Dav, and paintings in gilt frames that definitely are.

Standing at the base of the stairs, coiffed without being ostentatious, is a slim, tall woman in high-end jeans and a creamy knit sweater. Her hair is mostly gray, though by her face I'd guess she was a little younger than Mum, if she were human.

Of course, she's not.

I do the fist-heart-bow thing, which seems right, because it's returned by the dragon, and Dav does another round of introductions with rainwater trickling down the back of his neck.

"And this is Paulette Windsor Tudor, of the Line of Llywelyn, the Countess Plymouth, my mother," he finishes grandly.

"That's a mouthful," I say, before I can think better of it. I immediately wish the floor would crack open under my feet and swallow me whole.

Luckily, the Lady in question laughs. "It is indeed. Just Paulette will do, Favored of my beloved son."

"Yeah." I scratch my calf with the toe of my shoe. "I, uh, didn't expect so much ritual about, you know, titles and things." I turn to Dav. "You call me your Favorite, but what do I call you?"

"Just Dav will do," he says with a cheeky grin.

I tug him down for a quick bite of a kiss.

"Ow," he protests.

"You deserved that. I'm serious, is there some important title I'm supposed to call you?"

"If you like, you may refer to him as your boyfriend in public, and," Owain pauses to wink at Dav. "Your personal stuck-up pain in the arse with family."

"I am not stuck up!" Dav protests.

"You're a little fussy, babe," I say.

"That's not the same."

Owain laughs, hearty and unrestrained, and Paulette beckons us into a drawing room that's an eerie echo of Dav's public one. Though this one is in a warm palette, instead of Dav's light blues and daisy yellows.

"Oh, I see," Dav pouts as we follow his mother to a door on the far side of the room. "The humans plan to gang up on me, then?"

"How can we gang up on you when it's finally even numbers?" Owain asks.

"You know very well how," Dav waggles a finger at him. "Don't you be teaching Colin any bad habits, Father. You know how Frank is."

"Stuffy goat," Owain agrees, and seriously, I love this man already.

The second room we enter is cozy, more family-oriented, filled with bookshelves and sofas worth sitting on. Someone's laid out a tea service, and it's even got one of those three-tiered cake displays.

Oh, Christ. Here it comes. The Fancy British Stuff. I plan to let Dav take the lead on this one and copy everything he does, but Dav doesn't sit.

"Leave the lad to his refreshment," Paulette says, beckoning Dav to yet another door on the far wall. "Come up to the hatchery with me Alva, and greet your sister."

Before I realize what's happening, Dav is off, and I'm left with the father of the man whose dick has been in me. *Don't think about sex while you're alone with Dav's dad, oh god.* I hope my expression isn't giving anything away.

Owain pops one of the fancy finger sandwiches directly in his mouth, eschewing the tongs, the delicate plates, the embroidered cloth napkins. I do the same.

"Oh, man, that's good," I say around a mouthful of something eggy and crisp, and remember to cover my mouth with my hand so I don't spray it.

I'm trying to decide if a) I actually want tea this late and b) if it would be rude to pour for myself, when Dav's dad pops up, and heads for a table with a drool-worthy spread of decanters that my own father would have drooled over.

"You drink whiskey?" Owain asks.

"Heck yeah," I say, then, "Yes, please, uh, sir."

Owain cuts a mock-glower over his shoulder at me, and I relax. Okay, sure, no 'sir's here.

"Cherries?" he asks, and it's only then that I realize he's making Old Fashioneds.

I swallow hard against the unexpected lump in my throat. Owain would have gotten on *famously* with my Dad. I ask for extra, then stuff another sandwich in my face to swallow the embarrassing sniffle that's threatening. We're halfway through our drinks, making a good job of silently demolishing the pile of carbs, when the jetlag catches up with me.

"Up you go, son," Owain says softly, when I list to the side, the ice in my tumbler rattling. "The old wyrms will be takin' their time. I'll see you to your bed."

I make my reply in the form of a jaw-cracking yawn.

I'm too tired to do more than shuffle behind him up the stairs and through some corridors that, to my exhaustion-blurred vision, all look tasteful, oldey-timey, and worryingly identical. I am totally going to get lost in the middle of the night searching for the washroom.

Maybe I *should* feel worried, or maybe lonely, or maybe even abandoned, being left in the room I'm shown to alone. Instead, when I flop face-first onto the bed, still in my grimy travel clothes, all I can think of is how kind and welcoming these strangers (who will be my family for the next few centuries) have been.

And how lucky I am because of it.

# chapter Forty-Five

The house *does* look like a castle from the back. Where what Owain called the "new build house" (*only* four centuries old) blends into the older Medieval manor and fortified courtyard, there's a grand gray-stone gateway topped with pointy gables and archer's windows, bordered on either side with low round turrets, twinned with ivy.

"Thank you!" I throw my arms up at it. Yesterday's drizzle has let up, and this morning the stone glitters in the sunlight. "Finally. Something living up to the stereotype!"

Dav arches an eyebrow. "Are you disappointed I don't live in a drafty old castle, and sleep on a bed of gold with a princess I stole from a neighboring clan?"

"I mean, yeah?" I wrap my arms around his waist and slide my hands into his back pockets. "What's the point of having a dragon if you don't get the castle?"

"I note that you're not adverse to comparing yourself to a princess." He presses his cheek against my temple, nose buried in my hair.

"I know my role in this little fantasy."

"Fantasy?" Dav pulls back to catch my eye, his oblong pupils fattening with interest. "You didn't tell me it was a *fantasy*."

"Not like that!" I protest. Then I reconsider. "Okay, maybe a little bit like that."

Laughing, Dav pulls me down the wedding-cake-tiers of the slope towards the water, a cute little babbling brook with artificial waterfalls, and unnaturally straight banks in a lush, carefully manicured lawn.

The whole back of the building is an Italianate Garden, charming and rigidly wild in that uniquely English way. The carved dragon door is on this side of the building, which means that at one time this had been the main entrance. I imagine the stream being something wilder and mightier in centuries past, deep enough for barges to sail up from the bay and deposit visiting dignitaries at the bottom of the hairpin stone staircases. This door is carved with as much lovingly rendered detail as Castle Frank, but unfortunately most of the symbolism is lost on me. I do catch that the dragon carved at the bottom of the doors, head twisted up to breathe fire from which the rest of the little figures and scenes rise, looks exactly like Dav.

"That your Mother?"

"Grandfather," Dav corrects. "The family resemblance is strong."

"Speaking of, how's your sister?"

"Much further along than I thought," Dav says. "Her shell is lovely."

"What's the nest like?" I ask, wondering if the egg is in a literal nest of blankets and jumpers that smell like her dad, or buried in gold, or is in the back of a secret water-lit grotto under the house.

Dav laughs and wraps his arms around me from behind, resting his chin on my head as his hands cup my hips. He's slow and clingy this morning. I don't think he got much sleep. He was there when I woke up, but I don't know when he came in. I conked right out. I didn't even have the wherewithal to go poking around the room to see if we'd been put in Dav's childhood bedroom. There must be embarrassing trophies, or crayon drawings, or, ooooh, even an old stash of the Regency version of porn mags...

"Just a nursery," he says genially.

"But like, what does she look like? Do we call the egg a she, or an it before it's hatched, or...?"

"You can call her by her pronouns," Dav says.

"How do you know it's a girl?"

"How do human mothers know?"

"You ultrasound the egg? What's the egg like, is the shell strong enough for that?"

"Wouldn't do it otherwise, would they?"

"True. How big is the egg, is it—?"

"Darling!" Dav laughs. "Would you like to come meet my sister?"

I turn to face him. "Is that allowed?"

"You're my Favorite. Of course it's allowed. This way."

Dav leads me back into the newer part of the house. But he's unsure about the way, and twitchy, too. "I could have sworn there was a door over... oh, no, it's there." I squeeze his hand. "I am too used to Fynyth. But this is no longer my territory. It's uncomfortable."

"Itchy?"

"Yes."

"Roman itchy?"

"Not that bad. It's a matter of familiarity," Dav assures me as we climb to the top of the house. "The longer you are welcome in someone else's territory, the less itchy it becomes. Onatah visits me frequently with few problems, you'll note."

*One more thing to fix*, I decide. *We'll be visiting her, too. Onatah can't be the only one experiencing discomfort for friendship.*

We end up in one of the rooms graced with a pointy gable. The balcony it lets out onto is just large enough for two humanshaped folks, or one dragonshaped one. The stone balustrade is covered with deep claw marks, and I'd guess this is where generations of Tudors have made their first, fumbling attempts at flight.

Oh man.

*Flight.*

I've seen Dav in his dragonform a few times now. Sometimes he'll transform and flop all over me like a blood-warm, scaly St. Bernard. But I've never seen him as a crimson blur against the high, bright blue of the sky. I want to see that so bad. It'd be cool.

The rest of the room is exactly what Dav called it—a nursery.

A bucolic scene of idyllic Welsh countryside, replete with fuzzy lambs frolicking in the meadows and hedgerows, is painted on one wall. It looks like something one of the great Romantics might have created. As dragons do have the ability to annex anyone whose talents they value, it's possible that maybe one of them did. There's a rocking chair, a changing table, a low bookcase already crammed with well-loved board books and new stuffed animals. The floor is covered with soft, fuzzy carpets that look like they might be the end result of those lambs on the wall.

The only way in which this nursery is different is that there's no crib.

Instead, tucked into a recess built right into the chimney stack, separated from the hearth by a thick brick wall is, yes, a nest. It's low to the ground so any tumble from the deep arched alcove won't damage an egg or hatchling, but not so low that anyone can kick the egg by mistake. Dav pulls me over to sit on one of the poufs piled around the opening. The fire to the left of the nest is limpid, and Dav gently works it to get the flames leaping again.

Inside the alcove, a bundle of fragrant straw and woolen fluff holds the lady of the hour snuggly in place. There's a sort of prop under all the stuff, like a breakfast egg-cup, but porcelain and intricately painted to match the mural.

As for the egg itself, it looks perfectly, well, *normal*.

It's oval, and about the size of a newborn baby. Propped up on its fat bottom, it's creamy white, shot through with marbled veins of gold and red.

"It's... *she's* beautiful."

"You can touch her, if you like. She should know your smell."

"She can smell me through the shell?"

"At this stage of development, yes. And hear us, too." Dav turns his face to his sister. "Can't you, *wy bach*."

"*Wy bach*?" I repeat, deciding I better start on that Welsh language tutoring sooner rather than later. Dav winces a little, but clearly decides that now is not the time for a pronunciation lesson.

"Little egg."

Dav takes my hand and, gently, presses my fingers over the dome.

"It's... leathery." I pet down the side of the shell, and under the faintly pebbled texture, make out the subtle bumps of Dav's sister, curled up against the casing. "And damp."

"Yes," Dav says. "We're not birds. Our shells aren't brittle. She'll rip her way through when she's ready. There's water in the stand down there, do you see? Oh, hold on." From a small gilt hook on the side of the hearth, he fetches an ornate porcelain pitcher that looks like a watering can with a long, thin spout. It's painted to match the little cup that the egg is sitting in, and now that Dav's brushed aside some of the nesting, I can see that there's a trough in the side of the cup. Dav tips the spout against the trough, and the alcove fills with lavender-and-milk scented steam. "The bath was getting low."

"Do you have to do this for the whole time? Keep up the fire, fill the cup with water?"

"Yes."

"How long?"

"Oh, just a few decades," Dav says offhandedly, refilling the pitcher with fresh water from a huge metal cauldron on the hearth. He sprinkles more dried lavender into the pitcher from another matching porcelain bowl on the mantle—clearly it's an all-together baby-baking set—and sets the pitcher back on the hook. "She's had a trio of minders all this time, from Mother's hoard. They have apartments through there."

He points at a cleverly disguised door in the middle of the mural.

"Have we kicked them out?"

Dav sits beside me again and pats my knee. "They'll have heard us coming up the stairs and made a discreet exit. Probably taking a moment to catch up—they sleep in shifts."

"Intense."

Dav shrugs. "It's not the same people for three decades. Mother employs nursing students from Cardiff University."

I scoot back to let Dav have his turn with the egg, petting the shell and murmuring in Welsh. I don't mind waiting. It's nice to see him so content, so relaxed. We've spent way too much time stressed out and snapping at each other lately, and it's good to be reminded that we do actually like each other's company.

That what we have is worth everything we're going through to keep it.

When Dav's done, he leans back, and I shamelessly crowd onto his pouf, half in his lap. This will likely be the last time we'll get so much alone time for a while, and I want to make the most of it.

"Oh, hello," Dav chuckles, and scoops an arm around my thighs to hold me in place. "No funny stuff in front of the baby."

"No funny stuff," I agree. "Just... I missed you last night."

"I was there."

"Not until after I was asleep."

"I had things I wanted to discuss with Mother, and it was the right opportunity—"

"No, no. I get it. I'm just saying... I missed you."

Dav melts like the big softie he is, and pinches my chin between his fingers to hold me still for a kiss.

"My hopeless romantic," he accuses, as if he isn't the one who picks flowers out of his own garden for the vase on the table by our bedroom fireplace.

"Mm-hmm," I agree. "Still angling for that happily ever after."

"Working on it," Dav says, and kisses me. "Although."

I jam a finger into his chest. "Don't you dare change your mind."

"What? No, of course I'm not. I keep thinking..." Dav trails off, staring at his sister.

Oh my god.

*No.*

"If you tell me you're already thinking about getting me with egg, or whatever, you can just slam the brakes right on down, buster." I thwack him.

Dav laughs. "Draconic biology is not *that* different from humans, Colin. I cannot get you pregnant, and if we were to agree to add children to our family, it would not be without many months of conversation."

"Good."

My brain rewinds a bit.

Did Dav just call us a family?

I guess we are. Him and me.

How about that.

"So what are you thinking about, then?"

"Will you let me tell you, or will you interrupt again?"

I pinch my fingers in the air in front of his nose. "Smart ass."

"I'm clever, yes," he says smugly. "As for my ass—"

"Not in front of the baby," I remind him.

He gets thoughtful again. "Are we doing the right thing?"

"Changing the world?"

"Changing *her* world." Misery tugs at the corner of his mouth, tangling up in his Peter Pan kiss.

"Babe, look at me." He does. "Do you think we're changing it for the better?"

Dav hesitates for only a second. "Yes."

But he hesitated all the same.

"Are you *sure?*"

He scratches at his chin. "It will be different. Harder. She'll have to work more than I do. But I think she will be... happier than we are." He squeezes me tight against his side.

"Did you tell your mum?" I ask. "Is that why you were up here so long last night?"

"I couldn't accept her hospitality, and not explain what we intend."

"What did she think?"

"She was upset at first," Dav admits softly. "She didn't understand what was so *wrong*. Then she told me ..." He clears his throat, crackling out a small cough. "She says Da... there was a girl in the village. Da was set to marry her."

"She didn't know?"

"Of course she did."

"Then why—"

"Because it didn't *matter*." He arches his eyebrows significantly. "My mother picked, and my father was Collected."

"Your poor dad."

"Don't start imagining my mother snatched him away in her claws and ravished him against his will. But they met at a time when... if a dragon showed interest, you said yes. Because it would never occur to you that you were allowed to say no. Do you understand?"

I lay my ear against his waltzing heartbeat. "Yeah."

"And he's happy," Dav rushes to add. "They're each other's best friend. Mother's instinct was bang on. But I never knew that when they met, he would much rather have inherited his father's smithy than become a dragon's consort. I never *knew*."

"So after your mum was upset, then what?"

"She understood. She... wanted to know what we were thinking. What we were planning. And then she... she wanted to help. You'll have noticed she wasn't at breakfast."

"Yeah?"

"Mother has gone to Whitehall to petition the Queen for an audience on our behalf."

"Oh. No. Totally. Petitioning the queen in person." I choke on my tongue. "Of course."

Dav grins at me. "I have no doubts that we will be given an audience, you saucy thing."

"Saucy, am I? Gonna do something about it?"

Dav leans in, but instead of kissing me, he bites the tip of my nose and says, in a grumbling purr: "Not in front of the baby."

# chapter Forty-Six

"No," Paulette says, when she gathers us all in the drawing room three days later.

"No?" Dav repeats, bolting upright in his chair, teacup hanging halfway to his mouth. "But we're family! She really won't see me?"

Paulette's mouth twists sourly, the way Dav's does when he's got to say something he'd rather not. "Her advisers have been, hmmn, 'made aware' of the difficulties you've created with the coffee shop, and declined the request."

"Isn't it up to the queen herself to deny the request?" I protest. "Not her hangers-on?"

"Not if she never hears it," Paulette says, resigned, and flops back in her own chair. "I spent two damn days in that wretched palace and I'm convinced that not a single word I said to anyone made it any further than the ear it was spoken into."

"Simcoe," I spit.

"Simcoe," Paulette agrees. "I cannot say I'm best pleased with his audacity. Whitehall is far beyond his borders and the sphere of his Governorship."

"I spent so much time there as a child," Dav says, small and wounded. "We played in her apartments! She taught me the cotillion! And now she won't even *see* me?"

Dav never told me he'd grown up clinging to the queen's skirts. Christ. This is one secret I don't resent him for, though. I would have been *way* too intimidated to stick my tongue in his mouth if I'd known.

"Darling," Paulette says, sympathy and motherly concern radiating off her. "Please don't take this personally. This is political maneuvering. It's not at all about your relationship with Cousin Lizzie."

Owain takes his wife's hand.

Dav is *crushed*. His teacup, when he puts it back on the saucer in his other hand, rattles so badly that I take it away and set it on the table. Dav reaches for my hands as soon as they're free, a mirror of his parents, and I twine our fingers tightly. He breathes deep though his nose, eyes closed, collecting his calm, and I stay still to let him ground himself in my presence, like a good Favorite.

"All political maneuvering, may I remind you," Paulette says softly, when we've all had a good wallow. "Can be out-maneuvered."

Everything is a frustrating misery for the next few days. Prickly and unhappy, Dav and Paulette spend hours locked up together, calling, and emailing, and doing whatever else it is dragons do when they're trying to winkle favors out of one another. While I, completely useless and resenting it, do my best to stay distracted. But no number of garden walks, or castle explorations, or long calls with Gem and Stuart, or heading up to the nursery to have a good rambling conversation with the egg help.

"Alright, fetch your coat, lad," Owain finally says on day three. He grabs my elbow and drags me out of the library, where I've been trying and failing to choose a book for hours.

"I am not in the mood for another walk," I protest.

"No walks," Owain agrees, and hustles me into a waiting car before I have time to wonder why my de facto father-in-law is abducting me in the middle of the afternoon. "We're off for a cheeky one."

"A cheeky what?"

But we're already rolling down the tree-lined avenue, headed for town. The car stops fifteen minutes later opposite what the signage proclaims is Cardiff Castle. Or, from what I can see through the arched gateway, the ruins of it. I wonder if this one is a real Castle, or just another grandly named fake. How long ago did it fall? What happened to the dragons that ruled from that seat? Looking at the Welsh flag flying proudly from a pole in the stone courtyard, I have a pretty good guess.

Owain hustles me in the opposite direction, down a narrow cobbled street so old it has carriage tracks worn into the stone, and into a black-and-white half-timbered building. The sign above the door proclaims it *The Goat Major*, and our driver circles away silently as Owain holds the door to the pub open for me. We're greeted by a cheerful "Waheeey!" from the sparse spattering of patrons. The atmosphere is inviting—all hunter green leather, shiny brass fixtures, and low golden lamps. The walls are filled with military memorabilia and photos or paintings of goats alongside men in uniforms (whom I assume all hold the rank of major).

"Free by the fire, your Earl-ship," the bartender says, nodding us toward a little cozy, his tone mocking in a friendly way.

"Come here often?" I ask as we settle ourselves in a set of club chairs. My butt's barely finished making a dent in the leather when two fresh pints of some sort of deeply red beer are deposited on our table.

"Since the day it opened."

"So, a couple of centuries?"

"Aye. *Yachi da,*" Owain says, holding up his glass.

I repeat the toast. We spend the next few minutes correcting my pronunciation, and then lapse into contented silence.

"This is nice," I say at length.

"Mmm," Owain agrees, and, shit, yeah, this is the first time the two of us have been alone all week.

"Thanks."

"Hmmmm."

"It must have been hard for Day to leave here."

"Oh, no, lad," Owain says. "He was rarin' for the adventure. Spoke of nothing but coming back in glory." There's a touch of sadness in his words.

"And then he stayed?" I prompt gently.

"Aye, well." Owain sniffs. "That's all done now. When he told us he was trying to repatriate the territory to his friend, you know, we hoped... but he's got you, and a vineyard he's proud of. Sends us cases every year. We're just happy he's happy."

I set down my beer, nerves suddenly pricking. "You didn't drag me here to give me a shovel talk, did you? Because I promise you, his staff beat you to it."

Owain cracks one of his unguarded, jovial smirks at me, and the world tilts a little. It's weird to see a man who looks *so much* like my lover wearing an expression that I don't think I've ever seen on Dav.

"I'm not worried about you breaking my boy's heart," Owain says. "Nor am I worried he'll break yours."

"Oh." I force my fingers to stop twisting along the edge of my jumper. Dav had dug it out of a cedar chest for me, because the Welsh damp can sneak in and settle in your bones. The cabling is complicated, the ruby-coloured wool soft, and smells like a forest. "Thank you. So, why are we here then?"

"Oh, few reasons," Owain allows, finishing his pint and signaling the barkeep for another. "First, because the tension in that house was like to make me scratch my skin off. You'll learn that the more agitated the wyrms get, the more it makes *us* uncomfortable. One of the downsides to The Gift. We're meant to go soothe them, but I'm telling you now there's no soothing a Tudor when the bit's between their teeth. Best to just give 'em space."

"Going to a pub seems like overkill."

Owain thanks the waitress who drops off a fresh round for us, and we toast again, my pronunciation just barely improved.

"That's the second part of it," Owain says. "Absence makes the heart grow fonder."

"Is there a third?"

Owain reaches into his pocket and pulls out a ring box.

"I'm flattered," I laugh. "But I think Dav would be peeved if I married you."

Owain chortles and sets it on the table. "This belonged to Paulette's father's Favorite. It never suited me—" he shows off a broad blacksmith's hand. "But you've got them delicate fingers."

The ring is slender, but not girlish. The signet is stamped into a band of gold, the flower and the flames picked out in rubies. It's subtler than I had expected it to be when Dav had been musing about rings. And, unlike then, slipping it on doesn't send me into a panic spiral.

Dr. Chen would be proud.

The only finger it fits on, however, is my pinkie.

I decide to wear it on my left hand, where it won't get in the way. It has nothing to do with the fact that Dav almost always takes my left hand when we walk. Nope. Nosiree.

"Suits you, son," Owain says.

My chest is bursting with a kind of warmth I can't name, but don't hate. Pride swells in me. I feel like, for just a moment, my Dad is sitting here with us, approving, when Owain calls me that.

"Yeah," I agree. "It does."

Our dragons bluster in a few hours later, wind-swept and readjusting their clothes.

Dav crowds into the chair with me. It's way too small for both of us, so I end up perched on his lap. Owain and Paulette take over a sofa, too dignified to squish up like us youngin's.

"You smell like rain," I tell him.

"We came through a shower." He presses his cold nose against my nape and I yelp. I take both of Dav's hands between mine to warm them up, which makes the ring wink in the lamplight. Dav gets a good look at my new accessory.

"Da," he says, looking up at Owain. "This is yours."

"And now it's Colin's," Owain says.

Vibrating with a joy so profound I can actually *feel* it thrumming between us, Dav lays a thorough kiss on me.

By the bar, two of the old regulars whistle and clap.

"Good flight despite the rain?" Owain asks when Dav lets me up for air.

"Mmm, yes," Dav says. "Long time since I've done that."

"And I missed it?" I grouch, working up a pout.

"We'll go flying together when the weather's nicer." He shakes the water out of his hair like a playful puppy.

"Promise?" I ask. "The first sunny day?"

Dav exchanges a long, meaningful look with his mother. "Or when we're home." I pin Dav with a look, forcing him to elaborate. "Simcoe's connections are simply better than ours. Mother hasn't been to court in so long, and I've been absent for decades. We find that re-entering politics once we've recused ourselves from it so thoroughly, is a challenge we're having trouble surmounting."

I take a second to parse his meaning. "You can't *give up*."

"We are out of favors to cash in, and every string has been pulled. We've been denied."

"Yeah, but by *who*," I push. "Like, the queen hasn't actually told you this herself, has she?"

"No," Dav allows.

"Then, I don't know... we have to try harder."

"There is a blockage at her advisers," Paulette grumbles. "I do feel certain she would at least listen to your proposal, if you could—ah, but the court is so convoluted."

"So we find a way to cut through it. There's gotta be... didn't commoners used to petition royalty directly on open court days and, I don't know, give them a chicken for their table?"

"Genovia isn't a real country," Dav reminds me with a chuckle.

He steals a sip of my beer. I may be on my third, or fourth one, I don't remember, so I'm feeling tipsy and passionate, and yeah, a little horny watching him put his mouth right where mine was not a few minutes earlier.

"What about going to tea or something, then. A social call. Surely as family—"

"Invitations of that sort must come from the queen," Paulette says. "And we've rather tipped our hand."

"Shit," I say.

"Shit all around," Paulette agrees with me in her crisp accent, and joins Owain as they head up to the bar to fetch a round.

"So what now?"

"We wait for it to blow over," Dav says. "Come back to it when Simcoe thinks we've given up."

"How long will that take?"

"A decade, maybe a bit more," Dav says slowly.

"A decade," I repeat, aghast.

"You'll live to see it," Dav assures me.

"Yeah, but maybe not my Mum. Maybe not my *friends*. All the *good* you could do right now, and we're just supposed to sit around with our thumbs up our asses? Fucking hell."

Dav wraps his arms around me and sticks his face in my neck, soothing. It's soporific, the heat and the weight of my dragon curled around me, protecting me from the outside world and all its aggravations.

"I don't like it any more than you do," Dav assures me.

"Yeah." I run my palm along his jaw.

He needs a shave.

And maybe to sleep more. His puffy eyes rival Paulette's.

I've been sleeping like a baby. A happy contented full baby, the way I have been every night since Dav and I started having sex. Suddenly, I feel guilty for it. Here I am, getting every advantage of swapping spit with my lover, while every other person I love is dying by inches and I... I just can't... it's not *fair*.

"Excuse me," I husk out, and head to the door with no clear thoughts beyond needing a few minutes of fresh air to get my shit back together.

"Good morning, *mo leanbh*!" Mum's voice trills across the line almost before I realize that I've called her. "How's Cardiff?"

"Damp, Mummers," I tell her honestly.

For a brief millisecond, I consider telling Mum everything. About the enzymes, and the way that Simcoe whipped Dav, and how I'm trapped in a relationship with a man I love but in a structure we resent. About how the dragons who hoard us all could cure her of her need for hearing aids, and knowingly, selfishly, choose not to. About how they probably could have saved Dad—

But it's not fair to dump it on her.

Ignorance can actually sometimes be bliss.

Instead, I punch the wall until it starts to hurt.

With my right hand, of course.

Wouldn't want to damage my new ring.

"Colin? What was that sound?"

"Nothing—some drunks on the street," I lie as I shake out my hand.

"Tell me about what you're up to, *mo leanbh*," Mum hedges, not believing me. I tell her about the gardens at St. Ffagan's, and what little of the castle I can see across the road, rising above a stone wall topping a grassy berm, and Dav's forth-coming sibling.

"Haven't gotten out to see the sights, yet?"

"Dragons aren't big on straying too far from home," I admit. "Though maybe I can convince Dav to show me all the places they filmed *Doctor Who*."

"Oh. I suppose that's a shame, then. I was thinking how nice it would be for you to see your Auntie Pattie."

"Mum, Glasgow is on the other side of the island."

"Well, if it's too far, I'm sure she'd understand—" Mum stops when I groan.

No one can guilt-trip like a Scottish mother.

"Fine, but don't tell her, okay? Let me talk it over with Dav, see if we have time for it."

Our grand plans have been shot to hell.

We have nothing *but* time for it.

"She'll appreciate it so much," Mum enthuses, as if I've already said yes. "She hasn't seen you since you were in nappies."

Which is why I dread it. It's one thing exchanging letters and emails with a relative so distant you haven't touched them since you started kindergarten. It's entirely another to be forced to interact with them, likely in their house, sitting on a sofa smelling of mothballs and being told stories about other relatives you don't know, or care about.

After that, Mum and I chat aimlessly for long enough that my hand starts throbbing, and I begin to regret my tantrum. There's a split on my knuckle.

I know Dav can smell the blood, because as soon as I say my goodbyes and slump inside, his head jerks up. He inspects my hand, split-tongue licking the blood away like a cat.

"The wall will always win the barfight," he murmurs.

"I'll keep that in mind," I say, and try so hard for it not to come out glum. "Also, I... sort of told my Mum that we would go to Glasgow to visit my aunt?"

"I think that's splendid," Paulette interrupts us. "Get away for a few days and think about something else."

A thought occurs to me. "Could we *fly* there?"

Dav laughs. "It's too far, *Fy Nhrysor*. It'd take days for me to carry you to Scotland—we'd have to keep stopping for rest. Far faster to drive."

"Spoilsport."

# chapter Forty-Seven

Traveling to Scotland requires logistics. We take a few days to secure a B&B in an area of Glasgow that's supposed to be beautiful and historic, the tourist visas needed to hop across Hadrian's Wall, picking up enough Scottish Stirling cash from the exchange shop, and getting permission to cross through *dozens* of other dragon's territories via email forms, and then we're off. It's a seven hour drive, which we break up with a stop at a cidery in Manchester for lunch. I don't know Auntie Pattie's preference, but I buy a six-pack of scrumpy as a gift.

I thought she lived in Glasgow itself, but I guess it's been so long since I've sent her an actual physical letter that I didn't realize the return address on the packages had changed about ten years ago. She's in a walled medieval town called Renton now, a half hour or so's drive from the city, so not too far to pop down and visit.

Crossing the Wall is a breeze as we get waved through a special line, and the remainder of our travels in Scotland are oddly relaxing. Nobody on this side of the Wall gives a flying whatever who Dav and I are. It's refreshing to be anonymous again. If anyone even pegs him for a dragon, they don't say anything because it's nothing worth noting. Dragons are thick on the ground in the Old World. Not the way they are in the colonies, where there are so few territories occupying so much space that most humans will never cross paths with a dragon in their life, but they're recognizable from the news.

Auntie Pattie asks to meet us in a café on the far side of the city. The place is one of those ready-made-sandwich places, with run-of-the-mill coffee that can be charitably described as "drinkable".

We find a free table in the back and wait.

I'd had all day to tell Dav everything I knew about Auntie Pattie—that she was the daughter of Nan's terrible husband and his second wife, who had eventually kicked his alcoholic ass out; that Patricia and Mum had reconnected through mutual friends in Paisley where they'd both spent their childhoods; how Mum made a pilgrimage home every few years to spend time with her half-sister; how Pattie had some sort of government job that made it nearly impossible for her to get away long enough to return the visit; how Pattie had never married (and how I suspect her of being a big honking lesbian); how we swapped letters, birthday presents, and photos all the time.

So, we don't have anything left to talk about—except the merits of Scottish food and where we want to go for dinner. Neither Dav nor I have ever had haggis. So both of our heads are bent over my phone as we research restaurants when there's a chuckle—sounds just like Mum, eerie—from the other side of our table, and a: "I know I haven't seen you in decades, but I thought I would've got a wee bit of a warmer welcome than that."

"Auntie Pattie!" I'm delighted because for all that she had a passing resemblance to Mum, she's dressed less like a pottering older British lady, and more like Onatah.

Big honking lesbian, check.

Besides being blonde and blue-eyed like Mum, and having the same nose, Auntie Pattie doesn't look much like the rest of my family. Her eyes and mouth are creased with smile lines, and her features are finer. I might almost say we have the same cheekbones, but hers aren't as sharp and definitely don't come with my stupid ears. And her haircut is stylish, a trim glossy bob.

"Colin," she says warmly, and sets down her own mug on our table to wrap her arms around me. Gosh, it's a lovely hug. And spending as much time with dragons and hoard humans as I have, I'm starved for them.

"I'm so glad you called, young man," she teases. "Bless yer mum for bullying you into it."

"She didn't!" I protest.

"She did a bit," Dav says.

"And who's this fine ginger-snap?" Auntie Pattie asks, wrapping an arm over my shoulders and squishing me to her side to give herself a better view. She raises her eyebrow, clearly liking what she sees, then looks to me and raises the other one to join it.

"Right, sorry, yes. Dav, this is my Aunt Patricia."

"A pleasure."

"Same, hon."

"Auntie Pattie, this is Dav. He's my..." I hesitate, unsure how to describe our relationship to a mundie. "Well, he's mine."

"A pleasure," Dav says, offering his hand and then jerking it back at the last second like he'd been stung. It was an automatic reaction, I think, because he takes a second to stare at his hand as if he has no idea what just happened.

There's a long moment where Pattie and Dav regard one another, and Dav takes a long, deep inhale through his nose.

"I see." He inclines his head slowly, regally.

"Dav? Babe? What are you—"

My aunt, not even remotely plussed, presses her hand over her heart and offers him a slow, steady curtsy. Which looks, frankly, kind of silly in her shit-kicking boots and ripped jeans.

"Yours, you say?" Auntie Pattie says and tosses me a wink. "More's to say you're his, me lad."

"Wait, wait, wait," I splutter, looking back and forth between them. "Auntie Pattie, what the actual *fuck*."

"Language, *mo leanbh*," Auntie Pattie chides playfully.

"Is that what you meant?" I ask, scrambling for my phone and bringing up the email she'd sent over the summer in response to the first Instagram photo of me and Dav that went viral. "Runs in the family?"

"Calm down, Mine Own," Dav says. His gentle admonition has the opposite effect on me.

"It's perfectly reasonable for me to be *not calm* right now! Why didn't Mum tell me!"

"Because I haven't told Helen," Auntie Pattie says. "And you won't either, do you hear?"

"What? Why?"

"It's nothing shameful—" Dav starts, but Auntie Pattie puts up her hand to stall both of us.

The move makes the sleeve of her denim jacket fall back, and in the sallow fluorescents I see what Dav caught, and I missed. The bangle around her wrist is gold, shiny and bearing a thin plate in the shape of a shield. It's crisscrossed by a wide red x made of a different metal—copper, maybe? And the lowest quadrant bears the same little flame Dav's insignia does.

"It's nothing to fluster your mother over. Our Da, yeah? He had... *opinions* on dragons. He was old fashioned in the bad way, you know what I mean?" Unfortunately, I do. "Thought Georgius of Lydda shouldn't have stopped at one dragon, and said it loud enough he got banged up for it a few times..." She rubs her hand over her forearm, and I wonder if my grandfather broke or just sprained it. "And, you know, what you learn in childhood is sometimes hard to unlearn."

Dav lets out a puffing sigh of regret and pity. But he doesn't say anything, which I think Auntie Pattie appreciates. Anything he said now might come out as condescending, anyway.

Too little, too late.

"Mum's coming around," I reassure him. "Gem and Stu like you."

Dav grimaces all the same.

"Helen and her Mum left before I was born," Pattie says. "Helen was gone before she really knew what it meant to live so close with the dragons, to see that they really do care. They've got more of a wing in things here than in Canada, you see."

I think about the form letter I got with the electronic signature, congratulating me on my graduation. I wonder if Scottish territories are so small that the dragons actually attend the convocation ceremonies.

"So she was left with all of her dad's prejudices and none of the experiences she would have had when she was older to correct them?" I ask. "That's another way Simcoe has fucked his people over."

Dav makes a noise of agreement.

"So, explain, you're what, in a hoard?" I ask Auntie Pattie.

"Aye, just an employee, unlike you," Auntie Pattie adds warmly.

"How'd that happen?"

"Oh, well, there was a restoration project, and the team lead was impressed with my proposal, you know how it goes. I'm handy with a drafting table and a protractor. I was just out of uni and up to my eyeballs in student debt—I wasn't about to say no to a position that came with a free apartment, and enough money to pay off my loans in a year." She plays with the bangle around her wrist. "To be honest, I like it. It's kind of like having a big old family, you know?"

I place my hand over Dav's on the table top. "I know."

I do now, at least.

"May I see?"

"I'll show you mine if you show me yours."

We both stretch our left arms out, letting the other one turn them this way and that so our tokens catch the best light.

"It's beautiful, *mo leanbh*," Auntie Pattie says at length, then turns to Dav. "A Tudor then, are you, sir?"

"Distantly and only just," Dav says, voice croaking. "And your... ah, *employer*..."

He trails off, licking his lips, eyes darting to me.

"Don't leave us hanging, babe," I say.

Auntie Pattie smiles like a Cheshire cat.

"Raibeart Rìgh," she says gently. "Colin, dear, I belong to His Majesty, Robert the Bruce."

The volume at which I shriek "*What?*" gets us kicked out of the café, but that's fine with me because it means I have a lot of fresh open air in which to have my freak out.

I take a dozen or so minutes to pace the parking lot, back and forth across the banks of the river—fuming and grappling with the twisting, weird jealousy that washes through me each time Auntie Pattie bursts into peals of laughter at something Dav's said while they wait for me. They're standing a careful six feet apart, and I love him just that bit more for being so tender with my family, but he's *my* dragon. Finally, I stop in front of them, scuff my boots against the icy paving, shove my frigid fingers into my coat pockets, and grumble, "Okay. Yes. Runs in the family. Happy?"

"Delighted, darling," Dav says, all pleased sass, and I stick out my tongue at him.

He moves to grab it, but I dance out of the way before he can.

Auntie Pattie watches all of this with an amused expression but shrewd eyes.

"Well, now what?" I ask after Dav and I have scuffled ourselves out, and I've jammed my way under his armpit to take advantage of his draconic heat. Scotland in early winter is chilly in a way that's different than Canada. "Did you have plans for after you were outed to my boyfriend... lover... there's got to be *some* word for what Dav is to me. I'm his Favorite and he's my..."

Dav and Auntie Pattie share an awkward glance.

"If you tell me the answer is 'master', I'm kicking you into that river over there," I warn them.

"It's my turn to ask prying questions," Auntie Pattie says with a mischievous grin, changing the subject with the subtlety of a drunk elephant. "Why are you *really* over here?"

Dav and I squirm.

"Dav's sister is—"

"Oh, come off it, you numpty. You think the courts are so separate that nobody chatters? I have friends in Whitehall."

"And what are your friends telling you?" Dav ventures, wary.

"That you're agitating a fair few folk," Auntie Pattie says. And then she smirks. "But also that most of those being agitated deserve a good shake-up. Most of Liz's advisers are damn near as ancient as she is, if not older. Woosley spends more time asleep than awake, I hear. He'll be Turning Over soon."

"Turning Over?"

Auntie Pattie cuts a look between us. "Did he not tell you?"

Dav heaves a put-upon sigh. "No. I didn't want to overwhelm Colin with everything the microsecond after we kissed the first time, and it's caused a never-ending refrain of recrimination from everyone I know."

I pat his tummy consolingly, mocking him only a little. "Dav made a book for his first Favorite. Sat her right down on the ocean crossing and made her read it cover to cover before he'd let her accept his suit."

Dav startles. "Who told you that? Oh. Onatah."

"And he didn't do that for you?" Auntie Pattie asks.

"I sort of bumbled into the whole thing, you know, and..."

"Colin was already so... agitated."

"Freaked out."

"Discomfited."

"Freaking *the fuck* out—"

"That I thought it would compound the issue."

Auntie Pattie interrupts our playful banter. "But you could give him the book now?"

Dav shrugs. "I didn't know he was aware of it. And he hasn't asked for it."

"I'm asking now."

"It's at Fynyth."

"I'm gonna pinch you if you keep being sassy!"

Dav laughs. "No you won't."

I peck a kiss off his cheek instead. "No, I won't."

Auntie Pattie lets us settle, and then says: "Forgive me but... *first* Favorite?" Dav immediately goes still and silent. "Ah. My condolences."

"Thank you."

"Turning Over?" I prompt.

Auntie Pattie looks at Dav, leaving this one to him.

"Dragons don't die of old age," Dav says slowly.

"Oookay..." Are they pulling a prank on me? Though, when they would have had time to plan it, I'm not sure. Right, when I was pacing. "That's literally what happens when you get old but...?"

"For humans, yes," Dav says. "But ours..." he gestures at his own chest. "We solidify."

"Solidify," I repeat, deadpan.

"Turn to stone," Dav says after a pause. Then he takes a deep breath and plunges ahead, ripping off the band-aid: "Dragons are born in human shape, and as the centuries pass we spend less and less time on two legs, until it's more comfortable to be in dragonform all the time. And then the stone takes over, little by little. Cell by cell. We stop eating, stop making fire, and then, one day just... stop altogether."

I shudder, horrified by the image of Dav going still... forever.

"Normally the end comes with lots of warning," Auntie Pattie says gently. "Dragons will choose a cave, or a plinth, or the back corner of the Estate's Sleeping Garden, somewhere they'd like their remains to either be protected from the elements, or on display for their hoard."

I blink hard, eyes burning, throat closing up.

I hadn't expected to be smacked between the eyes with a frank discussion of Dav's fucking *death* today.

"And... and what about me?" I ask, voice trembling, and Dav splays a hand on my chest, over my heart, against my lungs. Reminding me. Breathe. Breathe into his hand. Just breathe. So I do. "Favorites live as long as their dragons. Do... do I turn into a goddamned statue, too?"

"You'll simply fall asleep," Dav says softly, pressing his nose into my hair. His voice is low, as much to comfort me as to keep this from being overheard by anyone else. "Not long after I do."

I judder once all over. There's something particularly morbid about knowing exactly how you're going to die.

"Okay!" I shake off Dav's arm and wipe at my face. "Okay. Topic change, please. Before I actually have a full-on meltdown."

"Actually, I'd rather we return to the first one," Auntie Pattie says, stamping her feet to warm up in the chill Scottish air. "What, exactly, are you two bully lads up to that's got every uppity priss twitching?"

Dav shoots me a look that says, *Can we trust her?*

My reply look says *After everything she's offered us? Yes.*

So we lean in close, make sure nobody is paying us too much attention, and we tell her everything. When we're finished, she shoves her hands in her pockets, rocks back on her heels, and has a good chew over what we said.

"Well, now," Auntie Pattie says at length, and then stops, thinking.

She doesn't go on, and we give her space to contemplate.

"Well, now," Auntie Pattie repeats, chewing on her lower lip, the same way my Mum does. Same way I do. But this time she finishes her thought: "Seems to me that if you cannae get in to see a queen, perhaps you ought to be seeing a king instead."

# chapter Forty-Eight

There's a delicious irony to the fact that Simcoe couldn't have had any freaking idea it would be *my* connections he had to worry about instead of Dav's. Auntie Pattie pulls whatever strings she has hold of, and late the next morning, Dav and I are making our way through the ancient stone halls of Cardross Castle.

We hadn't brought any clothing fit for taking an audience with a king, but a quick trip to the shops as soon as they'd opened had at least landed some decent off-the-rack suits. Mine is boring old black, though Dav has picked out a lux green shirt for me. His suit is a gorgeously on-trend floral pattern in shades of green and dusty copper that match my shirt, and sets off his perfectly-coiffed hair.

My boyfriend (fiancé? fella?) is such a clotheshorse.

(Is the term *really* 'Master'? Never in a million years.)

Auntie Pattie walks a few steps behind us, in a slick pantsuit. A few steps ahead, a footman in an old-fashioned livery blazoned with the same yellow-shield-and-red-x leads us through a vaulted gallery toward what is probably either going to be a) another fussy draconic parlor, b) some sort of conference room, or c) possibly a throne room?

I kind of want it to be C.

I've never been in a real throne room before.

It ends up being C.

Nice.

The room we're paraded through is at least four stories high, with intricate, painted columns and bas-relief covered in gold leaf which, I'm sure, have lots of important meaning to the people who can read them. To keep our visit as secret as possible, we were hustled in the servant's door this morning, so I don't know what Raibeart Rìgh's front door looks like, but whatever histories couldn't fit there seem to have overflowed to this ceiling. You always sort of expect medieval castles to be gray and lightless, but the arched windows are massive, filling the room with syrupy, slanted sunbeams. Dust motes dance in the air, and there are a few loose threads on the lush red carpet. It looks like someone actually *lives* here, which I like.

Dav and I pause at the base of a grand dais to bow – me with my hand over my heart – and Auntie Pattie peels off to the side to stand with a small handful of other people in equally smart suits and sparkling tokens.

At the top of the dozen or so stairs is a wide, ancient throne.

It's made of dark stone, carved with complicated Celtic knotwork. A dark red cushion on the seat supports another stone, lumpy and about the size of a wolf, and I wonder if this is the Stone of Scone that the draconic harlequins make a meal of.

And then the stone blinks.

It cracks a monumental yawn and I realize that this must be what Auntie Pattie meant by 'close to Turning Over'. Raibeart Rìgh's hide is craggy and as gray as the highland mountains, his eyes the bold violet of the heather that dots it. He's surprisingly...*fluffy* for a dragon. His long, thin tail, which I'd mistaken for tassels on the pillow, is feathered with curls. A mane starts around his ears and flows down over his shoulders to appendages that are rather more like paws than talons. He mantles his wings and raises his blunt-nosed head to get us in his sights.

"*An e seo an dràgon òg a tha airson an saoghal a shàbhaladh?*" he asks.

"Yes, my dear," a human says, stepping out from behind the throne. She's white, willowy, but short, and with wavy, brilliantly silver hair. At her throat shines an archaic necklace, heavy with gems and the king's signet. "Regrettably, the young Favorite only speaks English."

"Shame," the King says, the sound a cross between a thick Scots burr and the granite rumble of massive boulders grinding together. "Come closer, Dragon's Own. I am told you are descended of my hoard?"

There's a short silence, and then Dav elbows me.

Oh, *I'm* Dragon's Own.

"Er, my auntie's in your hoard, Your Majesty," I splutter. I take a few steps up, because the King is squinting and I wonder how good his eyesight is anymore. I just sort of hover there, not sure what to do with my hands, arms akimbo. "And my mother was born in Scotland."

"And yet you now come before me as the Favorite of a Welsh dragon," the King harrumphs and turns his head to Dav. "Little poacher."

Alarm clangs under my skin, but Dav, the bastard, just chuckles.

"Guilty as charged, Your Majesty. Had you seen how kindly and selflessly he serves his neighbors, how passionately he argues for environmental welfare, and how gently he loves his friends and family, you could hardly have blamed me."

"Doesn't hurt that he's handsome," Raibeart Rìgh chuckles.

My face immediately goes nuclear-red.

"Not in the least, Your Majesty," Dav agrees.

A loud cracking sound echoes through the gallery. It's the sound of a stone column collapsing. I flinch, but nobody around me is diving for cover, or looking up at the ceiling.

The sound was not the building shattering. It was the king standing.

Raibeart Rìgh climbs to his feet, barrel-chested and majestic. Even the stone-dust that puffs into the air glitters like fairy-dust.

"Bob, should you be—?" His Favorite asks, in a low, urgent whisper.

"We will retire to our study to hear the Marquess," the king says, amiable but firm. He pauses, eyes immeasurably sad. "The future comes faster than we'd like it to, *Mo Sheud*. And I wish to see my people cared for. In the best method possible."

"Wise, Your Majesty," Dav says gently.

"You don't need to flatter quite so obviously, little poacher," the king says affably. I'm not so versed in reading dragon faces that I could tell you exactly what his expression is, but I'm pretty sure it's amused. "Come with me now, Alva-draig Tudor. Margaret Banrigh sends her regrets, as she is promised elsewhere, but my son David Beithir waits for us in my chambers. Let us talk."

Dav gives my shoulder a firm pat, and starts up the stairs.

I move to follow him, but the king's Favorite is already coming down towards me with a grin. "This way, Mr. Levesque. We'll leave the wyrms to their chatter."

"But it... it's my plan, too," I protest, as Dav reaches the king's side and looks over his shoulder for me.

"Do ye not trust your dragon?"

*At least she didn't say "master."*

"Of course I do, but—"

"It's fine, Colin," Dav says. He pats his pocket where the flash drive with copies of all of our documents sits. We've been carrying a backup with us at all times, just in case. Good thing.

Not wanting to cause a scene, I wave him on miserably.

Dav gives me his sunrise smile, and places a hand on the king's shoulder and lets the ancient dragon lead him to a door to the side of the throne.

"Welp." I turn to Auntie Pattie. "Now what?"

"Now we take our ease, my friend," the Favorite says, instead of letting my aunt answer.

I don't know if it's a hierarchy thing, or a Being Favorites thing, but it kind of rubs me the wrong way. I didn't ask *her*.

"Off you go with Lady Isobel, boyo," Auntie Pattie says. "I have actual work to do, unlike you lucky lot. I'll fetch you for lunch."

"Uh, okay." I drop a kiss on her cheek, and scramble to catch up with Lady Isobel, who is already halfway down the gallery and walking with all the confidence of someone who is used to getting things exactly her way.

Not arrogant. Just so sure that it comes off as dismissive.

*I won't be like that*, I promise myself.

"And do you have a job I'm keeping you from?" I ask Lady Isobel when I catch up. She tosses an amused glance at me.

"My job is to see to Raibeart Rìgh's happiness and ease."

"Then shouldn't we be, you know, in there then? With our...?" I let it hang, wondering if she'll give me a term.

"No," she says instead. *Damn, foiled.* "They'll send for us if that changes. No need to fash yourself."

I'm not going to connect with Lady Isobel the way I did with Laura Secord.

Oh, Laura.

Man.

I haven't thought about Laura in weeks.

I want to call her.

I want to be her *friend*.

But Simcoe.

That's another thing I can't have because of him. I can't build a friendship with someone amazing, and clever, and insightful because... *This sucks.*

Lady Isobel leads me into a comfortably plush sitting room filled with jumbled groupings of furniture that look expensive but mismatched, probably cast offs from renovations. This place must have seen hundreds of updates in its time. A few other people are already seated in little groups, chatting and clutching cups. Everyone looks up and gives a respectful nod when we enter, but nothing so ceremonial that it makes me think there's some sort of protocol for greeting a royal Favorite.

Thank fuck.

Lady Isobel leads me to a little kitchenette, and asks me what she can make for me.

"Coffee," I say, and then, when she steps up to, honest to god, the most orgasmically beautiful fucking espresso machine I've ever seen in my goddamned life, I add: "Oh no, no, no, please. *Please*, allow me."

It starts to snow while I'm impressing the king's hoard with my latte art. When Auntie Pattie pulls me away from my adoring audience for lunch in the super-fancy canteen, the world outside is slowly acquiring a soft, calm blanket of white.

We catch up on family gossip, managing to entirely avoid talking about the exact reason we're both sitting at this particular table, until Auntie Pattie asks, out of nowhere: "Do you love him?"

Except not entirely out of nowhere, because I'm staring at my ring, watching the way it catches on the sunlight filtered through the whispering snowflakes.

"More every day," I confess.

"Even with all these... curve balls thrown at you?"

I drag my eyes back to hers. "As much as it pisses me off to be flat footed once a week, every week, Dav was smart to string out the revelations."

"Yeah?"

"I don't like being told what to do."

Auntie Pattie snorts.

"You grow up with twin older siblings, then tell me how sick of being bossed around you'd be." I cup my mug and tap the band of the ring against the ceramic. It's a soothing sound. "So it's... it's kind of nice. The revelations themselves aren't nice—actually, sometimes they are, but what I mean is... I'm not explaining it well." I take a breath to recalibrate. "Dav's first Favorite, Charlotte, he tells me she was the kind of person who loved to learn from books, right? I'm the kind of person who learns from doing—walking through the field, touching the vines, seeing the relationships between the environmental factors for myself."

"And Dav knows this about you?"

"He must have figured it out. Because if he had sat *me* down with a whole book of rules, and expectations, and an exact explanation about how we're both going to die in five hundred years, I'da run screaming."

"But he didn't," Auntie Pattie says. "And so you didn't."

"Which is lucky," I chuckle.

Auntie Pattie reaches over the table and pinches my ear.

"Ow!"

"Silly bugger. You think luck has anything to do with it?"

"Doesn't it?" I ask, rubbing my sore flesh.

"Your Dav is a military man, you said? Studied soldiery his whole life?"

"Yes."

"Being a commanding officer, the leader of a combat unit, being in charge of not only battles, but the logistics of getting everyone there in one piece, healthy and well-fed, and then getting what's left of them home again... you understand how much *planning* that takes?"

"Oh."

"Dragons who don't *think* don't keep their territories, and it's not all about battle prowess. Even if you outsource it by claiming the most talented humans you can in a field—" She gestures to herself, justifiably proud. "—you still need to find those people, first."

"So you mean like, Dav had a farm and a vineyard to run, so he chose a Favorite who could do it for him?" The thought curdles my good mood. I don't like the idea of being a conscious acquisition, even if it did result in us falling in love. I don't want to have started my relationship with Dav as a convenient and cultivated opening move in a chess-match to keep his territory intact and healthy.

I say as much.

"Ya ninny wee nugget," Auntie Pattie laughs. "I see the way he stares at you. It started with lust, pure and simple."

"Oh, well." I throw her a saucy wink. "It does make me feel better, knowing that he wanted to dick me down before he wanted me to oversee his production yields."

Auntie Pattie makes an undignified sound, shaking as she tries to hold in what I'm sure would otherwise be howling laughter. "I'm just saying, it's almost like he gave you what you needed, how you needed it. It's *almost* like he paid attention and figured out how to approach the first time in the best way possible."

"Oh no, that was a complete clusterfuck," I tell her, settling in to recount the full story. "Five seconds after we had our first real conversation, he stabbed me."

By mid-afternoon, the snow has slowed enough that I don't mind waiting beside the car parked at the front of the castle for Dav. Well, I *mind* because I'm still sore about being kept out of the meeting, but I'm not getting buried in a snowbank, at least.

"Fuck," I whisper, and beside me, Auntie Pattie gave me the stink-eye.

"I forgot to ask Lady Isobel what Favorites are supposed to call our dragons."

"Still picking at that?"

"Boyfriend sounds childish, and fiancé isn't right because we're not waiting for anything, but he's not technically my husband because we're not married and dragons can have spouses that aren't Favorites so like, what do I call him?"

Before she can answer me, everyone at the front door leaps into motion, cranking open the massive carven door.

"I think it's literally the least of your worries right now, kiddo." She drops a big kiss on my cheek. "Text me when you're back to Wales safe, and keep me in the loop, aye?" Then Auntie Pattie is off around the side, so she's not in the way of any formal grandstanding that might need to happen as Dav and I leave.

Which sucks.

I wish she could be here. She's my family.

But like everything else in my life now, apparently, there are freaking *optics*. And speaking of optics, Lady Isobel is the first one out the door, which surprises me. She's wearing a massive old-fashioned fur wrap, and carrying another.

"Marquess Niagara tells me neither of you brought coats with you," she scolds as she descends the steps and, another surprise, completely invades my personal space and wraps it around me. "November in Scotland? What were you think-ing?"

I smile at her fussing, pleased by this other side of her. In front of the other humans downstairs, she'd been aloof and politely amused by my showy barista antics. Now she's clucking at me like a particularly ruffled mother hen.

"I'm Canadian," I remind her. "This is barely out of shorts-and-tee-shirts weather. The snow's already melting."

Lady Isobel chuckles. "You aren't half-frozen, and that's all that matters. You'll be keeping the fur, lad."

"Oh no, I—"

"A gift," she says, with a sort of eyebrow wiggle that makes it clear that it's not only in bad taste to decline, but that it would *mean* something in the way that things among dragons always do. "From one Favorite to another, ye ken?"

"I'm beginning to." I fuss with the ends of the wrap—soft, smelling of cedar, absolutely older than I am, and, dear god, made of *real* dead animals—and giving her one of those little head nods that I'd seen humans offering each other on Halloween.

"Good fellow," Lady Isobel says. "Turn toward me, now smile wider, and there we are. That will make the press happy."

I heroically don't turn and scan the bushes that rim the grand entryway to the castle. "So this was a photo op?"

"As well as a chance to let you know that I think you're both daft. I can keep you warm *and* provide some handy symbolism to hammer the message home to Cousin Lizzie."

"And what are we, uh, hammering home?"

Lady Isobel smiles indulgently. "Marquess Niagara and his Favorite are protected by Raibert Rìgh. Quite literally." She pats the heavily jeweled clasp that could probably pay off the student debts of everyone in my cohort. "No matter what happens in the coming days, you will find succor and support at Cardross."

"Thank you." I swallow hard against a knot of fear and anxiety that her assurance shoves into my windpipe. Because you don't say shit like that unless you think someone's going to need it. "We are honored, Your Ladyship."

She cuts me a wink. Whatever little pageant we've just put on, I've performed admirably.

There's no goddamned way I'm going to ask her about what I'm supposed to call Dav *now*, not when I know there might be high-powered mics or lip-readers in the bushes. And then the doors open again, and there are dragons walking towards us. *Three* of them.

David Beithir looks like his father, only his scales are rich dark copper, his glossy mane shining in the sunlight. Next to him, Raibert Rìgh looks even smaller, and grayer, and dustier than he had in the throne room.

But between them, it's the third dragon who holds all my attention.

I've never seen Dav's dragonshape outside. I let myself stare openly, taking in the features I miss when he transforms in close quarters to sit on me for cuddles in the hideous orange lounge.

He's taller in the shoulder than the other dragons, I realize, more on the scale of an Irish Wolfhound to their St. Bernards. And longer by a lot, too. His tail curls and whips behind him, held up off the stone floor, undulating. He's not just red, he's *every* red. In the sunlight, his scales are brilliant carmine, glittering ruby, bright vermilion. His underbelly shines like new pennies, and as the cold air hits him, he stretches his wings up in a draconic yawn. The light through the delicate membrane turns them a glowing terracotta.

The first time I'd seen this, I'd been scared.

Not by the dragon himself, but by what getting to see his dragonform had meant. Seeing him now, unashamed and comfortable, I'm proud. Proud that this beautiful creature is mine. That I can look at him like this any time I like. That I'll have years, decades, to study every scale, examine every claw, kiss every little pokey spike down his back.

"Handsome," Lady Isobel says, catching my expression.

"Damn straight," I agree.

When Dav reaches the bottom of the stairs, he turns to offer the other two dragons some sort of elaborate wing-and-leg dip that I take to be a bow when they offer him a shallower version in return. When all eyes turn to me, I give an equally low, fist-over-heart bow of my own, and then the driver is opening the door for us.

We'd driven ourselves to Scotland in a rental, but Lady Isobel had insisted on loaning us a chauffeur and a roomy compact limo for the ride back to Wales.

"Do you want me to change back?" Dav asks as I clamber in. "My clothes are with our luggage in the trunk, I can step into the vestibule—"

The thought of being in the secluded rear of the car with this scaly, fascinating, beautiful version of my dragon sends an intrigued, pervy shiver up my spine.

"The poor lad is freezing," Lady Isobel says with a knowing grin. "You'd best be on your way now, and you can warm him better like this."

We're bundled into the back of the car—me in my seat, Dav sprawling on the spacious floor, tail curled around my waist and head in my lap—and then we're off. Straight back to St. Ffagan's, because *optics*.

Can't hang around the Scottish throne looking like panting beggars, is how Auntie Pattie had put it. It needs to look like it was a social visit, quickly done and quickly over. For the first few hours, we fill each other in on what our days have been like. I pet over his head, cataloging the difference in texture between the soft scales on the tip of his nose, the armored ones that surround his eyes, and the silkiness of his ears.

Lady Isobel was right, and I'm shedding the fur before long, the heat from Dav's internal furnace more than enough to chase away the Scottish winter.

Eventually our conversation tapers away. Dav dozes, and I must too, because I'm groggy when we stop for dinner. Dav, regrettably, changes back into humanshape and dons clothes so we can stop at a road-side restaurant.

It's almost midnight, and we're nearly back to St. Ffagan's, when I break the silence to ask: "Will you look like that?"

Dav is quiet, formulating an answer. It's snowing again. I loved driving with my Dad at night through the snow, because it looked like you were going warp speed through a sky full of whizzing stars. He would make starship noises, blooping all the buttons on the dash.

"Yes," Dav finally says. "But it will come on slowly."

"Okay," I say, because I can't change it, even if I hate the idea of having to watch Dav turn into a statue. "Does it hurt?"

"No, Mine Own." He leans over to kiss me softly. "I won't feel any pain."

"Okay," I say again, but this time I mean it.

Only the butler is awake when we arrive, and we tell him not to bother anyone else. It's nearly dawn by the time we've schlepped our bags upstairs, showered away the aches of a long car ride, and I've convinced Dav to return to his dragon-shape for bed.

Not in a kinky way. I'm not up for anything like that.

Not tonight, at least. (But definitely another time, oh yes, I am more than open to playing.) For tonight, I just want to feel the warmth and the weight of him, the physical promise that I'm his. That he's mine.

"So now what?" I ask as Dav lays his arrow-shaped head on my sternum. He yawns once, flashing wickedly sharp fangs, split tongue curling, then flopping out the front of his mouth in a draconic mlem. I tap it, and he grumbles and retracts it.

"Now?" he rumbles. "Now, we wait."

"Well, that's not going to be agonizing at *all*."

# chapter Forty-Nine

Dav's sister seems to hate waiting as much as we do. We're woken mid-morning by the sound of feet pounding up and down the stairs at the end of the hall, underscored by insistent knocking on our door.

"Get up!" Owain shouts through the wood.

"What's going on?" Dav asks. I didn't think dragons could get bedhead, but the scales on the side of his face are adorably askew. His ear has fabric creases on it. My heart clenches as I'm struck, all over again, with how much I adore him. I get to have this, this right here, for the rest of my life. "What's the fuss?"

"Nothing!" Owain says. "Unless you don't want to watch your sister hatch."

"She's hatching!" Dav exclaims joyfully, popping into his flesh so quickly I miss it between one blink and the next.

"Hey, hold on. Clothes!" I shout as he scrambles toward the door. He dives for the pajamas he'd left on the foot of the bed.

Hopping on one foot as he slides into the pants, he pulls the door open.

"How long?" he asks breathlessly.

"Your mother says you better come in the next ten minutes."

"Of course, yes," Dav says and smacks a kiss off his father's forehead. "Thank you!"

Owain looks past Dav, grinning, to where I'm still struggling to untangle myself. "Morning, Colin."

Oh god, I'm only wearing boxers under these sheets.

"Uh, yes, morning..." I mumble. "See you up there?"

He laughs. "Of course."

He closes the door, and Dav rushes around, fetching slippers, throwing on a robe, tossing mine at me, running into the bathroom to swish some mouthwash. I do the same, take a piss, and wash my hands thoroughly in case someone has the stupid idea to put a baby in them. Then we're joining the rest of the crowd of people upstairs, waiting breathlessly by the open nursery door.

Apparently a hatching is a whole-hoard affair.

By virtue of being the big brother, Dav and I are shuffled inside. We're herded to the poufs arranged around the ornate egg cup, which is now on the floor in front of the blazing hearth and surrounded by feather-down which will, I assume, catch any roly-poly babies and absorb any viscera that may escape the shell with her.

Dav greets his mother with kisses on the cheek, and as I sit, he clutches my hands.

"Do I have to, like, prepare myself?" I whisper, and he raises a confused eyebrow at me. "Is it gonna be ... icky?" *Don't be grossed out*, I warn myself. *Whatever happens, don't be rude.*

He smiles. "It's much cleaner than a human birth, if slower. It'll be—" and then he gasps.

I whip my head back around to watch as the top of the shell stretches, like thin leather, and then, suddenly, *pop.*

There's a tear in the delicate material, and a little, red, pointy nose is out in the world. The scaly nostrils flare as Dav's sister takes a few fortifying breaths, her first in the open air of the world beyond her shell.

"Come on, sweet one," Paulette encourages, leaning forward, her hands tangled with Owain's. "You can do it."

I realize that everyone is clutching someone else, likely to quash the desire to peel the shell back. Even I know that you gotta let the little babies do that themselves, when it comes to birds. Why should dragons be any different?

Dav's sister rests for a moment, and then seems to decide that she's sick of being in the egg. Her whole head emerges all at once. She looks like Dav in miniature, albumen glistening in the firelight. She huffs, exasperated with the struggle, eyes opening for the first time. I'm caught by how yellow her gaze is. Her pupils expand and contract as she adjusts, and she yawns wide enough to show off a mouthful of teeth like sewing needles.

Around her the shell deflates, and after a few tired struggles, the room erupts into cheers when she flexes her wings and rips free. She cringes at the noise.

"Oh, our apologies, my darling," Owain says, kneeling on the down to lift and wrap his daughter in a fine, soft blanket. It's embroidered with a floral pattern that matches the one painted on the rest of the baby-brooding set. "We're just happy to see you."

The baby settles with a few awkward wing flaps, allowing herself to be swaddled, and blinking sleepily up at her father. Then, still on his knees, Owain turns to Paulette, and the room drops into sudden, anticipatory silence.

"Paulette-draig Seren Addfwyn Windsor Tudor, Countess Plymouth, I present to you a child of our blood and our flesh," Owain says formally, holding the bundle of baby out like an offering. I think, for one moment, what it might be like for a dragon to reject a child presented to them like this, how easy it would be to dash the child to the floor.

Of course, Paulette would never do that—she's looking at the baby with happy, hungry eyes.

"I recognize this child as of our blood and of our flesh, and name it mine," Paulette announces, and then breaks the formality of the moment to flick her gaze first to Dav and I. "And beloved of my family."

"I give her to you," Owain goes on. "She is yours forever more."

"She is mine, forevermore."

Paulette takes the child—who has begun to fuss—and quickly tucks her against her chest. The baby settles, cooing, and presses her face as close to her mother's heartbeat as possible. Just like that, the trance of ceremony is broken. Owain hops back up onto the pouf so he can lean over his wife's arm to look into her face.

"Welcome, Carys-draig Tudor," Paulette says to her daughter, loud enough that everyone in the room can hear.

There's a collective sigh of contentment at the naming, and the crowd shuffles out. One of the nursery maids sets a kettle over the fire, no doubt for a baby bath, while the other opens all the windows, letting out the stuffy air.

"I thought you said dragons were born in humanshape," I whisper, waiting for Paulette's permission to get closer.

Dav can't take his eyes off the baby, vibrating with palpable impatience. "A human couldn't break out of the shell. Look," Dav breathes, and by the time I tear my eyes off his besotted expression, it's already happening.

Within minutes, she's a scrunch-faced, toothless, fleshy little bundle with wide buttery eyes and a thistledown wisp of frightfully ginger hair. I'm not one of those baby-hungry queers who coos and giggles over every womb-dropping they see... but, yeah, this one is worth some cooing.

"Should we take this as a sign?" I ask. "That she decided to hatch now?"

"Eggs tend to hatch when the whole family is present," Dav says. "I would have suggested we come visit for the holidays if we hadn't come now. It was about time."

"*I* think it's a sign," Owain says.

"Birth of a new world? Appropriate," Paulette says, and then, as soon as the nursery maids are gone and we're alone, adds: "Come greet her."

Dav is across the little room in a shot, kneeling formally before his mother, leaning down to rub his cheek against the baby's. It must be sticky with egg-stuff, but Dav doesn't care. Then he gently cups the back of her head and whispers, "Hullo, Carys. Welcome home, *wy bach*."

I make my way over more slowly, giving them a moment. Dav takes my hand and places my palm over the baby's fragile skull, lacing our fingers together to form a protective little hat.

"Hey, kiddo," I say. "I'm totally going to be the cool queer brother-in-law who talks to you about everything you can't talk to your parents about. But, uh, not the kind who helps you pick your prom dress. Sorry."

"He's really not," Dav chuckles, sniffling wetly.

"Hey, hey, babe." I hold out my arms so he can bury his face against my neck, and squeeze my ribs. "It's okay, don't cry."

"I'm so happy," Dav says, and I can't help the tears that spring into my own eyes.

It's fine though, because everyone else is already crying, and like, shit.

Yeah.

This is awesome.

It's even awesomer when a courier arrives a few hours later with a gift from Onatah—an entire boxful of baby-sized novelty socks.

The summons to court comes four days later.

Carys is laying on a play mat in the nursery, and I am totally laying beside her to get the perfect Tummy Time Selfies to send home to Mum, Gem, and Stu. Her face has started to look less squashed and more baby-plump. She's got her wings popped and it's the cutest damn thing. I can appreciate when my sister-in-law is being fucking adorable, okay? And I'm allowed to touch a dragon this young, which is nice because it means I get to play with her as much as everyone else.

"Two days from now," Dav says, coming into the nursery from where he'd gone downstairs to accept a letter addressed to him. It's old fashioned, hand-written and sealed with wax, and must have been hand-delivered. I give it a read over, then hand it to Owain, who has followed him up.

"They're giving you an audience?" Owain says.

"The throne is willing to hear us out. We'll speak to the queen first, and if she approves, we'll present to the Court of Peers."

Having little-to-no experience with royal *anything*, I ask, "So this is like a really fancy thesis presentation?"

Owain snorts so loud, Carys jolts and stares up at him with wide, scared eyes.

"Oh, no, cariad," Dav says, scooping her up before she can begin to wail, cuddling her close. "No monsters here."

"Me, a monster," Owain repeats, sarcastically. "Honestly."

I take the letter back, and read it again. "So, okay, an hour with the queen and if things go well, two hours with the peers. That's... not a lot. But I'm the champion of distilling a couple hundred pages of science gobbledygook into a compelling powerpoint. I just gotta... call Pedra. And finish that power-point. And, um, write a couple of abstracts. Like. Right now."

"Make sure you leave time for a fitting or two," Dav says as I pull myself up.

"Fitting?"

"It says court attire," Dav says. "My court suit is quite out of date, and we haven't had yours made up yet."

"Court attire," I repeat. "Like... ermine cloaks, and crap?"

Owain grimaces ruefully. "Afraid so."

"Right, okay, fittings," I mutter to myself. "Fittings, and power points, and physical copies in case there's no smartboard..." I pop up to my feet, and ruffle Carys' bright orange hair before doing the same to Dav. "I have work to do."

I'm so into my head about the whole thing that I nearly trip down the stairs.

Colin the disaster academic is back.

As a reader of historical romance, I know all about symbolism and the rigidity of Attire Laws as laid down by Elizabeth Regina. But as I prefer the historicals, it means I don't have much of an idea of what to expect in a twenty-first century Court Suit. My brain had flashed to ostrich plumes, wide panniers, capes with massive trains, and skin-tight buff-coloured breeches.

What I get is, I gotta be honest, ten times better.

And thank fuck, a *lot* more modern.

The morning of the audience, I'm in the foyer double checking the files, hand-outs, data sticks, and other assorted accouterments that I've stashed in the obscenely tasteful emerald-coloured leather briefcase that had appeared in our rooms. It matches my equally obscenely tasteful emerald velvet suit jacket—the cut resembles a modern blazer, though it still has the posture-improving old-fashioned back-set shoulders of Regency fashion. I talked the tailor out of going all-green, and opted instead for black trousers with a subtle pattern of Tudor roses, and a matching waistcoat. There's an emerald neck-cloth to go with it, but I've got it tucked into my pocket. In part because I have no clue how to tie it. But also because I'm currently drinking coffee and the last thing I want to do is drip.

*Dragon-roasted* coffee.

Because, like, I'm still in for that penny, right?

We'd grabbed some green beans in Cardiff when we'd gone to the tailors. My well-stocked briefcase contains little packets of coffee in different stages of roasting so we can hand them off to any scientists who want to experiment with them. Or humans who might want to try drinking it.

I snuck a cup of it this morning, and fucking hell, it's still amazing. I missed it. (Dav toasted me my first ever s'more last night and they are as fantastic as everyone said.)

"We're gonna be late if you keep primping!" I call up the stairs, when I reach the bottom of my mug.

"One moment!" Dav calls from the gallery. "I need... ah, there it is! Everything must be perfect, Colin."

"Come down, babe. I wanna see you."

"I look nothing as elegant as you," Dav complains. "Fashions have changed since I was last at court, and not in a way I expected. I blame Hollywood entirely."

"Shoooooow meeeeeee," I whine.

"If only to stop you from making that noise, Mine Own." Dav heaves a sigh, and then turns the corner of the landing and steps into view.

He looks (trust me, I have tried to find better ways to describe this and there are none) like the Empire from *Star Wars* vomited all over him.

And honestly?

It's a *good fucking look*.

Sinfully tailored black breeches tuck into knee-high boots. His jacket is a Regency cut-away with a double row of brightly gold buttons, fanciful frogging, and no epaulets. Otherwise, it screams military. It's in the firm cut of the shoulder, the tight mandarin collar, the rolled gold hems. A detailed gold waistcoat peeks out beneath the bottom of the jacket, and there's a tasteful row of ornate medals pinned over Dav's heart.

Dav's wearing a circlet across his brow, which instead of forming a full circle at the back of his head, wings out just past his ears into stylized maple leaves cradling four perfect pearls, two per side—the symbol of a Canadian marquessate.

And his eyes.

My god.

I have always loved me a dude unafraid to rock some guyliner at Pride. But Dav's lids are full-on caked with gold the exact shade of his freckles. His lashes are black with mascara.

Every cell in my whole body screeches with lust, and for a second I completely forget how to breathe.

"There's certainly less embroidery than my original court suit, see, there's nothing at all on the sleeves. But I'm told modesty is more the thing, now. It's my first audience since I've been created Marquess, and I want to make a good impression. Is it... is it not good?" Dav asks, as I stare at him, gawp-mouthed.

"The opposite," I say, all the sarcasm punched out of me. "Although..."

"What?" He asks, looking up, worry and self-awareness digging frown lines beside his mouth.

"Are you sure I'm the princess here?"

"Oh," Dav puffs out in a small chuckle. "Mine Own, I say this with the utmost love and affection, but..."

"But?"

He dimples at me. "Fuck off."

# chapter fifty

I am a very good boy and keep my hands to myself for the whole three hour car ride to Whitehall Palace. It is very difficult when Dav is looking so delicious. When we reach London, I'm distracted by the surprise of Christmas lights and holiday decorations in every storefront. The drive along the Thames is beautiful, and as we cross Westminster bridge, Big Ben and the London Eye both twinkle elegantly, attired for the season.

Have we really been over here that long?

Apparently, yeah.

Whitehall is Elizabeth Regina's nesting ground, the beating heart of a territory that encompasses a third of the world. The wall around the palace is tall, made of pale stone, equally historic and impressive as the rest of the city, and *smothered* with bas-relief carvings.

"What..." I ask, twisting my head to get a good look at them as we cruise by. "Is this all..."

"Her achievements and victories are too numerous for her door." Dav points to a specific section of the wall when we stop and wait for the driver to confirm our appointment at the front gate. "See there? That's Elizabeth Regina standing on the cliff at Tilbury, giving her speech to the troops before the Spanish Armada was engaged."

"Pfffft. She certainly has a high opinion of herself. Look—is that her *blessing* Shakespeare?"

"Everyone's histories are filled with bragging," Dav says. "There's a lot she's proud of."

My eyes catch on a section of the wall that appears to be the presentation to the queen of tobacco, potatoes... and Indigenous humans.

"Oh yeah. *Lots* to be proud of," I sneer.

Dav squeezes my knee. "We'll be on the wall after today. She'll get the glory, but we'll get the change."

He seems so sure. I hope he's right.

And then we're rolling through the massive iron gates.

"I was kinda hoping we'd be, like, turned away," I confess in a whisper, nerves surging.

"Why?" Dav asks, "We've worked so hard—"

"I never said it made sense," I interrupt, and lift his hand to my mouth to kiss the back of it. It's the only place on him I can't muss up. "It's just the brain weasels talking."

"Don't listen to them," Dav says gently. "There's nothing to be afraid of."

So, there's a little bit to be afraid of.

We're led not to a nice, intimate sitting room as Dav and I had assumed we would, but an echoing, circular chamber lined with arched windows, stone columns, and heavy curtains. The only people in the room are the queen herself, and three others. Two are about a decade older than me, but I've stopped trying to judge dragon-adjacent people by their apparent age. They're not servants, they're dressed too elegantly for that, but I can't tell if they're human because the thrall of the queen is overwhelming. Every organ feels suddenly magnetized toward her, every cell filled with a deep thrumming. It's not *uncomfortable*, but it's certainly *weird.*

The remaining person *is* human, and I do know this because he is slim, sloe-eyed, and appears to be around the same age as the queen. This is Robert Dudley, the Earl of Leicester, the queen's Favorite.

Like Raibert Righ, Elizabeth Regina greets us in dragon-shape. She's seated in all her shining glory on a chaise raised on a dais, which is the only piece of furniture in the room (Where am I going to put the briefcase down? Can I kneel to open it on the floor without looking like a child?)

The queen is distinctly serpent-shaped, long and thin, with a tail held in a tight coil. Her head is narrow, her nose studded with tiny horns that grow into a full fin along the back of her head. And she is *gold*. Not yellow, not orange, but straight up, blinding gold with black talons and horns.

So, an intimidating and chilly environment, check.

No sound at all but the ringing of our heels filling the void of the vaulted space, check.

And just in case we might have missed that fact, there are multi-tiered candelabras on either side of her, making sure she shines like a stereotypical treasure pile.

*Extra* intimidating, check, check, check.

This isn't going to be the friendly reunion and open-minded conversation Dav and I had been counting on.

Shit.

As we make our way across the chamber, to where the dais is set against one window, the queen *changes*. It's slow and showy, not the way that Dav does it, which is sort of all at once like a sneeze.

The queen sits up, her tail sliding around behind her, body turning paler and...

*That's a flex!* I think as I'm distinctly reminded that a dragon's clothing doesn't change with them.

We come to a stop a few feet from the base of the dais, and Dav slides down into a very deep bow with his painted eyes firmly aimed at his knees. I quickly do the same.

There's the rustle of fabric, and someone eventually says, "Rise."

Leicester finishes tying an elaborate cloth-of-gold wrap dress for the queen, and steps away. The queen's brilliantly golden wings stretch up and out, like an angel illuminated in stained glass, then fold slowly to nothingness behind her. Of course I'm familiar with the humanshape of my monarch—the famous strawberry hair, the severe brow, the imperious expression—but she looks older than her portraits. (Of course she does, that's how time works.) Her famous hair is now white, her heavily made-up eyes framed with the kinds of crows feet you can't get away with calling laugh lines any more.

Even still, she is scary as fuck.

Leicester nestles a tiara in the queen's hair. It's gold too, groaning with gemstones and filled with more symbolism than I can decipher. A quick glance tells me that the other two folks must be royalty as well. The guy's wearing a circlet similar to Dav's, with finials made up of a cluster of curly leaves, and many pearls; the woman beside him wears a subtler tiara. My brain catches up, and I finally recognize them from the tabloids my own unfortunate face has been splashed all over.

This is the Duke of Sussex, and his human, American wife.

Okay, so, royal family all around. Awesome.

Not even remotely intimidating.

Fucking *check*.

*Deep breaths, Colin,* I tell myself. *Don't fidget.*

And then the duke says: "Welcome, Lord Alva-draig George Tudor, blood of the two great lines of England and Wales, Marquess Niagara." Dav flinches at his middle name, which, fuck, that's cruel as hell to drag out right now. "Welcome, Colin Fergus Levesque, Dragon's Own, Favored of the Marquess Niagara."

I notice that my parentage isn't as important as whose property I am. Ugh.

"My thanks," Dav says, "on behalf of my Favorite and myself, Your Grace."

Oh, good. I'm actually happy the infantilizing traditions means that Dav's expected to speak for me, for once. My throat is so dry it clicks—I don't think I could have said anything if I wanted to.

There's not even any water available. This feels less like Elizabeth Regina is trying to intimidate us, and more like an active and deliberate 'fuck off.'

"And now that the formalities are over with," the queen says. "We shall begin the business."

Dav clears his throat. "Thank you, Your Majesty. It's a delight to be back. I have missed the court."

*Liar,* I think.

"And yet you accepted territory in Canada," the queen points out, amused.

Dav coughs discreetly, caught out. "The circumstances of that, ah, event are well known," he says, thrown off his patter.

"Yes, they are," the queen agrees. How much is actually being said under all the empty pleasantries? How much am I missing? "We celebrate your sister's arrival and the security of the Plymouth territory."

"Indeed, ma'am," Dav says. "And to the matter of territory, Your Majesty, my march borders the Onguiaahra territories, and I've had the great privilege of witnessing—"

Elizabeth Regina holds up her hand, palm out, and Dav trickles to a stop, confusion crawling over his face. My stomach drops.

*Oh no.*

"You misunderstand the point of this audience, Marquess," the queen says, and it's both vicious and gentle.

Pitying.

But acidic.

*Oh shit.*

And my poor sweet, earnest, *honest* Dav, hasn't gotten there yet.

"I think I do," Dav concedes after it's clear that Elizabeth Regina is waiting for him to reply. "I was given the impression that we'd been invited to present our research."

"No, Marquess," the queen says. "I have heard more than enough about your discussions with our northern neighbors to make up my mind about your research."

My brain catches on the word *about*.

About.

Not *from*.

My fear curdles into resentment.

"Then why request our presence?" I ask, feeling bold.

A small inhalation—not something so uncouth as a *gasp*—from the duchess makes it clear that I've probably broken some stupid etiquette rule, but I don't care. Not if they're going to treat us like this. Not if this is going to *end* before we're even allowed to start.

The queen turns golden eyes to me.

Dav flinches, ready to shield me from the queen's judgment with his own body. A flick of her hand nails Dav to the floor.

"I wanted to see the Favorite who so openly and boldly proclaims I am a failed and flawed ruler. Will you say as much to my face, I wonder?"

The noise that comes out of Dav is high and distressed.

Right.
*Right.*
I take a deep breath, screw up my courage. *Fuck, if my professors could see me now. This is way more nerve-wracking than a public thesis defense.*
Simply, and plainly, I say: "Yes, Your Majesty."
"Mine Own!" Dav hisses, horrified.
Leicester winces. The duke and duchess exchange a glance that comes across as... amused?
The queen sits, back straight, expression unreadable despite the narrowing of her eyes.
I hold up the briefcase. "But not just you, ma'am. The world has got it backwards. The Great Confidence? It's not *working,* and you know that as well as I do."
"Do you not fear our reprisal for this treason?" the queen asks.
"What treason?" I challenge.
Dav reaches for me, probably to haul me back behind him, but then stops himself, forces his hands behind his back, waits in parade rest.
*Trusts* me to handle this.
"Your Majesty, how can loving my fellow citizens of the Empire *so much* that I am risking my own wellbeing to bring them these truths be treasonous?" I gesture at my case. "How can wanting to improve the management of the land, of the resources, of the *people*, be treasonous? How can wanting to make my queen personally *happier* and better connected to your vast hoard, treason?"
Dav is vibrating next to me, he's so keyed up.
But the queen?
She laughs.
"What a flattering little gem you've found for yourself, Alva," the queen says to him. For the first time she sounds like she does actually hold the fondness for Dav that Paulette spoke of. "How well you've coached him."
"Oh, no, ma'am," Dav demurs, gasping for air like we've been physically sparring, instead of just verbally. "Please believe me, there's no telling Mine Own what to say or think. He is as stubborn as he is kind."
I try not to be annoyed at the way they all chuckle, like I'm some toddler who's just done his first, flopping cartwheel and expects applause.

"This is what I was trained to do," I say instead, yanking us back on topic. "In a school that's named for a general who defended your territory, I was taught to find ways to make the world a better place. How can using that education be a bad thing?"

"It is not the education, but the *daring* that I condemn. You requested an audience and we did not grant it," the queen says. Her voice drops low, a dangerous rumble which is likely meant to scare me. If I was smarter, I'd probably take the warning. But I'm too damned pissed off. "Some would take that as an answer."

"A non-answer is just cowardice," I offer boldly. "If you just consider what we suggest, I'm sure you—"

"Do *not* presume to know what I shall and shall not do," the queen interrupts, bristling. Leicester puts a calming hand on her shoulder, but otherwise doesn't intervene or presume to take attention or power away from her. All the same, the queen heaves a sigh and gentles. "My mind is not made up."

"But someone has been trying very hard to make it up *for* you," I point out. "The Lieutenant Governor of Upper Canada has a big part in keeping your empire running, and an even bigger investment in clawing in as much power as he can hold. His territory is massive. And from everything I've learned, it's *much* bigger than he can reasonably be expected to manage. He knows what he stands to lose—what *every* Empire-building dragon stands to lose—if we can get you on side. But I promise you, there are *benefits*."

"That's enough," Dav says, reaching out to take my arm, but I shake him off, take a step forward. Leicester matches it, getting ready to restrain me in case I like, I dunno, decide to be completely suicidal and lunge.

"Lost territories and insolent humans? No," Elizabeth Regina sneers down at me from the height of her dais and her position.

"Well then, what about taxes?" I counter. "Do you know how *much* you could save on public single-payer health care *alone* if you let dragons set up a monthly barbecue?"

"My advisers assure me that it's not feasible to—"

"Oh, your *advisers*." I cut a look at Leicester, who scowls. If the queen's going to bite my head off for being insolent, then there's no point in holding back. I'm headless either way, right? "Lots of old white conservative money-hungry pricks who've never made the welfare of the people they boss around a priority. It's easier for them to let us *die* of preventable diseases, to conjure wars, to think up an economic structure so ludicrous that the people who are supposed to be their responsibility are starving and oppressed, *by design*! Yeah, that sounds like they're fantastic advisors. No, totally, keep listening to them."

"You brazen—!" the queen starts, but I don't care. Leicester is already halfway down the dais to me, hand on the pommel of, yeah, yup, he's totally wearing an actual honest-to-god sword.

Whatever. Fuck it, fuck him, and fuck *her*.

"Literally the *one job* that dragons have is to look after humans! Isn't that it? That's what everyone keeps telling me, that's its evolutionary biology, it's in your DNA, it's your stupid draconic instincts! And *my* job is to give my whole entire fucking self to the dragon who owns me! In return for my freedom—"

"Mine Own, it's not *slavery*—"

"—it's his job to take care of everyone else! But you won't let *let* him!" I throw my hands up in the air, and the duke and duchess both flinch back. "You won't let *any* of them! So what the *fuck* is the point of this arrangement, then? What's the actual worth of any goddamned Favorite, huh?" This I direct at Leicester, who has frozen, wide-eyed, where he stands. "Nothing, that's what! What *good* are you stupid lizards if you refuse to do the one thing you are *biologically designed to do*."

# chapter Fifty-One

"**E***nough*!" The queen's wings snap out with a bull-whip-crack. The candles flicker. The windows rattle in their casings.

Leicester retreats to her side, hands free, at the ready.

Silence, thick and seething, descends on the hall.

I fold my hands in front of me, lower my eyes, bare the nape of my neck.

Theatrically submissive.

Because draconic instincts.

"I know you're scared," I say softly to the stone stairs. "And I know you were hurt by a human who took advantage of your trust and your youth," I add.

"You dared to tell him—!" the duke says, rounding on Dav in horror.

"He has a right to know *why*," Dav says. He lays a hand on the small of my back, supportive, claiming. But not quieting. Not anymore.

"But you can't take that out on every other human under your care, ma'am," I press on, daring to put one foot on the base of the dais. I tilt my head up, pleading. "Please. You keep saying that your advisers tell you things, but what is *your* heart telling you?"

"That I am a great queen, ruler of a great empire," she husks, eyes locked on mine.

"An empire that *hurts* people cannot be great. We're meant to be treasure, the most important jewel in your hoard, but empires don't value the individual life of each human. Only the number of them they've collected. Quantity, over quality. And everybody loses that way." I gesture to myself, placing my hands over my heart. "Humans suffer because there are too many of us in one territory, the distribution of wealth is uneven, the economy is lopsided and unfair. Indigenous dragons suffer because they're cut off from resources and cultural histories, suffer the trauma of their land and hoards stolen. And the settler dragons suffer," here I gesture to Dav. "Because they're forced to repress natural instincts to nurture and protect, taught—wrongly—that hoarding is better than *helping*."

The queen wavers. I can see it in the way her wings twitch, her eyes lower.

"My father..." My breath hitches, lungs tight, but I swallow around the grief knotting at the root of my tongue. "He died in the pandemic. Tens of millions of humans died. And they didn't have to. Ma'am, they didn't *have* to."

"If you think dragons can stem the tide of plague—" the duke starts.

"You could have done *something* more than *nothing*, though," I shoot back. "I never got to hug him again, I never got to... to *touch* him. We weren't even allowed in the same room. He... he was *alone* and I never—do you even know what it's like? For the 'Lasts' to come, like *that*?"

"The Lasts?" the duchess echoes. I choke back a sob, trying to keep my composure. It would not be cool to freak out now.

"I mean... the quiet terror, and sadness, and pain of not getting to *have* the 'Lasts'. With not being able to plan a good 'Last' that you won't regret. The sort of ripping inside you that happens when you realize that you had the 'Last' already, and didn't know it at the time. Suddenly. So you didn't set it in your memory, or-or choose not to argue over sour cream or be petty about the bourbon. The most terrible part about being told suddenly that what you thought was just one in a series has been frozen as the 'Last', forever. And you didn't know it was coming. And you hate yourself a little bit because you feel like you should have. Somehow. Irrationally. Illogically. And that's what dragons can give humans... better 'Lasts'. *Planned* 'Lasts'."

"*Fy Nhrysor*," Dav says gently.

I take another step up the dais, wipe my face dry. Her eyes are glistening, too.

Fuck, I don't want to make the queen cry.

But I will if I have to.

I will if it *works*.

"You once told the world you would never marry because you were already married to your people," I press on. Just one step below her now. "But isn't this, the hurt that you let other dragons inflict in your name, isn't that spousal abuse?"

The queen's wings lower completely.

I don't dare look at anyone else.

It feels like the whole room is holding its breath.

The whole *world*.

"Are you not Elizabeth Regina?" I ask. "Are you not the woman who has the heart and the stomach of a king?"

The queen's mouth twists in a sad, sardonic smile.

"That is a speech from an age long past, Dragon's Own. There are no more wars left to fight."

"There are hundreds of wars left to fight, Ma'am," I counter. "Corporate greed. Climate change. Corrupt politics. Cancer. Mental health stigmas. Institutional racism."

"Auntie," the duke says. "He has a point."

"I asked you to be present, hatchling," the queen says waspishly. "But I did not ask you for an opinion, nor gave you leave to speak."

Instead of cowering or apologizing, the duke rolls his eyes fondly and pointedly folds his hands in front of him.

"Please," I say again. "Let us explain. Pedra deserves to be heard. That's all we ask."

The queen takes a breath, opens her mouth, and—

The door to the chamber slams open, the crack of wood against stone as loud as cannon fire.

"Your Majesty!" Lt. Gov. WorstTimingEver bellows from the threshold, puce-faced and rumpled. "Don't listen to these...*bumbling, selfish fools*!"

"Governor," the queen snarls, eyes flashing.

Leicester draws up beside her, a literal human shield, in an instant. The queen flourishes, drawing all of that terrifying dignity back around her. As hastily as deference allows, I back down the steps, retreating to Dav's side.

It's everything I can do to keep from stomping my feet like a child.

I was so *close*.

Simcoe mistakes the queen's irritation for an invitation, and strides up the aisle. Before anyone can say anything, a guard steps out of the shadows behind a pillar, placing herself between Simcoe and the rest of us. Simcoe draws up short when it's clear that she has no intention of moving.

"Out of my way, human!" Simcoe snarls.

"You do not give the orders here!" the duke snarls back.

Simcoe didn't expect to be scolded.

I didn't expect it, either.

For a moment, we all eye one another, reassessing where we're each standing in this melodrama. Some of us are on the back foot when we expected to be on the front.

"Your Majesty," Simcoe says. He gestures at the guard, clearly expecting the queen to tell him it's okay to walk around her, or push her over, or even do violence.

"I find I prefer you and your insolence on the other side of a barrier for the moment," the queen replies, low and danger-ous. Leicester chuckles. "Were you not to *wait* in the hearing chamber, sir?"

*Hearing chamber?*

"The Court of Peers," Dav says, and then shivers once all over before taking a deep breath and forcing himself to regain his calm. "I see."

"I don't," I admit.

Dav shakes his head. "It is a court."

Not a royal court. A legal court.

Shit.

*Shit.*

"But... we haven't..." I look back up at the queen. "You can't be *serious*. So that's it, then?" I ask, and yeah, okay, it's probably pretty rude, but my ire is too hot now for me to cower. "That's all we get? You won't even *let* us talk and now you're, what, going to persecute us for even *attempting* to make the world a better place?"

"Yes!" Simcoe snarls with glee. The smooth demeanor of the social façade he'd struggled to keep up on Halloween cracks around the edges. "I came to investigate the delay—"

"A queen may take as much or as little time as she likes," Leicester corrects him.

Simcoe stops.

Swallows hard.

"Of course, Your Lordship," he simpers.

The queen hums thoughtfully. "However, now that you are here, perhaps it is time we joined the peers."

Simcoe grins triumphantly, and my hopes curdle.

"Your Majesty," Dav says desperately. "If there is to be punishment, please leave Mine Own out of it. All that he's done has come from a place of honest idealism and ignorance."

"And whose fault is it that he is ignorant?" Simcoe sneers.

"I take full responsibility," Dav says hastily.

"This is why you choose a Favorite from a coterie," Simcoe presses. "One that's *trained* already. First that girl, and now this. It's nothing but scandal after scandal with you, boy—"

"Hold on," I interrupt. "*You* chose Laura Secord."

"Hmm, yes," the queen says. "Interesting double standard, Sir Francis."

Simcoe flushes angrily but says nothing.

The queen descends, the duke and duchess at her heels, Leicester behind them. "Let's not keep the peers waiting."

We're led to something that's less courtroom and more fancy sports arena. Opposite the grand entrance doors is a gloriously appointed box for the queen, with less ornate but equally elevated chairs on either side of her, already filled with Favorites and dragons in either scales or flesh. Those wearing humanshape are as elaborately dressed as Dav, right down to the slutty, Pride-tastic eye makeup to highlight their wide array of flame-colored irises.

The floor is sunken in four concentric rings, the lowest of which is maybe triple the size of a boxing ring and made of bare stone. The next up is carpeted in a rich maroon, studded on either side with two clusters of tables, chairs, and a stone prisoner's box directly opposite the royal one. Simcoe strides to the left-hand table, where there are several other dragons already waiting, and Dav leads me to the other. I set down the briefcase, relieved that my self-sacrificing idiot didn't march himself straight to the prisoner's box.

The next ring is filled with three rows of intricately decorated benches. They're empty on our side, but filled with Simcoe's supporters on his. The final ring consists of balconies looming over our heads, broken up with the high, arched windows of the palace, and lined with rows of raked seats. They are absolutely *packed* with dragons in elaborate circlets and tiaras, and Favorites bedecked with jeweled tokens. I spin the ring on my pinkie, taking comfort in its protection, for all that I resent it means I'm owned.

Amid Simcoe's back-bench supporters is Laura Secord. She's subdued, the warm and generous woman I first met now dampened. The rest of the Favorites spark and shine, but even her clothing is muted, without any jewels, any metallic thread, any crystal. She doesn't indicate that she's seen me. She just sits there, stone-still, looking as tremulously furious as I feel.

The queen raises her hand, and the room goes silent.

"We are gathered to discuss the conduct of the Marquess Niagara, Alva-draig Tudor, seated before me thus." She cuts her palm in our direction, and Dav actually flinches. I reach out, under the table, and link our pinkies. "The Right Honourable Lieutenant Governor Lord Francis-dragoun Simcoe has leveled against him serious charges of territory mismanagement, and of breaking our most strongly-held taboos. The charge-sheet has already been read before the court."

Dav blanches. Laura flinches like she's been hit. Simcoe rises to his feet victoriously, holding a long roll of illuminated parchment aloft like the head of a conquered warlord. I want to punch him in the nose.

"However," the queen continues, before Simcoe can speak. "It has come to my attention that the Marquess' behavior has not been so dire as it has been painted by Lord Simcoe. In lieu of a sentencing, the esteemed honored peers gathered here will instead have the pleasure of first being made privy to the scientific research the Marquess and his Favorite have commissioned."

"*What,*" Simcoe hisses. He crumples the paper in his fist.

I turn to Dav, just to make sure I heard what I think I heard. He's looking at me with what I'd bet dollars-to-donuts is a matching expression of wide-eyed surprise.

"I beg your pardon, Ma'am...?" he asks.

"You have the floor, Lord Niagara."

"Your Majesty, the labor!" Simcoe splutters. "The interference! He went over your head to the Scottish King!"

I jump to my feet. "We were invited to visit my aunt, who is Collected and is part of His Majesty's hoard."

"You deliberately disrespected the queen's desire that you not speak about—"

"*My* desire, Lord Simcoe?" the queen interrupts him, and he flinches to a stop.

Laura's mouth tightens, but otherwise she doesn't react. I can't tell if she's more embarrassed *by* him, or by being *associated* with him, but she's definitely humiliated.

"As relayed through your advisers, Ma'am," Simcoe adds apologetically.

"Advisers that you, in turn, advised yourself," a dragon to the queen's right says, standing. She's clearly related to Elizabeth Regina, with the same pale complexion and serious eyes, but her hair is more brown than red, and holy shit, that's Anne Coronam Reginae.

"Ah," Simcoe prevaricates.

The crown princess leans on the railing of the royal box, elbows locked and eyes narrowed at Lt. Gov. ThornInMySide. "Had David Beithir not informed me that he had been visited by a dissatisfied Marquess of our court, who had been *denied* his right to petition an audience, we should never have known the Marquess of Niagara was seeking one at all."

A low murmur scurries around the room.

"Who are you to decide who may or may not speak with the crown?" the princess challenges.

"I was merely saving the queen the bother of—"

"*I* decide what is a bother to me, Lord Simcoe," the queen hisses. The princess sits, content that she's tightened the screws. "You seem to be in need of this reminder quite often, today."

"Apologies, Ma'am," Simcoe says with a bow. One of the dragons clustered around his table murmurs something to him as he straightens, smirk back in place. "But we all know that the rules about laboring for humans are a necessary evil. The population of humans is simply too large to sustain, and we—"

"That's Malthusian bull-shiii-crap!" I break in. "There's more than enough land, and food, and water for every living thing on this planet, Ma'am. The issue is *mismanagement*."

Simcoe bristles. "You have no *right* to interrupt me, your voice is worthless in this chamber—"

"Then I'm sure the paparazzi that must be hanging around in the bushes would *love* to put a microphone in front of me," I throw at him. "Do you have the ones on this side of the pond leashed, I wonder?"

Another round of shocked quiet filters through the room, only to be followed by the sound of the queen's amused chuckling.

"You were not wrong when you called him idealistic to the point of stubbornness, little drake," the queen says with an intimate softness, directly to Dav.

"No ma'am," Dav says, punctuating it with a put-upon sigh. "I was not."

Simcoe makes a noise like an overheated teakettle. "Surely you're not seriously entertaining proposals for territory management overhauls from this *human*. Let your more experienced counsel review the research and provide the suggestions. I would be happy to work with—"

"No," the queen denies him. "I find I don't much trust you to have the best interests of my empire at heart."

"Ma'am, with so many missteps to Niagara's credit, with his *temper*—" Simcoe tries.

"*What* temper, you toxic little snob?" I snap.

Dav hangs his head. "I do—"

"You *don't*," I insist. "You understand that he's gaslighting you, right? Classic tactics. He's trying to control you."

Dav blinks, stunned. "Dr. Chen suggested it, but I never thought—"

"Quiet!" Simcoe shrills, getting closer to unhinged the more he's shut down.

This is not gonna be good.

"You have no idea what you're—" Simcoe tries to backtrack, but that's it.

Laura-goddamned-war-hero-Secord has fucking *had it*.

She slams her hands, palm-down, on the bench. The sound claps around the stone room, dragging all eyes to her when she shoots to her feet.

"Of course he's made missteps!" she hisses at Simcoe. "Your father gave him responsibilities and territory he was unprepared for! And you haven't guided him because you *want* him to fail! Just the same way you lied to Hino'Hohawank, you lied to the Onguiaahra, and you drove them off the land *thousands* of them died protecting! Your father promised we'd respect their sovereignty, and you *didn't*!"

"Laura," Simcoe says dangerously. His expression tells me that this is very old, very dirty laundry she's airing. "Now is not the time."

"*No.* I have been silent too long. You've never loved, never treasured me for who I am. You only wanted to control what Alva coveted. The march! Me! And I agreed to it because I thought I could steer you... what a fool I was! Well, no more! I have watched both Upper Canada and this man suffer for your greed *enough*," Laura says, moving into the aisle, so they can meet eye-to-eye. "This is all on you, Frank. Everything he has mishandled was because he was *too young* to be given territory, and the only dragon in this room who doesn't know it is *him*!"

Dav blows a harsh breath out of his nose, and smoke curls up to the ceiling. "I was fifty-six, fully of age—"

"Just *barely*, Alva, dear," Laura says miserably. "One year out of your majority, that's so little for a dragon. They asked *too much of you*, too soon. And the moment you secured the march for Canada, this *scoundrel* began his campaign to steal it from you. That you continue to *stay* as a matter of honor, to protect the sovereignty of Onatah's territory, shows that you are *ten times* the man that Frank ever was."

A furious growl rips out of Simcoe, but Laura is uncowed.

Dav's spine, if possible, gets even stiffer. His chin wobbles but I don't think anyone but me is close enough to see.

Laura throws her arms wide, and lifts her face to accuse the gallery: "You sent hundreds of dragons out into the world, into war after war, for what? To collect a few measly acres of land into a vast empire? A grain of sand on a beach? A drop of water in an ocean? *Meaningless*. And when Alva fights to find meaning in it, you shut him down, shut him up, shut him away. You punish a child for being a *child*."

"Silence!" Simcoe snarls.

Laura flashes him a glare hard enough to cut diamond. "Everything good and humane happening among Alva's hoard, between Alva and his neighbors, is due to Alva's honesty and Alva's integrity. Not yours!"

Simcoe leaps up the few steps separating them.

"*Enough*, woman!" he growls, grabbing her arm so hard she gasps in pain. "You be *silent*, or I'll—"

"You'll *what*," I challenge, drawing his ire away from Laura on purpose. I've only ever met her once before, but that's humanity for you. We'll pack-bond with anyone if you give us a reason to. "You hurt her and I'll—"

"I rescind my token!" Laura shouts, yanking the black ribbon from around her neck. She throws the cameo into the middle of the pit, where it ricochets off the flagstone with an ominous *ping*.

# chapter Fifty-Two

**S**o apparently there *are* taksie-backsies.

Simcoe's expression catches in a rictus of fury. "You don't *dare*—you *can't*—"

"I'd rather die than spend another moment attached to you!" she confesses, heaving like she is bringing up black sludge with the words.

"Laura," Dav gasps, stricken.

"Let go of her!" I shout. "Somebody help her! Dav!"

"I... I don't know what to..." Dav stammers, curling his arm over my shoulder to keep me from launching myself at the abusive asshole.

"Can't *you* Collect her?" I hiss. "Can't you—"

"I don't know," Dav confesses. "Mine Own, I don't—"

"Enough, Frank," Laura snarls. "Isn't it *enough* yet?"

"Pick it up!" Simcoe orders her. Laura doesn't move. "I said *pick it up*, you stupid *bitch*!"

Above us, scandalized dragons hiss as one. Leicester springs over the rail of the royal box and scoops up Laura's token, before retreating back up the stairs with all the gravity of processing a dead body.

Simcoe remembers, suddenly, that he has an audience. He looks down at Laura's arm, then up at the dragons watching him. *Judging* him. Simcoe lets go. Then he whirls on us.

"Frank, *please*," Dav tries, placating. "Calm."

"Calm!" Frank snarls. He's got a new target now. "You and your snowflake feminazi *Favorites*! You never learn, Alva!"

"I'm not the snowflake here—" I protest.

"Control your mouthy little twink or I'll do it for you—"

"You will *not*!" I yelp.

"You never learn, Alva, you *never—*"

Laura gasps, scuttling up the stairs, breathing ragged, Jesus Christ, she's *bleeding*. There's a gash in her bicep. She's staring at the blood, dumbfounded. "You..." she gasps, sucking on the air like she's been drowning for two hundred years, and has finally surfaced. "You selfish...*fuck*."

Faster than I can follow, Simcoe whirls and lunges for Laura. She ducks away, but too slow, humanly *slow*, and everyone in the room surges to their feet, gasping in horror, because it's clear that he means to—that he'll—and she's his *Favorite*—how could—

Several of Simcoe's back-bench dragons get there first.

Simcoe draws up short when a woman hisses in his face, mouth sparking. The others shuffle Laura to the back of the courtroom, protecting the treasure that her own dragon has forgotten holds value.

"And *this* is the chaos that you will allow these two young *fools* to sow among our court?" Simcoe seethes.

"It is *my* court, Lord Simcoe," the queen reminds him darkly. "And we will have *order* in it."

"Your Majesty!" Simcoe protests.

The queen addresses me. "Your argument, Colin Dragon's Own, is that we should return colonies to the Indigenous dragons because they can manage them better than we can, isolated on our throne?"

"Yes, Ma'am," I say nervously, glancing between the queen, and Simcoe, and Laura. Someone in a paramedic's uniform is already seeing to her arm. Why don't they take her to safety? I don't—

"Master Levesque!" the queen says, voice like a whip-crack, and I yank my attention back to her. "Proceed!"

*Laura's safe*, I tell myself. *She's got a wall of scales between her and Simcoe.*

*I can do this. Laura needs you to do this. Focus.*

I step out from behind Dav. "Here's the thing, Your Majesty and, um, distinguished dragons and humans of the court, up there," I say lamely, craning my head up to the gallery and waving. "Hi, by the way."

Someone chuckles, but it's not mean.

Simcoe is so disgusted he spits. A smoldering hole appears in the carpet.

"Listen, I get it, there was Empire-mania going around. Europe's crowded. Territories are divided and subdivided and sub-subdivided. After centuries and centuries of nesting here, to be promised a wide-open New World devoid of dragons and rich with resources? It sounds tempting as hell, I *get it*, okay."

"But it was *not* wide-open, Dragon's Own," says the queen.

"No, Ma'am. It wasn't," I agree, turning back to her. "You were desperate to be the dragon sleeping on the biggest pile, so you—England, Spain, France, The Netherlands, Germany, Russia—you made like Rome. But we know what happened to Rome, right?"

Simcoe scoffs. "The Roman Empire failed because of the weakness of lesser dragons than Julius Cesar."

"The Roman Empire failed because it couldn't *serve* the territories it seized, which caused infighting," I retort. "I mean, also, the lead pipes helped. But you get me, right?"

One of Simcoe's still-loyal backbenchers sneers. "You believe we should withdraw, despite all we've done to develop the colonies?"

The sound of frustration I make is distinctly dragonish.

I hope Dav is proud.

"It doesn't matter who can manage the Territory 'better'," I say, with finger quotes. "That's the same damn excuse you used to steal it in the first place. It's a matter of what serves both the people and the land itself best, and that's not The Great Confidence."

"So you would have us walk among the people?" a dragon calls down from the gallery. "Labor for them?"

"Exactly!" I shout back up. "Dragons are happiest when their treasures are within reach—but you spend all your time shut away in castles. Doesn't it feel *unnatural?* Don't you secretly hate it?"

A murmur of agreement ripples like a swelling tide.

"It's shameful," I add. "You owe it to the dragons you displaced, you *murdered*, to do *better* than this. All of us Settlers do, not just the governments, not just the dragons! You have all this power to help. Instead you sit on it, squander it, hoard it, and for what? You'll still be wealthy when you give away a fraction of what you have, and it will make the world an immeasurably better place." I point to the briefcase. "If you would only *read* what Pedra and her colleagues—"

"The childish ramblings of a student?" Simcoe jeers.

"First, I'm not a student, I graduated with a degree in this shit! And so did everyone else who worked on this—they're professionals. And second, despite your middle name, I need you to literally choke and die right now, okay?"

"Colin!" Dav, yelps. "Manners!"

"*What* about my name—" Simcoe starts but I don't give him the satisfaction of getting out the rest.

"Sorry, it was Francis *Alibbed* Gwilliam Simcoe, wasn't it?" I seethe. Dragons and humans already in the know rustle as if settling uncomfortable scales, whispering to one another.

"Colin—" Dav tries to caution, but I'm too angry now.

"How apt would you say it is?" I sneer. "You gave Dav *George*. Famous slayer of dragons, meant to remind him of the one mistake he's ever made. " I hold up a finger, righteous, rigid. Then I tilt it down to aim it directly between Simcoe's eyes. "Do you know what I did when I learned that? I looked up yours. Alibbed? Isn't that IOld English? For *Survivor?*"

"I survived a battle that should have been my end!"

"Oh, I read about that," I say, theatrically indolent. "In Spain, right? Your father sent you away to fight under Wellington, and you think he should have kept you by his side. He didn't pick you as his second in command because you weren't *good enough*, Frankie. Dav was top of his class. So Dav was the one who marched dear-old-dad's forces all the way to Washington, and Dav was the match that burned their Presidential Mansion to the ground. *Dav* was the one who was rewarded with territory, with glory in battle, with your father's respect. While *you* barely escaped with your life. And you've spent the rest of it wondering if daddy *wanted* you gone. If maybe he gifted Dav a vital march because he didn't *trust* you with it. If maybe Dav was the son he always wanted. And doesn't that just *eat you alive."*

Dav grabs a fistful of my blazer, right at the small of my back. It's a warning. It's not necessary.

I know I'm on thin ice.

I've just decided I don't care.

"You let your *whore* speak for you?" Simcoe says. Laura's expression crumples in horror at the slur. "Is your allegiance to your own kind—"

"I owe you nothing," Dav rumbles. "Least of all when Colin's right."

"Upper Canada is *mine*. I inherited it, and *you* continue to hold territory within its bounds at *my* pleasure. You serve under *me,"* Simcoe snarls. His tongue is suddenly long and lashing, tail thrashing behind him, face slowly growing longer with every word. It's terrifying, this uncanny version of him.

And then he does the *unthinkable.*

Five things happen at once.

One: Simcoe leaps across the room and grabs me by the neck. Skin on skin.

It's so fast that his hand is gripping my chin viciously, the claws pressing into my cheeks, my back pressed to his front, before I realize what's happened.

Two: I get very, *very* scared.

Once, a long time ago it feels now, Dav had scared me. Dav's fangs, and claws, the way they slid so easily into my arm. It was just one moment, and never repeated. I never feared him again. Was shocked by it, yes. Swooned once, yes. Terrified *for* him when he'd frenzied, sure. But scared of Dav himself? Never.

I'm scared now.

Three: Simcoe hauls me into the sunken pit. My jacket tears off in Dav's fist. I freeze up as he drags me around, not daring to struggle with his claws so close to my jugular. His other hand slides across my chest, disgustingly intimate, before coming to rest at the base of my throat.

*Now is not the time for a panic attack,* I scold myself, even as my lungs burn and my whole body starts to shake. *Keep your shit together!*

Four: Silence falls so quickly it's as if the whole population of Whitehall has been sucked into a blackhole. And then, filling the void left by the horrified shock of watching a dragon lay hands on another's Favorite—lay hands with the intent to *harm*—a collective sound of disgust and alarm crashes across the rafters like a tidal wave.

Five: Dav screams. And I mean *screams*.

There is nothing remotely human-sounding in the noise. It's a shriek like tearing metal, filled with fury and fire. Literally. Sparks leap off his tongue. His eyes blaze golden, glowing with the fire he's stoking in his throat. His fingers curl into black-tipped, wickedly sharp talons.

I swallow hard, fighting against the impulse to surge forward, wrap him in my arms, calm and soothe his unimaginable agony at seeing his treasure so violated. But I'll be slashed open if I try.

Simcoe grips my face harder—why the face, it's such a weird and personal place to grab, so *showy*, but so awkward—and I suck in a stuttering breath that makes Dav pause. He shifts from foot to foot, like a jungle cat aligning his balance before pouncing, eyes wide, watching for his opening.

"He is *wrong*," Simcoe snarls, his voice right in my ear, his elongated tongue lashing hard enough that I feel it flick against the shell of my ear. I wince, and Dav's attention roots to that spot, lips curling back to reveal fangs. "Yet you insist on having him! I sought to release you from that, sought to *save you* from your terrible choices, and you *refuse* my guidance!"

*The handshake*, I realize.

"That's not for you to decide," Dav counters. "He asks only to be treated as my equal in an inescapable bond he unknowingly consented to."

"He wears your token! And yet you let him command *you*! Disgraceful!"

*Dav's temper.*

"I love Colin! I will not allow *anyone* to define the terms of our relationship," Dav hisses. "Least of all a poaching, heartless—"

"Poaching!" Simcoe laughs. "*Poaching*, boy?" He gives me a hard shake. A small prick under my jaw, and blood trickles down my neck. I don't dare lift my hand to wipe it away.

"Get your hands off him."

*He touched me on purpose.*

"Not until you submit to me," Simcoe snarls. "Not until you admit that your place is subservient to me."

"If you hurt him further I'll—"

Simcoe laughs again, harsh and cruel.

*He is touching me on purpose, right now.*

"You'll what?" he sneers. "Rip through him to get to me? Murder another Favorite?"

Another collective gasp of shock, another shrieking scream from Dav.

And then a sixth thing happens: I *understand.*

"You tried to make him *kill* me," I say. "Just like you made him kill Charlotte."

# chapter Fifty-Three

In literary terms, a 'climax' is the moment of highest point of tension in a storyline, often in a confrontation between the protagonist and antagonist. In this case, me, and the man who is one heartbeat away from literally slitting my throat. The climax resolves the main conflict of the story, in the moment the main character reaches their goal.

It is also, I recall as I swallow against the claws, sometimes when the protagonist *fails* to reach it.

Sometimes the hero tries to save the world and in the end... they don't. They can't. Sometimes they give up. Sometimes they die.

Lieutenant Governor Francis Alibbed Gwilliam Simcoe's hands are around my neck. I am on my tiptoes, straining, one hand on his forearm more for balance than because I have any illusions about my ability to pull his hand away. Chin up, eyes on Dav's.

*Poor Dav,* I think. *It'd destroy him.*

If this is to be my climax, if I'm going to perish like a literary hero trying to change the world that I damn well deserve to be, then I'm going to make sure everyone knows *why.*

"What were you planning for my accident, eh?" I hiss. "Another cliff? Paparazzi car chase? How were you going to make it Dav's fault this ti—*hurghk.*"

"I am going to *rip out your tongue*," Simcoe snarls, his hand tightening.

"Murderer!" someone in the gallery shouts, and the chant is picked up first by the Favorites, and then by the dragons. "Poacher!"

"I'm going to kill you, slowly, here and now, so he has to watch," Simcoe hisses against my ear.

The queen raises her hand and the chant stops just in time for everyone to hear me squeeze out: "Dav didn't kill Charlotte! You did, didn't you, Frankie?" I ask, because he seems like the kind of villain who would get off on revealing his dastardly plot. "Come on! Tell us how you did it."

My heart breaks for Dav when Simcoe proves me right.

"Yes! It was me!" Simcoe snarls, eyes rolling, teeth lengthening. "Alva-draig, the great strategist, the tactician so valued by my father, and I out-maneuvered him!"

"The rock wobbled," Dav gasps. "It was solid the week before, but when I stepped onto it—"

Simcoe laughs, high and shrill. "You're so *predictable*! It was *easy*. I knew where you'd be, that the river was far from civilization—"

"Hey!" I protest on Onatah's behalf.

"All I had to do was wait for you to do *exactly* what I knew you would... it wasn't as clean as I had hoped for, you didn't drown together, but I got to pin it on you anyway. Oh, Alva, if only you'd *left*, if only you weren't so foolishly *noble*, if only you cared more about your own people and less about those *savages*, we wouldn't have to do all of this all over again."

"Had your father killed, too, I bet," I husk out, reedy and strained. Okay, maybe I'm suicidal, I don't know, but like, fuck, if I'm going to die then I'm going to die making sure Dav knows the truth. "I don't know any dragon that dies of an illness. Survived *him* well and good, didn't you?"

"Outrage!" someone shouts from the back of the gallery.

"Betrayal!" calls another. "Treachery!"

I suck on another breath, heels kicking fruitlessly against Simcoe's shins. "You branded him a murderer, isolated him, tortured him, *for what?* You claim to keep Dav at the ready, a sword left in the sheath until it's needed. *Swords rust.* And when another whetstone came along, you couldn't *stand* to lose control. So you marked me."

"You threw me into the frenzy on *purpose?*" Dav howls.

Elizabeth Regina rises. Beside her, Leicester unsheathes his blade.

"Release him and explain yourself," the queen commands, voice ringing like a guillotine blade, raising one arm like a sword, pointing a finger like a pistol.

Simcoe quavers and seems to finally realize what he's admitted to. And in front of whom. He drops me to fold his hands earnestly over his heart.

I stumble forward. My dignity already well and truly dead, I use the forward momentum to throw myself at Dav. He catches me, presses his face immediately against mine, licking up my ear to eradicate Simcoe's touch, then at the nick under my chin to clean up the blood.

He's quick and efficient about it.

This isn't the time for a relieved, and lingering reunion. This isn't even the time for another frenzy.

That's not where we are in the story.

This is the climax, remember?

This is where the hero rises to their final challenge.

And this is also where the villain's hubris finally undoes all of his plotting.

Simcoe burbles, but the queen is having none of it.

"Speak again!" she commands, roaring like cannon fire.

"Your Majesty, I didn't—"

"You did!" I cough, ducking around Dav. "You planned both their deaths, and when that didn't work you engineered Dav's isolation, tailor-made his own personal mental fucking *breakdown* for him."

"Shut your mouth, you useless bedwarmer!" Lt. Gov Horrorshow snarls with increasing desperation.

Around the room, dragons rise to their feet, furious. Favorites reach across aisles to comfort one another. Laura Secord weeps. Her head is high, her posture rigid, her expression like stone. But there are tears running down her cheeks. And there is no one to hug her.

The remaining dragons on Simcoe's side slowly, deliberately, stand up. Walk to the back. Abandon him.

Good.

"Cowards!" he roars at them, then aims the accusation at the rest of the room. "Cowards! Do you know what we could do if we *took* what we deserve? We are the superior species, and *we*," he thumps his chest, "*We* have earned our place at the top! And you want to give away everything we've earned? Everything I've worked so hard for? It's *mine!*"

Another explosive noise of horror and protest crashes down on us.

Dav... I don't know how else to describe it. He *uncrunches*. He *uncrumples*. He seems to fill all of his skin, the power and the *presence* radiating off of him so intense that it knocks me back a step. Every cell in my body screams to throw myself at him.

This is the draconic magnetism Dav's been hiding this whole time?

*Shit,* it's strong.

He reaches up and, slowly, meaningfully, removes his winged circlet and holds it out to me. I take it, press it against my heart.

"Lieutenant Governor Francis-dragoun Alibbed Gwilliam Simcoe," Dav says, silencing the crowd's howls with his gravitas. "I, Alva-draig George Tudor, Marquess of Niagara and son of Y Ddraig Goch's own bloodline, do hereby charge you with the murder of my Favorite Charlotte Edith Woodley, and with the willful *repeated* violation of my Favorite Colin Fergus Levesque."

I blink to hear my name included in the list of his sins, but say nothing. This feels too important, too *formal*, to interrupt.

And it *must* be important, because Simcoe goes suddenly, shockingly pale.

"Alva, friend, you can't—"

"Silence!" the queen commands, and Simcoe curls in on himself, twitching. "Proceed, Niagara."

Dav dips his chin regally at the queen, eyes closing briefly, the gold paint on his lids glittering in the sunlight. Then he pins Simcoe to the floor with a gaze so filled with hate and fury that even I quail.

"I challenge you," Dav says.

But it's more like Challenge, with a capital C, with *meaning.*
"No," Simcoe whimpers.
In all the ways that Dav uncrumpled, Simcoe now seems to be pulling in on himself like a weasley, flop-sweating black hole.
"I challenge you," Dav repeats. "To a duel. *Now.*"
The noise that washes over the gallery this time is one of excitement.
Dav starts to undress methodically. He hands me each piece of clothing, one-by-one. Too stunned and confused to do anything else, I fold it and set it on the table. He wouldn't want it wrinkled; he always folds his clothes, even when we're in the throes of passion. So proper. A hundred-thousand questions press behind my teeth, but the most important, the most vital, blocks them all because I can't ask: *Promise me you won't get hurt?*
I try not to look at Simcoe, who hesitates before stripping far less elegantly than Dav. Enemy junk is nothing I want burned into my brain. But I do glance at him long enough to catch the raised, ridged gunshot scar that crawls across his back, ugly and deep.
Laura hasn't moved to his side to take his clothes. No one has. The only thing she's focused on is *me.* I don't know how to read her expression, but I think it's... pity? Sorrow?
For me?
Or herself?
A roar reverberates through the room, and I tear my attention back to the dragons in the middle of it. They're both properly scaly now.
Red as blood, Dav slinks down into the pit, his tail lashing in an ever-twisting Celtic knot, sunflower eyes now the bright glowing yellow of acid, black talons scratching at stone. One step up, Simcoe hunches on the carpet like a shivering dachshund. He's cinnamon brown, serpentine, but less armored than Dav. He turns pleading eyes up to the queen and she shakes her head.
His request has been denied.
A low, rolling growl fills the room, rising like foam on the sea. Dav is impatient.
I wish I had another Favorite here to squeeze, the way the other humans are holding one another. I wish Laura weren't so far away.
This is because of me.

This is about to happen because of me.

And it has *nothing* to do with me at all.

It's for Dav's pride, but it's also for his grief.

I want to stop the fight.

I can't stop it.

*Please be okay,* I think hard at Dav. *Please don't get hurt for me.*

*I don't know what I'll do if you get hurt.*

Simcoe uncurls, and steps tentatively down into the arena. Dav stops pacing. They both unfurl their wings, dip them at one another. Time stands still.

*One... two... three...*

They *fight.*

I hate to be stingy with my description of what happens next but first, I mostly read romances, okay? The fight scenes in those are usually a few shots fired in a field, or a few passes of a sword. I don't have the experience or language to describe it.

Secondly, it happens *so fast* that I'm not even sure what I'm seeing.

Dav lunges. After that, it's a swirl of tails and wings. Talons sparking off of hard scales. Tails twined together, and suddenly Dav is doing some sort of roll wrapping around Simcoe, *squeezing,* choking. Simcoe snarls, fangs flash, and Dav roars in pain. He shakes Simcoe off. Blood drips freely from a wound under his arm.

"Dav!" I cry, and I'm not sure what I mean to do, what I *can* do, but before I move, a dragon appears at my side. They lay a restraining hand on my clothed shoulder.

They're dressed in some sort of uniform that includes gloves and I think, *oh my god, they think I'm going to throw myself into the pit, and...*

*This is part of duels,* I realize. There's one of the liveried dragons standing beside Laura, too. *To keep the Favorites from interfering? Or from doing something stupid? Or is it to protect them from attack while their dragon is distracted?*

Fear and disgust curdle in my guts. I despise that owning people is so codified that there's someone *assigned* to keep me out of it. As if I was a fragile little bit of decorative spun sugar. As if I don't have a right to fight for the man I love, the way he's fighting for me.

Dav pulls himself to his feet, shakes to resettle his scales, and a thin spray of blood arcs across the pit. It splashes against the stone, hot enough to steam. Dav reorients himself, coils his tail behind him, eyes on his enemy. Only a twitch of his ear—oh, lord, his pretty soft ear is *torn*—in my direction betrays that he's heard me as I suck back a sob.

Simcoe licks my lover's blood off his chops.

"What..." I don't dare to turn away from the fight, but I have to know. I tilt my face up at the uniformed dragon at my side, eyes locked on Dav. "What happens to the Favorite of the losing dragon?"

"If they're lucky, age catches up with them, and they drift away," the guard replies.

"And if they're not lucky?" I ask shakily. Simcoe and Dav start pacing around one another in slow, serpentine circles.

"Forfeited to the winner, sir," they say.

Horror slams into my chest. "*No*," I gasp, whipping back around in time to see Simcoe look up at me, that bloody leer back in place. "That's barbaric—"

Dav catches Simcoe looking and lets out another furious roar. Too busy gloating, Simcoe is caught off guard when Dav charges, a whirlwind of teeth and claws. I've never, not once in the time since we've known each other, in the *years* since he sat in the café and watched me, *not-creepily*, seen Dav like this.

This?

This is the trained soldier.

Around the room, the sounds and the smells of the fight seems to be getting every dragon worked up. Beside me, the guard is panting harshly through their nose, scales sprouting out from the side of their face.

Every dragon's eyes *burn* as they lean forward. They're all waiting for something. Something brutal. Something bloody. Something final.

*Not to Dav. Please.*

Simcoe and Dav lunge apart and clash together again, and again.

Dav isn't the only one bleeding now. The stone floor of the pit grows slick with ichor and torn scales. The next time they separate, both dragons take a moment to breathe. Dav stalks back and forth, licking gore from his fangs, tail lashing. His low rumble builds into a ripping snarl and subsides again.

Every pore of my skin tightens, hair literally standing on end. And yeah, okay, watching Dav fight for me is getting me horny, not gonna lie. Dav stalks around to the far side of the pit and lifts his snout in my direction. His pupils blow wide and, yeah, okay, fine, fuck.

*Sure, let the whole room know how bad I want to bone you right now, why don't you.*

My fucking competence kink, I swear.

While Dav wriggles and shivers, agitated and ready to end the fight, Simcoe is panting hard, several gashes torn in his hide and one of his wings dangling the wrong way. He's leaning against the wall of the pit, one of his forelegs twisted, but a curling sneer pulling at his mouth.

"So easily distracted," Simcoe growls. "You've always been lead by your prick, you witless—"

The rest of Simcoe's insult is drowned out by the crackling roar of Dav spitting fire. It's not like the wide, orange flames he's been huffing up until now. The fire is so intense that it's yellow-white, a thin stream aimed at the side of Simcoe's ruined face. It's *focused*, it's...

It's the method of fire-spitting he'd developed to roast coffee beans.

Simcoe lets out a high, hissing shrill of pain, and tips over backwards in his effort to scramble away. If I never see another melting eyeball in my life, it will be too soon. My boner is well and truly wilted.

Simcoe writhes up the wall, but the dragons along the benches shove him down. He screeches again when Dav pounces on his back, ripping at the roots of his wings.

"Mercy!" Simcoe shrieks through a ruined mouth.

"Mercy!" Dav echoes scornfully. "Like the mercy you showed me when I was grieving Charlie? The mercy you showed your father when he was ill? The mercy you showed to Mine Own, when he was scared and new to our world? Pah!"

"Mercy," Simcoe begs again, too far gone on pain to actually hear what Dav is saying. He wriggles and cries, trying to get out from under Dav, but Dav bears him to the ground, sinks the wicked talons on his hind legs into the meat of Simcoe's thigh.

Fire sparking, preparing to strike that final, fatal blow, Dav stops.

Stops.

And looks to me.

The room holds its breath.

Waiting for me to speak.

Waiting for me to pass sentence.

Waiting for me to sob, and beg mercy, and end it peaceably. Well.

*Fuck that.*

I look across the room at Laura. She's standing now, the closest she's come to showing any loyalty to Simcoe during all of this. Her hands are locked around the back of the bench in front of her, mouth twisted in a grim line. Slowly, just once, she blinks.

*Once for yes.*

*Two for no.*

I wait for a second.

It doesn't come.

"Go on," I say.

Small noises slap against the vaulted ceilings. But nothing so vulgar as a gasp of horror.

"No skin off my nose," I add, when no one says anything else. When no one moves. "And it's not like he doesn't deserve it." I shake off the guard. They let me. I take a step forward. I'm not stopped. I take another, then another, and just like that, I'm at the top of the human-sized steps that lead down into that horrible, blood-stained pit. "If you want to do it. If this is something you *want*, then I'll support you."

"This is your life, your choice as well!" Dav says.

"I know." I want so badly to reach out to him, put my hand on his hide. But Simcoe is still trying to fight, muscles jumping, intact eye rolling, tongue lashing. I'm not actually stupid enough to jump in there like a romance novel heroine when there's still a chance Simcoe would crush me with his tail. "And I love you for asking me. But my choice right now is to follow your lead. Mine Own."

Dav's whole body shivers, eyes closing briefly. Then Dav rears up, throat sparking and clicking. Decision made.

"Alva!" Simcoe shrieks.

Dav *spits*. This close, the heat frizzles the hair on my face, slamming into me like a brick wall. It's so much like that morning in the kitchen that my scars twinge. *Hold it together!* I don't tell myself to take deep breaths, because they'll taste like charred flesh.

When Dav stops blowing, Simcoe is...

Simcoe is screaming, high and thready.

But he is *alive*.

# chapter 7ifty-7our

**D**av disengages his talons from Simcoe's ruined hide, and lifts his head so Simcoe's remaining eye can meet his. Simcoe's screams die down to a pained keening.

"Remember that a human you entrapped, and a dragon you betrayed, elected to let you live. *Together.*"

And then he walks away.

Limps, more like it.

I move toward him, feeling like I should be running in slow motion, but an authoritative voice cuts through the melodramatic romance of throwing myself at my victor.

"Give me the research, Dragon's Own," the queen says, holding out her hand. "I will give it all due consideration."

"That's all we ever asked, Your Majesty," I manage to squeeze out, frozen on the steps. I grope back at the table for the briefcase. The guard takes pity and pushes it into my hand.

Disheveled and still panting from all the excitement, I cross the stone pit. Sidestepping the blood, I hand the ruler of the British Empire the key to saving the world.

She stands slowly, and with no further word, departs. The members of the royal family follow in her wake.

I wait until the royal box is empty, for the full retreat of the crown, before I lunge at my dragon. He meets me halfway. I throw my arms around his neck, and press my face against the side of his, and hide a relieved sob against his scales. I'm pretty sure every person in the slowly-emptying room heard it anyway.

Dav and I are ignored while more of the paramedics descend on Simcoe with a stretcher. He's whisked out of the chamber faster than I thought it could happen—though I guess they'd have practice with this kind of thing.

On the far side of the ring, Laura Secord stands alone in the shadows. No dragon or Favorite is crowding close to see if she's okay. She is by herself in what I can only guess is her misery.

"Laura," I say softly into Dav's ruined ear. Laura Secord, Dav's only human friend besides me, is going to grow old and *die.* Quickly.

Dav twists his neck around, Simcoe's blood still painting the side of his maw. She offers him a subservient curtsy that looks so abjectly slavish that my blood boils.

"No," I tell him. "You can't take her like a *prize.* Dav, you can't—"

"She'll have no protection if I don't claim her for my hoard," Dav rumbles back, nosing at my neck, at what I am sure is already a necklace of developing bruises. "I need to—" Dav starts, but stops, making a frustrated noise. His tail is wrapped around my waist now, and he's sucking in lungfuls of my scent, bloody nose in my hair, wuffling under my arm. "Colin, you smell so—"

"I'll ensure she's secure," the guard says. "The withdrawing chambers are at your disposal, my Lord."

They point at a door to the side of the royal box, and then have the cheek to *wink.*

Getting duel-horny must be normal, because the 'withdrawing chamber' is built for fucking and nothing else. There's a big ass bed, a sofa, a bathroom, and, wow, a *basket* of lube and condoms. While Simcoe is fighting for his life and the queen is reading our research, Dav and I are *totally* expected to be getting it on. Strangely, knowing that every peer of the realm is entirely aware of the fact that I am about to have Dav's dick in me does not make me want to have his dick in me any less.

Shaky and parched, I let go of Dav's wing (the only part of him I could hold onto as we walked here) and make my way to a minifridge against the far wall. I drain a bottle of water all in one go. My skin feels too tight for my body, my nerves electrified. I shimmy out of my ruined jacket.

"Water?" I ask, turning back to Dav.

I expect him to be standing in the middle of the room, humanshape and covered in blood and shyly admitting that he feels disgusting and wants to freshen up. Alternately, I expect him to straight-up tackle me to the bed and start ripping at my clothes.

Either is fine.

I don't get either, though.

Dav is still in dragonshape. He's curled up on the floor, wings arched around himself like a tent. Sunflower eyes peer at me from the gap between them.

"Uh." I crouch in front of him. When he doesn't move, I tap the leathery membrane of his wing. "Hey, you okay in there?"

Dav rumbles but doesn't reply.

"Okay, so... have I done something wrong, then?" I ask.

"No!" Dav says, wings snapping back. He presses the side of his head to mine, knocking me on my ass.

At least the carpet is plush.

"Then what is it?" I pet up the bridge of his nose, pausing short of touching his torn ear. It's stopped bleeding, but if we're not gonna fuck, then I want to get some disinfectant on it.

Dav huffs and lays his head in my lap, eyes squeezed closed. "You're not disgusted?"

"The blood is kind of a turn off, I'm not gonna lie. I'd be happy to wait until you've showered. But humping has been more-or-less promised and I—you don't mean the blood."

The tip of his tail lashes back and forth nervously.

"Dav. Babe. Mine Own. *Fy Nhrysor.*" That last one gets him to open his eyes. "Don't look at me like that, I know how to use Google Translate." I keep petting his face, brushing off the flaking blood, straightening crooked scales, gently working loose the ones that have been ripped out. Soothing. Calm. "What's going on in that big lizard brain of yours, huh?"

"I'm mortified." Dav licks his lips, then grimaces when he catches some of the gore from the corner of his mouth. "You must find me so revolting. To be led so easily to such *violence.*"

"I knew you were a soldier," I remind him.

"Knowing and watching me half-kill a man are two entirely different things."

"And you're afraid that I'm...?" I leave space for him to answer.

"Frightened. I'm so much stronger than you, and I... I *know* you told me you never wanted me to hold you down, that you feared what I could do if I lose my head, and I was so *enraged* Colin, I lost myself to the fight so completely—"

"Whoa, wait up," I interrupt, tugging on his little armored ruff. I'm not strong enough to actually move him, not if he doesn't want to be moved, but he raises his head obligingly to let me meet his eyes. "First, you're being a self-pitying dumbass."

"Colin!"

"Well, you are. Secondly," I take one of his paws and press it into my lap. "I wouldn't have *that* for you if I was scared."

Dav sticks his nose in my crotch to get a good sniff.

Weirdo.

"After *all* of this, do you still not get that this is me *choosing* you, Dav?" I ask. "Your teeth are the size of a butcher knife and I am letting you near my junk. If this isn't trust, then—"

He grunts, swings his head away, smoke curling from one corner of his mouth.

"Fuck off," I say. "Don't pull that. Look at me." He does. "*Listen*, you big red idiot. I am *choosing* to be here. I love you."

"Even still?"

"Even still." I huff out a laugh. "I never stopped, even when you scared the shit out of me with stuff that I didn't understand, even when your cryptic bullshit frustrates me. Big old bleeding heart, pinned to my sleeve, staining my shirt; that's me. And I *love* you."

He licks my face once, gentle and sweet.

"Turn back," I say, giving his head a little shake. "Come on, I wanna kiss you."

He snorts.

"Fine." I roll my eyes and kiss his snout. Within seconds it's a human mouth, wet and opening under mine.

"Hi," I say, pulling away.

"Colin," he crackles out, engulfing me in a protective hug.

"Hey," I whisper. "How about we get this blood off, eh?"

"Yes, please," Dav says.

I hoist him to his feet shakily, and get him folded into the shower cubicle. Dav is exhausted, in too much pain to even raise his hands to wash his hair, so I strip down and squish in to give him a slow, gentle scrub. I don't mean for it to be sensual, not when he's so wrecked. But there is something undeniably sexy about taking care of your conquering hero.

Dragons heal quickly, so by the time I'm patting him dry, his ear looks whole, if crossed with an angry red line. The punctures in his hip and torso are scabbing over, but are ringed with dark black bruising. The gash under his arm is still nasty, but no longer oozing. While he towels his hair dry, I press myself to his back to kiss the worst of it.

"Oof, hello," he laughs. "Careful back there, it feels like you're about to stab me."

The image knocks the breath out of me.

"Can I?" I pant, clutching at his hips. "We've never... can we?"

He meets my eyes in the foggy reflection of the mirror above the sink. I knead the excellent flesh of his ass, and give him my best puppy-dog look.

He groans appreciatively. He folds the towel, rests it on the edge of the sink, and then sinks forward to prop himself up on his elbows.

"Fuck, *yes*." I grab the lube I'd optimistically brought into the bathroom. "Thank you."

"I didn't think you'd want to do it this way," Dav pants as I press in, slowly, with one slick finger.

"I didn't think *you'd* want to." I add a few bite-marks of my own to his back. "Control freak."

Dav reaches over his shoulder, sinks his hand into my hair, and pulls, forcing me up onto my tiptoes for a kiss. "Who says

I'm not in control?" he smears against my mouth, and I can feel him smirking, the jerk.

"Oh, yeah?" I ask, lining myself up. "Let's see if you can stay in control *now*."

"Colin, don't be ridiculous, I—" His protest cuts off as I slide in, and he arches back, groaning.

Nice.

"Thank you," Dav pants, as we find our rhythm. "For letting me stay."

"It's not about... hnnng... it's not about *letting you*, come on, it's... it's part of... holy, *fuck*, Dav I... ngk! Rule four! Relationships are work, right?"

"Rule six," he groans back. "Don't give up on soulmates."

"Oh, are we playing a game now?" I ask, straining against him, loving the way he's surrounding me, holding me safe. "Rule one?"

Dav huffs a laugh. "I think we're being pretty explicit right now, Mine Own."

"Fair."

"Rule seven," Dav cranes around and whispers against my mouth. I wait for him to go on, or to kiss me, or *something*. "Rule seven, Colin," he prompts, lips moving against mine.

"I am—" I start, but something hot, a surge of something big and wonderful and terrifying in only the best way, cuts my words off. I dig my fingernails into Dav's hips, press my tongue against his. Drag in a breath through my nose and smell sweat, and lube, and a ridiculously delicious whiff of black pepper and basil from the shampoo.

"You are...?" Dav presses, pulling away, teasing.

"I am..."

Shit.

I can't do it.

I wrap my arms around his waist, hide my face between his shoulder-blades. He pets over my arms. "Go on."

"Dav," I moan. I try to thrust, *something*, but Dav's planted himself. Immoveable. Using all that draconic strength to thwart me, and that's just not *fair*, the bossy little—

"Keep going, sweetheart," he says, low and rich with emotion. The same emotion that has a strangle-hold on my lungs, my heart, my mind. "Say it."

"I am..." I can't do it. I *have to* do it. The toppy bastard isn't going to let me come otherwise. "*Worthy.*"

"You are, darling." He resumes pushing back against me. It's sweaty, and slippery, and oh so fucking *good.* "My good boy, my handsome Colin. Mine Own."

"Dav," I complain, feeling my ears burn.

"Say it again."

"I'm worthy," I pout, arching and squirming... so close, so fucking *close...*

"Worthy of...?"

"*Love*, you big stupid lizard," I groan. "I'm worthy of love."

"You're worthy of love. You're worthy of everything. I would do *anything* for you."

"Even fight a duel, and destroy the very architecture of your society?" I tease.

As I knew he would, Dav laughs. "Yes, Mine Own. Even that."

He twists around for another kiss, but I get my fingers up between our lips. His nose scrunches in confusion, adorable and so *not-polished*, and I love it.

"You too. Say it."

"I am also worthy of love," Dav parrots diligently, sending a shiver of delight up my spine, and a hot surge of lust *down* it.

"Damn straight you are." I move my hand so Dav can have his kiss. I love that split tongue. I reach around him to clean the fog off the mirror. He raises his head so we can both watch the way the flush rises on his chest. God, those big, beautiful honeyed eyes. "Mine Own."

"You know," he pants, "Only dragons are supposed to say that."

"Give me a better word, then," I demand, but he's suddenly too overcome to answer.

Dav makes his *I'm close* sound and shudders.

"Almost, sweetheart, almost there," I promise him, gripping hips, hard, hard, grasping and pressing marks in as I fuck into him slow and sweet. "You first."

"Oh, Colin, Mine Own, you feel so... so..." His words dry up, focused and intense, knuckles white where he grips the sink.

I can't stop looking at his face reflected in the mirror. A lock of his hair has fallen down into his forehead, his eyebrows knitted together in effort. When he realizes I'm watching him, his face relaxes, and he smiles.

"Look at yourself," I say, gently. His prick's bobbing, red and leaking. He swallows hard and reaches for it. "No. Not yet. Just look. You're beautiful."

I go quicker, harder, and Dav braces himself against the wall beside the mirror, rutting back against me. It's almost too much to see him like this, stretched out and on display, just for me.

"Colin, I'm—!" Then another "*Colin*!" punches out of him, like it's the last word he'll ever get to say.

"Go ahead, sweetheart," I tell him, and Dav curls over the sink and comes *hard.*

*God, that's hot.*

And then, the bastard, he *squeezes*.

"Wait, uh, I'm supposed to be... ah! Augh, *Dav*!"

When I've come down from my own orgasm, I smack his arse. "Bossy jerk."

"*Your* jerk," he agrees.

"Absolutely. All mine. My dragon. My gorgeous, beautiful, badass dragon. Mine Own."

"You really can't say that, darling."

"What *am* I supposed to call you then? This is getting stupid."

"There's really no term," Dav says. "Not one that anyone would find polite, any more."

"Ah *ha*! It *is* 'master', isn't it?"

Dav's face scrunches up.

"Forget it," I tell him. "Not happening."

"No, I agree," Dav says. He turns in my arms. We share another lingering kiss.

"Hey, you know what," I say softly, heart beating a mile a minute. "I just figured out the perfect thing to call you."

"And what's that?"

Feeling absolutely ridiculous, completely buck-naked, covered in sex, and without a ring, I get down on one knee. "How does 'husband' sound?"

Dav smiles like a sunrise. "*Coc y gath*."

# chapter Fifty-Five

And this, dear reader, is the part of the story that we call the denouement.

From the French "unknotting", this is the part where—after the resolution to the conflicts occurs, like winning a duel against a sadistic prick, or convincing a queen to read your friend's awesome research—the remaining complexities of the plot unravel.

Hm, how do I explain everything that happened in the next few months without getting super '80s coming-of-age-film about it?

Nah, fuck it, I'm gonna do it.

First off, not that you care, Simcoe survived.

Yeah, I know. He's sure not as pretty as he once was, so that's something. And he's not Lieutenant Governor anymore, either. Dav was terrified that they were gonna make *him* do the job, which, no thanks. We just want to spend the rest of our lives farming our little patch and revolutionizing the world.

Thankfully, instead of appointing a new lieutenant governor, the queen let the province of Upper Canada elect their leadership for the first time. I mean, not the humans... we didn't get a vote. Not *yet*. But the dragons voted—*all* of them, mind you, not just the settlers—and a term of service was placed on the new Lieutenant Governor. The incumbent was charged with figuring out a way for *everyone* of legal age regardless of species to vote in the next election, to be held in a few decades.

Convincing a queen to overhaul a whole system of governance may only take one bloody duel and an afternoon with some research papers. But *implementing* those changes takes a lot longer.

Luckily, dragons live for centuries.

Centuries that Laura doesn't have. Laura confessed to me a few weeks later, one evening under a maple tree she'd helped Dav plant at the farm half a century earlier, that she thought Fynyth was going to be a fine place to die.

Which, fucking tragic, right?

"I'm open-minded," I'd replied hastily. "I'm not gonna get jealous over some spit-swapping if you and Dav want—"

She'd hushed me, thanked me for the offer... and declined it.

"I'm done now, I think," she'd said softly, looking older and grayer already. "I'm ready to go."

"But not too soon, okay?" I begged, kissing her knuckles.

"Not too soon," she'd agreed.

The next thing that happened was the start of The Conversation.

"It's not our job to dictate how reconciliation and repatriation should go," Dav had said, over tea with the queen the day after the duel. I was so damned proud of him. Especially by how primly he was seated in front of her Majesty. You'd never know that he'd woken up with an inability to sit down at *all*. "That's the same problem all over again: telling the Indigenous dragons what we'll give, what we'll take, and when, and how. No, it's our duty to open the dialogue and then be silent. To listen to what the people we've wronged want and need. Not to be high-handed and control it."

The queen had taken his advice to heart, and sought out Onatah's guidance. Onatah called it The Conversation, in that bluntly subtle way of hers, and it had caught on. With the help of Indigenous dragons from all over the colonies, they began to map out a plan to reach out to peacefully repatriate territory, and cede control of the land and the people in such a way that no further injustices and insults occurred, and the humans were kept in the dark.

There would come a time, as Pedra had once said, for the whole of humanity to be let in on the truth. But not until the territories were redistributed, not until the problems inherent in draconic wealth hoarding—food deserts and waste, poverty, unequal access to health care, wage gaps and unethical labor—were repaired. And like Dav had said, *also* once upon a time, that could take decades.

Change sometimes has to come slowly to make sure it's done *right*.

Dav and I ended up staying at St. Ffagan's until the snow began to melt. We decided that my family didn't need to know literally every gory detail of how, exactly, Dav and I got engaged. All they knew is that I had popped the question, and Dav had turned into a blubbering, emotional mess and cried for ten minutes on the floor of Whitehall Palace before I got a 'yes' out of him. So it only made sense to have Mum and the twins join us in Wales for the remainder of the Christmas holidays.

It's not like Paulette and Owain didn't have the space, and Carys was absolutely delighted to be spoiled by the whole Levesque clan. Mum and Auntie Pattie spent the whole holiday glued at the hip, and Owain, Gem, Stu and I escaped down to *The Goat Major* every time the dragons got it into their heads to either butt horns, or start wedding planning.

And what about Onatah, to whom we owed so much of our success and happiness?

As Dav promised, as soon as we got back to Canada, the contract they had drawn up to return all but his nesting grounds to her went into effect. And she, in return, had surprised both of us by immediately handing the portion that had been Dav's marquessate down to her daughter Anwaatin.

Yes, you read that right.

*Daughter*.

Turns out Onatah has a whole goddamned family of dragons who co-manage her territory, in the Onguiaahra way, and she plays shit close to the vest. So close that I have yet to meet Onatah's Favorite, the gloriously stingy bitch.

I like Anwaatin, and she likes me, and seeing as we're closer in age than I am with Onatah, we spend a lot of time at

Beanevolence just talking shit out and sending proposals back to Pedra and the senior adviser teams in both the Scots and British courts.

You know, just casually exchanging texts with royalty.

As you do.

Pedra was immediately offered a place in Elizabeth Regina's hoard, celebrated for her initiative and research (*offered*, not simply Collected.) With my Auntie Pattie to guide her, she'd accepted, and immediately became tangled up in consultations, flying all over the world to collect enzyme samples from dragons of all nationalities, ethnicities, and creeds.

Let me see, who else...

Katiya and her fiancé came back from their backpacking trip to find our shared apartment spotless, and me totally moved out. As well as a brand new sofa in the living room and their rent paid for the next year, because Dav is a goddamned romantic like that. Mauli seems to have no clue that Anwaatin has started to sniff around them, and I've tried to drop info about what being a Favorite means as often as I can without being obvious. Dikembe thinks it's hilarious, and Min-soo won't stop batting her eyelashes at me and sighing, absolutely enchanted with k-drama and the romance of it all.

And Hadi.

Well.

Hadi now had not only the permission to sell dragon-roasted coffee again, but a royal seal of approval. Dav handed the reins over to Anwaatin, who actually *is* a morning person, so you know, good for her but also, ugh, morning people. What started as roasting lessons every day slowly petered off to once a week, until Dav bowed out, leaving Anwaatin to labor in service of her new hoard without him.

The return of The Coffee Of The Summer heralded a return of the insane line-ups, and Hadi ended up needing to hire not just a social media manager, but a security gal on weekends who made sure the queue stayed orderly. Last I heard, the run-off business had boosted the downtown core so much that the BIA had given her an award. A few corporate folks offered franchise opportunities, but Hadi, the grumpy thing she is, said no.

"The whole point of this 'serving the people' thing," Hadi had said over drinks at the Brass Monkey, "Is that we *serve* them." She sent a glance toward Anwaatin as she said it that made me think that Mauli wasn't the only one being courted.

"Not some McCorporation. This shit's gotta come from the heart, right?"

"Hear hear," Dav had said, and raised a toast to the coffee shop that had brought us all to this point, right here, right now.

And Dav.

My beautiful, selfless, generous Dav.

I'm not going to lie, leaving Beanevolence, and the sense of purpose that he had there, left him bereft in a way he'll never admit to. With me overseeing the farm upgrade and liaising with the courts, and with Sarah taking over most of the wedding planning, Dav was at loose ends.

"Hey, babe," I'd said one morning, shortly after he'd completely given way to Anwaatin. It was just past dawn and he was already dressed and sitting on the end of the bed looking like an abandoned puppy.

"Colin." He'd planted a kiss on me, despite the stale morning breath. "Morning."

"Been up long?"

He'd made a nondescript gesture.

"Sulky pants," I'd said, nudging him with my foot from under the sheets.

"I'm not sulking."

"You're sulking. Go cook me breakfast."

Dav had raised an eyebrow at me. "You know I will be smacked with a spoon if I meddle."

"I didn't say *make* breakfast. I said *cook* it."

Dav's eyes had gone wide, and then narrow. "I'll burn your bacon."

"As long as you don't burn the coffee."

Dav had furrowed his eyebrows. "We don't have any green beans."

"Yeah we do." I'd hid my face in the pillow. "I ordered them Saturday. They're in the pantry. Shoo."

Dav shooed.

It became a habit. Dav now gets up early every morning and roasts coffee and cooks everyone breakfast. It's a start. Of course the farm renovations aren't going to keep him busy forever. I'm going to have to find him some charity committees and boards to sit on soon, for his own damn good. Maybe get him started in local politics, if it's something he's interested in. He has no desire to be Governor, but 'Lord Mayor of the Niagara-on-the-Lake Alva Tudor' has a nice ring to it. If he wants it.

I'll help him get it.

I'll help him get *everything* he wants.

Because he's already given me everything I never knew I did.

But that's *my* job, isn't it? To keep my dragon—my fiancé—my husband—Mine Own grounded. To make sure he has the ability to do what he needs to, to the best of *his* ability.

His job is to serve everyone.

My job is to serve him.

And our shared job is to make the other as happy as we can.

So, that's where everyone is, and what everyone is doing.

Tah-dah.

Cue the credits, play the soppy top 40s love ballad.

Except.

Well.

There's one more part to the ending of a love story, and I'm sure you already know what I'm talking about. As Lord Byron once said: "All tragedies are finished by a death. All comedies are ended by a marriage."

The sunrise alarm clock is just begging to be smashed.

"Get up," Gem says.

"No." I roll over and smoosh my face into my pillow. I reach for Dav but he's not there. The bastard has left me to my sister's evil clutches. "Y'r not the boss o'me."

"No, the boss of you is already up and dressed," Stu says from somewhere near the door. I yank the sheets up. "Already seen your ass, bro."

"I am a valued and celebrated member of Her Majesty's Council, and a trusted consultant to Canada's Environmental and Draconic Affairs ministers," I pout. "Which means I get to sleep in if I want to."

"Not today, you don't," Gem says and runs her hand through my bedhead gently. "Come on, my lord."

"M'not a lord," I remind Gem.

"And you never will be if you don't get your ass in gear," Stu says.

"*Why* are you talking about my ass so much today?"

"*Why* are you flashing it at me?"

I groan and finally sit up. "There, happy?"

"Ecstatic," Stu deadpans. "Shower and shave. Go."

"Whyyyy?" I whine.

"Because *somebody* decided that it would be, and I quote, 'awesome to do the brunch thing with, like, our nearest and dearest before we have to go do the big media-frenzy roy-al-wedding-of-the-century bullshit'," Gem says in a scarily accurate impression of me.

"Also, because your friends are already here and they're driving me crazy," Stu says.

"Friends... why..." I say, and then my brain finally comes online.

Oh.

I'm getting *married* today.

"Ah, there he is," Stu says, and comes into the room to ruffle my hair, too.

"Fuck off," I mutter, batting them away.

"Such elegant language for such an elegant lord," Stu laughs, as Gem throws my bathrobe at my head.

"Come on," she says. "Things to do, people to tie your life to."

"Yes, drill sergeant," I mutter. "You both gonna stand there and watch?"

Gem rolls her eyes, but drags our brother out of the room. Alone at last.

I seriously consider crawling back under the blankets, but I can hear voices in the house below. I can *feel* Cook and Sarah's patience running thin from here, so I slump to the ensuite to start my day. I've only got an hour before the brunch starts, so I pull on my wedding suit, knowing that someone will stop me somewhere between the bedroom and the ballroom to tie my cravat correctly.

Last night, Dav and I had taken a moonlight stroll through the vineyard and exchanged private wedding gifts. I'd given him a lovely golden ear cuff, the same color as his freckles. It was dripping with rubies the shade of his scales, and citrines that matched his sunflower eyes. I'd seen a similar design on several of the dragons at court, and I wanted to proclaim my adoration of this man to everyone who saw him rock up to the noble sessions in his sexy-ass court attire.

In return, he'd gifted me with a Marchon's circlet, a head-band meant to be worn across the brow the same way he wore his. It was silver, etched with a simple stylized streams of fire, and and wreathed with hammered metal grape leaves which cradled the four pearls of a Marquisate. Little embedded chips of emerald made the leaves shine when I tilted it to catch the light. While the design was too masculine to be called a tiara, exactly, it still fulfilled essentially the same purpose.

I slide the circlet over my arm, which feels like a stupid way to carry it. Unfortunately, our second, distinctly more fleshy exchange of gifts last night meant that I'd been too caught up in the afterglow, and I'd accidentally left the fancy cushioned box somewhere out among the grapes. And I'm not supposed to wear the circlet until Dav puts it on me in the ceremony, so... actually, I should find Hadi and make her look after it as my Best Man.

Best Lady.

Best Friend.

Ugh.

*Coffee.*

I'm not the only one desperate for caffeine. When I make it to the kitchen, there's a handsome, ginger-haired dragon standing in front of the gloriously fancy espresso machine that had been gifted to us. Dav's huffing and muttering to himself, wrenching on the steamer wand like a cranky toddler.

"You'll break it," I say from the doorway, and Dav jumps, mouth sparking guiltily.

"This wretched thing... I'm sorry," he says. "I cannot make it give up anything palatable. I think Raibeart Rìgh sent it to tease us."

"It works if you do it right," I tell him, hanging my jacket and circlet over the back of one of the chairs. "Shove over." I hip check my fiancé out of the way when he moves too slow, and he slaps my ass in retaliation. "Careful now, you're gonna want that in pristine shape for tonight. Get some mugs."

As Dav does, I start the Americano, press the espresso, line up the wand, tap out twenty-seven seconds with the toe of my chucks as the machine hisses.

"Caffe Tobio for you, sir."

Dav takes a sip and sighs in delight as I start a caramel latte. "I'd ask for a scone to go with it, but I don't think burning down the kitchen this morning is a good idea."

"Ha fucking ha. Nice suit by the way. Clothes horse."

"Just because I come from an age when men wore high heels and actually cared about their appearance—"

By then I'm done at the machine. I set both of our mugs on the counter, and he takes my hand. He presses five soft kisses against the dime-sized scars on my bicep. Which becomes a kiss on the shoulder. Which becomes a sucking kiss on my neck, low enough that my collar will cover it later. Which becomes—

"Oh my god!" Gem shrills. She's in the doorway with Carys in her arms. The baby clamps her hands to the side of her head. "What are you two doing?"

"Having sex in the kitchen?" I say, at the same time Dav blurts, "Just getting coffee!"

Apparently our guests were thinking the same, because Owain shoves past Gem to wag a finger at us. "You shouldn't even be looking at him! It's bad luck!"

"Neither of us is a bride, Father," Dav snorts.

"Still bad luck," Laura tuts, following him in and heading for the cupboard to take down mugs.

"That's not fair!" I whine, gesturing at Dav's *every-thing*. "He's evolved from a Snacc-Dragon into a full-ass three-course-meal."

Hadi rolls her eyes as she elbows past me to get at the espresso machine. "Okay, who wanted what?"

The rest of my family, the rest of Dav's, and all of our friends pour into the room.

Before I know it, Mum's got my waistcoat buttoned, Paulette's got my cravat, and my throat, in her claws, and my caramel latte is *so far away*.

I hold out my hand and make gimmie fingers. Dav takes pity on me and hands me my coffee. He pulls us as far away from the rest of the group as possible, right into the bay window. He helps me shrug into my jacket and loosens Paulette's choke-hold knot.

"Oh my god, thank you," I tell him. He leans back against the sill and opens his arms for me to hide. "This was possibly not a good idea."

"Overwhelming?"

"Loud," I agree. "All these *people*. What the fuck are they even all doing here, anyway?"

"Celebrating us, more's the pity," Dav says with mock seriousness. "I'm afraid manners dictate that we're not allowed to kick them out until we've at least given them dinner, cake, and a few dances."

"Boo hiss," I sulk, sipping my latte.

God, this shit is good. Nothing will ever be better than dragon-roasted coffee. Except, maybe, the dragon-smoked chocolate he's started to experiment with. Which I can actually *eat.*

"If it's any consolation, it's worth it to see you all trussed up like this for me. What's this?" Dav asks, running his thumb along the edge of my new lapel pin.

It's the Tudor Rose, but instead of floating in a white field, the rose is now on a flag held aloft by the curled foreleg of a lamb—the traditional standard-bearer, I learned, of the Levesque coat of arms. It's still banded by laurels, and joined at the bottom with a lick of flame.

It signifies the joining of the Tudor and Levesque houses—equal and balanced.

I say as much.

"Your father would have been pleased," Dav says, and that little stab is back.

That one where you don't remember, for a second, that someone you love is not here to share this moment with you. Until you do.

But it's okay.

I mean.

Obviously not *okay.*

But Dad is here, in a way. Here on my lapel.

Here in my heart.

Here, with his name on my husband-to-be's lips.

Nice.

"Yeah." I lean against Dav's chest, craning to meet his sunflower eyes. "But this will still be good."

"And what's 'this'?" Dav repeats, only now we're not talking about my pin. He links our pinkies. "What part of the story are we in now?"

I lean up to press my lips to that saucy corner of Dav's mouth, right at that not-quite-a-dimple. Hoarding his Peter Pan Kiss for myself, for the rest of forever.

"I thought it was obvious," I say, palming his ass.

I can feel my wedding band in his pocket. I can't wait for him to slip it on, warm from the heat of his fire and strength, the tenderness burning at the bright center of the man I love.

"Tell me anyway, Mine Own," he says softly, linking our pinkie fingers together behind him.

"This?" I bite his lower lip just once, teasing. "This is the bit of the story with the Happily Ever After."

I don't really have to tell you what happened next.
But I will, anyway.
Hey, reader?
I fucking married him.


The End

# Acknowledgements

I wrote the dragon's share of this book during the cycling lockdowns of a global pandemic. I kept my sanity by going on long rambles, exploring the ravines, cemeteries, and forgotten niches in my corner of Castle Frank / Rosedale neighborhoods. The history of these places galaxy-brained (along with my desire to write a heavily queer, deliciously fanficcy, and tropey romance for my next offering) into this novel.

My first and most important and heartfelt thanks goes Ruthanne, without whom I don't think I would have ever finished the book. Your honest and enthusiastic interest in this story is what teased it out of my brain when I was too bogged down with grief to want to create. You are the best sounding board and cheering squad a writer could hope for, and who always made sure that in writing grand battles and fights I didn't forget the emotional heart of each gesture and confession. Thank you for the hours of video chats, the late night text exchanges, the way you fought to make Dav's inner life rich and Colin's anxiety real. This book wouldn't be a tenth of what it is if it wasn't for you.

My next thanks goes to Adrienne, who as always and as ever is a great brainstorming partner, springboard, and writer-in-the-trenches friend. I value your feedback and advice more than I can say. Without you I would not have had the emotional and mental bandwidth to sit down and write when, in the middle of the whole world catching fire, it felt like there was no point.

Also to: Stephanie, now living her own Coffee Shop AU, which inspired this one. I certainly hope yours is less fraught. Anna and Real Colin for their suggestions and enthusiasm, and for helping want to continue the story when I was feeling like a fraud and a failure, and for coming up with the history of the Scots Dragon Kings.

More thanks to:

Mom (the best proofreader on the planet), Elize, Rose, Brienne, Cory, Scott, Rob, CJ, Ninja-Muse, Ibrithir-was-Here, TeejayStumbles, Just-Add-Butter, illustrator Chris, bookseller Chris, Bianca, Allison, Tao, and everyone else who provided the images for the book; or helped me finesse my pitches and understanding of the book's genre, marketing appeal, and blurb; or taught me all about self-publishing my first book from scratch; or just waved pom-poms as I worked. It takes a village, it really does.

The NaNoWriMo Crying Room chat, but especially Dreaming Blue and Mer; the Storm the Castle discord group, with special thanks to Rodney and Deb; the Tuesday Night Broadview Dinner Writing Group; and the Toronto Indie Authors Conference.

Patrice Sarath for naming the coffee shop Beanavalance when I asked for suggestions on social media.

My sensitivity readers Jimmy the Welsh Viking, Peachii Dany, and Joe and Brad, who helped me navigate the topics and portrayal of their own lived truths and cultural histories as authentically as possible. Jaimie Oliver and Jimmy Doherty, who provided an overview of coffee roasting. Lucy Worsley, Ruth Goodman, Alice Loxton, and Eleanor Janega, whose amazing podcasts, videos, and television programs continually inspire and teach.

Shout outs to: The real Leacock Museum in Orillia, the real Ludology Boardgame Cafe, the real Brass Monkey, the real Twenty Wine Bar, and the real Goat Major. Sadly, Beanevalence isn't real.

And my immense and deep-felt gratitude to The Woodcock Artists' Grant, which helped me gain some financial breathing room so I could focus on revisions, and the Toronto Arts Council Works In Progress Grant. This isn't the novel I intended to write with the TAC grant, but with the world shattering the way it did, this book begged to be written first, and I was so grateful that the grant gave me the ability to do so.

I acknowledge the land this book was written on is the traditional territory of many nations including the historical Onguiaahra and Iroquois who settled around what we now call the Niagara Region; the Mississaugas of the Credit, the Anishnabeg, the Chippewa, the Haudenosaunee and the Wendat peoples. This land is now home to many diverse First Nations, Inuit and Métis peoples. I also acknowledge that Toronto, where I have settled, is covered by Treaty 13 with the Mississaugas of the Credit.

This is sacred land, and has been a site of human activity for 15,000 years, far before the forming of the nation of Canada as we know it today. It was the subject of the Dish with One Spoon Wampum Belt Covenant, an agreement between the Iroquois Confederacy and Confederacy of the Ojibwe and allied nations to peaceably share and care for the resources around the Great Lakes.

Today, this meeting place is still the home to many Indigenous people from across Turtle Island, and I am grateful and humbled to have the opportunity to contribute the rich history of storytelling in this place.

# Also by J.M. Frey

*Triptych*
*The Dark Lord and the Seamstress,* a coloring storybook
*City By Night*
*Hero Is A Four Letter Word,* short story collection
*Lips Like Ice,* as Peggy Barnett
*Worldbuilding Through Culture: A Workbook for Storytellers*
*Time and Tide*
<u>The Accidental Turn Series</u>
*The Untold Tale*
*The Forgotten Tale*
*The Silenced Tale*
*The Accidental Tales,* short stories from the Accidental World
<u>The Skylark's Saga</u>
*The Skylark's Song*
*The Skylark's Sacrifice*

www.jmfrey.net

# About the Author

J.M. Frey is an author and lapsed academic. She writes queer speculative fiction and fantasy. Her debut novel TRIPTYCH was nominated for two Lambda Literary Awards and garnered a place among the Best Books of 2011 from *Publishers Weekly*, and her most recent novel TIME AND TIDE was named one of *The New York Times'* Best Romances of the Year. Her life's ambition is to step foot on every continent–only three left! She lives in Toronto where she is surrounded by houseplants, because she is allergic to anything with fur. Like her main character, she is also allergic to chocolate. But not wine.

www.jmfrey.net